A PERFECT DIVORCE

• • •

ALSO BY AVERY CORMAN

Kramer vs. Kramer

The Old Neighborhood

50

Prized Possessions

The Big Hype

Oh, God!

ST. MARTIN'S GRIFFIN ≈ NEW YORK

A PERFECT DIVORCE

. . .

AVERY CORMAN

For information, address St. Martin's Press, 175 Fifth Avenue, New York, N.Y. 10010.

Design by Gretchen Achilles

www.stmartins.com

Library of Congress Cataloging-in-Publication Data

Corman, Avery.
A perfect divorce / Avery Corman.
p. cm.
ISBN 0-312-32983-0 (hc)
ISBN 0-312-32984-9 (pbk)
EAN 978-0-312-32984-6
1. Children of divorced parents—Fiction. 2. Teenage boys—Fiction. 3. Divorce—Fiction. I. Title.

PS3553.O649P47 2004
813'.54—dc22 2004046819

10 9 8 7 6 5 4 3 2

For Judy

ONE

• • •

Kim Greenley was crying. The word spread through the classrooms, the corridors, and by evening nearly all of the 125 seniors at The Bantrey School and a substantial number of parents knew that Kim Greenley, a B-plus student, whose rendition on Music Night of "When I Marry Mister Snow" had received a standing ovation, whose father was an orthopedist and whose mother was an administrator at Lenox Hill Hospital—how bona fide can parents be—Kim Greenley, of the sweet, round face and blue eyes, a little chubby perhaps, but why should that matter, Kim Greenley, with a boyfriend at Cornell, which placed her off limits to the boys and nonthreatening to the girls, bright, likable with serious credentials, left the office of the college advisor for the crucial beginning-of-senior-year college assessment meeting, crying. Her parents solemnly followed her, the father biting his bottom lip, the mother grim and looking close to tears herself. Outside the advisor's door they paused for a few words between themselves along the lines of how could this possibly happen, as Kim moved on, shaken.

The next group waited on an oak bench, Karen and Rob Burrows and Tommy, their seventeen-year-old son. Tommy had known Kim since kindergarten and rushed over to her before she descended the stairs out of the building, wanting to offer solace, something; her parents had momentarily abandoned her. She looked at him through wet eyes, her world collapsing.

"Tommy, he said I'll never get into Brown."

The Burrows family was on deck to see the college advisor with this bleak foreshadowing, like the Lenny Bruce routine of the comic who bombs at the London Palladium, the comic just about to go on and the female singer on stage ahead of him asks the audience for a moment of silence for the boys who went to Dunkirk and never came back. Not a good sign for the Burrows group, this Kim Greenley business. The advisor's secretary, a middle-aged woman of no discernible charm, appeared poker-faced as in I've-seen-them-cry-before, and said, "Mr. Kammler will see you now."

They filed in. Karen Burrows was a slim brunette, forty-nine, dark brown eyes, a patrician nose, a thin, elegant face, nearly professionally beautiful, who could have qualified for one of the Ralph Lauren ads where they finally deign to show women of a certain age. She was wearing a charcoal suit, a business meeting suit, and what else was this other than a business meeting? Rob Burrows, a former miler for the University of Pennsylvania, was six feet tall and still slim at fifty-one, with light brown eyes, and thinning brown hair which he cut short, an athletic man with a rugged face and firm jaw, a New Yorker who resembled someone from the heartland, which served him well in his business. Twice a week, or more often when she could, Karen went to a gym before going to work. Twice a week Rob ran around the Central Park reservoir, only once around, about a mile and a half, but he ran with his miler's stride faster than anyone else his age or virtually any other age, his attempt to beat another kind of clock.

They had been divorced for four years and communicated for the past three weeks leading up to this meeting with e-mail, a boon for ex-spouses who wished to spend as little time as possible on their exes, but needed to get a certain amount of ground covered. In this case, when is the meeting, when will you get there, what will we ask, what will we say? Tommy officially lived with his mother. A joint custody arrangement was modified on request of the parents in the second year of the divorce when they realized the logistics of his shuttling between apartments turned him into a spinning bear in a penny arcade. Rob, the more substantial wage earner with a playground equipment manufacturing company, paid the big-ticket items like Tommy's private school tuition. Karen, with a crafts retail store in SoHo, handled most of his day-to-day bills. Generally, Tommy spent weekday nights with his mother, every other weekend with his father. They alternated his school vacations, but the last summer he had been away as a counselor at the children's camp in Vermont where he had spent his camper summers. He was spindly, five feet ten, long brown hair, with his mother's slender face, his father's light brown eyes, the good-looking son of attractive parents. He walked with an athletic grace, ironic since he was a young man with little interest in athletics. He sometimes ran around the reservoir for exercise and occasionally joined his father when Rob ratcheted down his speed a couple of notches to accommodate him. Tennis instruction in camp revealed him to be a possible player. After talk of his trying out for the Bantrey tennis team Tommy learned the squad was picked by the contenders playing each other winner-take-all, which he found too competitive. With his noncompetitive nature, honed at the noncompetitive summer camp he attended, he gave up the idea of the team, so there would be no varsity tennis line on his college applications.

Martin Kammler, the college advisor, was in his fifties, a stocky man of five feet eight who had taken to dyeing his hair reddish to get the gray out. An unimposing person physically, he was at this time of year arguably the most powerful person at The Bantrey School. The rumors. For their graduating class, June of 2001, the competition for colleges was going to be even worse than the year before. That a conspiracy exists. That Mr. Kammler makes deals with the admissions people at the colleges. That he steers students away from schools to make slots available to other students—someone who is a shoo-in to get into Harvard or Yale is asked not to apply to Brown where he might block the one who might get in, but might not get into Harvard or Yale, and so on down the line. That the colleges give him quotas. That he's guaranteed a certain number of slots. That he'll say to the admissions people, take this one or don't take that one, and they listen to him. That he has his preferences. If he likes you, he'll fight for you. How else to explain why Bantrey, not a boarding school like Exeter, simply a Manhattan private school, placed so many students with the top colleges? And never, never ignore his advice. If he says apply to Columbia, early admission, rather than wait and try for Princeton, that's it, he knows, he can make it happen.

The office was small, spare, a few bookcases with college catalogs and college guidebooks, professional certificates on the walls, the room a charmless laboratory where the doctor of colleges made his prognoses.

"So, Tommy, Mr. and Mrs. Burrows," the voice warm, friendly, a paradox considering the verdicts rendered here. "I see your grades are pretty consistently C pluses and B minuses."

"Could be I'll do better this year." The remark for appearance's sake. He had no expectation of doing better in his senior year. He did what he did year after year, an average student at Bantrey with no peaks and no valleys, but no peaks.

"Tommy is conscientious. I can't remember the times he's missed school," Karen said out of anxiety.

"Good attendance is a given," Mr. Kammler said without even looking at her. I was told, don't be aggressive in the room, Karen thought, let Tommy be the focus. I shouldn't have said that.

"Your SAT score," referring to Tommy's file. "1020 the first time. You *are* planning to take it again?"

"He is," Rob said quickly then caught himself. Damn it. We talked about this. Don't volunteer anything. Mr. Kammler didn't look at Rob either.

"You should," he said to Tommy. "Have you been tutored?"

"Yes."

"Years ago we never officially recommended SAT tutoring, but then everyone was doing it, so we capitulated. Now I can't see an argument against it. I'd like to see you improve on your score."

"All right," Tommy said.

"There's a new company, Power Testing. I'm not fond of the name, but they do very rigorous tutoring, one on one. Expensive, but they get results."

"We'd be prepared to pay for it," Rob hurried to say.

"The issue is whether Tommy is prepared to do it," Mr. Kammler said.

"I would do some more tutoring," Tommy said.

"Good," Mr. Kammler responded. "Now what else do we have?" thumbing through his folder. "You did your community service at an after-school program in the Bronx?"

"In a rec center."

"I like the feel of that. And there's cartoonist for the school paper. You did a good one last week, Tommy. What was it again?"

"Two kids are talking and one of them says, 'You think I can list my SAT tutoring as community service? My tutor is, like, poor.' "

The slightest trace of a smile appeared on Mr. Kammler's face.

"So it's social observation."

"Yes, Mr. Kammler."

"Too bad there's not a way of quantifying 'social observer.' We'll have you list 'cartoonist for the school paper' and submit some of the cartoons. That should give you something."

Mr. Kammler paused, considering Tommy's possibilities. Karen and Rob leaned forward slightly. Tommy, in his Ben and Jerry's T-shirt, jeans, and sneakers, was trying to sit still in the chair. Mr. Kammler appraised him and his T-shirt before speaking.

"My favorite ice cream," Mr. Kammler offered, pointing to the T-shirt.

"Their factory is up where I worked in camp."

"What work did you do?"

"I was a counselor."

"You should put that on your applications, too. Along with the recreation center, it might mean something."

"He was a very good counselor," Rob said, eager for something to contribute.

The remark didn't seem to register with Mr. Kammler.

"So—this is the moment everyone gets to eventually. Now you must realize, this is just my opinion. You control your own applications." No one in his audience believed him. "We allow you seven applications. What we have to do is create a pattern that maximizes your chance of acceptance in a range of schools that makes sense for your level of candidacy."

New York School of Dog Grooming occurred to Tommy as a little comic remark to break the tension, but he knew it wouldn't go over too well here.

"Have you given thought to large school or small, region of the country, or what you might be interested in studying?"

"Small rather than large, I think. Anywhere, really. And liberal arts, more on the English side. My math and science scores are not the greatest."

"Fair enough." He kept looking through Tommy's material. "We advise an approach where you select a couple of reaches, two or three middles and a couple of safeties. I don't think I would advise early admission anywhere. They should take time with your application." He pondered, made some notes on a pad. "I would say Colby and Hamilton as your reaches, but I wouldn't hold out too much hope there. Lafayette, Gettysburg, and Marlowe as your middles, with SUNY Albany and Clark as your safeties. And I think you'd have a shot of getting in somewhere."

There it was, the years of his parents anticipating how he might fare in these sweepstakes, Rob the previous spring pushing Tommy to visit colleges he wanted him to see like Wesleyan, Brown, and Middlebury. Dad, it's a joke, I don't have a prayer of getting into those places. Just to see, to get a base line. Karen reprimanding Rob, you're setting up false expectations. The anxiety, the restless nights, the repetitive conversations that left everyone numb and, finally, the prognosis from Mr. Kammler. Tommy had "a shot at getting in somewhere."

"They're good, small liberal arts colleges, except for Clark and SUNY, and in the case of Clark it's called a university, but it's smallish. What do you think, Tommy?"

"Sounds good," Tommy responded, relieved to have any list.

"All right then," Mr. Kammler said. "We've got a plan."

They stepped outside the office. The next group was waiting, Tommy's friend, Jill Fleming, and her divorced parents making an uncommon appearance together for this meeting. They looked apprehensively at the Burrows family.

"New York School of Dog Grooming," Tommy finally got to say. Jill laughed. The adults did not. Tommy then said, "He thinks *someone* will take me."

They adjourned to the parents' association lounge. Karen and Rob had lived for years with the knowledge Tommy was an average student and no amount of the subject-by-subject tutoring they tried periodically seemed to help. They anticipated that he wasn't going to get into a college with the prestige of their schools, the University of Pennsylvania and Barnard, which they attended after Stuyvesant High School and The Fieldston School respectively. They tried to find a comfort zone—he was a good boy, the way he worked with children in the Bronx and a good counselor at camp and no drug problems they knew of, and honest, too. Hardworking usually went with honest, but they weren't certain how hardworking he really was. Healthy, though, they were deeply grateful for that, the main thing considering the children in wheelchairs, the children who can't run because of their asthma, the children with life-threatening illnesses, you shouldn't have to go to those comparisons to feel comfortable about your son, to think of others who have such disabilities, but they did go there, they were lucky with Tommy, and if he would never get into a prestigious college, they had the fact that he was a good boy and honest and healthy to sustain them, only it did sting more than a little, to see the pattern they identified over these past years confirmed. Hamilton and Colby, his reaches, were schools Bantrey students attended, but the others, they never heard of anyone from the school going to any of them.

"It's a well-rounded list," Rob said. "But I think you can lose the dog grooming joke. If you keep saying it, it'll put you in a bad mind-set on this."

"You mean I'll think less of myself and I won't apply myself?"

"You know what Dad means. It's too self-deprecating."

"Okay. But the dog grooming *is* there as a backup."

"Tommy—" Karen reprimanded.

"All right. Dogs smell when they're wet anyway."

"We should take a look at these schools," Rob said, all business.

"Absolutely. I have no idea what they're like," Karen said.

"Let's get the brochures, the applications. So it was Hamilton and Colby . . ."

"Those are the reaches, Dad, *very* reaches," Tommy said.

"Still, they're on the top of your list. Then there's Lafayette, Marlowe, Gettysburg." Rob was suppressing his own bias; he didn't know anything about these colleges. They had names he had only seen for football scores on the bottom of the television screen on ESPN. "And the safeties?"

"SUNY Albany and Clark."

"If he lets you apply to seven, it might be a different seven. These are just suggestions," Karen offered.

"Mom, Mr. Kammler doesn't suggest. These are the ones he wants me to apply to."

"How do you feel about the list, Tommy?" Karen asked.

"Hey, we know I never was going to Harvard."

Tommy went to his next class. Karen and Rob stood outside The Bantrey School, located in a five-story white brick building on 78th Street between Park and Lexington Avenues. The student body numbered 1250 students from K to grade twelve. In its earliest years Bantrey attracted mainly the children of the Upper East Side, old money. Around the 1970s this gave way to new money, mainly Wall Street people and working professionals, as well as actors located in New York and the occasional music business star. The star parents were now increasingly from the business world, including one falling star, a CEO caught in what the *Daily News* characterized as "corporate hanky-panky." Karen and Rob were somewhere in the middle of the parent population in income and school involvement, Rob on the athletic committee, Karen on the annual auction committee. They originally selected Bantrey for Tommy thinking the emphasis on "the whole development of the child" was good for their rambunctious little boy. And looking ahead, Bantrey had the reputation for getting students into good colleges. About the time of ninth grade, when Tommy appeared to be firmly located in the middle, his parents talked about, but decided not to, transfer him. Essentially he seemed fairly well adjusted to Bantrey, merely in the middle.

"Did we make a mistake?" Rob asked Karen. "Maybe he would've been better off somewhere else."

"It's possible he is who he is," she said. "He's never going to be a great student and never could've been."

"I'll get on this tutoring thing. Whatever it costs."

"Three hundred fifty dollars a session with those people. Sessions run an hour and three quarters."

"How do you know this?" Rob asked.

"I looked into it. I wasn't going to bring it up until we had the meeting."

"Okay then. We'll get this done."

"We'll get this done."

They paused a moment before parting and looked into each other's eyes with sadness—this is our boy, his first words, his first steps, his first everything belonged to another time, as did innocence. Not only of their love, but of Tommy himself and who he was—and now this professional was saying, by the standards used to measure these young people, he was not on the level of most of his peers. So there was disappointment, but they loved his kindness, they loved his wit, they loved his physical grace, they loved him. Whatever the directions of their lives, he was of them, born when they were special together, and in the rush of these shared feelings, Rob leaned over and kissed Karen on the forehead. It was the first time they had touched in any meaningful way in four years.

1980. Reagan versus Carter. Karen and Rob were volunteers on the Carter campaign in the New York Democratic Party office. They discovered they both owned early Bob Dylan albums. People with early Dylan albums didn't volunteer for Reagan, they agreed while working a table distributing Carter campaign literature on 72nd Street and Third Avenue. Rob was thirty-one, a graduate of Penn with an MBA from the Wharton School of Business. He worked at MayPole, the company he was later to buy. Karen was twenty-nine and had taken her anthropology major at Barnard into Appalachia for a thesis and eventually became a promoter and wholesaler of Appalachian crafts. By the time of the Carter campaign she had opened a retail store on the Upper West Side called Homegrown with crafts from around the United States. She had just spent nearly two years with the eternally noncommitted Charlie Miller, as he was referred to by Karen and her friend Polly Dresner, her roommate from Barnard. Charlie was a civil rights lawyer, fighting the good fight and thoroughly self-involved. Karen and Charlie lived together for four months. When Karen moved out she told Polly it took Charlie a week to realize she was gone. Even if eternally noncommitted Charlie had become committed, it was a question whether Karen would have accepted anything permanent from the relationship. In her background was her own parents' marriage. Her mother was a schoolteacher in a Harlem elementary school who had imbued Karen with the idea of doing good deeds in your life. One good deed for Karen's mother was being married to Karen's dentist father, who turned out to be a fooling-around-with-the-patients philanderer. He finally left Karen's mother after twenty-five years, not for a patient, for Magda, his thirtyish, bosomy, bleached-blonde dental hygienist whom Karen regarded as close to a character in a vaudeville skit. "That is such a joke, Dad," she told him. "It's ludicrous." But however she characterized it, the reality lingered for her that despite her mother's day-in and day-out decency, her own parents' marriage couldn't survive. Still, she would have liked the option with Charlie to consider a permanent relationship. She had nothing to work with—eternally noncommitted Charlie made it clear he was not going to commit and she decided she was limiting her possibilities with him. After Charlie she went through a couple of years of interchangeable single men and a couple of married men prowling around with weak promises that one day they were going to leave their wives. When Rob walked into the Carter campaign offices she was susceptible. He was good-looking, intense about the campaign, the Dylan albums didn't hurt, and if not a pure civil rights man like Charlie, he had his own particular moral base. At Stuyvesant High School he initiated a program tutoring younger inner-city children in track. At college he continued the thought and helped develop a mentor program of Penn track-and-field athletes with Philadelphia schoolchildren. The sense of social responsibility seemed to have come from within rather than from his parents. Rob's father was a nose-to-the-grindstone costume jewelry manufacturer, the quality of the jewelry and the profits generally modest. His mother worked in the showroom. They traditionally voted Democratic, but were uninvolved with social issues other than to have been readers of the *New York Post* back from the days when it was on the left. Karen, who was intent on creating cottage businesses for crafts workers among the poor, found in Rob a kindred spirit, as he did in her. When the marriage was in trouble, they still respected each other's social concerns, but with all else dragging them down the early Dylan of it was not enough.

The first years of the marriage were storybook material, the photos neither of them looked at anymore now in the bottoms of drawers, vacations before Tommy was born, of radiant-looking people in love, and then the baby pictures and the toddler period, and young Tommy as he got older, happy faces, this happiness looking like it would always go on. They were earnest parents, they read about parenting, they had intense conversations with other parents, they loved the good parts, watching your child's development, nurturing, playing, taking trips as a family, and Tommy rewarded them: He was rosy and energetic.

With Karen's encouragement Rob bought the company from his boss, who had been looking to retire. She held her husband's hand literally and emotionally as he deliberated over managing a long-term note and a bank loan. When the contracts were signed she had a party store make a maypole, which she set up in the apartment. They drank champagne under the maypole—and the company was his. And then their respective careers made increasing demands on them and they couldn't stop and didn't want to. They felt they were doing good work and it was not to be shortchanged, not everyone could do what they did. The work required travel and it became a major issue in the marriage. Rob was going to other cities on a regular basis to make deals for the company. He had thirteen people working for him in a loft in Long Island City. As for the actual physical creation of the swings, slides, climbing equipment, he subcontracted the manufacturing to a company in South Carolina. His clients were schools, parks departments, municipalities, developers, restaurants, apartment complexes, day care centers. He was competing with regional manufacturers and his mileage added up and was matched to some degree by Karen's. She was well beyond Appalachia with her network, the Amish country, the South, inner cities, searching for artisans, developing cottage industries and featuring them in the store.

Their housekeeper, Maria, a Hispanic woman in her forties, came in weekdays. Neither Karen nor Rob wanted a live-in housekeeper, both clinging to the idea that it was best for Tommy to have one or both of his parents around nights and weekends. They couldn't quite make it work and their squabbles about who was guarding home plate increased as neither was prepared to cut down their work schedules.

When Tommy was eight they went to see a marriage counselor, a studious man in his fifties who urged them to write everything down so there were no surprises if one or the other was planning to be out of town or working late. A day's advance notice was requested on late hours, the first casualty—they were always working late. There was a separate schedule for

Tommy—who was designated to spend time with whom and when, the time it was Karen exclusively, Rob exclusively, and a column for "entire family," all of which worked in theory, not in practice. Circumstances changed, crises arose, blame was assigned, and the arguments fed on themselves. They sought another therapist when Tommy was ten, in the twelfth year of the marriage, a woman in her sixties, Elsa Futterman, the author of several books, well regarded by the news media, who would call her for quotes on the matrimonial woes of celebrities. She was confrontational and forced them to be so. The result, over the year and a half of twice-a-week sessions, was that nearly every feeling and complaint did not go edited or unspoken; you kept nothing to yourself no matter how petty. Communication was supposed to be paramount and they became skilled injustice collectors, the therapist's office was their theater. Grievances did not pass, they were expressed.

When they were together they were safe in discussing Tommy, how he was doing in school or with his friends, or movies and plays were fine to talk about, or people, or current events. These subjects did not impinge on the main issues—who is home, when, how much do you give over to your career before you are ignoring your spouse, ignoring your child, who says a woman can have everything, and who says a man can have everything anymore, I told you I was going to be in Texas, I told you I was going to Boise, who goes to Boise, if I went out on the street and I asked a dozen people, nobody would have ever gone to Boise, it's just a school play for sixth-graders and he has three lines, it's not like he's doing *Hamlet*, and when you missed the Christmas show because you were in West Virginia, that was all right. Furious, someone would say why don't we just end this, and the other would say, Oh, don't be stupid, or I'm not ending it, or don't make a bigger deal than it is, and they soldiered on.

New York magazine was doing a piece on two-career couples and would they be interviewed and photographed? Karen thought it was good visibility for the store, relocated from the West Side to a large space in SoHo. Rob thought you don't do this, not when you've been having trouble juggling two careers, you don't boast about how clever you are about your two careers. They finally agreed to the interview and when the piece appeared he thought it was a sham. She called it negative thinking, they should use this image of themselves, inaccurate as it might be, as the ideal for themselves and they went through another descending spiral. The marriage proceeded as with a low-grade illness. Rob found himself thinking more of his parents, who had a lifelong undertone of nastiness to their relationship—Oh, yeah, tell me about it, is that what you think? Well, you're the expert, listen to Professor Einstein here. He didn't know why his parents stayed together. In the beginning, for his sake probably, but they just drifted along. And Karen and Rob drifted along. Their sex life never completely went away, fueled by physical need rather than any particular expression of affection, at some point you gotta have it, and if you're not cheating, this is where you go, Karen told him bluntly one night after sex. Here's how the world has changed, he said in response. Now it's the woman who says things like that, and she didn't disagree.

Then Ol' Ru surfaced. They stopped seeing Elsa Futterman, so at the time of Ol' Ru they were working without a net. He was Rufus Peabody, seventy-eight, a retired African-American house carpenter from Wheeling, West Virginia, who painted on discarded lumber, shingles, plasterboard, milk cans, corrugated boxes—rural scenes in a classically naive style. Karen thought he was a find and this was confirmed by a couple of folk art dealers she knew, and she decided to promote Ol' Ru. She featured him in her store, managed to get an appearance for him on the *Today* show, curated an exhibit for him in a folk art gallery in East Hampton. There was plenty to go around, he did a large amount of work. Overseeing the marketing of Ol' Ru was time-consuming along with everything else for the store that was time-consuming and they fell back into their pattern of accusation and counter-accusation, but I'm contributing here, he never would have been discovered but for me, fine, except when are you here for us, for me, let Ol' Ru go, he isn't Grandma Moses, he's not that good, he's just Ol' Ru. How would you know, can't you be a grown-up, can't you be a wife, and around and around until finally Karen said—maybe we should just call it quits. And this time, for the first time after eight years of these arguments, there wasn't any, Oh, don't be stupid, or I'm not ending it. He said, Fine.

In an emergency session with yet another marriage counselor before they came to a final decision, Rob said softly maybe the dirty little secret is that two-career marriages don't work. Maybe when you're rich or when one of those careers isn't really as important as the other they can work. Or when there's no child. Or when the child is older. But not when you're like us and they're all-out careers and you're looking for a fair share in the house and the other person, because these are, after all, two careers, is always letting you down, and nobody's willing to give up a piece of their action, maybe they just don't work. And Karen said, maybe they don't.

The idea of annihilating each other in the divorce settlement never occurred to either of them. They spent a considerable amount of time discussing Tommy and how they would divide his care. Joint custody seemed to have been invented for them. This was, as Rob's lawyer described it, the most humane settlement he had ever seen. You really sure you want to do this, he asked, and Karen's lawyer asked the same thing. But they were exhausted by the marriage, from trying to deal with what was appropriate to expect of a marriage partner.

Polly, Karen's friend from Barnard, was a public relations consultant to foundations, married to a political consultant. A tall, thin woman with a hawklike intensity, she peered at Karen when told Karen and Rob were breaking up, looking for the mouse in the field.

"There has to be another woman," she said. "Men never leave unless there's another woman."

"We're both leaving. We've long gone. Actually, I was the one who brought it up first."

"You've both brought it up before. That doesn't mean you do it."

"We don't really get along is the truth of it. Life is too short for this."

"Everybody has problems. Joe and I have problems. Don't do it."

"It's not like I'm doing this now. It's just acting on what's already done."

Rob's friend Seth Coleman ran a small advertising agency. A former track teammate of Rob's at Penn, a sprinter, still wiry, five feet six, a jumpy and abrupt African-American and the father of two girls, eight and six, he was not any more supportive of Rob.

"I'm going to put a citizen's arrest on you. Karen is beautiful, she's goddamn valuable, the work she does. She's not the woman you leave. If anything, she's the woman you leave *for*."

"It's a lousy marriage."

"Make it better."

"We've tried."

"Try harder. Jesus, does she have someone?"

"I don't know. I don't even care. I'm just worn down. What I've been missing is the marital version of labor peace."

"That's the stupidest thing I ever heard. Married couples fight. Where do you get your information from, Hallmark?"

• • •

Consistent with the-best-interests-of-the-child, they met with a child psychologist to figure out the best way to tell Tommy and try to fashion strategies for the daily life to follow. They read a book with the blatant title *How to Tell Your Child You're Getting a Divorce.* They spoke to other school parents who were divorced. Half the children in Tommy's eighth-grade class were listed on the class contact list as children of parents with different addresses.

"That's a good thing," Rob said to Karen in her lawyer's office. "If half the kids in his class went through it, he won't feel like it's something to be ashamed of."

"Possibly. Kids talk. Maybe he'll have a kind of support group."

"I'm sure."

"A terrible statistic, fifty percent," she said, "but maybe out of its terribleness it'll make it easier for him."

They were following the professional advice to tell your child in the morning, on a weekend, not at the end of the day when the child might be tired from school and would have to go to sleep on the news. Don't feel awkward about making notes or scripting it, or even rehearsing aloud before you tell the child.

A Saturday morning. Thirteen-year-old Tommy finished watching a PBS program on wolves. He seemed alert, intrigued with the show. Karen sat on the sofa next to him, Rob in a chair. They had rehearsed.

"Tommy, I don't know how aware you are of the way Dad and I have been arguing over the years."

"Oh, that's nothing," he said.

"It isn't nothing to us," she said, "and we can't stop it. We've seen marriage counselors. They help you talk about your problems. We did that a lot and we talked it over and over, how we can get along better. We love each other, but sometimes loving each other isn't enough."

"Why not?" Tommy asked.

"You get to the point in a marriage when you have these arguments," Rob said, "and when they don't stop, then the fact you can't stop them makes them get bigger, and when the people disagree more than they agree, then you have what they call irreconcilable differences."

"So you're getting a divorce."

They were stunned.

"Well, yes, but it's not as simple as that," Karen said.

"Why not? You're getting a divorce or you're not getting a divorce."

"We can't stay married," Rob said. "We've tried."

"We've been running on wishes for a long time. Wishes that we could have a better marriage, wishes to get along better, it's not like we don't love each other. We do. We just can't find a way to live together."

"If you love each other then why would you get a divorce?"

"Because we can't find a way to live together and we have these irreconcilable differences, like Dad said, and the truth is it isn't the same kind of love anymore, what we have for each other."

"Love is love."

"There's a love where you respect the other person and value all the things that you've had together and will always be important to each other because your love created a beautiful child, and that's the love we have," Karen said.

"What's wrong with that?"

"It isn't enough," Karen continued. "Because the love you need to keep a marriage going is the love where all those things are true, but also, and this is very important, also where you can forgive the other person everything and we can't. We'd like to, but we end up hurting each other."

"We're like a team on a bad losing streak," Rob said, "and we can't turn it around. Each of us feels as badly and as much to blame as the other. It's not one of us or the other who's more at fault. We don't love anybody else, there isn't anybody else."

"We'll always be this amazing combination of people, you and your dad, you and me, and on the important issues, the three of us together, because we're going to stay in each other's lives always. And to do that, you'll live half of the time here and half of the time with Dad."

"Because we both love you more than we could ever express. So you'll be here with Mom. And I'm going to have an apartment where you'll have your own room."

"Joint custody," he said and they blinked at his familiarity with the term.

"Yes, that's what they call it," Karen responded.

"Billy Waldman has joint custody."

"The most important thing is," Karen said, "we'll both always be in your life."

He pondered the information, more solemn than they had ever seen him.

"So now I'm just like all those other kids."

TWO

• • •

Homegrown was located on Mercer Street in SoHo between Spring Street and Prince Street, a dramatic space with high ceilings to the second floor of the building, the walls adorned with quilts and throughout the store, baskets, trays, bowls, toys, cutlery, weathervanes, handmade furniture, knitted goods, art by naive artists like Ol' Ru and Native-American crafts and sculpture. Karen's talent was to nurture artisans from rural areas and inner cities and encourage them to draw on their roots to create superior crafts work. Although not a major profit center, not with SoHo rent and employee salaries, Homegrown was a respected enterprise and she was respected.

After the divorce Karen remained in their two-bedroom rental apartment on Lexington Avenue and 91st Street and Rob rented an apartment across town on West 96th Street near Columbus Avenue. He found the place through a building owner he met on city-related business. The owner received a variance for placing a vest-pocket park on commercial property and Rob supplied play equipment for the site. Rob gathered his clothing, some books, and personal belongings and walked away from the place he had shared with Karen for fifteen years, conceding that nothing of the quilts, the paintings, the handmade pieces by Karen's people would have come into his life without her. He certainly didn't want to divide the few pieces they owned by Ol' Ru.

Seth's wife, Carlotta, an art director at Seth's advertising agency, offered to help Rob get settled in. Carlotta, thirty-eight, an African-American woman of five feet six with hazel eyes and high cheekbones who had helped pay her way through the School of Visual Arts by modeling, was a stylish woman who knew her way around off-beat resources. She urged him to take time. She was prepared to go with him to antiques dealers, auctions, SoHo, NoHo, Tribeca, order from catalogs, start him fresh, but with taste. He was not interested in a protracted decision-making process. He just wanted to get in fast. They went to ABC Carpet, the smartest home furnishings place she could think of for him, and in three hours he purchased everything he needed for a two-bedroom apartment. Tommy joined them the last half hour to pick out furnishings for his room. He didn't like anything there, it was too fancy for him, and they went to Macy's, where he selected some modern white pieces for his room. Done. Tommy had his room, Rob had his apartment, and he was in.

He sat with Carlotta in the new apartment, the two of them assessing the day.

"It's going to be serviceable, Rob. The place is going to need a little more character."

"You might argue so am I."

"The walls. Always a dead giveaway on divorced guys. After a while, they may get out of the cardboard boxes when they move in, but they don't get anything up on the walls."

"I'll buy some posters."

"Right, bullfight posters? Just out of college? It's stunning to me, in terms of gender. The woman in this situation is in an apartment with beautiful things and the man is going to be in a place with ordinary posters."

"Photography then. I always liked New York photos. I'll get some good ones, Berenice Abbott, Helen Leavitt."

"Great photographers."

She became teary-eyed, startling him.

"Why did you have to do this, Rob? Couldn't you work it out?"

"We couldn't. We just couldn't."

The arrangement was for Tommy to spend two weeks on and off with each parent. Their business travel wouldn't fit neatly into the schedule and they understood that flexibility was going to be required. What they didn't understand was how unsettling it would be for him to be shifting back and forth every two weeks, an urban gypsy. As a concept, joint custody sounded fair and responsible. The child could count on his parents, they loved him, didn't the sharing demonstrate it, except the child had to keep moving. He became increasingly unhappy, letting slide hints and sighs until one Sunday night packing up to return to Karen's apartment, the second time that month, the twentieth time that year, he said to Rob, "Going back and forth is a pain." Karen and Rob talked about it at length, went to the child psychologist for a session, and emerged with a new plan, Tommy staying mainly at Karen's apartment. He seemed relieved.

Karen skated through advanced-in-age versions of eternally noncommitted Charlie, never-married men in their fifties and sixties, what is your problem, or they were widowers who deified their late wives, "a saint," one of them said to her over dinner about his deceased wife, or the recently divorced who really wanted to be with younger women and spent a token evening with someone like Karen to prove to their female friends they weren't shallow. Single life in New York for a woman in her forties was not the subject of a television series on HBO. Occasionally she had sex with one of these players, the highest up she could find on the mental health charts. By choice, no one stayed on her dance card very long.

After three years of divorced life Karen was convinced she would never marry again. The first time, building a family was folded into the equation. What was the point of marrying now? She accepted, intellectually, the advantage of being in a mature marriage, two adult people with no intention of having children, living the good middle years or the golden years upcoming, with the wisdom and freedom to enjoy themselves. They showed commercials on the nightly news for those kinds of couples walking along the beach. She was running a business. She had no time for the beach. And what would she want with a man who did?

"What I *am* ready for is a semi-meaningful relationship with a clean man who has his own teeth." She was at breakfast with Polly at Sarabeth's on the Upper East Side.

"They all have their own teeth. It's today's dentistry. They screw them in or something."

"You know what I mean. Not old-old. And who can actually come up for air from talking about himself."

"Gay is all right?"

"Temporarily. It's still good now and then to, you know . . ."

"I may have your guy. He was seeing someone, but his lady friend just moved to Johannesburg."

"Johannesburg? That is so *Masterpiece Theater*."

"I'm telling you. She has family there and wanted to go back, he wouldn't go, and it looks like they broke up. I don't know if you can say 'broke up' when the guy is sixty-six, but let me poke around, find out if he's available."

"Sixty-six is close to the outer edge."

"A young sixty-six. Bill Withers. Retired executive from Time-Life. Runs a small foundation now and he just became a client. I think you can get a semi-meaningful relationship out of him."

"I might also be in the market for a meaningful semi-relationship."

Polly invited Karen and Bill to dinner at her apartment. Polly's husband, Joe, several inches shorter than Polly, balding, with watchful, darting blue eyes, a consultant who ran aggressive political campaigns for Democratic Party candidates, was aggressive this night on what he regarded to be the political cynicism of the Bush administration. The others inserted comments when they could, which he mainly disagreed with, a lively and somewhat disagreeable evening serving to disguise the fact that the two "singles" were there to meet. Bill was six feet two, thin, with all his light brown hair and an alert, unsagging face.

"Do I deliver?" Polly whispered to Karen when they had a moment in the kitchen. "What do you think of Gregory Peck?"

"He's nice looking. He's not *that* nice looking."

"Everyone's not Rob. And I'm sure he has his own teeth."

Bill dropped Karen off at her apartment in a cab that night, asked if he might call, and they started with a dinner, another dinner, then theater on his subscription tickets, which, alas, dated back to when he was married to his wife who died of a heart attack ten years earlier, giving Karen a peculiar feeling. I guess you don't give up the tickets if you like going, but still—I'm in her seat!

He had been a marketing director and was currently running the Watkin Foundation, a family foundation funding literacy projects. Polly was going to help raise the visibility of the organization. Karen told Polly she was looking for clean. This man was also clean professionally, which appealed to her. Of crucial importance, he seemed to understand the nature of her days. In the later years with Rob he had stopped seeing the store as anything other than the major problem and it might as well have been the other man. In the beginning Rob was wholly supportive and she didn't think she could ever have gone forward without him. It was Rob, perhaps naive about how time-intensive it would be, who encouraged her when she was considering moving to the larger SoHo location from her small West Side store. He brought in his colleagues from work to help with the design and contracting requirements. Photos of the proud couple at the opening night cocktail party—and it was Rob who threw the party for her—were among the pictures she never looked at anymore.

Bill liked that Karen had this life. When he first walked into the store a couple of weeks after they met, he said, "My God, the scope of this. The detail. And you have a great eye."

"Thank you. Thank you for recognizing it."

"This is like a crafts museum."

"Better not be or I'll go out of business."

He looked at a star quilt hanging on the wall.

"I'd like that for my daughter."

"Whoa. Do you know anything about this?"

"Only that I like it."

"There are new quilts and antique quilts. Antique quilts run higher. Before 1950 it's considered antique. And this is around then. From Ohio."

He noted the price tag. Three thousand dollars.

"I'll take it."

"You can't do that."

"I want it for her."

"I can't sell it to you. Here." She handed him a hand-painted tray. "Take this, a gift from me."

"I'm buying the quilt, Karen. Are you here all the time?"

"Not all the time."

"I'll come back when you're not here and buy it then."

"No, Bill."

"I'm coming back."

"Well, I can't sell it to you retail. Fifteen hundred dollars—it's what I paid for it."

"A deal."

"Just this time. This could be a very expensive relationship. For us both."

He walked around the store, reading the various descriptions and biographies that accompanied the crafts pieces, understanding he was not just looking at merchandise, there were personal histories here and she had unearthed them. He took everything in, turned to her, and said, "It's like looking into someone's heart."

• • •

When they first began to have sex she made it a house rule, never at her apartment while Tommy was there. Tommy had a girlfriend at school and she suspected he was having sex, or some version of it, and whether he was or was not, she felt it psychologically incorrect for her to entertain there. Karen's apartment was decorated liberally with crafts pieces. Bill's apartment, a two-bedroom place on Madison Avenue in the Eighties, studiously interior-decorated as the decorator might have advised, was in a style thirty years old, antiques, traditional art on the walls, landscapes and still lifes, not by famous artists but a few cuts below, the man living in his former wife's decor.

He was the experienced hand. After fifteen years with Rob where everything was speeded up, build the business, make the sale, get on the plane, and the tedious arguments about building the business and making the sale and getting on the plane, Bill was a welcome change. He stood apart from the other men she had spent time with, as well: Polly's hectic and aggressive husband, Joe, and Rob's friend, wired Seth.

Bill had his routines, he played tennis, he swam in a health club to stay in shape. He was calm. He ate carefully, watching his weight and his cholesterol. This required an adjustment for her. Rob was cholesterol-reckless, a red meat guy. The sex with Bill, if not spectacular, was sex. He was capable.

"What is it like to make love to a man that age?" Polly said over lunch at a Japanese restaurant in SoHo.

"You can't ask that."

"Yes, I can. I was around when you had sex in the dorm with Tino Gurelli and I had to lean against a car on the street until you were done."

"I was nineteen. And sex with Tino Gurelli was terrible."

"That sex I don't care about."

"It's personal. Not personal about me, about Bill."

"Come on. I fixed you up. It's a simple question. How's your sex life with this guy and how does it compare with your ex-husband?"

"That's a simple question?"

"Give me a general answer so I don't feel my friend of thirty years is pulling away from me."

"What a lousy argument. All right, just to shut you up—"

"This lunch is getting good."

"He's attentive. An attentive lover. With Rob, everything was an athletic performance."

"Athletic. I would take athletic. Although attentive is good. Better than absent."

"Better than absent."

"Good. I don't feel cheated."

"And we mentioned your client. You can write this off."

Karen's store manager was Pam Delaigh, a lively twenty-six-year-old crafts enthusiast whom Karen trusted sufficiently to get away on a weekend now and then when Tommy was with Rob. Karen and Bill went to a quiet inn in Connecticut Bill liked, tranquil weekends, in keeping with the man. They attended the theater often, and not only the subscription series; Karen ended up sitting in seats without a connection to the deceased wife. He looked like he was proud to have Karen on his arm. He appeared to glide into restaurants with her. Usually they spent Friday and Saturday nights together. The rest of the time they were on their own.

Bill's daughter, Cindy, thirty-three, was a dermatologist in San Francisco, married to a doctor. She came to New York for a medical conference and they went to dinner, Bill prideful of the daughter and of Karen. Karen could see a resemblance to her mother from photographs Bill kept in the apartment, Cindy, a brunette with soft features and pale white skin. Karen became aware of staring at her, not because she was so beautiful, rather because she was a doctor while Tommy was embryonic.

Bill's relationship with Tommy was formal, somewhat remote on both sides. At times, in the reverse situation of the teenager who has to fill time talking to the father while the daughter gets ready, Bill talked to Tommy while Karen was in her bedroom. Largely, they were cordial to each other, nothing more. I don't even want to think about this guy doing my mom. I'll go crazy. Karen seemed to be happy with Bill and that was all right, he supposed. If he had his choice, though, the man wouldn't be around. I can't say I like him. I can't say I hate him. There's nothing I can do about it.

In the hours following the crucial meeting with Mr. Kammler, Karen was useless in the store and sat in her office not taking calls, preoccupied. Tommy's English and history grades were only slightly better than his math and science grades, and he was using the thought that he was no good in math and science to choose liberal arts. What did that mean for him, liberal arts? She and Bill had plans that evening. A new Italian restaurant opened near his office and he was eager to try it. She was so preoccupied with Tommy they might as well have been eating at the Vince Lombardi rest stop on the New Jersey Turnpike. Bill made a weak attempt to match Karen's preoccupation but he was scrupulously making his way through his endive and goat cheese salad and his swordfish Milanese as though he were the restaurant critic of *The New York Times*.

"We should close this off," she said. "A tough day and I need to go home. I shouldn't have put this on you."

When Karen was back home she thought it was exactly what you should put on the person you're with, why else would you be with someone? The person she needed to speak to was Rob.

"It's me. Did I disturb you?"

"I'm already disturbed," Rob said.

"Me, too."

"As it gets closer, it gets scarier. He says he isn't as good in math and science. It's not like he's hitting it over the wall in anything else."

"I was thinking the same thing. So it's not just a school, it's where will he grow. Where will a smart, witty, underachieving kid do best?" she asked.

"Karen, what if he isn't underachieving?"

She wasn't prepared to argue; she didn't know.

"Then he's still got to find the right school."

"He has to get his SAT score up," he said.

"If he can."

"He has to. He's with you most of the time. You have to stay on top of it."

"Oh, great. What a trip to put on me."

"I'm worked up, that's all."

"I hear that. So am I."

"If someone walks into the store who's a trustee at Colby or Hamilton—"

"Right. Let's just hope he can do better on his SAT."

The next day she arrived at the store to find Pam, her manager, looking grim.

"What's wrong?"

"Coach is coming down here with a new store. Karen, I've been offered a job to manage. It's a twenty-five thousand a year raise. I have to take it."

"I can't match that."

"I know. It's not like I was in the market, looking or anything. This guy I met, he works for them and they called—"

"It's out of my range—"

"Maybe we can work together, do tie-ins, where there's a display and it's stuff from here, which we give you a plug for."

"At Coach? That's apples and oranges."

She was scheduled to see Bill that night. She couldn't go through a dinner with him, or sex, or anything. She just wanted to decompress by herself at home. Bill convinced her to join him at a bistro in her neighborhood. In addition to losing her manager, troubling Karen was the idea that it represented a raid by another heavily budgeted operation dipping into the SoHo waters and jeopardizing individual places like hers. The very person she relied on to free her up a little, her most reliable employee, was leaving. Bill said she should take comfort from the fact she found and cultivated Pam in the first place, someone without experience in this area. If she could do it once, she could do it again. Karen was obviously gifted in this regard, too, in training people, as she was gifted with the store. Bill, not much of a help on the subject of Tommy, was good on business, and she appreciated the counsel.

Dean Jacobson, the SAT savior from Power Testing, three hundred fifty dollars a session, came to the apartment. He was unkempt with wild hair, hopeless clothing—I-have-no-idea-what-I-am-even-wearing and who cares—paint-stained dungarees, a ragged sweatshirt, work boots, a knitted hat with flaps, towering over them at six feet six, a vision of disorder, bearing one overriding credit he managed to insert right after the hellos. "I guess I should get this out of the way so you know where I'm coming from. I went to Bronx Science and I aced my SAT and I went to Harvard and I know how to get people through this." Tommy withdrew to the room with Dean and came out an hour and three quarters later.

"Dean was really helpful, Mom."

"Good. We'll see you next week then?"

"Fine with me. Call the office." Turning to Tommy. "Do that work."

"I will."

After Dean Jacobson left, Tommy said, "Remember *The Cat in the Hat*? He's the Cat with the Flaps."

"Tommy, you're up for this?"

The brightness in his face suddenly faded.

"I'll try," he said.

"I know you will."

At about one in the morning, unable to sleep, Karen came to his room and peeked in on Tommy's sleeping form. Is this a good sleep? What are we doing to you? If we lived somewhere else would it be easier for you? But this is where Dad's work is and this is where my work is and this is the world you have to live in. Sometimes I wish it weren't so, but this is who we are.

THREE

• • •

When a marriage is in decline and finally ends, the man always has someone he was seeing waiting in the wings. Or he has a fantasy about someone he would like to have been seeing and acts on the fantasy. In the aftermath of the divorce Rob learned these were standard assumptions about failed marriages and people he knew were surprised this was not his circumstance. He came to think the fact he had no one was an indictment of the marriage, it collapsed under its own weight.

At the opening of a renovated playground in Queens featuring May-Pole equipment he met a television producer for a local cable news company covering the story, Ronda Rapasso, late twenties, lively, all energy in bed, out of bed, good for repatriating the older guy fallen out of a marriage, his first sex in fifteen years with anyone other than his wife. Ronda was hired by *Good Morning, America*, a career victory for her. They went together for four months. Half the time she was traveling on assignments. She had a sublime preoccupation with any story she was working on, crop-duster pilots in the midwest, the free-range turkey industry. She could speak of little else when she was working on a piece. He found her subjects mildly interesting. She announced to him that she couldn't see him anymore, she was getting engaged to a news producer at the network. He was nonplussed, assuming she had been sleeping with them both at the same time. New rules.

A woman closer to his age, a copywriter in Sean's agency, Robin Winfield, forty-two years old, gym-every-morning fit, was someone he found attractive. She had never married, was droll with a self-effacing sense of humor. "I've been dating for twenty-seven years and still haven't hooked up permanently with anyone. Do you have any idea how incredibly cut off I must be?" Over a four-week period they went to museums, galleries, movies. She started breaking appointments, then he couldn't reach her on the phone, Sean explaining, "When guys get too close she bolts."

"Four weeks. How close could we have been?"

He met Vickie Carstairs in the unromantic circumstance of a zoning dispute in New Rochelle. She was the attorney for a day care center. Rob had been contracted to supply playground equipment for the center. She was thirty-five, five feet four, chesty for her small frame, a slim waist, red hair with a pug nose and light blue eyes. Men, even on the other side of the dispute, could not stop looking at her.

Several local homeowners, white, resented the idea of the day care center expanding with an outdoor facility. The center serviced nonwhite as well as white children. The homeowners didn't have a problem if the children stayed indoors where they could not be seen or heard. The day care center people believed they had the right to develop their own property, the locals did not. On the board of directors for the center was an investment banker who knew Vickie when she worked at Pickens, Wright, a Manhattan law firm. When he learned she was running her own office he called her and she agreed to represent the day care side. Rob was to testify as to the work they were going to do and he and Vickie were in contact with each other over a couple of days. She was impressive fighting in court and in the local papers, and the day care center won their dispute. He asked to take her to dinner to celebrate. She warned him she was a single parent with two small children and did he still want to have dinner with her? Rob dismissed her caution flag and took her to Le Bernardin.

"This is an occasion place, birthdays, anniversaries," she said.

"It is an occasion. You won, we won."

"Well, don't get any ideas from how much this dinner is going to cost you. I have to tell you right off I don't go to bed with a man until the second year."

"Next time we eat in a luncheonette," he said.

He asked to see her again and she agreed to meet on a Friday night if it could be an early dinner, she had a baby-sitter who couldn't stay late. They went to a simpler restaurant this time, a pub in her neighborhood. She invited him in for a nightcap, releasing the sitter. Vickie lived on West End Avenue and 70th Street, in a rambling apartment in an old building. The decor was tasteful, modern pieces with some care taken in assembling a collection of graphics. She checked on the children and they were pretending to be sleeping. They exploded out of their rooms when they saw her, two boys, Tod, six, and Keith, seven, redheaded mops. She needed to read books to them and calm them down. Rob was in the living room, pensive, and when she returned she found him in this mood.

"Just remembering my son when he was a little boy. Seems like another life. It is another life."

"We've done the zoning dispute, my practice, your business. Dare we do our marriages?"

"Is it obligatory?"

"We should get on the table the lies we tell ourselves."

"Are they guaranteed to be lies?"

"I suppose we try to be truthful."

"My ex-wife runs a store called Homegrown."

"I know that place. It's fantastic."

"It is, fantastic, but somewhere along the line it got between us—and my business got between us. That is major oversimplifying."

"We just met, Rob. We're not going to be complex."

"We couldn't . . . we never got out of the hole. We saw shrinks. Didn't help. My son, Tommy, was thirteen. He's sixteen now. We had joint custody the first year and we stopped it. It wasn't working out. I get him every other weekend."

"What's he like?"

"A good boy. He's been stiff-upper-lip through all this."

"And how do you get on with your ex-wife?"

"It's a correct relationship. Correct is the word for it. And that's not a lie. Let me hear about yours. You said you were married to an actor."

"Tim Grove."

"Really?"

"We met at Northwestern. He was studying acting. I was a law student. He came to New York. I finished law school and followed him. He did some theater, television, and then he got rolling from independent films."

"Didn't I see something in the paper the other day? He was with—"

"He's always with someone, Winona Ryder, Sandra Bullock, Gwyneth Paltrow, people like that. I'm sure they make distinctions in the movie business. They're all the same girl to me."

Vickie had been married for six years and divorced for four. She described her ex-husband as the definition of charismatic. Women who saw him on the screen wanted to make love to him and, unfortunately, that was also true of women who saw him off the screen, and vice versa as far as he was concerned. So she set him free for the population at large. She had custody of the boys and their father made appearances, they had no formal arrangement. He kept an apartment in Greenwich Village and popped in and out of New York in keeping with his general style.

Her parenting had a serious impact on her advancement within the law firm. She couldn't find the hours required to push her way up, not as a single parent with children this young. With illnesses and housekeeper emergencies and baby-sitter no-shows, she could never compete with female single lawyers, or male married lawyers. She chose to practice the real estate law that was her specialty freelance, renting space within a law office.

"It's admirable of you. To make that choice."

She read his bias immediately.

"Unlike your ex-wife? Don't think I'm so admirable. I had no choice."

"Still, you put your children first."

"I'm divorced. And my husband is like the wind. This is what I had to do. You gave yourself away a little there."

"Did I?"

"You sincerely believe women should work and fulfill themselves, but not if it means doing it all the way like you guys get to do."

"This sounds like an old argument I used to have at home."

"I'm not a lawyer in a law firm because I can't be right now. I don't want you to see me as your dream girl because I constructed my life this way. Don't think I'm easy—culturally, I mean."

"None of this is easy."

The evening sent him tumbling into self-doubt. Here was an impressive woman he just met who, in barely any time, exposed him as a sexist. "You sincerely believe women should work and fulfill themselves, but not if it means doing it all the way like you guys get to do." He thought he had always been supportive of Karen, particularly with the SoHo store, and it wasn't as if he was a guy who needed his dinner on the table prepared by his wife. He was there for her when it counted. Their commitments got out of hand and they couldn't survive them. He called Vickie at home the following night to justify himself. He made his argument about the difficulty of sustaining two full-throttle careers in a household with a child. Maybe if one party subjugates needs they can survive. Or if both do. But if neither does, you get perceived injustices that undermine the marriage. She agreed about subjugating needs.

"If I didn't *need* my husband to be faithful we might still be married. Richard Rodgers' wife. She just looked the other way and they stayed married forever, which was smart from a royalties standpoint."

"Maybe it's about a kind of faith. When you're fresh and new you have faith in each other and in the marriage. When you lose the faith, you've lost the marriage."

"Why are you so wound up on this?"

"I don't want you to think I'm an old-fashioned male chauvinist pig."

"Does it matter so much what I think of you? We just met."

"It matters because it goes to what I think of myself."

"Okay. That makes sense. That's pretty self-aware."

"For a guy."

"For a guy. Look, it's not an exact science. We're all muddling through. I wouldn't call you a male chauvinist pig. Just a guy who never worked it out."

"Fair enough."

"This is all a little heavy for so early on, but I'd say we're off to a promising start. We've shot past small talk into who am I—"

"—and where did I go wrong?"

"Stay tuned. That thing I said about not sleeping with a man until the second year. I may be willing to make an adjustment."

Sex was restricted to his apartment when Tommy was not there and was off limits in her apartment, her boys were always there. Rob came by for her one evening, her sitter cancelled, and Vickie was unable to leave and ordered pizza. Rob was entertained by an auto show courtesy of the boys, specialists in vroom noises. They ended up having pizza from three different take-out places because the place Tod liked it from was too oily for Keith, and the place Keith liked it from was too spicy for Tod, and Vickie liked it from a third place where she preferred the crust.

"This should make the 'Dining In' section of *The New York Times*."

"What's that?" Tod asked.

"What this should be in, a newspaper."

"Do you know my daddy?" Keith asked.

"I've seen him in movies."

"He likes it from another place."

"I'm sure that's a world record," Rob said.

"If Rob comes back, should we let him pick pizza from his own place?" Keith said.

"Okay," Tod responded.

Vickie smiled over at Rob.

"This passes for acceptance."

Acceptance possibly, nothing compared to the real thing for these boys. Rob was meeting Vickie for a movie and dinner. The sitter was late and Vickie asked Rob to wait with her in the apartment until the sitter arrived. Unannounced, her ex-husband buzzed up. He was on his way to the airport and wanted to drop some stuff off for the boys. They began to jump up and down, shouting, "Daddy! Daddy!" He entered, they leaped onto him, and he took them both in his arms.

"Tim, this is Rob Burrows."

"Quite an entrance," Rob said. "Omar Sharif in *Lawrence of Arabia.*"

"And you do?"

"Playgrounds. MayPole Manufacturing."

"A businessman. Nice," with just enough condescension to go noticed.

He had a shopping bag with him and headed straight for the boys' room as they pulled on him in excitement. He only stayed ten minutes. Rob and Vickie labored through a conversation, treading water. Mainly they listened to the squeals from the boys' room. He sailed out, the boys still clinging to him, Tim giving a peck on the cheek to Vickie and a cursory nod for Rob, and he was gone. He was tan with thick, curly, blondish hair, a lithe six feet two. He was so dominating for these children, anything that followed their father's appearance would have been a disappointment. Vickie was unsettled by the suddenness of his entrance, the flamboyance, and she apologized to Rob, but she couldn't go through with the rest of their evening.

For Vickie, Rob was the balanced man her ex-husband was not, a businessman, as Tim patronizingly characterized him, and yet a creative businessman. Most men were frightened away by her children and a couple of months into the affair, Vickie asked him why he was not.

"I like kids," he said. "I have a son. I do work that revolves around kids. They don't scare me."

"But if we were ever to get involved?"

"We are involved.

"Seriously involved."

"We can have our relationship. With your guys I'll never be more than somebody around." By now he had been present for another grand entrance by Tim. "They have their father. And he's the sun and the stars to them and always will be."

His assessment continued to be accurate. Rob read them books when they needed someone to read a book to them, he watched them as they demonstrated their cars and trucks and games when they wanted an audience, he went to the circus with Vickie and the boys. He reached the point in their household where he could special-order his own pizza. He was somebody around, while Tim rushed in and out of the boy's lives like a great main course chef.

They had been seeing each other four months. Rob was logging in his usual long hours at work. Since his time with Vickie was limited to weekends for the most part, and portions of weekends at that, his work schedule was not a serious issue in their relationship. They emerged publicly with a few evenings scattered between Seth and his wife, Carlotta, and a woman lawyer, Dori, with whom Vickie worked in her previous law firm, who joined them with her husband, Jim, a reporter for *Newsday*.

Rob and Vickie felt it was time for her to meet Tommy. The Legal Aid Society was running a benefit, a cocktail party and screening of a movie on Ernest Shackleton's *Endurance* adventure in the Antarctic and Vickie intended to buy tickets. She asked if Rob would like to invite Tommy, assuming the story would appeal to a sixteen-year-old, and this might be a good way of meeting the boy.

Tommy was at Rob's for the weekend, a drop-in. He had plans with friends and would be sleeping there and not much more. Rob had taken to booking him in for events, buying him a shirt, going to an early afternoon movie with him, renting a video to watch together, whatever he could create. He knew Karen fared little better. Tommy appeared in cameos.

"In two weeks when you come, can you hold Friday night out? I told you I was seeing somebody and she'd like to invite us both to a movie on Shackleton."

"We talked about him in school."

"Good. It's in a movie house at Union Square. There's a cocktail party before in the lobby, which is not important. We can get there for the last few minutes, then we can see the movie. You'll be out by ten."

"Uh-huh. And *why* would I go?"

"A way for you to meet my friend. And see the movie."

"Is this an important friend?"

"Important enough that I'd like you to meet her."

"Okay, but afterward I have to split."

"Go right ahead."

A portion of the theater lobby was cordoned off for the benefit crowd and they found Vickie near the door. She was wearing a black dress that showed off her cleavage, pearls around her neck, her red hair loose around her shoulders. Tommy stared unduly at her. Whatever he might have been expecting, somebody not as sexy, younger, taller, more like his mother, she was a surprise to him.

"Tommy, this is Vickie Carstairs, Vickie, Tommy."

"Very nice to meet you, Tommy. Know much about Shackleton?"

"Some."

"I look forward."

"Me, too."

"Your dad said you covered him in school."

"A little. They knew the movie was coming out, so they talked about it in history. I think they're going in," and he took the first ripple of movement toward the inside of the theater to cut this off.

During the movie his attention went in and out. Here was the first sighting of his father, of either of his parents, free in the world, romantically, sexually. The movie ended and they paused in the lobby.

"So?" Vickie asked.

"It was good."

He stood in silence and she and Tommy studied each other. Vickie was fascinated. He did not have the paws-too-large puppy look of most teenage boys who have not yet occupied their full bodies. He was physically comfortable within himself. This did not mean he was being social. He was not giving anything. Both adults sensed they could stand there all night and he would not say another word. Rob filled the void.

"So he was a great hero, but he also took risks," Rob said.

"He did. People could have died because of him," Tommy suggested. "But—"

"Yes?" Vicki asked.

"If he stayed home there wouldn't have been a movie."

She chuckled, assuming he meant to be witty, and he stared at her, the teenager having the capacity to freeze the adult. He was, however, just staring at her.

"Gotta go. Thanks greatly."

He stiffly shook hands with Vickie, Rob kissed him, and he scurried away.

"He's gorgeous, Rob. And he hates me."

"He doesn't. He's a teenager."

"No, he hates me. Children in divorce always have the wish their parents will get together again. I'm like this redheaded symbol that it isn't going to happen."

"It isn't. So the sooner he gets it, the better in the long run."

"Except it must be very painful."

Tommy reached the doors and turned back for a last look at them, at her, at the woman who was not his mother, not anything like his mother. Vickie happened to catch his eye and she raised her hand, a little wave good-bye with a slight smile, an empathetic smile that said, I understand. This was to be the key moment in her relationship with the boy. From then on she dealt with Tommy with compassion, never allowing him to think she was trying to replace his mother, concerned, but never overly parental, trying to be his friend in court.

Tim Grove's parents were real estate brokers in Los Angeles and he was planning to take the boys to see them and tie in a trip to Disneyland. With a week's time open for Vickie without the children, she asked Rob if he would go to Paris with her. A client offered her an apartment, she had frequent flyer mileage, Rob needed only to show up. He paused before answering and she said, "Would Paris be too intense?" teasingly, to deflect her fear he was about to say that he couldn't go.

"To tell you the truth . . ." and he paused again and she wondered if this was the moment when you push too much, when everything is going along well, so long as you stay exactly where you are, and if after these eight months you try to advance it a little and he's forced to confront that little change, it falls apart.

"Paris is where Karen and I went on our honeymoon."

"I see."

"I don't know how comfortable I can be there."

She thought about how convenient it would be to say forget about it, and yet it was an opportunity, to be in Paris together and compete with the memory of her, deal with it as they were going to have to do if they were ever to move forward.

"New York is the city where you lived together and every day you're here without her and we've done things here and we've been okay. So I'll overlap with Karen and your Paris. Maybe we'll create *our* Paris."

"You're a good lawyer."

"I'm not lawyering. It's an opportunity—for both of us."

They went to museums in Paris and ate and walked and made love. The city had seen people arrive with extra baggage before. It rained every day, a gray mist, but these were beautiful days for them. When the plane landed in New York, trying to be charming, he said, "We'll always have Paris."

"What do you mean?"

"From *Casablanca*."

"I know where it's from. Humphrey Bogart says it to Ingrid Bergman because it's over."

"No, I didn't mean it that way. I mean we'll always have Paris. We have *our* Paris now."

Vickie won a victory for a real estate company in Tribeca on a mixed-use site to house a charter public high school and rental apartments. Similar to the objections in the New Rochelle dispute, a group of condo and co-op owners tried to block the school from coming into their neighborhood. After she won, Vickie gave a statement to a *New York Times* reporter. "The people who fought this probably have very strong views at dinner parties about education. And they're in favor of education for children less fortunate than they, so long as they don't go to school in their backyard." A few days later she was featured in a piece in the Metro section of *The New York Times* in the "Public Lives" column. The woman reporter was intrigued. Vickie was the ex-wife of Tim Grove and a woman who left a major law firm in a conflict between advancement and time at home with her children. Vickie was characteristically direct. "I'm not a role model. I do what I have to do. If the legal profession had been more enlightened a few years ago, I'd still be in a law firm." On the subject of her personal life Vickie offered that she had "a male friend," and it appeared that way in print, Rob not mentioned by name.

• • •

"I *am* the male friend?" he said over wine at his apartment.

"Protecting your privacy. I wouldn't want to blow your cover in case you have rambling feet."

"I don't have rambling feet. But it's a year now. And I feel we're still sort of sneaking around."

"Doesn't feel like sneaking around to me."

"I think we could improve on the zoning. Like be under one roof."

"You're looking for a real estate metaphor?"

"Not very well. I love you, Vickie. Whatever that means. Not to take anything away from saying I love you. But, you know . . . What I'm trying to say is, will you marry me?"

"Rob, that is so lovely."

"That's not a response.

"It is so. A lovely thought."

"But—"

"But I come with so much—"

"So do I."

"Not like I do. Marriage? No middle ground? No living together?"

"I think we deserve a marriage."

"Do we?"

"We do."

"My boys—it's only going to get bigger to deal with. They're only going to get bigger."

"Believe me, that is something I know."

"I'm approaching the limit, Rob. Would you want children? I've got to ask."

"No. I would say I'm pretty booked."

"Sounds terrible to ask. Did I just blow the romance of this?"

"The romance of this would be to say yes."

She took his face in her hands, kissed him, and said, "Yes. I would love to marry you. And I love *you*. Whatever that means."

A formal wedding, a civil ceremony, the parents present, no parents? Weeks of discussion. Vickie's parents lived in Cleveland, her father a chemist for a pharmaceutical company, her mother a librarian. Previously on a visit to New York they had met Rob, Vickie making dinner at home. Her parents were small in stature, conservative in their dress and manner, a matched salt-and-pepper shaker couple. Her father, Pete Carstairs, asked a few perfunctory questions about Rob's business. Her mother, Joan, was mainly interested in Rob's first marriage—and why exactly would you say you broke up? They were somewhat cordial. He understood that compared to Tim, he was not a star for these people either.

Rob wanted his parents to meet Vickie, and they came down by bus from Kingston, New York, where they lived in a retirement complex. First, they spent the afternoon with their grandson, who was at Karen's apartment, and went for lunch and a movie. Tommy agreeably spent the time. The miracle of grandparents and grandchildren. Rob's parents were congenitally sour. With Tommy, they were sunshine. Their relationship with Tommy carried over to Karen, with whom they were always cordial, to the extent Rob's parents could get out of each other's way.

He took Vickie and his parents to dinner at an Italian restaurant Rob liked in Little Italy, Pellegrino's, a place so unpretentious he thought the friendly atmosphere would overcome the chill he anticipated from his parents. Rob's father, Frank Burrows, eighty-one, five feet ten with a full head of white hair, who still possessed the handsome features he passed on to Rob, was stooped with the weight of his years and his confusion. Why am I still with this woman, why aren't I richer, why can't I remember everything? The former jewelry manufacturer was now plying wares at flea markets, relying on his wife to remember prices, facts, and the day of the week. Rob's mother, Anne Burrows, was five feet eight, stout, a beauty-parlored woman, wrinkled at seventy-eight with the outline of a pretty face depleted by time, as well as a lifetime of disapproval. She was not embarrassed to let it be known to all concerned that, if not for her, the Mister wouldn't remember half of anything. It gave an interesting glow to the proceedings. Rob caught his mother in little disapproving glances in Vickie's direction and his father peering at Vickie, as well, but at her bosom. They got through the meal, Vickie smiling so hard she might as easily have been in a booth at a sales convention.

Rob and Karen received the clear message that each team of respective parents preferred the ex-spouses and by a wide margin. Here were the odd spillovers in divorce, the ex-sons-in-law and ex-daughters-in-law with the ex-fathers-in-law and ex-mothers-in-law. Karen probably got along better with Rob's parents than he did. Less was at stake and she was the mother of their beloved grandchild. Rob liked Karen's mother very much; he just never saw her anymore. In Tommy's early years, Grandma Sally was around often. She was working in a Harlem elementary school, a getting-on-in-years white woman holding the fort on academic standards for fifth-graders, keeping her eyes on their prize. She taught school through the breakup of her own marriage with the philandering husband, after his death, and then retired to Delray, Florida, to be near a sister. In character, she took a job five days a week at a senior citizen's center while a senior herself.

Two years after the divorce Rob was in Miami on business and drove to Delray so he could meet Sally for lunch. She was in her early seventies, a still elegant-looking woman, five feet seven, erect, with Karen's dark brown eyes. They went to a restaurant and talked about Tommy and he assured her how well he and Karen were handling matters, a patient account of the need to abandon joint custody. She made inquiries about Rob's business and she filled him in on her activities at the center. To Rob, the lunch went well. He always respected her tremendously. Rob dropped her off at the center and stepped around the car and kissed her on the cheek. She looked closely at him and shook her head.

"You two," she said. "You broke my heart."

They decided to have a civil ceremony at City Hall, invite the children, a few friends, and that would be it, except they needed to find a larger apartment for the times Tommy would be with his father. Rob appealed again to his landlord contact who promised him the next three-bedroom to come up in the building was his. Two months later they had the apartment, which meant they could have the marriage.

"Why would you go into that lion's den?" Sean asked when Rob made his official announcement to him in a sports bar in Midtown.

"I love her. And I don't enjoy being single."

"You were only out there a few years before this woman. You've been with her a year. You haven't lived."

"It's enough to know. I couldn't stand the start-up time with new people, the wasted time, you show me your résumé, I'll show you mine, and the getting to know each other, and then when you do, they get cold feet, or you get cold feet and you start up again. Who needs that? Vickie's the one."

"Well, you've got it over Karen. Nothing wrong with me, kiddo, I'm whole, I'm healthy, my new sweetie's got two children, that's what a great guy I am, and I'm getting married, fuck you."

"This is not some revenge fantasy."

"You never should've broken up with her."

"That doesn't get me anywhere. We were toxic for each other."

"Two children? Rob, you doing research for a sitcom?"

"I know she's not going to want any more and that's a good thing. With somebody else, maybe they'd want a child. Marry a younger woman and that's practically a guarantee. The truth is, if I had another kid with someone, I'd feel I was being disloyal to Tommy."

"You've got too much rattling around in your head."

"Then marriage will get me organized," he quipped.

The next time Tommy was at his apartment Rob went into his room and told him he was marrying Vickie, that it would be interesting for all of them and hopefully rewarding, extending the family. Tommy said congratulations so softly it was barely speech. Rob was getting another apartment with a room for Tommy—and he wanted him to be his best man.

For several days Tommy considered whether he would want to ever stay in the new apartment. A consultation with his two pals, Jill Fleming and Brian Dobson, convinced him it was not a bad idea to have another place to get away to when it gets too tight with the custodial parent.

On an autumn day they convened in the City Clerk Chapel Room in the New York City Municipal Building, Rob, Vickie, Tommy, now seventeen, the two little boys, Sean, Carlotta, Vickie's friend Dori, and her husband, Jim. Rob was wearing a blue suit, Vickie an antique white dress, Tommy a sport jacket and tie, and the children in little-boy blazers. Their group, even factoring in the children, was by far the oldest in the room. The waiting area was institutional with gray walls and rows of worn molded-plastic chairs and yet it was bright with the promise of new marriages. A Hispanic couple, still in their teens, the girl in a beige satin gown, the boy in a dark suit with dark shirt and tie, eight people in their party, excited, animated. A couple no more than twenty-five quietly speaking Italian, with the girl's mother looking on, the girl pressing an inexpensive bouquet of mixed flowers to her lips. An Asian-American couple in their early thirties with three friends, already celebrating, taking pictures of each other in various poses. A stiff WASP-looking man in his late twenties with a delicate Indian girl his age in a sari and a woman friend along, the friend holding a suitcase for their getaway. And Rob and Vickie, the older crowd, waiting as each group of these young people entered the chapel with their dreams.

"This is New York," Rob said to Vickie.

"It's perfect."

Their names were called, and they filed into a small room where an American flag and the flag of the City of New York were displayed. A female clerk in her forties performed the ceremony at a lectern. *We are gathered today to unite Rob and Vickie . . . If there is anyone present with any legal reason why these people should not be united, speak now or forever be silent . . . As a token of your love will you place the ring . . . By the powers invested in me . . .* It took no more than three minutes, they kissed, Carlotta took their picture, and they were married.

Rob phoned Karen and she was surprised, hoping her surprise didn't show, and offered her congratulations. She assumed Rob would always favor his traveling-man side and she wondered how he would reconcile it with a new wife with two young children. Rob and Vickie went on a honeymoon to Morocco and returned to New York and their complicated extended families.

A month after the wedding Vickie called Karen and asked if they could have lunch. Karen agreed, thinking it extraordinarily civilized; curious and dreading it. They went to Jerry's, an informal restaurant near Karen's store, Vickie in a suit for her meetings that day, Karen less formally dressed for the store in a skirt and sweater. Karen did not expect to find Rob's new wife so dramatic, the red hair, the theatrical bosom and figure. She was fascinated, this is the look of the woman Rob chose, wondering if it was a comment on her, that ultimately he thought her to be dowdy. For her part, Vickie didn't think Karen would be so elegantly beautiful. She wondered if she looked gaudy opposite her.

They discussed the store and Vickie's practice. Articulating for both of them, Vickie said, "This couldn't be more awkward."

"I agree."

"I thought it was important because of Tommy. Sometimes he'll be staying with us. And I hoped there wouldn't be tension."

"Why should there be tension? Just because you married my ex-husband?" Karen said directly, and it was so direct Vickie laughed.

"Well, there needn't be extra tension."

"Okay."

"I have two little boys of my own, seven and eight. They take up space and attention exponentially. But Tommy is going to occupy some portion of our household. It's important for me to tell you, I have my boys, and whatever relationship evolves with Tommy, I will never look to replace you in any way."

"Thank you. The best interests of Tommy."

Vickie said what she wanted to say and they had little to do with each other from then on, a few words on the phone concerning Tommy's movements. No animosity. No friendship.

In the beginning period of the new marriage Tommy seldom stayed in the new apartment. It's too weird, he told his friends. Gradually he found it convenient, as they suggested. Vickie was cautious with Tommy, not imposing herself. He came to enjoy her children. When he was there he played with them, read to them, took them to movies. They worshipped him.

The tutor from Power Testing, Dean Jacobson, was at the apartment for a session.

"How are you doing?" Vickie asked Tommy when he left.

"Better, I think."

"He's good?"

"Went to Harvard. Interesting looking guy, huh?"

"He's overdoing the grunge thing for my taste, but if he's effective—"

"We'll find out."

"What school are you leaning toward, Tommy?"

"Any place that'll take me."

She was upset by the exchange. She sensed Tommy was bright, no matter how he was faring in the rating system, and unusual in the way he related so comfortably with her children. Before she and Rob went to sleep that night she said, "I read some students defer a year before they go to college. They take a break, get some life experience. Maybe that'd be good for Tommy."

"He's in with other kids now and they're all going through the SAT and everything, so he's game. If he delays, down the line he may not be as motivated."

A rational response. But with the scores, the applications, the lines to be filled in, from her viewpoint, there was no way of properly presenting this boy to colleges. As far as she was concerned, by the rigid standards used, he had already fallen through the cracks.

FOUR

• • •

The three friends, Tommy Burrows, slender and composed, Jill Fleming, small and perky, and Brian Dobson, taller than Jill, shorter than Tommy, rotund and ungainly, were together as often as their school schedules would allow. Jill went through boys as if the supply were inexhaustible, Tommy had an occasional girlfriend, Brian, hapless in social encounters, lived dateless, but they were the constant for each other. They had been so since a sixth-grade assignment had required them to work as a team charting jaywalking patterns on Fifth Avenue, the results long forgotten, but here was the real result, these pals.

The captain of the field hockey team, having briefly lost a boyfriend to Jill, dubbed them "The Three Stooges." The nickname didn't last. Students at the school tended to hang out in various combinations and this was another. And you couldn't take the "Stooges" appellation seriously when Brian was in there throwing off the curve with a perfect SAT score of 1600.

Brian's mother, Marjorie, was a fundraiser for the New York State Republican Party and a frequent head shot in the New York newspapers. Her second husband was Ralph Bettman, of Bettman, Rangerly and Corvin. He defended lawyers in lawsuits. Bettman, sixty-eight, a dapper man in Brioni suits, talked about retiring. Business was too good. Brian's father, Paul Dobson, a bankruptcy lawyer, once worked at Bettman, Rangerly and Corvin. Marjorie Dobson, a sultry woman in her forties, half Brazilian, with nearly black hair, pale skin, and almond-shaped eyes, had had an affair with Bettman for two years, while never missing a beat in sleeping with her husband, now and then. Bettman was in the clear morally, his wife had passed away six years before. In her machinations, Marjorie announced to Bettman she was breaking it off, she couldn't live the lie any longer and, as she planned, he urged her to divorce her husband and marry him, and she did.

Paul Dobson moved out, all the way to Chicago, where he joined a law firm and within six months married a physical therapist. His animosity toward his wife, his desire to have nothing to do with his first marriage, took the unfortunate form for Brian of the father distancing himself from his son. He started a new family in Chicago and was more attentive to the two little daughters from his new domestic arrangement than to Brian. Since the breakup of the marriage Brian had seen his father a smattering of times. Paul Dobson never seemed to work out regular holiday visits for his son. With the onset of e-mail Brian hoped he might develop an e-mail relationship with his father, little messages to keep the lines of communication going. Days would pass before Paul answered and sometimes he never got around to it. Brian did not consider his father to be on his "buddy list."

Brian lived with his mother and stepfather in a Fifth Avenue co-op on 67th Street, an apartment with world-class antiques and formidable art on the walls. He had a room an apartment's length away from them with a small TV, a DVD player, and his computer. He wanted no part of the big screen TV or elaborate stereo system his mother and stepfather had in their end of the apartment. He never used the home gym they installed in one of the rooms. This was an attempt at independence, to reject their toys. He came and went through the back door, the servant's entrance. They were on the New York social scene A-list for people of their station, benefits, benefit committees, dinner parties, out nearly seven nights a week. Brian could go four days without seeing his mother or his stepfather. He usually ate alone. They employed a housekeeper and Brian had little contact with her. He was a latchkey child in a luxury co-op. His friends, who accepted him fat, who accepted him socially unacceptable, were, in a way, his family.

Jill Fleming lived on Second Avenue and 65th Street in a two-bedroom apartment with her mother, Lonna. Lonna had been a communications major at Syracuse University, where she met Jill's father and worked in public relations until the marriage ended. With the divorce Lonna went into a slide and quit her job. Realizing her torpor was a terrible model for her daughter, who was urging her to open the blinds, she rejoined the company she worked for and became a functioning single parent. She was replaced in her husband's life by "Miss Fitness," a model featured in the television advertising of the company Jill's father owned, Super Health Centers. The happily remarried Marv Fleming lived in an East Side town house with the former "Miss Fitness," Chappy Lawrence, twenty-seven years old, very fit. Chappy was taking singing lessons and through a connection Marv managed to get her club dates in a couple of Greenwich Village venues. He asked Jill to see her perform "The Songs of Billy Joel by Chappy Lawrence." For support, Jill brought her support team. Tommy thought she wasn't bad for someone who wasn't a singer yet. Brian said she wasn't bad for someone in a karaoke club, only she wasn't in a karaoke club. Jill thought she was the worst singer she had ever heard in her life, except for Brian.

When Tommy was a little boy Rob brought him along to playground dedications if MayPole donated equipment. His intent was not to proselytize about civic responsibility, although taking him did result in awareness in the child. Mainly he wanted to include Tommy in what he did for a living and give him a chance to play on the equipment he manufactured. Karen ran special events in her store featuring crafts for use in children's rooms, hiring clowns, balloon makers. The artisans came with their children and grandchildren and Tommy mingled with them. Tommy grew up in contact with children from inner-city neighborhoods. Influenced by his parents, Tommy volunteered in the recreation center in St. James Park in the Bronx, doing crafts projects with elementary school children. Influenced by Tommy, Brian and Jill also signed up. Brian taught chess to the children, Jill ran an exercise class for the senior citizens. They had been doing this for three years, beyond the school requirement for community service. They understood by volunteering they got more out of it than the people they were assisting. They didn't want to be labeled as they might have been by youngsters less privileged, as private school kids, rich kids. These young people lived on a tightrope, maneuvering between their parents' life decisions, trying to find a balance for themselves.

Jill played on the girls' field hockey team and started to write about the team for the school newspaper, eventually attracting Tommy and Brian to the newspaper. Brian wrote movie reviews, scholarly treatises with detailed cross-references to other movies. It was Jill who suggested, since Tommy couldn't draw, that he make social observations and run them under the stick figures. They were happiest in their little group. But as independent as they might like to have thought of themselves, they were still under parental control. They needed to go to college and needed their parents for college.

Brian's stepfather had attended Harvard and Harvard Law School and so had Brian's father. With his high grades and perfect SAT score, the community service, the movie review column, the social positioning, Brian was certain to be accepted at Harvard and was applying for early admission to be done with it. As Tommy pointed out, "Yale is your safety."

Jill was leaning toward Tufts. She wanted to continue with French in college and the school was supposedly strong in foreign language studies. She was a B-plus student and her SAT score was 1430, above the median average for incoming freshmen, as indicated in the college guides the Bantrey students studied. She also liked the idea of going to school in the Boston area.

"To sit with your boyfriend along the Charles River—"

"It's not about boyfriends and the Charles River. You need to be in *a* school, don't you?" Brian said, the three eating lunch together in the cafeteria.

"That, too."

If either Clark in Worcester or Marlowe in Pittsfield accepted Tommy they could conceivably see each other on weekends. He couldn't count on anything, though. It could end up being Gettysburg deep in Pennsylvania. Brian tried to help him with the SAT, but he didn't have a good technique for teaching a friend, he just knew answers. So Dean Jacobson was the ticket to raising Tommy's score. He seemed to know what he was doing and on the practice SAT tests Tommy was performing better.

Tommy needed a sense of the colleges that were on his list. He visited the Web sites, wrote away for catalogs, and was ready for his college visits.

Karen and Tommy left the city on a Friday afternoon to see the two Pennsylvania campuses, Gettysburg and Lafayette. They were going to stay at a motel in Gettysburg Friday night, visit the campus in the morning, and drive north to visit the Lafayette campus later in the day. Tommy spent part of the time on the drive working on a practice SAT. He set the test aside and plugged a Bruce Springsteen album into his Walkman. Karen wondered if kids Tommy's age listened to Springsteen; she thought it was people Springsteen's age. Tommy, one of these places *has to* want you.

Karen asked him to put it on the tape deck of the car. Driving along, listening to Springsteen, she was reminded of Bob Dylan and then she thought of the first time she learned Rob Burrows, the cute guy on the campaign, knew the words to all kinds of Dylan songs. Dylan, now Springsteen, time gone, the marriage gone, their boy sitting next to her.

Karen and Tommy picked a particularly good moment to visit the Pennsylvania colleges. The leaves were turning, crisp air, a bounce to the students' steps. At Gettysburg they joined with other high school students and their parents for an orientation session by an admissions officer and a tour led by an I-love-this-school-more-than-life-itself student guide. On the drive north to the next on the list, Lafayette College, Tommy said, "Looked really nice. A little quiet."

"I think that's the idea."

"The fraternities. That's such a stupid idea. I don't know if I want to be in a place with fraternities."

"Not everybody joins. Lafayette has fraternities, too."

"Were you in a sorority? Was Dad in a fraternity?"

"We weren't. Actually, Penn still has fraternities and it's considered a good school, so I'd say you can coexist."

"I know what you're thinking. I can't make too big a deal. If the place I can get into has fraternities, I'd have to go and just not join."

"We may be surprised. You may end up with more of a choice than you think."

"I heard some kids are getting their essays ghostwritten."

She had heard. An insidious idea.

Tommy laughed softly and made a note on a slip of paper.

"What?"

"Idea for a cartoon. Kid says, 'My mom helped me so much with my college applications *she* got into Wesleyan, but I'm going to Tufts.' "

She chuckled and glanced over at him. His lightness passed quickly.

Lafayette College was another sylvan campus graced by autumn. The tour guide was a young woman from the soccer team in love with her surroundings. Following the tour Tommy went to a coffee klatch of high school visitors with Lafayette students, free time for the parents. Karen sat on the library steps and read a newspaper. A man in his forties approached her.

He wore an expensive-looking brown tweed jacket and slacks and an open-necked beige silk shirt, stylish for a college campus, brown hair and eyes, a well-trimmed beard, someone who would stand out in the city, certainly he did in this setting.

"Visiting here?"

"My son's looking at schools."

"That is a fabulous bag."

She had a crafts bag from her store made out of quilt material.

"Thank you for noticing."

"A great day to be looking. Your son interested?"

"I doubt that he knows yet."

"I'm Peter Briggins. I teach here."

"Peter Briggins. Do you write?"

"I do."

"I read a book of your stories."

"Head of the English department is a friend of mine. I've taught in a couple of places and he said, why not us, so I'm here for the semester."

"Good for them."

"And for me. I got divorced, not an easy time, and this is a good place to park for a while."

Karen wouldn't talk to anyone in the city who approached her. In the store she maintained a distance with customers. This seemed more informal.

"Your name is?"

"Karen Burrows."

"Your husband couldn't make it?"

"He's working *and* remarried."

Jesus, this feels like I'm in a bar.

"I'm new here, but anything I can tell you about the place—"

He offered to buy her a cup of coffee. Conflicted, should I, maybe I'll learn something valuable for Tommy, is that an excuse, he's coming on to me, is that a crime, oh, what the hell, she went with him to the cafeteria. He gave her his impressions of Lafayette. He asked about her work and she told him about the store. She mentioned Tommy's cartoons for the newspaper and he was interested. If Tommy would send some to him perhaps he might write a letter of recommendation attesting to his creativity and that might help his application.

She smiled slightly and he immediately picked up on it.

"Worrying if it's unethical because we just met and I don't really know your son—and what's my motivation?"

"Sort of."

"I do get into New York. I'm sure you knew that was coming. But I'm also interested in creative students and if I think there's a spark there, I'd be willing to say so. But there has to be something there."

"I'll talk to Tommy about it."

"A lot of this is fake fair. Like Olympic skating. Not everyone who gets into a school is better than the one who doesn't."

"I don't think I want to hear this. It *was* a beautiful day."

They walked back to the library steps and Tommy was waiting.

"Good?" Karen asked.

"Interesting."

"This is Peter Briggins. He teaches writing here. Tommy Burrows."

They shook hands, Tommy studying him.

"Your mother told me about these cartoons you do—"

"They're really noncartoons. Line drawings with sayings."

"Would you send me some? Not promising anything, but maybe I could help on your application."

Tommy looked at both of them.

"Okay."

"What do you think of it here?"

"I like it."

"Anything you don't like?"

"Fraternities. Not much of a fan."

"Neither am I. Why don't you send me the drawings."

Sensing he had reached the end of the segment, he shook hands with Tommy and then with Karen and walked on.

"Peter Briggins. Didn't you read—"

"A book of his."

"How did you meet him?"

"We just got to talking."

"Oh. Well, I'm done here."

"So am I."

On the drive home Tommy went through some of the material he had accumulated at the two campuses.

"You think I should send the cartoons to that guy?"

"I don't think it can hurt."

"Mom, how are you doing with Bill?"

"Fine. *You* know. He's a very nice person. And what about you, young man? Anyone special?"

He was so noncommunicative about his social life she rarely knew much about his activities. She didn't know whether it was true of boys or just Tommy.

"I was hanging with somebody from Trinity. She got too possessive and I broke it off."

"How long were you together?"

"A couple of months."

She couldn't do the math, whether that meant they were having sex. Something must have gone on.

"I'm going to take a nap now," ending the discussion.

He said that she got too possessive. The remark disquieted her. Should she connect the divorce to Tommy running from a relationship? My darling, did we do this to you? Did you run? Are you going to grow up to be a runner?

Driving back to the city, Karen reflected on the encounter with Briggins. He approached her and she allowed it to go to the next stage. Minor, a cup of coffee, nonetheless the next stage. She could have declined. He was younger than Bill, more age-appropriate. She was attracted to him. But Bill is dependable, not someone like this guy, needy, coming off a divorce and isolated on a college campus. I am all over the place.

She was eager to be home. Bill was waiting with an order of sushi and a chilled bottle of white wine. Tommy was not in a storytelling mood. Karen filled in and, as if to confront her confusion of the day, she said, "We met this writer, Peter Briggins, who teaches at Lafayette, and he said if Tommy sends him some cartoons he might give him a letter of recommendation. We'll see. It's up to Tommy."

"Sounds like a nice guy."

"Seems so," Karen said.

She offered no more and prodded Tommy to answer a few questions about the courses and the facilities at the colleges for Bill's benefit. After ten minutes on the subject of the trip she could read in Bill's face—okay, I got it, as if he were the one who had the long day, and he made a transition to a rough session on Wall Street. Tommy slipped off to his room. Not a great performance for Bill. About a C plus, she estimated, unhappy with herself for grading him. What's worse here, she wondered, his withdrawing or me grading him? Still, a C plus.

• • •

The next leg of Tommy's college visits was to be Rob's—the safeties, SUNY Albany and Clark University in Worcester, Massachusetts, with one of the middles, Marlowe College in Pittsfield, Massachusetts. Then the learning disabled issue surfaced at Bantrey. Karen called Rob at his office. She had to get together with him immediately. He was leaving for a sales call in San Diego and would be away five days. She shook her head slightly on the travel announcement, a pain memory. But he was someone else's problem now. When he returned to town they met for a drink after work, Rob suggesting Gallagher's, a Midtown steakhouse where Rob was known. Karen had never been in a steakhouse with Bill. Is the world divided between men who eat steak and men who won't because they're worried about cholesterol?

They ordered drinks and she asked, pro forma, "How was your trip?"

"All right."

It was similar to the empty exchanges between them in the past about his business travel and might have been lifted right out of the end of their marriage. This stood for what it was, a token icebreaker.

"I was at the school last week," Karen said, getting on with it, "auction committee stuff, and I overheard something that's very disturbing. About a half dozen of Tommy's classmates are going for a disability exemption on the SAT."

"A disability exemption?"

"They get extra time on the test with a note from a doctor saying they're learning disabled. They can get up to five hours instead of three. The scores used to go in with an asterisk. But now they don't have to, so if you've got the exemption you can take more time to finish than everyone else and the college doesn't know it. The colleges only get the score."

"These are students who are not learning disabled, I take it."

"That's the idea. Their wonderful parents buy a diagnosis from a willing doctor."

"For God's sake."

"Three of his classmates that I know about are doing it. From what I hear they've never shown any signs of dyslexia or attention deficit disorder or anything. They do better in school than Tommy."

"How did you find this out?"

"One of the parents. Her sister's a doctor. She talked to someone she knew who was accommodating people and had an attack of conscience and stopped. Can you believe it, they're buying time on the SAT."

"Which costs?"

"A couple of thousand to get an evaluation that will stick."

"Really?"

"Tommy's competition isn't Brian and Jill. His competition is—if one of *these* kids is close to him on the SAT. And if Tommy wants to go to a school and they want to go to the same school and they get in by doing this and raising their score, they've blocked him out."

They looked at each other, neither committing to the next leap. Do we dare consider this for Tommy?

"In principle, where is this disabled thing different from hiring a tutor like we're doing?" he said.

"Everybody in Tommy's world hires tutors, so if you don't you're foolish," she said.

"They don't at three hundred fifty dollars a session in Harlem."

"And as Mr. Kammler said, Tommy's not in rural Indiana, either. The kids in *these* schools are his competition. That's the playing field he has to play on. But this tips the field. So there. I vented. I needed to get it out with you and I did."

"Insidious. What are we in?"

"We're not going to do it for Tommy, of course. We're not that kind of people. He's not learning disabled. He's just—Tommy."

"What kind of lesson can it even be for your child?"

"Oh, I don't think these people care about lessons. They care about scores."

"Vickie said something about his delaying a year, maybe pick up a little time to mature."

"It's not a good idea. He'd never go back to school."

"That's what I said."

They would not diminish themselves or their son by playing the learning disabled card. They were synchronous for the moment, divorced people working with the remnants of what had once been a marriage.

FIVE

• • •

Whenever the economy was sluggish, playground equipment dipped below the horizon line. Rob was obliged to increase his travel and was away at minimum a week each month. Vickie was busy with her real estate clients and, depending on the rhythms of her work, she could glide past Rob's absences, or try to do so. But a potential crisis developed over celebrating their first wedding anniversary. Vickie asked her parents to come in from Cleveland and stay with the boys for a weekend; she and Rob were taking a trip to Bermuda to celebrate. Rob was in Seattle, where bad rains were playing havoc with a playground installation and he was obliged to stay on to placate the local officials. The project was the first in a geographic area he wanted to cultivate and he thought it would be a poor business decision to break off too quickly and go back to New York. He was supposed to fly home, be there a day, and then go on to Bermuda with Vickie. He kept delaying until everyone in Seattle was satisfied with the installation. He took the last red-eye possible, narrowly avoiding missing their first wedding anniversary celebration, which would not have been acceptable behavior. He was cutting it so short he had to meet Vickie at the airport for their Bermuda flight.

"I don't know whether to kill you, or to kill you," she said.

"I am so sorry. Let me take you to Bermuda to make up for it."

"Rob, this is crazy. And I'm not just talking about this trip."

"Never again."

"Right. Least you didn't say, I'll meet you in Bermuda."

They enjoyed two spectacular weather days in Bermuda and the crisis was averted.

Vickie was developing an even-tempered relationship with Tommy and it was logical for her to ask to come along on the next round of college visits. She had the opportunity because Tim was in New York and she prevailed upon him to take care of the children for a weekend. She was supporting him with a sleep-over sitter so he wouldn't have to be on full duty. Rob and Vickie drove north toward Albany in the no-nonsense Volvo sedan they owned, a carryover from his marriage to Karen when, for safety with a child, they owned Volvos. They stopped along the way in Kingston to see Rob's parents. Saturday morning and his parents were working a flea market in a church basement. When they entered the hall Frank was sitting listlessly in a canvas chair while Anne stood over their wares, three folding tables with scattered merchandise. The display was eclectic, costume jewelry, kitchen items, lunch boxes, picture postcards, vinyl albums, crystal ware. On seeing her grandson, Anne let out a yelp, rousing Frank.

"What a delight," Anne said. "You're looking at colleges?"

"SUNY Albany's first today," Tommy said.

"That's not far," Frank responded. "We'll see you if you go there."

"To be announced," Tommy answered.

"How are you, folks?" Vickie asked.

"Could be better. Could be worse," Anne said. She looked at Vickie peculiarly as if she expected Karen to be along with Rob on this excursion. "Your children, are they with you?" Anne asked, an unmistakable tone, her son's second wife had her own children.

"They're with their father for the weekend."

"I saw his picture in *People* magazine," Anne said. "He was at a Hollywood party."

"No doubt. He's in New York for a party."

"How's the show going?" Rob said.

"Starting slow, but you always hope for the best," Frank answered.

"He wouldn't know if it's starting fast," Anne had to say, "but it's starting slow."

"Come with me, my big boy," Frank said, his arm around Tommy and he led him to a nearby booth.

A browser stopped to look at a Flintstones lunch box, a man in a work jacket, jeans, and boots. Rob was intrigued: There's a market for this?

"How much?"

"Twenty-five dollars," Anne said.

"I'll give you ten."

"You'll give me twenty or you'll give me nothing."

"I'll give you nothing." And he walked away.

"Very effective, Mother," Rob said.

"He'll be back. It's an antique."

Anne showed Rob why it was an important Flintstones lunch box, ignoring Vickie. Anne couldn't be more obvious, you are the second wife, you are an outsider, you are not the mother of our grandchild, you have children of your own. Vickie looked over to the booth where Frank had led Tommy. Frank proudly fit a vintage Yankees hat on Tommy's head. He nodded to the dealer, we'll settle later. Tommy came back to show off his present in front of his proud grandfather, then he turned to Vickie. She tugged on the brim affectionately and Tommy gave her a warm smile. Anne seemed offended they were even relating. Frank stared at Vickie after her exchange with Tommy. He shook his head in the affirmative, having come to a decision, picked up a rhinestone bracelet, one of the better items in the display, and handed it to her.

"For you."

"I couldn't."

"What, you want a Yankee hat?"

"Frank! You don't give away the merchandise," Anne reprimanded.

"It's for her!" Never taking his eyes off Vickie, shaking his head—if you're all right with my grandson, you're all right with me.

They stayed awhile and then needed to get on their way. Kisses all around, Anne maintaining her iciness toward Vickie, even more so now. As they walked away, Frank caught Vickie by the arm, drawing her away from the others.

"He's going to be all right with this college business, my Tommy? He's not so good in school, I hear."

"He's a wonderful boy. They have to discover him and they will."

He was reassured by the response.

"She makes out like I don't know anything. The bracelet, *I* found it. Enjoy."

They left the building, Tommy ahead of Rob and Vickie.

"You made headway with my dad," Rob said to her.

"I'll take it."

"My mother, she still hasn't accepted *me*."

"They're difficult. But you have to give them their due, they keep themselves busy."

"That could be us one day," he said puckishly. "We can be a team, without the undercurrent."

"A sweet thought. Maybe one day."

He was back from the road, she was along on this junket, and she got past his parents. She was abundantly aware of the extent he had been traveling. She didn't realize she was caught in an old Rob flight pattern.

The State University of New York at Albany with its undergraduate population of nearly twelve thousand was the other end of the spectrum from the nearly dreamy small liberal arts campuses of Gettysburg and Lafayette. The campus was spread over a couple of locales and there were students everywhere. People were headed in various directions looking as though each of them had purpose. The school was known to be strong in political science, given its proximity to the state government in Albany, and in English. Mr. Kammler was watching out for Tommy's concern about coping with science and math. The school also featured fraternities, a football team, and in its attempts to be a rounded university, plays, films, lectures, concerts. It was his main safety, the place where he might very well land. For the first time in these visits he understood, through the very size of the place and the number of people moving about, that it was a necessity to own something of his own, to choose a major, to have purpose himself. I'm not about anything. Jill has French. Brian has history or any damn thing he chooses. And all those people, they're on their way somewhere. I'm not anywhere.

Marlowe was their next stop and in the car he said, "I think it'll help if I'm an English major."

"Sounds sensible," Rob said. "Can be the foundation for any number of things."

"And I *speak* English, so that's a start."

"I think you speak English very well," Vickie said.

Marlowe College in Pittsfield, Massachusetts, had been created thirty years earlier by Roger Marlowe, a former owner of Cadmium, an electronics company in Waltham. The main goal of the college was to develop computer scientists who had wide-ranging interests or, as one of the college guides said, "Computer nerds who can read a novel." The computer science program was outstanding, but the departments in the humanities were fairly strong. The scuttlebutt in the guides was that for its specialty, computer science, Marlowe was very difficult to get into, but humanities majors who were needed to balance out the campus could slip in on less impressive scores and grades. At twelve hundred students it was one of the smaller colleges in the northeast, with a pocket-sized campus Marlowe converted from a boys' prep school. Stone buildings from the prep school days were augmented by newer versions. No football team. And no fraternities. In keeping with its mission, the college offered a first-rate schedule of cultural events, film, theater, concert and lecture series popular with the students and the Pittsfield community.

The newly minted English major-to-be could see himself here. And with the cultural activity he didn't think he would feel isolated, the offerings interesting enough so that Jill and Brian might even come over to visit him. The tour guide looked like a computer nerd, but he was low-key, a change from the boosters at the other colleges. "We actually discourage people from coming," he said. "We only want the people who really want to be here." Tommy was already counting himself as one of them. He figured if he could squeeze another hundred points out of his SAT he might have a shot at getting in as one of the token nongeniuses.

They stayed at an inn near Worcester and discussed the day over dinner. Tommy was enthusiastic about Marlowe, and he had a major now, something to shoot for; he was feeling optimistic. The next morning they visited Clark at Worcester, with about nineteen hundred undergraduates, the size of many small colleges. Again, Mr. Kammler's list held up. Clark, the second of Tommy's two safeties, looked like a good place for a student with Tommy's academic record, a respectable school.

"What do you think?" Rob asked as they headed for the car after the visit.

"Possible. I'd rather go to Marlowe. I'd say it's my first choice."

"You can't know that yet. You've still got to see Colby and Hamilton."

"Those were my reaches, Dad. Mr. Kammler didn't hold out much hope."

"People visit their reaches, don't they?"

"I don't want to spend the time. If I get in, I'll visit."

"But it'll affect the way you apply."

"Dad, they're in a book, *The Hidden Ivies*, that they're these underrated schools, as good an education as Ivy League. They're not going to take me. I'd rather spend my time working to get in where I have a chance."

"That's totally defeatist and it's not playing it out."

Rob turned to Vickie for her opinion.

"It's up to him, Rob, if that's how he wants to spend his time. People do visit once they get in."

"I disagree with both of you."

They stopped at a diner for lunch and Tommy went on about Marlowe and how clever Mr. Kammler was to put it on the list and how you never know, maybe they'll get overstocked with brains and they'll need someone like him to integrate the place, a cheerful riff which made Rob feel better about things, but Rob still felt he should go to the top of his list and take a look at Hamilton and Colby. In his business he would be out of business if he didn't make calls where it was a long shot.

Karen and Bill went to a movie at the Angelika Film Center downtown, where most of the people in the lobby were considerably younger and Bill seemed to be the oldest man. Was it age, then, that held him off from being interested in Tommy? Was he too old to care about high school senior problems? Over drinks after the movie she tried to pass on Rob's report to her about the last college visits and Bill looked to be barely listening.

"This is important to me."

"I realize that, but I really don't have much to offer. It's all different from my daughter's time."

"You tune out."

"I just think . . . He liked Marlowe. And a couple of the others. That's a very good start."

"You just think what?"

"Nothing."

"Bill—"

"I just think a lot of this turmoil you and Rob go through over the boy is unnecessary."

"Is that a fact?"

"My opinion—these children, eventually they all find their own level."

"I see."

"So it's not that I don't care about him, or about your worries about him, it's the reverse. It's just that I have this really strong opinion—"

"That they find their own level. Eventually."

"Right."

"But we don't know what that level is. Or what he might need to get there."

• • •

Dean Jacobson was in now for two sessions a week, Dean also tutoring Tommy in calculus to keep him afloat in his schoolwork. Tommy sent off a batch of his cartoons to Peter Briggins at Lafayette and geared himself for the next try at the SAT. He did a cartoon for the newspaper. One student says to another, "I think they should grade the SAT pass-fail."

Karen was considering a new store manager. He was from New York and last worked in Scottsdale in a Native-American arts gallery. John Fox was thirty-two, five feet ten, blond with a male model's features. She liked his work experience, which related to her merchandise, except he had no background in managing a store.

"We'd be starting from scratch. I'd have to teach you everything."

"I went out to Scottsdale and didn't know anything about Indian crafts."

"What brought you there?"

"A boyfriend. He was in real estate there."

"You only list the gallery. No other jobs?"

"Are you hiring dancers?" he said.

"Where did you dance?"

"The Joffrey. I was injured. I adapted."

His knowledge of at least one area of crafts was a plus. His lack of managing experience in a store, a significant minus. Bill was coming downtown to meet her for dinner and she seized on the opportunity to have Bill meet this prospect. Here was the kind of support she could count on him for and she invited John to join them for dinner. Before they went out, Karen took Bill aside and gave him a quick briefing on John's background, then they went to the Mercer Grill, a nearby restaurant. Bill spoke to him exclusively about his dance career, the pieces he danced, his opinions of choreographers, his taste in ballet. John went on his way afterward and Bill strolled along with Karen.

"That was curious. Not a word about managing a store."

"You're going to have to teach him, which you can do. If he can bring a portion of what he feels about ballet to your business, I'd give him a lifetime contract. Also, and this is important, he accepted the discipline of ballet into his life and he was a working dancer. He can handle being the manager of a store."

"Thank you," she said, kissing him on the lips.

"That's what we're here for." I can do this. Don't press me so hard on Tommy, was the implication.

She hired John Fox. He was off to a notable beginning, a quick study, effective with the salespeople and the customers, a major problem solved with an assist from Bill, whose strengths were his strengths. She avoided discussions of Tommy and college, not pressing Bill on the subject, no tests.

Smiling a good-looking-guy smile at one of the young saleswomen in the front of the store, wearing a brown tweed suit with a bright yellow scarf twirled around his neck, Peter Briggins walked into Karen's place near closing time. She was surprised to see him, an unwanted reality for her—physical attraction, the possibilities of what it might be like to be with a man younger than Bill, someone who knew what her son was going through, who lived in that culture—and how stable was it with Bill if all this is cascading through my head just from the look of the man, puffed up in his English squire motif, but impressive looking, you have to give him that.

"What a tremendous store," he said.

"Peter Briggins. Looking very town-and-country."

"I was in to see my publisher and I thought I'd take a chance you might be here. I brought a letter for your son."

"Did you? That's very, very nice of you."

"I thought we might talk about it over a drink."

"One drink, Peter. I have plans tonight."

He suggested they go to Fanelli's, a SoHo hangout for artists established well before SoHo became gentrified. He knew his way around. She sipped a glass of wine while he drank a Grey Goose vodka straight up with a twist, nothing Lafayette College about his drink, he was in a New York state of mind. He concentrated on her, on the store, how she got into the business, what she liked best in these crafts areas, tell me about yourself, honey, type of talk. He appeared to her far more experienced in these opening round gambits. If she were a bookbinder he would be asking right about then which adhesive she preferred in bookbinding. She directed the attention away from herself. He was in the city for a couple of days, then was going back to the campus. She judged him to be someone you have on the side when you're married, or on the side when you're in a relationship that has room for opportunity. I would give us three months, tops, under any circumstances. Karen decided to get to the letter for Tommy and wrap this up, not the time for a dalliance. Bill, on the comeback trail, offered stability and culture and had proven how valuable he could be and was reliable while this man with his smile and his technique was unreliability personified.

"What did you think of Tommy's work?"

"Clever. Obviously he can't draw a lick so he does these simple drawings. But the one-liners are pretty good."

"I agree."

"But here's the problem. I can't, as someone who teaches writing, as a writer, go hog-wild over one-liners. It would look phony."

"We don't want phony."

"With that as a disclaimer, something was there. Here's what I wrote for him."

He removed a letter from an envelope inside his jacket pocket and handed it to her.

"As the author of several works of fiction and a member of the faculty at Lafayette College, with previous positions at Middlebury and Wesleyan, I believe I can recognize creativity in young people. Thomas Burrows in his clever, insightful observations of high school life for his high school newspaper demonstrates genuine creativity."

"Could be helpful. Much appreciated."

"And please, not just for Lafayette. Use it for other schools."

"It's very nice of you."

"Now—think we could make a transition to dinner? How firm are these plans of yours?"

"Firm. And frankly, no disrespect intended, so is my relationship with the man I'm seeing."

"I was just suggesting dinner. What does he do?"

"Runs a foundation. Promoting literacy."

"Noble. I'd expect no less of you."

"That's a nice compliment."

"You run quite an operation, Karen. I admire you."

"And I admire your writing."

"Well—a rain check on dinner."

He remained at the table as she left. Her assumption was that Peter Briggins would try his luck with the general population, beginning with whoever wandered into the place. She now had a letter of recommendation for Tommy to go with letters from his faculty advisor on the newspaper and the director of the recreation center in the Bronx. Impossible to know what was decisive within the lunacy. She looked at the letter again. The language was restrained. Briggins's restraint made sense to her: He taught writing and these weren't schoolboy short stories that would have been in his area of expertise. They were something different, wry observations. To his credit he didn't sell out a piece of his reputation to curry favor with a woman. Perhaps there was more to him than a guy cruising in good clothes. His fiction actually seemed more complex to her than he did. She was comfortable, though, with her decision to get out of there before his second drink. Her plans that evening were not firm, she had no plans. Bill was in Boston on business.

MayPole Manufacturing was located a few subway stops away from Manhattan in an industrial building in Long Island City. The showroom was created by Rob's chief designer, Lars Olaffsen, forty-two, a hulking man of six feet four with a craggy face, and in keeping with Rob's athletic leanings, a former linebacker from the University of Pittsburgh who had transferred to Carnegie Mellon. Lars was married to an architect and they had a daughter, Toby, a tenth-grader at the Bronx High School of Science. When she was a little girl Toby played on MayPole equipment at playground dedications just as Tommy had done, and Rob was privy to her schoolgirl triumphs over the years. The college frenzy had not yet reached the Olaffsen household. A marriage intact, a high-achieving child, talented people, Rob admired the Olaffsens, but kept his distance socially, which he felt was correct for the business relationship. His style was to remain distant from all his employees. His wife, to some degree, his ex-wife, and his friend, Seth, were the only ones he opened up to and he was not about to admit to anyone at work how much he worried about his son.

The MayPole showroom was an outdoor space indoors. On display were bucket swings, tire swings, tunnels, birdhouses, trains, fire engines, cars, castles, adventure towers, ships, chutes, seesaws, gingerbread houses, all for climbing and wriggling and whatever. Rob positioned MayPole as the high end, quality manufacturer of playground equipment. The image of the company was reinforced by the trade advertising, the company's catalog, the sales promotion material, and its Web site, all executed by Seth's advertising agency.

Part of Rob's travel time was devoted to drop-ins and schmoozing with the dozen construction contractors who supplied installation workers on a need basis to install equipment anywhere in the United States. He never thought Karen understood the necessity of keeping his network intact, and now Vickie was getting restless with him. He didn't see a way out; it went with the territory.

His staff consisted of two assistants to Lars, an engineer and a designer, including a secretary for that group. A production manager in his thirties, efficient and important; he was the liaison with the plant and responsible for overseeing installation scheduling. He had a secretary. A specifications manager, someone who dated back to the time of Rob's boss, a man in his sixties who managed the endless specifications for safety requirements. The company lawyer, a woman in her forties, a single mother with two teenage daughters, who had been with a large law firm and came to work for Rob, who was flexible about her hours. A secretary for the lawyer. A salesman in his late twenties, a graduate of NYU, Marty Rosen, a chunky five feet six, who did not fit Rob's athletic profiling, but had tremendous energy and traveled more than Rob did. Rob sometimes thought of Tommy in relationship to Marty. Tommy was interested in MayPole, he listened when Rob discussed the business. He didn't seem to be cut out for a business life at a company like MayPole, if Marty was the standard for ambitious young men. Schools, parks departments, communities, and municipalities were largely Rob's domain. Marty was responsible for the accounts Rob chose not to handle—developers, apartment complexes, and the restaurants in malls and near highways that sometimes maintained play equipment. A woman in her fifties, a widow, who had been with Modell's, was Rob's comptroller. She had a secretary. And Rob had a secretary, another holdover from the previous regime, Molly O'Connell, sixty-six, married to a retired postal worker, a grandmother of four, who may have lost a bit of efficiency since the time when she was the secretary to Rob's boss, making up for it by being endlessly optimistic.

MayPole was a model for a lean, efficient small-to-medium-sized business, and over the years Rob had been invited to address various business seminars. He enjoyed an advantageous long-term lease in the building. The cost of manufacturing via Atkins Welding, the Sumter, South Carolina, company that produced the company's products, was eminently fair. His sales promotion material and advertising were created by his buddy, Seth, at bargain rates. But sales had been sporadic since the decade had begun and the downturn was industry-wide.

• • •

Rob was with his inner circle in the MayPole conference room, his comptroller, his lawyer, Lars, and Marty. They were reviewing the weak sales for the last quarter. The windows for the offices were at the end of the loft and faced the New York City skyline with the industrial landscape that was Long Island City in the foreground. A heavy rain was falling and the skyline couldn't be seen, a dark, brooding day inside and out. Nobody wrote songs about Long Island City in the rain.

"It's not good, guys," Rob said.

For the past several years they had been mapping strategies, trying to expand their customer base. Within the past few months Marty managed to sell mini-playgrounds to Taco City, a new fast food chain in ten locations. Rob sold a revamping of playgrounds in Wheeling, West Virginia. MayPole was doing business, but not nearly enough. They sat at the conference table and Rob looked at the rain falling and was silent. He thought of the first time he made a sale for MayPole, the first time he met a payroll, the first time he took little Tommy to a dedication of MayPole equipment, a playground in the Bronx, and he climbed into a tree house and called down, "Look at me, Daddy, look at me."

He became aware of the silence in the room.

"Were you waiting for me?" he said to the group. He turned to Marty. "I guess we'll just have to travel more."

SIX

• • •

Rob scheduled a three-week sales trip through the South. He had just been away for two weeks, back for one, and he was leaving again. Vickie was working on a project for a real estate developer for a shopping center in Brooklyn and she would be kept busy, but as she pointed out, when she was busy, she was busy in New York. He tried to make his case to her. The Internet expanded everyone's possibilities. Prospective customers could surf Web sites and view playground equipment from their desks for companies they might not have dealt with before. For manufacturers it increased the business possibilities, but also increased competition. No one had a distinct geographic advantage in their region of the country any longer and anyone could look like a major player with effective graphics. He needed to get out there and see people face to face, particularly since he was from New York. You had to defeat their prejudices about doing business with a New York firm. You had to show them you were a decent, responsible supplier, not out to screw them because you *were* from New York, especially the new ones who didn't know you, and she nodded and said she understood, but it was the old look, Karen's look.

He lay awake at night. Did they credit you for being on the road and not doing a Willy Loman, not taking up with the availables, the airline stewardess, the car rental clerk, the other travelers, young businesswomen on the make in their careers, away from home, traveling on company money and feeling free. AIDS was not a deterrent, things happened in these hotel rooms. Willy Loman loved his wife and still . . . but it's not something I do, despite the opportunities. So when I come to a city I don't get laid, I run. I find a track in a park or at a school or I just run through the streets near the hotel with the sun barely up. How ascetic is that? The running monk. Do I hold some kind of record, some dumb-guy record? Into my second marriage with all my time on the road and I have never cheated on either of my wives.

"You're just feeling sorry for yourself," Seth said to him at lunch in their sports bar hangout when Rob expressed his complaints.

"This is true. There is nothing more unsympathetic than a misunderstood man. But I am misunderstood."

"You're Willie Nelson, on the road again. You leave her with an empty bed and you're supposed to be *her* new start, *her* clean slate."

"I can't rely on New York City for business. There's always an underbidder and the red tape kills you."

"I understand, but I'm not married to you."

"Her little boys are even starting to look at me with sheep eyes."

"It was the same when Tommy was growing up, as I recall. How's he doing by the way?"

"Better, I hope."

Seth sighed palpably.

"What?" Rob asked.

"Just Tommy."

"What about him?"

"He was such a sparkling little boy. And with school, you never heard a peep that anything was off. Then you guys get divorced and all of a sudden he's not doing so great."

"He was thirteen when we got divorced. The work gets harder."

"Possibly. Rob, I'm going to say the unsayable and you can hate me for it, but there's a reason for me saying it. The divorce may have beaten him up. Everything falling apart in his world and the custody thing. Maybe he hasn't done better in school because most of his energy has gone into—coping."

"Just what I need to hear."

"Here's the point, here's why I'm saying it. It could reverse itself by his ultimately coming to peace with what's happened."

"This is your old theme again? We never should've gotten divorced?"

"You never should've. There aren't any no-risk divorces and you're living with the consequences and I know you hate me right now—"

"What about his friends, Jill and Brian? Their parents are divorced and Jill does fine and Brian has a goddamn perfect 1600 on his SAT."

"Tommy's emotional DNA just may be different from theirs. And maybe they weren't as tight with their parents. But don't lose the point here. When he gets older, when you don't need your parents so much, this may reverse itself and you'll find he's the grown-up version of the sparkling little boy you always thought he was."

"He was asleep at the apartment and I was up, I've been sleeping lousy, and I peeked into his room, and it was like a movie, like his image morphed into the child who used to sleep holding his alligator. It was heartbreaking."

"Yeah, well, we none of us can stop time. What I'm saying is right now you're worrying over every breath he takes. There could be light at the end of the tunnel."

The waitress arrived with their food and this discussion came to an end. Seth had business to talk about. The drop-off in sales at MayPole caused him to reexamine the company's advertising and promotion. He wanted to create a new campaign featuring children of various ethnic types posing with MayPole playground equipment as though they were proud homeowners standing in front of their homes. Each ad would present a different piece of playground equipment with a different group of children. The copy line would be, "These are our true customers." A thin block of text along the bottom of the ad would carry the nuts-and-bolts for ordering, rendered in the clean typography associated with MayPole. Rob knew it was good business practice to jolt the advertising at this point and this was a solution that could work. But the divorce may have had absolutely nothing to do with Tommy's performance in school. He might just be an average student. If you take every kid in his school whose parents split up, that's half the school and they're all going to college and some very good ones. If you take every kid in his school who's got a more prestigious list than Tommy, you're going to find divorces in there, too. I couldn't stay in that marriage. I knew it and Karen knew it and she couldn't stay in the marriage either. You're an outstanding advertising man, but that doesn't mean you know what the hell you're talking about when it comes to Tommy.

"Are you listening?"

"You're an outstanding advertising man, but that doesn't mean you know what the hell you're talking about when it comes to Tommy."

"Maybe I don't. It's an opinion. But if it's so, it might help you in the long run."

"What did Keynes say, in the long run we're all dead."

"The divorce is in, man. You did it. Just file away what I said. Look for the silver lining and now let's focus on the campaign."

"It's very good. You're very good."

"I know. How can you hate a guy who gives you quality advertising on the cheap?"

"He's a good boy, isn't he? I didn't totally screw him up, did I?"

"I never said that. He's a great kid. You must have done something right when you were around, Willie boy."

Rob called Karen in the store and asked if he could meet Tommy for dinner that evening, nothing important. Tommy wasn't due to be with Rob for another week and he just wanted to spend a little time with him. Karen didn't understand, why out of the blue in the middle of the week? Did he have something to say to Tommy about the colleges? Perhaps they should discuss it together. He assured her he wouldn't do anything without consulting. He had no motive and even dropped the notion of the Hamilton and Colby visits, he wasn't pushing that any longer. She didn't object to their getting together. They didn't run a punitive schedule against each other; it wasn't the way they ran their divorce. He left a message for Tommy on his answering machine and he called Rob back later and said it was fine, he wasn't doing anything in particular that night, so Rob took him to a neighborhood Italian restaurant. Rob had nothing much in mind. He told Tommy about the new promotion campaign, Tommy responding that it sounded cool. Tommy gave Rob an update on his applications. He walked Tommy back to the building, kissed him on the forehead and returned to his apartment, and that was it. Rob just needed to look at him.

Karen admitted to Polly she didn't know if she was a prude or being sensible, but Bill had never spent the night at the apartment with Tommy at home. She and Polly speculated on whether it kept the relationship at a distance and that was intentional—fear of commitment on Karen's part. Nonetheless she still couldn't make love to a man with her undoubtedly sexually active teenage son in the place at the same time. That Tommy might hear them in sex or wake in the night and see them sleeping in bed together was beyond her capacity for sophistication.

Tommy was having difficulty writing his personal essays for the college applications. Dean Jacobson advised him cynically, "It's not important to nail yourself. It's only important to give them somebody they can identify. They're assembling a class." Of the books Tommy read in high school,

A Death in the Family most affected him. He didn't equate the tragedy within the story directly with his experience. The boy in the book was six when his father died. Rob was alive. And Tommy was so reserved and protective of himself—you can't lay a glove on me—he would never be so self-dramatizing to see himself in the story. Yet something about the loss in the book communicated itself to him. And he did see himself in the "Knoxville, Summer 1915" prologue, where it described all the people loving the boy, and no one, not anyone will ever tell him who he is.

Brian's stepfather had a niece, Merry, a senior at Horace Mann. Brian avoided her whenever possible, a fashion-minded girl with an active social life. She was having a birthday party at her apartment and Brian's mother pressed Brian to go, bringing it up whenever they saw each other, which was every few days or so. The party, by default, was the only major point of discussion between them. Merry was tall and slim and Brian felt fat with her, or fatter than usual, and she was always bragging to him at family events about how many guys dropped dead in love with her and how her girlfriends were so terrific looking they were like a SWAT team when they came to a party. Brian's mother got to the we-don't-ask-you-to-do-very-much stage. Apparently Brian's stepfather felt there should be more family unity among the young people and Brian finally allowed himself to be recruited and, in turn, recruited his pals.

Merry lived in an apartment on the West Side overlooking the Hudson River. Her father was a real estate developer, her mother a real estate broker. The apartment was a shrine to expensive bad taste. Brian, Jill, and Tommy were fascinated by the voluptuousness of the decor and statuary. Merry greeted the trio and said to Brian, "Thanks for coming. Maybe you'll get lucky with one of my girlfriends," offered with a sly smile, a thinly disguised putdown, he didn't have a chance, Merry's girlfriends were very pretty, as advertised, and did not look their age. Merry motioned Brian toward the bar and moved on.

Tommy, Jill, and Brian drank beer and eavesdropped, nothing they hadn't heard before, guys coming on to girls, girls flirting, the activity whirling around them, with a couple of people making moves on Jill. "I could put together a book of awful lines from guys just being around you," Tommy said. "You're supposed to learn from them," she said and slipped off to the bathroom. After a while she hadn't returned and they went looking for her. She was talking in a corner of a bedroom with a girl in jeans and a sweater, delicate features, soft brown eyes, a marked contrast with Merry's turn-up-the-volume friends. Jill introduced them. She was Abby Altman, also there as a courtesy. Her mother was a business associate of Merry's mother.

"Jill tells me you're a cartoonist for the school paper," she said to Tommy, Jill doing his advance work.

"A sort of cartoonist."

"He's the finest social observer of his generation," Brian said.

"He means in my building," Tommy added.

Brian suggested they leave, he had put in his obligatory time. A revival of *Paths of Glory* was playing at the Film Forum, Brian was eager to see it, and they planned to go together. Tommy asked Abby to join them. Afterward they went out for Chinese food. She was a senior at Stuyvesant and a serious pianist hoping to attend Juilliard. Tommy was smitten. She lived farther downtown, he offered to take her home, but she was determined to go by herself. He asked if he could call her.

"I'm sorry. You rescued me from that terrible party and I had a good time, but I can't get involved with you."

"We're not up to 'involved.' "

"But we will be. You're cute and fun and we will be and it'll come to an end and be awful and we'll both get hurt."

"You're, like, incoherent. How did you get into Stuyvesant?"

She laughed and said, "That's what I mean. I'm sure I'll like you, but I know about it from my older sister who's also a pianist—people like us, we have to be with people who understand music. That's why so many musicians are with other musicians. It's a common language and we don't have it, Tommy."

"This is amazing. This is like an end-of-going-together scene without the going-together."

"It's better this way. Thanks for including me tonight," and she hailed a cab and disappeared from his life as quickly as she entered. Morose, he returned to Brian and Jill and they walked along and critiqued the rejection.

"I wish I were that smart," Jill said. "She could tell it wasn't going to work out. I always think it's going to work out."

"This is not over," Brian declared. "They have those books you can buy, *Learn the Harmonica in Three Hours*. You can play yourself into her life."

"Brian—"

"Or those albums they sell on late-night TV, 'The Romantic Piano

Concertos, $19.99, plus shipping.' You can study up and have enlightened, romantic piano concerto discussions."

He managed to elicit a smile from Tommy.

"Look, her standards are too fussy," Brian said.

"It was totally nonnegotiable," Tommy responded.

Here was the best girl he had met in a while and not interested in him. He allowed the rejection to stay with him for the next few days. It was motivating and made him want to count for something, so it might not have been so easy to dismiss him. More than ever he wanted to have a purpose, get into a decent college, study, be smarter. The next time he was with Dean Jacobson for a tutoring session he had never been more focused. What he needed now was a good day with the culture-driven and unavoidable SAT.

He didn't want to be in the room with the people he was in direct competition with, so he elected to take the test at the Dalton School, where he was less likely to know anyone. He was scheduled for one last session with Dean Jacobson the Thursday evening before the test on Saturday morning. Just before they broke off, Dean said to him, "I feel like Don Corleone going over the details with Michael. We've been over this before, but remember, it's a test that penalizes wrong answers. Better to leave a question blank than guess wrong. If you *are* guessing, eliminate the ones you know are wrong off the bat and guess from there. Don't answer questions in order. Answer the easy ones first, get the right answers in, then go back. And when you walk in that room you've got the knowledge you've been scoring much higher on the practice tests than you did when you first took it in the spring. Be calm. Take a deep breath if you start to get a little tense. You're not going for a sixteen hundred. You don't have to be perfect, but you have to be calm and disciplined and you've been that, you can pull it off. All my students do."

Tommy was at Karen's apartment the evening before the test. Like most teenagers with working parents, he was a specialist in take-out food. Not for this night. Karen made sure to be home early, and prepared lasagna, one of Tommy's favorite dishes. They both knew from the college guides he would be wiser relaxing than cramming and he rented a comic movie, *This Is Spinal Tap*.

Rob wanted to weigh in with his best wishes and he had a pep talk in mind for Tommy. When Rob was competing for Penn they were entered in the Penn Relays, an important event in track and for the school. During the week he felt a twinge in his hamstring, sought treatment from the trainer, and spoke to his coach about the possible injury. He was running a leg of the four-mile relay. If he dropped out, Penn had no real backup. A two-mile runner would have to drop down from his event and compromise his own specialty. The coach asked Rob to try, he shook off the twinge, and running the opening leg produced the best mile of his life, 4:08, an excellent time in those days for his school. Penn came in third, a major feat against quality track teams, and the team rejoiced on the infield for a third-place finish. Rob thought the story was about persevering and about competition. Sometimes not coming in first, but competing at your best is winning the gold. Karen and Rob were partners in the college process, so he tried the story out on her. She listened to it and said, "You told me about that. When we first met. I think it was to impress me and it was wasted on me, since I didn't know a 4:08 mile was a good thing."

"I told it to you? And you remember? I don't remember."

"You did. Rob, it's a good story. But it's all about you. If he's going into a big test tomorrow he doesn't need to hear how his father did this great thing when he was on an Ivy League track team."

"You're right. It's a stupid story."

"It's not a stupid story. I just don't think this is the night for it."

"I'll just wish him well."

"That'd be fine."

"Thanks for this."

"It's okay. Checks and balances. Call him on the other line. I'm sure he'll be glad to hear from you."

"Good night, Karen. Appreciate it."

"4:08. Wow!" she said, teasingly. "You were fast."

He called back on the line in Tommy's room.

"It's me. How are you doing?"

"Watching *Spinal Tap*. It's funny."

"I just wanted to say good luck tomorrow."

"Thanks, Dad."

"It'll be fine. Sleep well."

"Okay. Talk to you."

" 'Night now."

Just what it should have been and he was grateful to Karen. He would still be droning on about himself.

In the early years of photography, the film we use today had not yet been invented. In 1851 an Englishman, Frederick Scott Archer, developed the collodion process whereby a chemically treated glass plate was exposed to an image and the glass plate became the negative. Paper for printing the eventual photograph was placed against the glass plate and a paper image was created. The photographic equipment was unwieldy. Early photographers huddled under the canopies of their cameras, which were mounted on tripods, and yet studio photographers of the day were eager to take their cameras into the world.

In America this reached a high point when the studio photographer Matthew Brady led a team of photographers into the battlefields and behind the scenes of battle during the Civil War. Their photographs from the early 1860s are a somber chronicle of the fierce struggle. Among the photographers working under Brady was Timothy H. O'Sullivan, whose photograph of fallen Confederate soldiers taken on the morning of July 4, 1863, was among the most famous images of the war.

In 1867 O'Sullivan joined a government-sponsored survey of the West led by the scientist Clarence King. The purpose was to inform the country and its leaders about the nature of the land in the West, its composition, mineral value, and agricultural possibilities. O'Sullivan had to handle the unwieldy photographic equipment, transported by mule and wagon under arduous conditions of weather and terrain.

He took hundreds of photographs on this expedition. In 1873 he joined a similar expedition led by Lieutenant George Wheeler. The photographs were taken to provide a record of the West and serve as a reference point. Artistry was not the principal objective.

By now, O'Sullivan's eye and his sense of perspective and light were highly developed. Although he was taking what were essentially documentary photographs, he was among the most experienced and gifted landscape photographers in the world. One of his photographs, of Canyon de Chelley in Arizona, with light and shadows raking the awe-inspiring canyon wall, is one of the great images of the frontier West and appears in several books on the history of photography.

O'Sullivan was taking photographs for a photographic record and yet, by dint of his pure talent and vision, they have become art. O'Sullivan's photographs of the West are cherished by collectors and command high prices in galleries and auctions as examples of great artistic landscape photography, though created out of the exigencies of government-sponsored expeditions.

The primary purpose of this passage is to:

(A) tell us about the history of collodion wet plate photography
(B) describe early photographic techniques and the special achievements of one nineteenth-century photographer
(C) inform us of the arduous nature of photography in the Old West, given the unwieldy nature of early photographic equipment

(D) establish the place of Matthew Brady, the Civil War photographer, and his colleagues in the history of the photographic medium
(E) demonstrate how little was known of the West in the nineteenth century even as late as twenty years after the Civil War

Tommy huddled over his test booklet, and darting across his consciousness was a memory. They were in Canyon de Chelley during a school vacation. It was raining and they were wearing ponchos, his mother on one side, his father on the other, and they looked up at the canyon wall. He must have been eight or nine and he could remember their faces, how pleased they were for him to see this place, the high wall, the Indian ruins. Both his father and mother had rain dripping off their noses and he laughed at how they looked, he remembered the noses, he remembered how happy they were . . . He dared not drift. His job was to dig out the answer and move on, always keep moving. The answer was (B), he was sure of it. At Dalton he didn't know anyone in the room, which he thought was good, nobody's eyes were on him. An hour and fifteen minutes on the verbal—

Choose the lettered pair that is related in the same way as the pair in capital letters. ABSTEMIOUS: PROFLIGATE
(A) intransigent: obdurate
(B) jocular: humorous
(C) cautious: wary
(D) laconic: garrulous
(E) irate: obstreperous

On a break he spoke to no one and tried to stay relaxed. An hour and fifteen minutes for the math—

In a college in Pasadena of 3400 students, 41% are from Pasadena. Of the remaining students, 28% are from north of Pasadena, 34% are from south of Pasadena, and 38% are from elsewhere. How many students are not from Pasadena?

If 4x x 2y = 24 and 7y/2x = 7 what is the value of x?

A square is enscribed in a circle with a diameter of five. What is the ratio of the area of the circle to the area of the square?

During the morning while Tommy was in the test room Rob was in the apartment, cross with the children for playing the television set too loudly, abrupt with Vickie, who asked him to run a couple of errands for him. He was repairing a broken vase. Couldn't she see he was busy? "It'll be over soon enough," she said knowingly.

Karen was in her office in the store. A nonbeliever in psychic anything, she sat at her desk, closed her eyes, and imagined her love enveloping Tommy as he sat in the test room, an aura of warmth surrounding him as he labored.

"Hi, Mom, all done."

"And?"

"Can't tell. Didn't feel like I screwed up. We'll see. A week from Thursday. I'm going home now and taking a giant nap."

He placed a call to his father.

"Dad, can't say I aced it, but I didn't faint or anything."

"All right! Congratulations."

"Thanks. Speak to you."

Dean Jacobson expected a call from him.

"Don Corleone?"

Dean did a very poor Brando impression. "Did you follow my advice, Michael?"

"I did. It felt okay."

Normal voice. "I'm sure it was. Look, Tommy, now that it's over, the schools you're applying to, they're going to factor in all the elements, class work, and where you're strong, extracurricular, community service. What we needed to do was just get you to where the SAT doesn't stand out, just get you competitive. I'm sure we did."

"Let's hope. Thank you, Godfather."

Tommy called eight business days later and received his score by phone: 1170. "Yes!" he said out loud, pumping his fist. He had increased it 150 points since the first SAT. He called Karen in the store and she let out a shout of exultation. He reached Rob on his cell phone and he was overjoyed. Dean Jacobson wanted Tommy to know it was an excellent result and he was in the ball game. Brian said Tommy had done so well he was convinced he *could* learn the harmonica in three hours if he put his mind to it.

Karen likened the end of the SAT to the earlier phases in Tommy's life, like the day he was done with his crib and it was discarded, and you never thought about a crib again. He still had to get his applications in and his essays completed. Dean Jacobson was going to continue working with Tommy to see that he didn't fall off the calculus bridge. He needed acceptable grades in his fall semester. But the SAT part of his life was over. The score was going to be submitted by the school. Tommy and his parents would never have to worry about it again, think about it again, would never again have to say SAT.

Bill received an invitation to a conference of foundation executives in New Orleans and was trying to persuade Karen to join him. A long weekend was involved. John, her new manager, was proving to be more than capable. Karen needed the SAT to be over before her head was clear enough to make a decision. With the test score in, she agreed to go. She had gone to New Orleans once before on business. And when she was married to Rob they talked about going there. During the downslide they never managed to make the trip. In retrospect, she thought they should have taken a few more vacations toward the end, either with Tommy or the two of them, given themselves over to simply having fun or trying to have fun. The vacation pictures they accumulated went up to a point and stopped.

Bill and Karen stayed in a hotel in the French Quarter. He was busy in sessions during the day. She used the time to meet with a couple of suppliers in the area whom she had never met. One was a cabinetmaker of children's furniture with a studio on the outskirts of the city, Tony Blake, an African-American in his thirties with a gift for whimsy who created colorfully painted furniture in the shapes of animals. He was a soft-spoken, gentle person, a Mozart concerto playing in the background. He sold to a half-dozen retail stores with Karen his outlet in the northeast. They talked about children mostly and how he designed for them. He had twin boys of six. His wife was a school nurse.

"I can't imagine doing anything better for a living," he said to her and in the service of his craft she was able to say, "Neither can I."

Her next visit was to Amelia Hotchkiss, a pillow maker, who turned out to be a wealthy woman living alone in a Garden District house. She was a demure person in her sixties whose late husband, she informed Karen, was very big in canning. Karen never knew anyone who was big or small in canning, whatever canning was. She showed Karen her workroom, which contained a large collection of fabric she used for the Victorian-style pillows Karen sold in the store.

They sipped tea in the garden and Amelia said to her, "I don't do all the sewing, mind you. But all the designs are mine."

"And beautiful they are."

"They've kept me busy after Mr. Hotchkiss passed. I don't see a ring. Are *you* married, dear?"

"I was. We were divorced. I *am* with someone now. We're here together, which is why I'm in town."

"Someone like you shouldn't go unattended."

"No, I'm not. And I have a son, seventeen."

"My children are grown. A daughter, she's a teacher, and a son. He, too, is in canning."

"Well, you do wonderful work and it's lovely to meet you."

"Same here. And you have your own business. Good for you."

A reaffirming day. The costs of career seemed worth it on a day like this—to have your own business, to be able to accommodate vastly different people of talent.

Karen and Bill went to dinner in a Creole restaurant recommended by somebody at the conference. Bill was interested in her meeting Tony Blake and Amelia Hotchkiss. His was also a worthwhile time. He attended two panels on the business of foundations he found to be valuable.

Karen was luxuriating in a bath when she suddenly felt faint and nauseous. She staggered out of the tub and barely reached the bowl in time to throw up. No sooner did she finish heaving when she was stricken with diarrhea. She was moaning in stomach pain, sickened by her own stench, and began to throw up again. She lay naked on the bathroom floor. Bill came into the bathroom and gently stroked her hair and said he was going to call a doctor. The front desk told him a doctor was on call and they could have one there within fifteen minutes. Bill crouched over her, trying to soothe her. He took a wet cloth and placed it on her forehead, then covered her with a robe. Her head was spinning. She had never been so sick. Can't be from two glasses of wine. Had to be bad. Botulism. People die from it. This feels like dying. What happens to Tommy? He lives with Rob. He'll be all right with Rob. He's a good dad when he's there. He has to be there. He can't be running off so much when I'm not around anymore. The store is over. A sale. The money goes to Tommy. Rob can put it away for him. Rob will take care of college. Rob will look out for him.

The doctor was young, looking as if he had been out of medical school for the fifteen minutes it took him to get there. He asked her a few questions, what, when, and where she ate, what she was feeling, how was her vision, and in the middle of answering she threw up again, then lay on the bathroom floor.

The doctor checked her pulse and blood pressure.

"Ma'am, these are symptoms of food poisoning. I don't think you have to go to the hospital. I'm going to give you something to help with the vomiting. You need a few hours. It should get better." He helped her to sit up and gave her a liquid medicine and turned to Bill. "Call me if she doesn't improve in the next hour and we'll take it from there." He wrote his number on a piece of note paper. "This will flush out. Your system is working and you'll be amazingly better. Try to sip some water. A little later nibble on some toast. Okay?"

She managed a slight nod. They guided Karen to the bed and she lay in a fetal position. Bill saw the doctor to the door and sat next to Karen on the bed. She looked up at him. His empathy was palpable. A few minutes earlier all she could think of had been Rob. Rob would be there. Rob would look after Tommy. Rob would take over for her. But this was the person she was with, sitting next to her, looking guilty, in pain himself. "You're a good man," she said, as much for herself.

SEVEN

• • •

Death of a Salesman *was a play Rob studied in a course in college on modern American drama when his interests were unformed and his future indistinct. He would find, as an adult, glimpses of his life in the play's scenes fifty years after it was written. To varying degrees he was an administrator, designer, strategist, marketer, and salesman, yet he could not separate himself from being a Willy Loman when he was on the road. The scene when the son fires Willy was redolent of too many sales calls when he found himself across the desk from someone younger than he and indifferent to his and the company's history.

He was in the office of the vice president in charge of purchasing for School 'n' Play, a chain of privately financed preschool centers in Houston. The company was new and expanding to five centers from their original two. Rob was ready for the sales call. He ran in the early morning through the streets near the hotel, showered, ate breakfast, read the newspapers, and walked into the office for his ten A.M. meeting feeling fit. The buyer was Don Terrell, late twenties, wearing a blue Dacron suit with a white shirt and knit tie, a no-frills uniform for a seriously unfriendly young man with a buzz cut and a thin, unfriendly mouth.

"Mr. Burrows, I have ten minutes."

He said it in such a cold, flat voice it sounded computer-generated. Rob flirted with saying he had twenty-five years in the business and it wouldn't take ten minutes to tell him to screw himself. Business wasn't good enough. He made his pitch. MayPole was the premier company in the field with thousands of installations, from a seesaw to an entire playground complex. A newly expanding business like School 'n' Play should place themselves in the hands of people who had won industry design awards and safety awards for decades. These were some of the terrific designs they featured and he went though the catalog and with his laptop computer showed a three-minute sales film with scenes of children at play on May-Pole equipment. Terrell watched dully. Rob did his local-contractor sell; they were a national company functioning regionally. Rob said he could offer testimonials from satisfied customers, but he didn't have enough time since it would probably take several hours. The unfriendly Mr. Terrell did not change his expression. He wanted a breakdown on costs and Rob showed him the figures, no reaction there either. Rob did his own computation. In apportioned costs it was about a thousand dollars for Rob to be sitting in a room with this person for his ten, now stretched to twelve, minutes. What was his background, how do you get to purchase equipment for a new company in the child care and education area? Is it in purchasing, did you go to college for business, do you really think this cool you're affecting is in any way unique? Rob recalled a story Karen told. She was first starting to develop crafts people for her original store and had the idea of being a wholesaler and took a booth in a crafts show featuring some of her artists. A woman in her sixties from a store in Boston, a grande dame, stopped at the booth and Karen tried to sell her graphics she was displaying, charcoal rubbings of New York City manhole covers. The woman said wearily with a slight European accent, "I have seen everything rubbed." It became a catch phrase between them, an earlier "been there, done that." Well, I have seen everything rubbed, buddy, and your cool is playing very tired even at ten fifteen in the morning.

"We'll let you know," Terrell said. "May I keep this?" and he held on to the catalog and price list.

"By all means. Call me, e-mail me, write me. Anything I can do to answer your questions," with a warm, engaging smile and a firm handshake. You don't say, screw yourself. You don't call him on his attitude and that he hasn't been in the business long enough to make a sound decision, but this is the salesman's life, and at this time of day, in this room, in this city, he was not the well-regarded head of a respected company, not the subject of articles in the trade press, not a guest lecturer, he was a salesman selling. He was about to leave the office when Terrell said, "You know, I purchase everything from the computers we use to the equipment for the children. And some people, some who might be your competitors, are prepared to sweeten the pot a little bit."

"Cut prices?" Rob said, pretending naiveté.

"Not exactly, if you follow me."

Rob began working for MayPole with advice from his boss, Phil Grant, a shrewd, cigar-smoking man, who had the diction and bearing of a bookie. Not the ethics.

"Never bribe anybody. Even if you're desperate. Even if you figure you can take it out of your commission and I'll never know. Never do it. Because sometimes you'll be calling on public officials, parks commissioners, and like that, and it's a bribe, and it's illegal. And it'll get you and us in trouble. And it never stops. So we give Christmas gifts. A hundred dollars cash value, tops. And that's it. We rise and fall on our product."

The speech his boss gave him was the same speech he gave to Marty when he started with the company. And now this guy in a Houston office was looking to shake him down to influence a sale.

"We're the crème de la crème, Mr. Terrell. The new mini-castle, it's fantastic. The new climbing equipment, rhesus monkeys would love it. Children certainly will. We can put in great equipment the children will love and make you look great. As far as what our competitors are doing, I don't give a damn." He gave him a definitive nod for emphasis. "I'll follow up. We're in your best interest." And he walked out the door.

He tracked down inquiries from prospective customers gathered from the Web site, from the catalog, and from advertising. He moved through the world of airline terminals and delayed flights, misplaced hotel reservations and we're sorry, all the nonsmoking rooms are booked, of room service and tepid food, of being awake before the wake-up call, of the women with the fellow-traveler smiles. He once saw an interview on television with the lyricist the late Sammy Cahn, who answered the question about which came first, the lyrics or the music, by answering, "The check." The sale came first. Everything derived from the sale. The reputation of the company couldn't be based on showroom samples alone, no matter how well executed. Eventually buyers wanted to see equipment in site placement, with photographs, sales films. Business was needed to generate other business.

He shared with the early peddlers who sold pots and pans and bibles and dry goods the survival mechanism for salesmen—deny rejection. Keep moving, nothing personal if they turn you down or even try to shake you down. Stay positive, see enough people, cast a wide enough net, and you'll get business. He had been running this company for seventeen years and it *was* the crème de la crème. Doing a selling job on himself for reassurance, he worked his way through Dallas, Jacksonville, Birmingham, Atlanta. He called Vickie twice a day, knowing it wasn't compensation for her.

He was in Atlanta, the last stop on the trip. In New York, Vickie was dealing with a double case of flu with her boys and was less than a hundred percent herself. She reported that Tim stopped by, in town for a few days, and was so concerned about not becoming contaminated he wore a surgical mask when dropping off games for the boys. "He looked like he was still playing a doctor in the soaps." Her friend, Dori, visited with chicken soup, reported matter-of-factly, Rob hearing the subtext—it would be nice if you were around at a time like this. When he spoke to people in the office he liked to be a booster, everything was promising. With Vickie he admitted the trip was mixed, trying to justify the need for him to travel.

"I can't wait for you to get back. I miss you. The boys do, too."

He supposed they did. They had an appetite for attention. Still, it was nice to hear it.

"I miss all of you. A few more days. Tell them I asked for them and I hope they feel better."

"You could pick something up for them."

Damn! I would've forgotten.

"Sure."

"Good luck in Atlanta."

"Vickie—"

"I know you have to do this. We'll get through it."

The address for the Atlanta sales call was a trailer next to a large lot in an African-American neighborhood. The lot was the size of a city block, rubble, mud puddles, and mounds of sand surrounded by a chain-link fence. The homes nearby were in serious need of repair and any attempt at reversing the conditions would be undermined by the lot, an open wound. He was to see a Ronnie Blakemore. A uniformed security guard sitting in a chair outside the trailer checked his name on a clipboard and passed him through. At the end of the trailer was an African-American woman in her early thirties in a bush jacket behind a desk. She rose when he entered and smiled in greeting. She was movie-actress beautiful and looked familiar as if he could have seen her in something.

"Mr. Burrows, Ronnie Blakemore. We've met, you know?"

"Yes?"

"I was at Columbia. Teachers College. And you were on a panel on recreation. I spoke to you afterward—"

"Right. That was—"

"Three years ago. I got my master's and came back down here. I grew up a couple of blocks from here. Come outside."

She walked with Rob along the chain-link fence around the sorrowful lot and briefed him on the project. She was the director of the Restoration for Play Foundation and had a budget for new playground construction. Working with a financial officer who was currently in Washington, they assembled a combination of federal, state, and municipal funds with additional financing from foundations and private individuals to create playgrounds for lower income families on vacant lots and blighted properties in Atlanta. This was the largest site and would be the first. She took him by car to three other prospective sites, not as fully cleared, with condemned buildings still standing. The site clearance and capital construction of surfacing, benches, fencing, rest rooms would be handled by a newly created construction company employing local workers. The playground equipment, since it was a specialty, would be under contract to a manufacturer she would determine.

They stopped for coffee at a diner and she said, "I can't believe you're here. I can't believe we got this far."

"It's a truly admirable project."

"I want it to be more than admirable. I want it to be wonderful. I want people to know they may be poor and their children may be poor, but they count for something."

"I have a short sales film on my laptop I can show you."

"Not necessary. I could have any number of companies do the work. I could divide it up between companies. But MayPole, you're the best, and I want them to have the best. Not equipment that's going to rust out or break down and it should be beautiful. You do such beautiful work. The castles. I want them to have castles." She almost lost her composure. "Sorry. This cup of coffee is a long time coming. So I'm going to give you the blueprints for the sites. I have a pretty good idea of what I'd like going into them, and what it should cost, but of course I'd like your recommendations on top of mine."

"Of course."

"The first site, the big lot, should be surfaced within three months, the others cleared and ready, I'd say, over a two-year period. We have the money. An amazing four words. We . . . have . . . the . . . money. Will you do it?"

"I'd be honored. Ms. Blakemore, this *is* wonderful. *You're* wonderful."

He picked up some toy cars for the boys in the terminal. On the plane back to New York he couldn't stop replaying the encounter. It was a project at the highest level he could imagine for his company, castles for the poor. This beautiful woman was an angel for her community and for him. She reversed the sour beginning to the trip with the weaselly Mr. Terrell. And it reinforced his feeling that he needed to be the point man on these sales trips. She wanted to meet him, she knew who he was, his particular stature in the field was at the heart of MayPole getting the job. The company was all of them. But I still have to do this part of it.

Tommy was coming for the weekend. What in any of this could Tommy do? He never even wanted to work in the place over a summer. He was a counselor at camp and Rob conceded that was excellent for him, decent work, too. Why am I back to thinking of Tommy like this? Because it's my company and I have a son and I think about it. An English major. Where does that lead? I bet every parent of every son who ever said he was going to be an English major asked the same thing. He could oversee marketing. Work with Seth. Tommy could do the marketing in-house. Not design or specs or sales, but marketing is a possibility. Or after college he could go to law school. English majors go to law school all the time, and he could be the MayPole counsel, which could position him to be the head of the company one day. He goes to college and then to law school and comes and works for us. It's a good day for dreams.

Periodically the shade was lifted, a college permitted a journalist in on the admissions process, and a report emerged saying the essays were actually read, although no one on the admissions side was prepared to offer a precise assessment of their weight. Karen was aware of the legitimacy of the essay in the procedure and encouraged Tommy to take time in the writing, believing it was the one area to present his character. The colleges' strategy was to get the applicant to talk about himself and their essay questions varied, describe a risk you took, tell what you think you will be doing in twenty years, how do you think you can contribute to the life of this college, describe a person or something you read that influenced you. At a loss earlier for a theme, Tommy now wanted to write about his sense of discovery during the college search, his realization he could do better and wanted to do better. He found a way of weaving the theme through the essays for all of the schools. Dean Jacobson wasn't sure it was the best approach.

"It's too goody-two-shoes for me. 'I really want to learn.' "

"But it's true."

"I think you find a terrific thing you did and describe it and then they get to say, oh, he's the one who did the terrific thing and that positions you. Like some child you helped when you were at the rec center."

"That's very obvious. And kind of fake."

"Just my opinion. They're your essays."

"Right. My essays. And this is a way I can write them."

"Then do it. Maybe honesty will count for once."

Stores like Banana Republic, Ralph Lauren, Armani, and Prada had transformed SoHo in recent years, not merely in the way the area looked, but in the rents landlords could charge. Karen's landlord was not a person, it was a corporation, GDBC, fronted by a manager, Ray Miller, early thirties, preppy in blazers and rep ties and a false smile that seemed store-bought to Karen. Her lease was up for renewal at the end of February, 2001. She was paying $10,000 a month. Ray Miller knew, along with whoever else was behind the GDBC Corporation, that if Homegrown, in a prime SoHo location, couldn't afford a substantial rent increase, a well-financed new brand-name store could be slotted right in to replace her. Smiling—how could he smile, was there some disconnect in his head, she wondered—he stood in front of the store and offered to renew her lease for three years at double the rent she was paying, to $20,000 a month. She was livid, it was unconscionable. He said it was below market. For whom, for Prada, she wanted to know, and he casually replied that Prada *was* the market. GDBC had just put her out of business in her location. This was confirmed by her accountant. Fred Otterman was virtually retired, Karen his only account. He was a hardy seventy-four-year-old, five feet four, behind thick glasses. His services were originally offered to her by his wife, one of Karen's first customers in her West Side store. His eyes were sad, a man living with a wrenching incompleteness after his partner of forty-six years died. He was with Karen in her office and said gently to her, "My dear, Karen, this is the way of the world today." He held out little hope for the negotiation of better terms. Fred worked with an attorney, his nephew, who was with Halliwell and Company, developers of commercial real estate. The nephew looked out for Fred's legal needs and those of his one client. He was mainstream and capable, but he could not move the intransigent GDBC beyond an additional six months on the lease, which was meaningless to Karen.

She asked Bill for his advice and he came over to the apartment. On the table in her small dining room were the listings she accumulated, classified ads for retail stores and printouts from the Web sites of commercial real estate brokers. So many people relied on her, the artisans whose work she sold, the employees who worked for her, and she herself was defined by the business she created, that she was trying hard not to be engulfed by anger.

"These seem to me the options," she said. "I move to another location in the general area, so I don't lose too many customers. Or I relocate—Brooklyn, Westchester, Long Island. Or I do mail order from catalogs and a Web site."

"So you keep the store name and that's your branding."

"Right."

"It's something I know about. You'd still need warehousing, but it wouldn't be retail rent. You could hold on to your store manager perhaps. You will need personnel."

"I understand. And I guess the last option is to scrap it. Do something else, whatever that might be."

"Let me think about it. I wouldn't want to just barrel in with a judgment."

She sent him home. She was fatigued.

Bill was diligent over the next few weeks in trying to form an opinion that would be useful. He accompanied Karen on her first excursions with brokers of retail stores outside the main SoHo area. They went to Tribeca, Brooklyn, Westchester, Long Island, finding problems with all of these areas. Either they would add difficult travel time to her day, or the pedestrian traffic was too light, or the store just didn't seem to fit. If she continued with a store, Manhattan seemed to be the only logical place, with the area east of SoHo in the emerging area around Elizabeth Street as the best possibility.

Karen called Fred and told him about her alternatives.

"Care to weigh in?"

"You're a unique person, Karen. Whatever you do should be unique."

"I'll try, Fred."

"My Martha said you were a beautiful girl with a beautiful eye. I'm talking to you and looking at a quilt she picked out from your first store. It's little houses."

"A log cabin quilt. I remember."

"She brought lovely things into my life."

The sadness in his voice, the sense of loss, forty-six years of marriage and alone in his apartment, he was still touched by his wife's taste. How do you get that kind of feeling and longevity? I admire you so much for that, Fred.

Now that she was looking outside the SoHo area, particularly along Elizabeth Street, she found retail stores in that area were created not out of factory buildings with their large spaces, rather out of tenements. She was being offered sites that had been grocery stores, candy stores, hardware stores. When larger space resembling her current store was available, the rent was prohibitive. She thought about the possibility of combining two small stores to give herself enough room to operate. Even at that, she could no longer have such an extensive collection of merchandise. A new store would have to be closer to a small art gallery in feeling, a boutique. Karen was troubled by the possibility of eliminating artisans in a new space, many of whom she cultivated, several of whom relied upon her for income. She thought a running video presentation of crafts that were not physically on display might allow her to continue offering these suppliers.

"A video is modern," Bill said to Karen in her office. "It's the opposite feel from your merchandise."

"But I'm thinking the look of the store would *be* modern, recessed lighting, white walls, like a gallery."

"So you'll just be selling on the high end."

"No, it would still be a variety."

"Karen, I've been considering this. And for me, honestly, mail order is the best idea."

"Really?"

"I've questioned myself—whether it's my bias because I know something about it and I might be able to help. But I'd like to see you get out of a retail store in these economic times. Mail order through a Web site and with a catalog makes better business sense."

"I wasn't leaning that way."

"I understand. A store is what you've been doing. This way, you still hold on to your suppliers, but wonder of wonders you're not in retail anymore. No more rent, no more expenses, no more salespeople calling in sick two days before Christmas, no more overhead, no more listening to the weather report and worrying how it's going to affect store traffic. And best of all, no more retailer's hours."

"I see."

"You don't want to hear this."

"I'm listening."

"Then that's my conclusion. Get out of retail. Go Internet and mail order and you keep your career and what you love and you'll make out better in the long run. Now, it's not perfect. You have shipping and returns and broken merchandise claims and lots of headaches you don't have face-to-face with people, but I bet you aren't without headaches now."

"True."

"Homegrown, the catalog, the Web site. Not a hybrid store that tries to mix crafts with video presentations in a neighborhood that's also a hybrid."

He showed her a presentation folder with a business plan for Homegrown as a mail order company, projected costs, list acquisitions, printing, fulfillment expenses. The unknown for a new business of this kind was a projection for sales, but Bill was providing a baseline on start-up costs. He argued that Karen could use the opportunity of a cycle ending to create a new cycle and capitalize on everything she knew and everything she was for a new beginning. They went back to her apartment and talked until midnight.

The following day she attempted to sort it out. She went to her store, trying to look at her own place as though she had never seen it before and she carried the image with her along the streets just outside SoHo. She would have to deal with a reduction in space anywhere she went. And yet she still thought with good design she might be able to carry it off. "The hybrid store," as Bill characterized it, didn't seem so ill-conceived to her. He was a person with a good business mind, though, and he was voting against the idea of another store, saying the catalog business was feasible, providential. She was thoroughly confused.

Tommy finished his first essay articulating his eagerness to do better in college than in high school. He showed it to Karen, who liked it very much, and he e-mailed it to Rob, who thought it was outstanding and called

Tommy to say so. Tommy told him he didn't feel he needed to show the other essays to Rob and Karen. They would be similar and he was going to run them by Dean Jacobson. Rob didn't object and said Tommy had the situation under control. Rob called Karen a while later.

"It's really good."

"I think so, too," she said. "He did an excellent job."

"Excellent. We don't have to worry about *that*. Karen, I read an article that said retailers are jumpy. How's Christmas looking?"

"It's my last Christmas in the store. My lease is up in February and Fred says I can't stay on."

"That's not good. What are you going to do?"

"I've been looking at space east of SoHo. Anywhere I go, what with rents, it has to be a smaller operation, but I have some ideas about that. And I'm also considering going mail order. Drop the store and sell from a Web site and catalogs."

"Drop the store?"

They were standing in the raw space of what was to become her current store on Mercer Street. She was shaky. How would she fill it, how would she do it, would people come? He put his arms around her and drew her close to him and said it was going to be the greatest store of its kind anyone had ever seen and she was the one to do it. He remembered.

"Tactile," he said on the phone. "That's the key word, as far as I'm concerned."

"What?"

"You're a tactile person. You love the wood and the ceramics and the fabrics and being able to feel the workmanship. You love when people pick up a basket or a piece of pottery and hold in it their hands and turn it over. You love it when they buy something and you see the light in their eyes when they're happy that they chose this thing that you found. And when they're looking for a gift for somebody they care about and they hold it and it feels just right and you're there to see it—you don't get that in a mail order business or from a Web site. I have a Web site and I still have to be in a room with people. A Web site, it's electronic. A catalog is impersonal. You need it happening in front of you, seeing it, touching it. You don't want to run a business behind a computer. You're not mail order, Karen. You're tactile."

She couldn't speak for the moment, never expecting such concern from him. Still a bond, Rob, even now.

"Appreciate the interest," she said.

"No problem. See you, Karen."

"See you."

She called Bill at work in the morning and told him she was not doing the catalog business. She was going ahead with another store.

EIGHT

• • •

Bill was living as much in the moment as if he were an uncommitted single man in his thirties. He was comfortable with his privacy and his independence. He and Karen were together for portions of weekends, staying at his apartment or hers depending on Tommy's whereabouts. He saw his daughter in San Francisco whenever possible. His free time, when he was not with Karen, was spent largely with books. Bill was a history buff and a casual collector of first editions by historians. A man of refined taste, he considered the relationship with Karen to be eminently civilized. He and Karen never discussed marriage. He didn't see the merit. It was legally complex and more than he was prepared to commit to—and Tommy made marriage even more implausible. He regarded Tommy a high-maintenance teenager, a boy of mediocre ability and overanxious parents. In a marriage Bill would be drawn into his problems. He worried about being too old for Karen. He knew he was too old for Tommy.

Bill's wife had been a children's book editor. He thought of the relationship with Karen as an homage to his wife; he was involved with someone she, too, would have respected. He was concerned now about his standing with Karen. She unequivocally rejected his advice about the store and he saw it as a rejection of him. The biggest decision she made since they were together and she dismissed his opinion. He never gave Rob much thought. He was now feeling competitive with him. Rob had been there when she first went to SoHo and established herself with the store. Bill was offering her a way to not only break with retail, but with a residual part of Rob, to do something new, something within *his* orbit, and she declined.

Bill played tennis throughout the year at the Midtown Tennis Club. Mack Friedman, a chunky five feet ten, sixty-eight, was Bill's regular doubles partner and his closest friend. A retired principal of Seward Park High School, after a thirty-five-year career dealing with the bureaucracy, the union, the parents, and the students, he was perceptive and blunt. They completed their weekly game and the two of them went to a bar near the courts.

"You get into a pattern, just going along," Bill said. "Every once in a while there's a chance to be valuable to the other person and this was the chance."

"You said, 'Sweetie pie, trust me, I know what's best for you' and she said, 'I don't give a damn what you think is best for me.' "

"*And* she's making a mistake."

"That you don't know. You won't know for a while. This relationship is important to you?"

"It is."

"You know this is really about aging. You want to feel relevant to her, so she won't think you're old."

"Where did you get that from? Maybe you're talking about yourself."

"Seems to me you can be the big smarty-pants and keep telling her she's making a mistake because you know best and then you'll really be irrelevant. Or you can encourage her. You'd be doing her the service she needs from you." He sat back, pleased with himself. "This is why I was such a good principal."

"I can do without the self-congratulation."

"*I* can't. So that's my best thought on the subject. You want to be relevant to her, old-timer, be on her side."

Bill followed Mack's advice and didn't express reservations about the choice Karen made, signing on, affirming it was the right decision. Karen brought up the mail order question again, asking if he thought she might be able to do both, relocate to a new store and use the Web site and a catalog to generate sales. If she did go into a modified mail order operation, then his expertise might make him more valuable to her. He answered her honestly. A good mail order business was time-consuming. Given her hands-on style, she would find herself overinvolved with layouts, copy, photography, lists, fulfillment, returns. She might consider using limited mail order, flyers at holiday seasons. She should focus on the store.

A broker found a location for her that was coming vacant at the end of the year on Elizabeth Street between Prince and Houston, a few blocks east of SoHo, the area a blend of new, upscale boutiques and old stores in tenements. The desirability of the store for Karen was that it was adjacent to another store of the same size and the broker thought the occupant of that store was leaving at the end of his lease in March. Karen could combine the space of the two stores and have a double window. The rent for both was $6,500 a month and she signed a letter of agreement, contingent upon the second store coming available. Bill came downtown to see the space and gave his approval; he was unlikely to offer anything less. Karen called it a precelebration dinner and they went to a funky Cuban restaurant, her suggestion, nothing fancy because the space was not yet certain.

Tommy used the school vacation to get the last of his applications ready and he sent them off. Nothing anyone could do now but wait until April 7th, when the seniors heard from the colleges. He was at Rob and Vickie's and she brought out little cupcakes after dinner and put a candle in one for Tommy to blow out. Her boys didn't understand, was it Tommy's birthday?

"No," she said, "it's like Tommy ran a long race and he finally finished so it calls for a cupcake and a candle."

"I like the cupcake and candle. Even a Carvel cake would be too much. The Carvel cake is when I get in somewhere."

Students at Bantrey were advised not to blow off their senior years, that colleges were on the lookout for slackers and a dip could be decisive. With his newly discovered Main Idea about improving himself, Tommy was acting on the thought, performing at a higher level in some of his classes.

For New Year's Eve, looking to mitigate some of the stress his travel had caused, Rob suggested an evening to include Vickie's children. He knew someone with the Walt Disney Company through a project he worked on involving Disney characters and he made a call that produced four tickets to *The Lion King*. The children were enthralled with the show. Rob remembered how rewarding it could be when a child was filled with wonder at something you took him to see. He went with Tommy, who was about five, to a performance of The Paperbag Players at the 92nd Street Y. Tommy's eyes were wide with delight. He could see the same look with the little boys. And when Tommy was older they went to Mets games, father and son, before the divorce, before Tommy became disinterested in baseball.

"Did you like it?" Vickie said to the boys when they left the theater.

"Great."

"Really great."

The words at their command couldn't express what they revealed in their faces. As they moved with the crowd onto the street, Vickie placed her arm inside Rob's and said, "Great's the word. This was great of you."

They went back to the apartment and before the boys went to bed, and unprompted by their mother, they came into the bedroom where Rob was reading and each kissed him on the forehead. It was the first time they had ever kissed him like that. Rob and Vickie opened a bottle of champagne, toasted in the new year, made love. Before he fell asleep he thought of Tommy, as he so often did—this time in a different sense, in terms of Tommy's theme for his essays, relating it to himself. I can do better here.

Tommy, Jill, and Brian were invited to a New Year's Eve party of Bantrey seniors and assorted others in a weekend home in Peekskill belonging to the father of a girl in their class. Some of the guests were bringing sleeping bags and they brought theirs. They took a train from Grand Central Station and then a taxi and entered at ten to find the party under way with people drinking beer, liquor, smoking pot. The chaperone for the event was a Labrador retriever named Smokey.

By midnight the house was jammed with young people. Jill announced boozily to Tommy that since they arrived she already had two complete relationships, without sex, with beginnings, middles, and ends, and she was going to start the new year celibate. Brian was sitting on the steps to the second floor with the object of his desire, Monica Feld, a saucy classmate he had always had a crush on. Tommy was on the floor in the living room, observing the proceedings, smoking a joint. Tommy considered himself an occasional pot smoker and the general detachment he felt about most of the revelers made this a pot occasion. Brian had to pass Tommy on the way to get a couple of beers. Monica's boyfriend broke up with her that very week, Brian informed Tommy. "He stranded her New Year's Eve, the scoundrel," Brian said, raising his eyes in mock expectation. Brian and Monica slipped into a guest bathroom, causing unhappiness among the guests who wanted to use the facility. Tommy was sitting by himself chuckling over the barred bathroom. Jill came by and sat next to him.

"You okay?"

"I'm good. Brian is in the bathroom with Monica and it's a half-bathroom so I don't imagine they're taking a bath. Let's hope Brian is starting the year off on a high with Monica. I am already on a high."

A young woman joined them, five feet ten, coltish, with short blonde hair and pale blue eyes—Ricky Burns, their classmate, and a celebrity at school for being a part-time model.

"This is the worst year of my life," Ricky announced.

"That's funny. The year is twenty minutes old," Tommy said.

"Brendan broke up with me. I came alone."

"This is the very Brendan you kicked our Tommy over for, only two months ago, and he broke up with you already? Very poignant, Ricky."

"Jill, don't be so arch," Ricky said.

"Arch? Who uses a word like arch? You still studying for your SAT?"

"Tommy, I need to speak to you. Would you excuse us, Ms. Archness?"

Several beers along the way herself, Ricky took him by the hand and led him upstairs. People were occupying the bedrooms, so she selected a clothing closet in the hallway. She pushed the coats back with her rear, closed the door, and began kissing him passionately. They had been involved for no more than three weeks when she took up with her Brendan, a twenty-four-year-old actor. Now at her instigation Tommy and Ricky were about to have sex standing up in the clothing closet, pushing against the coats. Trying to adjust a condom from his wallet, Tommy said, "Houdini couldn't have done this." When it was over, Ricky said, "Don't assume anything. It was just the mood I'm in."

"To coin a phrase, whatever."

Ricky curled onto a corner of a bed where coats and ski jackets were piled up and immediately went to sleep. Downstairs, Monica walked away shortly after she and Brian emerged from behind the locked bathroom door. Brian didn't know where she went and refused to say anything about the bathroom episode. The party had evaporated and Tommy, Jill, and Brian unrolled their sleeping bags and slept on the floor of the living room.

They nodded off on the train going back to the city in the morning, Jill with her head on Brian's shoulder, Tommy in the seat behind them. He awoke first and looked at his friends. It's always the three of us, basically.

At breakfast in a MacDonald's Tommy floated a plan. When school was over they should both come and work in the camp where he was a counselor. They would be going off to different colleges, so it was the last time they might be able to be together. With the rec center experience they wouldn't have trouble getting jobs there, he would see to it. They agreed, the summer together. "The Three Musketeers," Brian said. "The three friends," Tommy responded more soberly.

Karen and Bill attended a New Year's Eve party at Polly and Joe's apartment in an apartment house overlooking Washington Square Park. About two dozen people were there—couples, singles, some of Joe's Democratic Party colleagues, friends of Polly's from her public relations business. A centerpiece was their Christmas tree, elegantly decorated with ornaments created by a wood carver in Maine whom Karen had found.

They mixed with people, the guests ranging from mid-thirties to mid-seventies, the age of Joe's parents. Emily, Joe's mother, was a poised-looking woman in a black dress. His father, Milt, was a robust man of five feet six wearing an ancient pinstriped suit. Emily was a head taller than Milt, the pair an uncanny replica of Polly and Joe. He held forth to a huddle of guests about the Republican control of Congress and how "the Dems" had to find a strong party leader. He told the group he was a former assemblyman from Brooklyn and a former handball champion in Coney Island. He was unquestionably the father to pugnacious Joe. He came over to Bill at a table set up for a bar.

"I'm Milt. Joe's father."

"Bill Withers. Happy New Year."

"What brings you here?"

"Your son and daughter-in-law. I'm with Karen Burrows."

"No kidding. Good for you," with a sly expression.

"Yes, it is," starchily, given the man's tone.

Milt leaned forward, he had something confidential to share.

"It's good for guys like us to get out and mingle with some of these kids. They can learn something from us. 'Cause they don't know shit about shit."

Joe retrieved his father for introductions to some friends of his who had arrived. Bill leaned against a wall. Guys like us.

In the way people who dislike cats feel cats have a way of finding them, everywhere Bill turned, Milt was there. He tried to adopt Bill as his soul mate. He introduced him to his wife and Bill was entrapped in a conversation about how well Joe and Polly were doing in their careers, Bill standing with the two oldest people in the apartment. Bill extricated himself, talked to Karen, but it was a party, people moved around, other people came over to Karen, and Milt was back. He shared his views with Bill on "the Dems" finding a strong party leader and did Bill know he was once the handball champion of Coney Island? He didn't want to be Milt's buddy, to be seen with the most visible senior citizen of the night. To get free of the man Bill inserted himself into a small group where Joe was holding forth. Sports team owners who extort municipalities for sports complexes should be run out of town. The cities are always left with the bill. Milt pushed in. He agreed with everything his son said, delivered with his arm around Bill, his new friend.

"What do you think, Bill?" Milt asked, including his pal.

"I'm not sure."

Not good enough for Joe.

"You must have *some* opinion," Joe said.

He should have declined. He knew it the moment he started to speak. But he did have an opinion.

"Sometimes a city benefits. We got a nice park out of the world's fair in Flushing Meadow. And we got public courts out of the U.S. Open. If venues are built for the Olympics, they remain and the public gets to use them."

"What?" A *what* from Joe that sounded like he had just heard the stupidest thing ever spoken. "Thirteen billion dollars when we can't pay the firemen or the cops, where kids can't read and there aren't enough classrooms or school buildings and you want to spend money for fucking racing sculls and cycling!"

They were saved by the countdown for the New Year, the hour was struck, people kissed, champagne was poured. The tolling of the New Year could not break Joe's train of thought.

"We can't be passive. The vote comes up in 2005. We have to let them know, those corporate connivers, that the people of New York City don't want it, the construction delays and the cost overruns and the entire charade, and your argument for post-event benefits is ludicrous, Bill. I'm fucking surprised at you."

"Are you always right?" Bill said with a smile, hoping it would be read as playful and if not that was fine, too.

"Yes," Joe answered.

It got a laugh. Karen emerged from another room at the tail end of this and led Bill away from the group. They were both ready to leave. In the elevator Karen said, "That's his blood sport. You don't get into a contest with Joe."

"I should know better."

If his idea was to not appear too old in a room of younger people, he failed spectacularly. They made love and, as luck and his emotional state would have it, he was premature.

"Not to worry," she said. He pretended to sleep, concerned about her feelings about his overall performance on this night. She was awake herself, not over him, over the prospect of the coming year. I can design the space, make it look good, but I have to know it isn't the same pedestrian traffic over there and probably never will be. I just have to think of myself as a pioneer in the area and hope business will follow. You don't get the same type of shoppers or as many tourists. I'll have to . . . He was not foremost on her mind.

Rob was unable to avoid going back out on the road. The Atlanta project required his participation for follow-ups. Marty was in a dry spell and Rob had to compensate. The first months of the year he was not away as often as periods in the past, still it amounted to several weeks' time. As compensation, he attempted to be more attentive to the boys when he was home. On weekends he took them to a few children's movies and plays, just the guys. He was overpowered, though, by their father whenever Tim made one of his star turns.

Tim was with the boys on a Saturday. He arranged with Vickie to pick them up in the morning, keep them with him all day, and was going to return them around six. Vickie went off to do chores and some shopping. Rob was in the apartment using the time and quiet to work on a sales presentation, rust never sleeps. Tim called at three. Was Vickie around? No. Then could Rob help him out? He just got a call on his cell phone from a director he had been trying to get together with for the past few days. The director wanted to meet him for a drink right away since he was going back to L.A. that night. Tim was strapped for time. Was it possible for Rob to come downtown and pick up the boys after a matinee at the Victory Theater on 42nd Street at four? Rob granted that getting the boys uptown and then going back downtown would cost Tim an hour and he agreed to be in front of the theater at four. He stood on the sidewalk waiting for the handoff. Also waiting among the bystanders was a young woman with sunglasses in a sheepskin jacket, jeans, and boots. Tim emerged with the boys and his eyes met the young woman's. He led the boys to Rob. They were disappointed in not getting every minute out of the day with their father. They gave Tim large hugs and kisses in saying good-bye, beyond anything they had ever managed for Rob, and it was writ large as the news crawl on the Times Tower, ROB IS OKAY, BUT THIS IS OUR DADDY AND HE IS OUR STAR. They shook hands, Tim said he appreciated it, and Rob took the boys in tow and led them away. He turned back for a moment to see Tim walk away with the young woman.

With the college applications submitted, the tense phone calls and the furtive get-togethers between Karen and Rob were over. They continued to call each other concerning Tommy's comings and goings and they still used e-mail, but the frosty e-mail relationship that preceded the college search also ended.

Rob's travel time was building inexorably. Vickie needed to know why he was the one who had to do the traveling. He brought his job sheets home and spread them on the dining room table, a contentious performance. He went over every project in-house and the sales calls projected from inquiries.

"Right," she said reluctantly.

"If I were in the navy, I'd go to sea."

"If you were in the navy you'd be home months on end."

He did want to do better and initiated a ritual. They began to work their way alphabetically through the Zagat restaurant guide and go to as many different restaurants as they possibly could when he was around. He also checked the newspapers for children's events and took the boys for more men-only outings. And he continued to travel.

The second store came through on Elizabeth Street. From a person uncertain and confused, Karen was excited, revitalized. She met with a store designer, Mary Hong, who created some of her favorite interiors for boutiques and began the design process. The designer had a team of construction people to do the work and Karen began to go back and forth between the two locations, overseeing the new store while running a relocation sale at the other.

"This is exquisite timing. It may not even touch me."

She was going to have her grand opening on the day of her fiftieth birthday.

"It's brilliant," Polly told her. They were eating a brown bag lunch at the desk in Karen's office.

"I'll be completely self-absorbed, so involved with the store, this birthday will barely cross my mind."

"We wanted to throw you a party. We still do."

"Thank you, no. Fifty. Jesus. Judy Collins sang that song, 'Who Knows Where the Time Goes?' "

"To only good things," and Polly raised her paper coffee cup in a toast.

"I'm really up for it. It's going to look great. Small, but classy. And they'll find me. If they don't, their tough luck." Then she added, "And I'll go out of business."

"No, you won't."

"No, I won't."

Karen's concept was for the store to look like a prestigious museum shop for a crafts museum. Spotlights illuminated some of the higher-priced merchandise. Other items were displayed on counters organized by material—wood carvings, ceramics, knitted goods, with descriptive copy about the crafts work and the artisans accompanying every item in the store. Karen followed through on her idea of a video presentation, hired a video company to make a short film, and stored the items in the basement, where they could be produced on demand.

The first store had been described as a "cornucopia of crafts items" in one of the shopping guides to the city. The new, smaller store was called "a jewel" by *New York* magazine in an article the week before the opening. *The New York Times* also sent a reporter and photographer down and a complimentary piece with a photograph of the interior appeared the day before the opening. At least in these two major news sources Karen had made the transition to a smaller space for her business without sacrificing prestige.

On the morning of the opening Rob wanted to send flowers, except it was, of course, also Karen's birthday.

"You don't send flowers to your ex on her birthday," he said to Vickie. "Not when you're married."

"You can. Send them from both of us and make sure the card says 'Congratulations on the new store.' "

"That's all right with you?"

"I'm all for good relations with divorced spouses."

• • •

He had to be in Manhattan that day for a lunch meeting. Curious about the place, hoping it worked out for her, he stopped at the store before returning to Long Island City. Several shoppers were there at three in the afternoon—pretty good, he judged from his old vantage point as husband of the retailer. He looked at the double windows. Nice use of display space, he noted.

"This is so sweet of you to come," Karen said as he entered. "Thanks for the flowers!"

"The store looks terrific! Very smart."

"Let me show you."

She took him through, pointing out pieces, some made by artisans whose names he remembered, some of whom he had met.

"Love it. All the best here, Karen."

He kissed her on the cheek, took a last look around, and left.

She watched him until he turned the corner. I might not have done *this* either without you.

Rob walked at a deliberate pace toward the subway. Seeing the store, how she was able to create it after some words of encouragement from him, but nothing more, nothing like the last time when he was there for every step, seeing how beautiful and well conceived it was, how totally independent she was from him now, made him realize a marriage doesn't end with the divorce papers. It ends in slowly descending waves.

NINE

• • •

Thick envelopes were good, thin envelopes were bad. Thick envelopes had forms to be filled out, information. Thin envelopes contained merely a letter. A letter wasn't good. Rejected. Or wait-listed, which wasn't altogether bad, but wasn't good.

Tommy entered the building short of breath from anxiety. He removed a stack of mail from the box for the apartment, shuffled through it, some thin, some thick with a thick envelope from Marlowe College in Pittsfield. He tore it open to find a letter of acceptance and collateral forms. He held his arms above his head in triumph and raced back out of the building. He wasn't going to call his mother, he wanted to see her. He hurried toward the subway looking through the rest of the mail. He was accepted by SUNY Albany and Clark, wait-listed at Gettysburg and at Lafayette, even with the letter of recommendation by Peter Briggins, but he didn't give a damn now, and rejected by Hamilton and Colby, and he didn't give a damn about that either. The night at camp with Betsy McCallister on the ball field, his first time, was special. This was special in its way. He burst into the store.

"Mom, I got into Marlowe! I got in!"

"I'm so happy for you."

"I did it."

"How smart are they to know how great you are."

To celebrate she was going to take him to dinner at Pig Heaven that night, his favorite Chinese restaurant, where they not only served excellent spare ribs but ice cream sundaes, a wild juxtaposition and under the circumstances perfect for the occasion. He went into her office and made his calls, reaching Rob on his cell phone.

"Marlowe, Dad! Aces!"

"Fantastic!"

"You owe me a Carvel cake."

"I'll be home Friday night."

"I'll be there."

"I'm so happy for you I'd buy it right now, but they do have a tendency to melt."

"How about it, huh, Dad?"

"You're terrific."

Tommy didn't offer the other results and Rob didn't ask for them, the happiness in Tommy's voice was sufficient.

He called Jill and Brian. They shouted their congratulations. Jill was in at Tufts, Brian at Harvard. They were all going to be within range of each other, they would come and see him, he would come and see them, they would sit and have lunch by the Charles River. Next he called Dean Jacobson, who did his Godfather voice again in congratulating him, overdoing it, only Tommy was not about to complain. Tommy returned to the apartment, changed into his jogging gear, and went running into Central Park, circling the reservoir, gliding along with the view of the Midtown skyline; it was like flying. This less than outstanding student finally emerged from the overcomplicated process feeling there was nothing wrong with him.

Businesses flowed into businesses in SoHo, restaurants generated customers for art galleries, the art galleries generated customers for retail stores, and it doubled back on itself. In Karen's new location, several blocks east of the main SoHo hub, the flow of pedestrian traffic was considerably lighter and more uneven. Weekends were far busier than weekdays and to capture any available business Karen followed the example of many boutiques in the area with store hours from ten A.M. to ten P.M. seven days a week. Her salespeople from the original store stayed with her by making adjustments in their schedules. Many of her former customers found her. And the stores along the street attracted a number of people browsing. As she told Bill, some happened to be collecting bottles and cans, but some were shoppers.

Tommy didn't require his mother on weekends, he was functioning as an independent entity. Bill, though, was marooned. Wanting to be the supportive, relevant good guy, he couldn't very well complain about the hours Karen was devoting to her business. She did not go in to the store Mondays and Tuesdays, which had no impact on his life with her. She used that time for personal needs or to do whatever traveling was required acquiring merchandise, extending to Wednesdays and Thursdays if necessary. Weekends she was obliged to be in the store into the evenings, which upset Bill's construct of what their relationship should be, no more Saturday night plays or concerts. After she left work on Saturdays, usually around nine P.M. they went to dinner at a restaurant in the area. Depending on Tommy's whereabouts they spent Saturday nights at her apartment or his. Sunday mornings they often went out for brunch and then she headed downtown to the store.

"This isn't forever," she told him on a Sunday as she was about to head for the store. "Eventually, it'll start to run on automatic pilot like it did before."

"You're happy and it's doing well. I'm happy you're happy."

"Good." She kissed him and scurried off to get a cab.

He had a book to read; he always had a book to read. He was a self-contained man. And he had a business life. The arrangement did feel empty to him, however.

Polly dropped by while doing some shopping in the area. They sipped coffee in the small back office of the new place.

"I left Bill looking a little beleaguered," Karen said. "I always end up in the same place, with the man feeling neglected."

"Yes, but look what they get when they get it."

"Are you talking sexually?"

"I mean you. I mean everything."

"Rob would've hated these hours."

"Rob had his own hours."

"It's good Bill is patient. Anyway, we're not married."

"Do you want to be?"

"No. I don't need to be. I couldn't be right now."

A few days later, in perfect tune with himself, jauntily strolling into the store in a beige linen suit, tan shirt, and a yellow knitted tie was Peter Briggins.

"Karen—"

"Hello, Peter."

"They told me in your old spot where I could find you. A French war surplus store? What kind of place is that?"

"It's not war surplus, it's fashion."

"*This* is neat, though." He looked through the merchandise, nodding his approval. "Good going."

"Thanks, Peter."

"A person in the admissions office told me your son was wait-listed. Apparently his grades weren't good enough on the first go-round. But I was told he has a chance off the wait-list."

"He's been accepted at Marlowe. He's going there, but thank you for the information."

"Marlowe is good. Maybe I didn't write a strong enough letter, but under the circumstances—"

"For all we know it tipped it for him at Marlowe," she responded generously.

"We have things to celebrate, this store, your son. Squeeze me in for a drink?"

Flattering, to have this roguish guy flitting about, but she had qualms about shortchanging Bill, and her business responsibilities placed Peter Briggins in a distant category.

"Peter, I have so much on my plate, even a drink with a man as charming and good-looking as you could send the plate skittering to the floor."

"Is that a compliment? Just a drink. Here I am alone in the big city."

"Flirtations are not entirely unwelcome. It's nothing I can act on these days."

"One of these days?"

She had a gathering of flowers in a vase near the cash register. She removed a rose and pinned it to his lapel. He smiled in appreciation.

"Good luck in the new store. And good luck to your son."

"Good luck to you, Peter."

Would someone who advertises like that, who gives off such sexual energy, be a dud in bed? Not likely. Oh, well. There's work to be done, a decent man to be respected. Triage.

Bill and Karen celebrated his sixty-seventh birthday with a dinner at the SoHo bistro Balthazar, and with a silk shirt as a present from Karen. He would like to have avoided the birthday entirely. Sixty-seven was getting closer to seventy. Was Karen going to be keen about being involved with a seventy-year-old man? But she had given him a present he was unaware of in her dismissal of Peter Briggins.

• • •

Vickie needed to be in Queens for a Saturday meeting and was relying on Tim, who said he would be in town and could take the boys for a few hours. He left a message on Vickie's machine saying he wasn't coming. Rob was in Chicago on business. She couldn't find a sitter on short notice and called Tommy at Karen's apartment and asked if he could stay with the children.

"I'm desperate. I'll give you a thousand dollars. Just kidding. I'll give you a really nice dinner next time you're here."

A working mother, Vickie's meals tended toward short-order. She was a fine cook; she seldom had the time for it.

"Lemon chicken."

"A deal."

"But I've got to get to the library with my friends. The boys have to sit quietly for a while and then I can take them to the Museum of Natural History or something."

"Sit quietly? My boys? All right. I'll make sure they do."

He arrived at the Mid-Manhattan Library with first-grader Tod and second-grader Keith. Jill and Brian were interested to see the children, whom they had never met. They all sat at a long table, the boys subdued by the quiet of the place. Forewarned by their mother, they dared not speak. Vickie had filled their knapsacks with books to keep them busy and they kept themselves occupied for about a half hour until they became restless. Tod said something to Keith, who shushed him loudly and they started to giggle about the solemnity, the no-talking of the place, and Keith giggled in turn and they couldn't stop giggling. Tommy and his friends had covered some of the work they needed to do, a sampling of speeches by Eugene V. Debs for their history class. Brian said they could finish without him and Tommy left with the boys, who were apoplectic from trying to suppress the giggles, Tommy having trouble himself. He took them to the Museum of Natural History and back to the apartment, where they watched a Muppets movie. Vickie returned, grateful. Tommy brushed it off and went on his way. His ease in taking care of the children merely masked problems among the adults. Vickie left a message for Tim to call her back, it was important for them to speak as soon as possible. He returned her call three days later.

"Sorry I didn't get back to you. I'm working and with the time difference—"

"All right, I have you now. Tim, you can't get their hopes up that they'll see you and then not show. How many times is it? I've lost count. And there's no pattern to when you do show up."

"There's no pattern to the work."

"Then at least if you say you're going to be there, be there. You're starting to create chaos in their lives."

"Maybe if they were with me all the time we wouldn't have this problem."

"What are you saying?"

"If you're so pissed with my behavior, well, if *I* had them, there wouldn't be an issue."

"Are you reading lines from some movie you're going to be in? That is truly childish—watch out, lady or *I'll* take the kids? Nobody would ever award you anything, Tim. You couldn't take care of a cat."

"Just back off, Vickie. I do the best I can. And it's not like there's nobody around. You *are* married last I looked."

"I'm asking you to try harder."

"I'll try harder."

"Good. I'll speak to you."

She needed to get off the phone. He scored heavily against her without realizing it, hitting a nerve on her marriage to Rob. Rob and the boys had their outings together. He fell short of compensating for their inconstant father. He was away too much of the time.

At a stand in a street fair on Lenox Avenue Karen discovered the work of a talented African-American quilt maker, Lena Hattersby. Karen started selling "Ms. Hattersby's Quilts" in the store. A customer for one of the quilts was an African-American woman in her thirties, Jessie Parsons, a well-dressed, slender woman with delicate features and a warm, ingratiating smile. The smile disarmed people, which she found useful in her work. Among those she needed to disarm were the students at Martin Luther King High School in Manhattan, where Jessie was a guidance counselor. When Karen learned her customer was a collector of quilts and her job was working in a high school, it came together for her, Lena Hattersby, Jessie Parsons, high school girls. She suggested they follow the tradition of groups of women assembling quilts. Lena would be the master crafts teacher and they would recruit teenage girls to be the quiltmakers, with Jessie a participant—as a guidance counselor. The girls would work on the quilts under Lena's instruction and as the talk drifted among them, Jessie, in the room with the others, would offer informal but pointed observations for the girls, guidance counseling while making a quilt. Jessie was intrigued by the idea and she knew a church that would be amenable to offering the space, the Amsterdam Baptist Church in Harlem.

They began with nine girls, ages fifteen to seventeen, the daughters and granddaughters of church members. Karen stopped by occasionally for a few minutes, but was not a participant, she meant it to be their project. She planned to sell the quilt and future quilts in the store and donate the proceeds back to the church. Lena was passing on skills she herself learned from older women when she was a child in the South. She was eighty, a small woman with a wrinkled face that seemed to carry within its lines a larger story than her own. The archetypal grandmother, she was wise about her craft, loving to the girls. Jessie was like a savvy aunt who came in with her pointed remarks as the girls talked about boys, sex, clothes, music, school. In the first weeks three girls dropped out, unwilling to make the commitment of a two-hour session each week.

Karen was proud of the project and the girls, China, Tamara, Kadeesha, Dana, Shannon, and Tonya. The quilt, an abstract design of bright colors, was to be completed within a week with a public showing and party in the church basement. Tonya was a lively girl of sixteen, four feet eleven, with some flair; she favored black and white outfits, high-top sneakers, and baseball caps turned backwards. She had not been present for the last couple of weeks. Jessie knew Tonya lived with her grandmother, a church regular, who worked at cleaning apartments. Tonya's mother was killed in an automobile accident when the girl was twelve. She didn't have siblings. Jessie never learned about the father and presumed Tonya wasn't in contact with him. She thought the grandmother must have been reliable since she persuaded the girl to come to the church, a venue not high on the list for most teenage girls. Tonya went to DeWitt Clinton High School and hadn't been in class either for the last couple of weeks, which Jesse learned when she called the school. The guidance counselor at the school said Tonya was a good student, they had hopes of her going to college. They were concerned about her absence and a social worker had been working with the police, but no one had seen Tonya or her grandmother recently. The New York public schools, Jessie told Karen, was more of a transient culture than was commonly known. In any given school year many of the students who started the fall semester were unaccounted for by year's end, their parents relocated, the relatives they were living with left the district or the city, students dropped out. Karen and Jesse decided it was slightly encouraging that both grandmother and granddaughter had not been seen, that Tonya alone was not a missing child.

Two days before the party Jesse called Karen at home.

"They have a letter at Clinton requesting her school records. They've moved to Birmingham, Alabama."

"Birmingham?"

"She's in school down there, for now anyway. The grandmother spoke to someone at the church who called me. This is sad to say, Karen. Tonya is pregnant. The grandmother apparently took her out of school, out of the environment to go down there."

"Damn."

"The grandmother didn't say who the father is and I doubt she cares or she wouldn't take her away. I'm afraid we've seen the last of Tonya."

"She's sixteen!"

"She talked about boys . . . I didn't see it coming."

"What happens to her?"

"She'll probably have the baby and I don't know. A black unmarried teenage mother—she's just a statistic. With luck, she'll finish high school. I wouldn't count on it. And I wouldn't count on college anymore."

"So much for this concept."

"The concept is fine, Karen."

"Can we find out where she's living?"

"Probably."

"I want to do something. Send money."

"You can," she said in a resigned voice.

"You don't sound like I should."

"Go right ahead."

"What, Jesse?"

"My experience is you try to keep them on the tracks, as many as possible. Better to help the ones who are on, or teetering. One of them goes off the tracks, the likelihood is you'll never get them back on. We got five girls to finish the project."

The showing attracted a few dozen people from the congregation along with church officials. The quilt hanging on a wall looked beautiful to the guests. The five girls were very proud of themselves and said they would like to do another one. Karen bought each of them a little corsage. A bittersweet event. Jessie came over to Karen to cheer her. "Karen, it's a success."

She managed to get an item into the *Village Voice* about the quilt, which she sold in the store that week for five hundred dollars, donating the money to the church. The item indicated the project was going to continue and ran with the names of the quiltmakers. Karen included Tonya's name on the list. She sent the article with her own check for three hundred dollars to Tonya's grandmother, an address that Jessie unearthed. She received a note back from the grandmother, thanking her for the money, not understanding the reason, but they could use it, and that Tonya said hello. At the beginning of the following school term Karen sent a picture of the next quilt created by the expanded group of girls. In her note she said Tonya had helped the tradition get started. She included another check. The envelope came back "addressee unknown."

Bantrey's school tradition for the senior prom, although old-fashioned, became a point of honor for the students. The idea originated with a student dance committee during the sixties to ensure scholarship students wouldn't be priced out of a prom and people without boyfriends or girlfriends could still attend. Rejecting the black-tie-and-gown, students-hiring-limos style of many high schools, Bantrey held a square dance and people dressed country-style in jeans. Some scattered to private parties and clubs afterward; it was not the purpose of the evening and anyone could attend the square dance and it would be sufficient; they could feel they had gone to their school prom. The night featured line dancing and in the current era gathered up not only scholarship students and students without dates, but the gay students, as well. Jill had just broken up with someone at Columbia. Brian was at large, no Monica Feld. Tommy wasn't seeing anyone, and the plan was for them to go as their regular trio. Ricky Burns was back with her actor boyfriend, but he refused to come to a high school event. Ricky asked Tommy if she could join them and they were going to meet at Tommy's place. Karen stayed home so she could take pictures of them on their prom night. Jill and Brian were well known to her. She had seen Ricky in the school as the girl was growing up. She walked in the door wearing eye makeup, a flannel shirt, and tight jeans on her long frame, looking like she walked out of the dance line of *Oklahoma!*

Karen took pictures of them in different poses as they clowned around and sent them all off with the obligatory "have fun, be careful, not too late," in keeping with her position. As they were leaving, Tommy took a step back, aware of the way Karen had been staring at Ricky.

"We were together for a little bit, now we're not. We're just friends," he said and joined the others.

He was with this stunning girl? He never mentioned her. She couldn't be sure who he really was socially.

The Bantrey School, lacking the space within its own building, held its commencement ceremony in the auditorium of the Ethical Culture Society. In earlier times the event took place within the school. The rising divorce rate directly affected seating. With half the parents of the graduates now divorced, seats were needed for stepparents and, in some cases, step-grandparents. Each graduate received six tickets and the students made deals with each other depending on whether they needed or did not need the allotment. Tommy's six tickets were going to Rob, Karen, Vickie, Frank and Anne—Rob's parents—and Sally, Karen's mother. This group had never occupied the same space before. Bill was not attending, obliged to spend the day in meetings with members of the Watkin family, who funded the foundation. Karen was disappointed and he didn't like being out of the loop for her. But he didn't mind being able to avoid the scrutiny of Rob and Rob's side of the family.

The graduates sat in caps and gowns on the stage, the auditorium at capacity. Dealing with their own complications, Jill's mother was a few seats away from her ex-husband, separated by her parents. His wife sat on the other side of him holding his hand, Jill's mother sullen. Ms. Fitness looked as fit as when she appeared in the fateful commercials that began to unravel the marriage. Brian's father was not present; neither was his stepfather. Brian's mother was his only guest. Throughout the auditorium were broken families pieced together in ill-fitting combinations.

The school orchestra played excerpts from "Appalachian Spring," a decent sound with no honks or squeaks. These student-musicians, private school children, were the products of years of music lessons. The principal spoke in praise of the graduates, their spirit and sense of volunteerism. The student speaker was Monica Feld, slightly below Brian in her grade point average, en route to MIT, chosen ahead of Brian by the student commencement committee because she outscored Brian in extracurricular activities. Monica delivered a humorless self-referential speech. An alumnus spoke, an eighty-two-year-old retired Wall Street executive. With a cracking, sincere voice, he implored the students to find their own way in an ethically muddled business climate. Kim Greenley, headed for Wesleyan, sang "Wind Beneath My Wings." Lastly, a class parent, Ed McBride, an English professor at Hunter College, invoked a passage from *The Once and Future King*, in which young Arthur's animal friends exhort him to draw the sword from the stone, rooting him on out of love. He told the graduates that speeches at high school commencements were not high on the list of things one remembered as the years went by, but they should remember their families were there on this day rooting them on out of love. Altogether a dignified, sometimes moving ceremony and then on to the celebration lunches as the graduates and their families scattered through the city, the intact families and the families consisting of people who barely spoke to one another.

Rob made a reservation at an Italian restaurant, Petaluma, which Tommy enjoyed for the thin-crust pizzas, and it was his day. As if he had scripted the lunch out of fear they would go into free-fall, Rob talked enthusiastically about the graduation ceremony, how well he thought it was structured, and the others pitched in with their comments. Sally stole a few glances at Vickie, the woman who replaced her daughter with her ex-son-in-law. Rob made a toast to Tommy for being all-around terrific. Karen gave the next toast, her voice choked with emotion as she said how much she loved him for everything he was. Sally offered how grateful she was to see her grandson graduate from high school. Frank gave an addled toast about Tommy going off to college, creating an embarrassed silence as he had him attending college in Albany. Anne corrected him and gave her own good wishes for Tommy starting off on a successful life. Vickie, as the stepmother, was cautious about offending any of these people and chose to speak last in this little bureaucracy, and said she was happy to know Tommy and that he had enriched her life. Tommy thanked them all and said he, for one, was going to remember everything said on this day. Rob was worried any moment one of his parents was going to say something outrageous and explode the lunch. He could see Sally was uncomfortable, although too fine a person to be indiscreet. He wanted to accelerate, get through the meal, get the bill, and get out of there so Tommy could come away with an unmarred celebratory lunch. He steered them into a safe, bland discussion of the academic program at Marlowe. He paid the check and they scattered. Rob paused for a moment with Vickie away from the others.

"We got through it," he said. "After the graduation the family goes out and we did it."

Karen took her mother downtown to see the new store. Sally hadn't known what to expect. Karen warned it would be much smaller. She was very much impressed with her daughter's creativity. Tommy came along to spend a little extra time with his grandmother. He showed her how the video offered merchandise for work not displayed on the floor. Sally sat in the rear of the store chatting with her grandson and then he broke off from them. He was getting together with his friends for a party.

By arrangement, Bill came by so Karen could introduce him to her mother, the first time they had met. Sally had not been to New York since the relationship began. She scrutinized him as if he were eighteen and dating her sixteen-year-old daughter. They went to a Starbucks for coffee, the conversation largely between Sally and Bill, a retired teacher and a man who funded literacy projects. Karen was charmed by her mother's undiminished erudition and Bill's rapport with her.

Sally was staying at Karen's apartment that night and they talked in the living room.

"He's a lovely man. Very refined," Sally said.

"Yes, he is. He's a great reader of history and he collects history first-editions."

"And this leads to?"

"Next week and the week after."

"Will you ever get married again?"

"It's not in my immediate future. The store is pretty dominating right now."

"Rob is a workaholic. Didn't stop him from getting married again. Karen, if you'd listened to me—"

"Don't start, Mother. I couldn't stay in that marriage."

"So you both said. I would've stayed in my marriage for all your father's philandering. Because it doesn't go on forever. They get older. They get sick. I've seen it happen. They need to be taken back sometimes and if you love them enough, you forgive them enough, and you grow old together."

"I'm not the romantic you are."

"I don't know if it's being romantic or practical. In any case, he left. I would've taken him back, though, if I had the chance. He was very smart, your father. Never should have been a dentist. Something else in medicine or a professor possibly. Too handsome, that was his shortcoming. You know she died?"

"She did?"

"I just found out. Cancer. There's no trace of their relationship anymore. Ironic. I'm the custodian of his memory."

"God, you did love him."

"In your case, Rob wasn't even cheating on you, as far as we know. This man is very nice, he does something worthwhile, but it's a modest little foundation. What you do when you're retired and want to keep active. He's not on the front lines like Rob. He doesn't have Rob's stature."

"Please—"

"What can I tell you, my beautiful girl? I'm a believer in marriage."

"You think this does me any good? Rob and I are divorced. Mother, get over him."

Tommy was able to get his friends jobs in his camp, White River, in Vermont. He had taken his experience working with children in the recreation center, researched books on children's crafts, and the previous summer managed to make himself into an arts and crafts counselor. He returned to the job. Jill was a counselor for the twelve-year-old girls, who revered her for makeup tips and inside dopester stuff about boys. The sleeper among them was Brian, who became one of the most popular counselors in the camp. He was assigned the youngest children, seven-year-olds, and also helped oversee the weekly camp newspaper, a witty publication under his direction. He also became an unlikely role model for the similarly nonathletic boys in the camp. They saw that even if you were ungainly you could still be smart and funny and get into Harvard, which they knew was a big deal. Betsy McCallister, Tommy's first, was back as a counselor, but unavailable; she had a boyfriend at another Vermont camp and Tommy didn't connect with anyone over the summer, nor did Brian. Jill managed a little love affair the second half of the summer with Werner Haas, an archery instructor from Berlin, who was returning to Germany at summer's end. With new beginnings at Tufts, Jill was not too broken-hearted about losing him. "Tell you the truth, this is perfect," she said to Tommy and Brian. The summer was exactly what they wanted, a chance for them to be in each other's company for an extended period of time. They took days off together, saw each other at night, Werner trailing along at the end.

Tommy's eighteenth birthday came up the next to last week of camp. He received presents from parents and grandparents, checks to be used at college. Camp custom—everyone sang "Happy Birthday" in the dining room. By the time they went home, they were ready to be college kids.

Sales in Karen's store stayed at a steady pace throughout the summer. She wouldn't take the chance of being away from the place for a vacation. Bill took time from the office on some of her Mondays and Tuesdays off and they made a few trips in a two-hour-drive radius from the city.

Vickie sent the boys to a day camp and it was a busy summer for her and, as always, for Rob. He took his entire staff on a trip to Waterbury, Connecticut, so they could see the results of the work they did, MayPole equipment in use by children there. Courtesy of a slightly more responsible Tim, who showed up and stayed with the boys for a few days, Vickie and Rob went for a weekend to a hotel in East Hampton.

Throughout the summer Karen and Rob were conscious of the date, August 29th, when Tommy was scheduled to leave for college. Since most of his belongings were in the apartment with Karen, her place became the point of departure. The drive to Pittsfield was about three hours. If they went up in one car it would decrease the amount of room for Tommy's things and the parents would have to spend the return trip, just the two of them in the car together. They may have been able to handle the drive, but it seemed to both an unnecessary intimacy. Tommy would go up with Karen. Rob would drive separately in his own car. He was going to tie the trip to a sales call the next day in Boston. In her own carryover from the marriage Karen, too, drove a Volvo.

Tommy's residence was Torrington Hall, a modern three-story building with exterior accents designed to relate to the overall neo-Georgian architecture of the main buildings. Rob arrived first and sat on the front steps waiting for them, observing the incoming freshmen and parents lugging cartons, suitcases, duffles, computers, printers, trash bags, television sets, sound systems, portable refrigerators. The computer products were a change from his college days and added to the bulk. Some of the parents carrying their children's possessions looked like overburdened bearers on safari. Karen drove up and Tommy burst out of the car, excited, giving his father a high five. They went to his room, located on the first floor. Tommy's roommate was already there and fully moved in. He was a sturdy six feet three, broad shoulders, blond crewcut. The roommate's appearance and the baseball bats in the corner told Tommy he was rooming with an athlete, Tommy who barely looked at the sports pages. Well, I run. Freelance.

His name was Kevin Wilkins. They spoke briefly the week before and arranged for Kevin to supply a portable refrigerator, Tommy a television set.

"Hope you don't mind if I settled in, but I got here early."

One of the beds was close to a bay window with a built-in bookshelf under the window and more space on that side of the room. The accommodations were not equal and he had taken it upon himself to appropriate the better space before his roommate arrived.

"No problem," Tommy said, not wanting to make an issue out of it, although it was informative about his new roommate.

"You play?" Rob asked him, noting the baseball bats.

"Left field."

"You're already on the team?"

"I'm on," he said coolly. "I'm going to let you guys get settled. Tommy—" and he walked out.

"Kevin—"

They carried everything from the cars into the room. The roommates needed a vacuum cleaner and Karen was prepared to buy it for them. Tommy also needed a lamp to read in bed. They went to the college bookstore, which had a department for household items. Karen and Rob began to squabble over the vacuum cleaner. Karen wanted the most expensive, highest-power vacuum, Rob said it would take up too much space in the room, a subject they had never discussed in their lives and suddenly they were both experts on which vacuum cleaner a college freshman needed. Tommy didn't care about a vacuum cleaner and couldn't deal with their squabbling. He walked away to browse through the store. Karen's point was that all the vacuum cleaners on display were meant for these students' rooms. If they were too large they wouldn't have been on display in the first place. Rob threw his hands up and said she could have it her way. They looked at lamps and they couldn't come to an agreement there either. Rob thought a clip-on lamp affixed to a bookshelf above Tommy's bed would give him the best reading light, Karen wanted to buy a floor lamp that would look better in the room and could still give enough light. Tommy returned and rather than make this larger in front of him they agreed to buy both lamps. They carried the items to the room, did some more unpacking, and everybody was ready for lunch. They walked to a nearby commercial strip where another skirmish broke out over where they were going to eat. "Cut it out, you guys!" Tommy said. He interceded and chose a take-out sandwich store so they could eat on the grass on campus as some of the other students and parents were doing.

Tommy was exasperated by their behavior. He didn't understand the college drop-off had become the very symbol of his parents' divorce, the two coming up separately, competing to make it go smoothly, the right vacuum cleaner, the right lamp, the right lunch before they left, needing it to be a wonderful college drop-off, for nobody to ever have had a better college drop-off, saying to themselves—we may be divorced, but you weren't affected by it, you don't have any problems, you're in the school you wanted to go to, you're starting out with everything just right, everything is fine, you're fine, it will all be fine—and they kissed and hugged him and left the campus with blinders on.

TEN

• • •

Separation anxiety was a condition Karen associated with children, the puckered lips as they went off to nursery school or the first time to summer camp, not the distress of a mature woman off-stride because her son has left for college. She was accustomed to his absences, the times he stayed at Rob's, summers when he was away. At home he tended to be private, but he was a presence. And now he was gone. For Rob, Tommy was not the sole other person in the apartment for him. Still, he felt a change, if not as pronounced as Karen's—his son was off to college and he would be seeing less of him now. By and large, Karen was the custodial parent, a single parent whose child had just left for college and it was lonely without him.

She expressed her feelings to Polly, who immediately invited her to come over that night for dinner, she was making an informal meal, meat loaf, mashed potatoes, comfort food; Karen would feel better.

"What you have to know," Polly said at the dinner table, "is it's a very short school year. Every time you turn around they're standing in your living room."

"I'm surprised at how much I seemed to have relied on him to just be around."

"Then this is a message," Joe said. "This is your life."

"She doesn't have to hear that."

"Yes, she does. It's you, your store, and this Bill."

"Don't say 'this Bill,' " Polly reprimanded.

"Tommy's not going to be around much anymore and when he finishes college he's going to really be off on his own and how much his mother, any mother, can be a factor in a young adult male's life is questionable. So you have to make sure you have the best setup for yourself and ask yourself whether this Bill should be part of it."

"You should do a cookbook," Karen said. "*Meat Loaf for Suicides.*"

"Karen, Tommy going off to college is a wake-up call," Joe said, relentless.

"I just came for a cold, Doctor."

"Ease up, Joe."

"He's being Joe," Karen said. "And it is a wake-up call, I suppose. I ran into a Bantrey mother on the street. Her daughter went to Vassar and she was telling me how happy the girl was at school and how she called at midnight to read her an English paper she wrote and I said, 'Wait a minute. Your daughter *called* you?' "

"He doesn't call?" Polly asked.

"Sunday nights. He's got that worked out for himself."

"You call *him*?"

"I started to, but I only got the machine."

"Is he okay there?" Joe asked.

"Seems so. They do four majors. He's taking contemporary American short fiction, a survey course on the Vietnam War, a computer course on Web site design, and Italian."

"That's great," Joe said.

"I know. So, onward. If this is my life then it's a lucky life, I'd say. It wouldn't be appropriate anyway for me to go up every Sunday to bring him spare ribs from Pig Heaven."

On September 11, 2001, Karen was in the store early doing paperwork. She kept a radio in the office and it was tuned to WINS, the all-news station, when the first report of the disaster came through. Her manager, John, called from home. He had been watching television and in these early moments there was still uncertainty as to the events. She told him to stay home, knowing this wouldn't be a day to be open for business, not anticipating how calamitous a day it would turn out to be. Tommy called on her cell phone and she assured him she was out of harm's way, the site was far south of the store. She fielded other calls, from Bill, Polly, her mother, and Rob, as well, and assured them she was all right. As people covered with dust, many dazed, began to stream north through the streets, she joined with other retail store neighbors, including one who owned a grocery, and they set up a table on the corner of Elizabeth Street and Houston Street and distributed bottled water to the survivors. Her feelings of separation from Tommy were even more acute—this was a time to be with family, to be together. Students from New York were not going home, he informed her the next day. The college was trying to support their community from within. All classes were canceled for a memorial service and he was going to attend.

The store was closed for two weeks while the downtown area was blocked off for rescue operations. Karen and John helped out at a sandwich and coffee stand for workers at the site, then on reopening Karen donated 25 percent of her receipts to the victims' fund over the next month. As with nearly everyone in New York there was a degree or two of separation from the tragedy. A woman in Harlem who knitted baby sweaters for Karen lost her husband. A man John went to high school with was gone, as was a former salesman of Rob's who had become a bond trader.

Tommy talked to his parents more often than he might have in these first weeks and then evolved to a once-a-week call to each of them. The adjustment to college life, the newness of everything, distanced him from the tragedy in New York, and he told them he felt strange about it, but the mood at school was to concentrate on school.

Rob was on a business trip to Rutland, Vermont, and sent Tommy an e-mail, could he meet him for lunch, he was coming through that way and it was easy for him to stop by in Pittsfield. Tommy sent him an e-mail Rob picked up on his Blackberry, lunch was all he had time for, but it was okay. They went to a pub and Tommy was eager to know how the city was coping. Rob told him people were trying to get back to normal, but there was a constant, rolling sense of mourning.

Tommy felt he picked the right courses for his first semester. He was hoping to get together with Jill and Brian on a weekend. He had too much work. The largest negative was his roommate, a disagreeable jock with a surly temperament. He had a sophomore girlfriend and the guy seemed to think it bestowed him with status. Tommy thought Rob would be interested to know he had been jogging. About three times a week he ran along a roadway encircling the campus, close to four miles. This certainly did interest Rob and he asked if Tommy might consider going out for track, possibly cross-country.

"I don't think so," Tommy replied. "I don't want to be on a team, I just want to run when I want to run."

"It's good you're doing it. All sounds excellent."

"Now if I can do the work. You think it's only about getting in, but they have this thing and it's called college."

"My money's on you."

"What it's costing you, it should be."

Rob met Karen the following morning at a Starbucks near her apartment and gave her a report. Tommy seemed to be well-adjusted and seeing him in the setting of the school was far more reassuring than Tommy's brief phone calls. He looked healthy, was exercising, working hard, apparently. She couldn't stop herself from feeling jealous. He gets to just drop in on him. It's what Joe was saying about mothers. A boy isn't going to want to have his mother drop in on him.

Rob particularly wanted to meet Karen so they could deal with the upcoming holidays. With Tommy away at college, Karen and Rob no longer had a workable custody arrangement. Tommy had been living with Karen and was supposed to stay with Rob every other weekend. If he wasn't with Karen, when exactly would he go to Rob's and how would that be scheduled? They never argued over custody and weren't territorial with each other; they simply didn't have a practical plan any longer. Thanksgiving, as a family holiday, seemed more important to people after September 11, and their respective relatives were willing to travel so they could be together. Vickie wanted to have a Thanksgiving dinner and invite her parents from Cleveland and Rob hoped to have Tommy with them. But Karen also was planning a Thanksgiving dinner. Bill's daughter and son-in-law were coming in from California, and Bill made a special request of Karen to have a holiday meal. She wanted Tommy at her place.

"What some people do is just divide up the school vacations," Karen said. "And they split Thanksgiving and Christmas."

"Except the Christmas break is longer."

"Beats me, Rob. Why doesn't he come to me for Thanksgiving and you for Christmas part of the time? Mid-semester break he can split any way he likes, since he has a vote in this by now."

"I don't want to end up where I never get to have him with me because it's so much easier for him to be with you."

"His father is not going to be deprived of seeing him. We'll do it by feel. If it feels like you haven't had a fair share, we'll just say to him, 'Tommy, it's time to spend a few nights at your Dad's' and I'm sure he'll go along."

"So he stays with you, as usual, and we'll look for a practical equivalent to the every-other-weekend thing."

"That's a good way to put it, a practical equivalent."

The unpleasantness of the college drop-off, which had been fueled by their anxieties, receded in this time Tommy was away at school. Here were the enlightened Karen and Rob, trying to be fair and not create any frictions contrary to the best interests of the child. They did not quite have an agreement, though.

"It still leaves the issue of Thanksgiving," Rob said.

"I'll have the Thanksgiving dinner and you can have a Christmas dinner."

"Only Vickie is very, very eager to do Thanksgiving. And we'd like Tommy to be there."

"And Bill is very, very eager that I do it. And I'd like Tommy to be there."

They sat without speaking for a few moments.

"Why don't we stagger the times?" she said. "I'll do a lunch. You can do a dinner. And he can go to both. We'll be stuffing *him* like a turkey, but it's a solution."

"All right, you take one meal, I'll take the other. Peculiar, but okay." He started to smile. "I read a book once with quotes from people in Hollywood and Oscar Levant said, 'Affairs are all right, but it's the second dinner that kills you.' "

"Why would you remember that?"

"Because it's amusing."

Did you have an affair, Rob? Is it leaking out? All of a sudden this little slip?

The way she was looking at him, ignoring the humor of the quote, it was obvious what she was thinking.

Think you caught me in something? No, Karen. As if it matters now.

"It's semi-amusing," she said.

"Amusing and that's why I remembered."

"So who breaks the news to Tommy and what if he doesn't go along with it?"

"*You* can," Rob said, chuckling.

They had a new custodial agreement.

• • •

Tommy found the idea to be odd, but agreed—he would have a Thanksgiving lunch at Karen's apartment at one P.M., then move over to Rob's for dinner at seven. He was also planning on seeing Jill. They never managed to get together in Boston or in Pittsfield during the first part of the semester. Jill's father and his wife were on a cruise and Jill was spending the holiday with her mother. Brian was excited to be going to Chicago to visit his father and his father's family. His mother and stepfather were in Bilbao.

Tommy appeared at Karen's door the night before Thanksgiving, the first time she had seen him since the day he began college. His hair was a little longer, his complexion clear, healthy. His eyes even seemed brighter although she knew that was a contrived thought on her part.

He gave her his account of school to date. The work load was difficult, not unmanageable, but difficult. The roommate continued to be annoying. He had been to some parties, wasn't seeing anyone in particular yet. She tried to read between the lines. Do you have any friends at school? He told her the college ran a literacy tutoring program for elementary school children in town and he signed up. There were a couple of guys in the program, sophomores, whom he liked and that served to assuage her concerns a little. He had met people.

On Thanksgiving morning Tommy received a call from Brian. He never got to Chicago. His father called the night before and said one of the children was coming down with something and the Thanksgiving dinner was called off. Brian was supposed to fly from Boston to Chicago and decided to come into New York rather than be at Harvard by himself over Thanksgiving.

"I've got more Thanksgiving meals than we can even eat," Tommy told him. "Lunch at my mom's. Dinner at my dad's. And later, if we want, we can go out to eat."

"Dinner sounds good. There's a movie I want to see in the afternoon."

"You got it. After dinner we'll hook up with Jill."

"Do you have to clear it?"

"It's okay. I'll just tell them you're coming. I'll pick you up."

"Thanks, Tommy."

"No problem."

Tommy didn't know Brian's father. He only knew he was a bastard.

• • •

The Thanksgiving lunch was the first time Karen had met Bill's son-in-law, Jed, a gastroenterologist. He was a blond of six feet three with a sturdy frame. She thought he could have been a California surfer when he was younger. She asked out of curiosity if he had ever surfed and he said he still did. She smiled privately at Tommy. Here was a cultural divide. They didn't know any surfers in their family.

Bill was eager for the lunch to go well and he moderated like a talk show host. With his daughter and son-in-law both doctors, he steered the conversation to current events in science, abortion rights, stem cell research. Tommy pretended to be very interested in everything the doctors had to say and they were not timid about expressing themselves. Getting bored, he asked Karen about the store and she talked about the quilt-making project. No one had directed their attention toward Tommy, which was a relief to him. He escaped as far as dessert. Cindy asked the old standby, what are you majoring in and when he said English, he knew what was coming next—what are you going to do with it, and he launched into what was a stump speech for English majors, he wasn't sure, but it was a building block for any number of choices, and he reached the finish line, the end of the meal. Bill was pleased, it went smoothly. Everyone had gotten along, a pleasant Thanksgiving meal that included his family. Karen had come through for him. Tommy helped Karen clean up after the others left and then she released him, he was going to meet Brian at his apartment before going to Rob and Vickie's place.

"I noticed you ate lightly," she teased. "So what did you think of Cindy and Jed?"

"A little boring."

"I agree."

"Is there something different going on between you and Bill? Why was this so important?"

"He just wanted a get-together for Thanksgiving."

Having cleared out the are-you-two-getting-married line of questioning, he departed.

Tommy met Brian at his apartment. Alone in a large apartment on Thanksgiving, Brian looked to Tommy less like a wealthy teenager than an abandoned child.

• • •

At Rob and Vickie's place they walked into a squall, the boys shouting about seeing Tommy again. Vickie's parents were there and Vickie introduced them.

"Mom, Dad, this is my stepson," she said proudly. He couldn't remember being in a situation with her where a formal introduction was required and she said "stepson." He didn't mind hearing her say it that way, she was so pleased about it. "And this is his friend, Brian. Don and Joan Carstairs." They shook hands and her parents appraised the boys.

"So you're an English major at Marlowe, I hear," Joan said. "I'm a librarian so I like that. And Brian, where are you in school?"

Tommy noticed them both looking hard at Brian. Pinched, precise people, they were having difficulty with Brian's appearance. Despite wearing a blazer, shirt, and tie, the Brian belly was dominant, the portliness overwhelming his tailoring.

"Harvard."

"Really?" Joan said.

"That's very nice," Don added.

Tommy noted the power of the college name in defusing any lurking disapproval.

If lunch with Bill was the science section of *The New York Times*, dinner was the *Daily News* Sunday comics. Except for the turkey, everything was "yuck" to the boys, the squash, the cranberry sauce, the brussels sprouts, especially the brussels sprouts. Keith feigned eating one and spit it out, causing his brother to laugh, and when they were reprimanded severely by their mother they sat silently and that made them laugh. Finally, they calmed down. Brian, the natural camp counselor, encouraged the boys to talk about what they liked on television, which led the adults to a general discussion about television and everyone offered their opinions. Don then directed a tough line of questioning at Rob about his business as if he had just shown up in Vickie's life. Rob was diplomatic. The lack of enthusiasm for him on the Rob vs. Tim comparison chart was obvious. The boys left the table, coming in and out pushing fire trucks along the floor. Brian went inside with them and they watched a video together; he seemed content to be with the children rather than the adults.

It was finally time, the two meals completed. Rob came to the door as Tommy was leaving to tell him he was a good sport for doing this. Tommy reprised his early jest to Brian, saying they were going out to grab a bite.

They met Jill at a party for Bantrey graduates and Tommy returned to Karen's apartment. Everyone seemed to get what they needed out of the day. Tommy was pivotal for these adults. In the desire of his parents and their partners for an ideal Thanksgiving family holiday, he was needed to complete the families.

He lay in bed that night without a sense of having done anything particularly noteworthy and without a good feeling about the day. Two Thanksgiving meals, one serious and stage-managed, the other noisy and uneven, meeting new people—Bill's daughter and son-in-law, Vickie's parents—none of it had the impact for him as the lingering image of his friend, Brian, alone in the large, empty apartment.

Faced with a paper he needed to write and final exams in three weeks, Tommy cut short the weekend. He took a bus back by way of Kingston, New York, stopping off to see his paternal grandparents, who were unable to make it into New York for Thanksgiving. Rob's father had badly sprained an ankle and was on crutches. Tommy spent a couple of hours with them, they had lunch at the house, and he took the bus to Pittsfield.

He opened the door of his dorm room late afternoon and found his roommate, Kevin, in bed with his girlfriend, a muscular, buxom member of the swimming team, her full breasts in view above the blanket line. They were asleep, as was Bob, a friend of Kevin's from the baseball team, whose girlfriend was sleeping against his leg, Bob naked, the girl partially covered by a ski jacket. Scattered about the room were empty beer cans, spilled potato chips, and a limp condom in a loafer. A cardboard container from the beer, a couple of empty cans, and an open bag of potato chips had been tossed on his bed and he swiped them onto the floor.

"All right, folks, party's over."

Only Kevin stirred. He opened his eyes, looked at Tommy with a superior smile that was a DO NOT DISTURB sign and closed his eyes again—get lost. "Hey, time's up!" Tommy raised his voice.

They stirred, but were not about to rouse themselves. He returned to school early specifically so he could get work done and didn't want to waste time dealing with these people. He dropped his carrying bag on his bed, opened the refrigerator, found a cold beer, shoved it into his jacket pocket, and left with his knapsack. He worked for two hours in the college library, which was sparsely inhabited, then went to a pizza place off campus, bought a couple of slices, and returned to the campus with the pizza in a bag. The night was mild, a starry sky. He thought the most private place he could enjoy his pizza and beer would be the area behind the college bookstore, a loading zone he knew would not be in use on the Friday night of Thanksgiving weekend. He sat on the rear steps of the building with his private meal. He thought he had given them enough time. When he finished he was going back to his room to clear them all out.

A campus security car cruising the campus pulled into the area. The security officer behind the wheel shined a spot on him and he was trapped. Campus regulations prohibited the consumption of alcoholic beverages, even beer. Students drank; the idea was not to get caught. He chose a place so remote it was on the campus security police's patrol route. The uniformed officer emerged and walked over to Tommy, who stood up. The officer was in his early twenties, several inches shorter than Tommy. He was overweight, puffy, and he spoke in a thin, high voice, a post-adolescent who would not be mistaken for a tough guy on a television cop show.

"ID."

Tommy handed over his student ID and he looked at it.

"Not allowed to drink on campus, you know."

"I'm not drinking. Just a beer with my pizza."

"I'm going to have to report this."

"It's Thanksgiving weekend. Nobody's around. I wasn't bothering anyone, just having a beer by myself."

He didn't look sympathetic and Tommy was getting a bad feeling, the security officer was too young, a town-gown confrontation, and Tommy knew this was serious when he said, "This is my job. I have to do my job."

"It was nothing, really. I'm sober. Look at me. Let's just forget it, okay?"

The officer ignored him and went to the car and called in his report to the main security desk, where they had a roster of students' names and dorm rooms. He was informed that another officer had been dispatched to Tommy's room and was there now. He walked back to Tommy, who had thrown away the damning beer can.

"We're going to your room."

"This is so nothing. Why don't you just let it be?"

"Get in."

As they drove to his dorm Tommy continued the unsuccessful attempt to convince the officer it was a simple beer with pizza. The dorm room had been strewn with beer cans when Tommy left. He doubted his roommate cleaned up since then. He did not want to walk in there with this officer. They entered the building and a woman was shouting, "My father's a lawyer and he'll sue your ass!" They reached the doorway and another uniformed security officer was writing notes on a clipboard as the girl continued to rail at him. It was Kevin's girlfriend, now dressed, as were the others. The second officer was older, in his forties, tall as Kevin and not sympathetic to these students. He was ignoring Kevin's girlfriend. In the room was Calley Shea, the dorm advisor, a senior who lived on their floor, a heavyset girl with stringy black hair, a computer science major with a dull personality and a stickler for dorm rules. Tommy knew if Calley Shea was there, it was not a good thing.

"What's up?" the younger officer asked.

"Ms. Shea here smelled marijuana in the room. Asked to enter and they wouldn't open up. So she called us in. And we didn't do anything illegal, miss. You opened the door and we just observed." For his colleague's benefit he said, "Alcoholic beverages." He led him to the window. On the ground was a scattered mess of beer cans, which they had hastily tossed out the window before the officer appeared. "They missed these from under the bed." He had two beer cans on a coffee table. "No drugs observed. Must have been consumed."

"This is the roommate. Caught him drinking beer behind the bookstore."

Kevin saw the opening and seized it.

"He brought the beer in," Kevin said.

"What?" Tommy was flabbergasted.

"It's his beer."

"Is that true?" the older officer asked.

"No! This was not my party. I was by myself. Isn't that how you found me?"

Tommy, furious, glared at Kevin, who gave him a palms up—don't look at me, buddy.

"Tell them the truth. One of you got the beer," Tommy said. "I didn't."

"Wasn't one of us," Kevin's girlfriend said.

"But it was here. Are you denying alcohol was consumed on the premises? And that I can't ascertain pot when I smell it?" Calley said.

"Fuck you," Kevin's girlfriend said.

"We'll let the discipline board sort this out," the older officer said.

"Can we go now?" the other girlfriend asked.

"You can go. I seem to have everything."

He handed back their student IDs.

"But I would advice prudence the rest of the weekend."

"Who gives a shit what you advise," Bob said as he and the two girls pushed their way past Calley, Bob making contact with her, bumping her as he left. The guards followed them out and Tommy slammed the door behind them, leaving him in the room with Kevin.

"You lying sonofabitch."

"Hey, man, your beer. That's my story. And if it gets to pot, your pot."

He grabbed his knapsack and pushed past Tommy to leave.

"I'm not getting framed by you, you sonofabitch. I came in, I could've called security and you would've been up the creek, you were all so zonked. But I wouldn't do that."

"Well, good for you."

Kevin hurried out of the room and Tommy grabbed him by the arm.

"What are you going to do, Tommy, beat me up?"

Kevin saw the older officer in the hall going over his notes.

"Hey, this guy's looking for a fight and I don't want any trouble."

"What's going on?"

"All I want to do is leave the building and he won't let me go."

"I strongly suggest you return to your room and allow him to leave," he said to Tommy.

"This guy is a lying snake."

"You can take it up with the board. Go back to your room."

Triumphantly, Kevin walked down the hallway. Tommy did not see him for the rest of the weekend.

The Student Judicial Board of the college held jurisdiction over disciplinary matters on campus not serious enough to involve the Pittsfield police. A hearing consisted of three students out of a rotating pool and a faculty advisor as an administrative observer. Tommy's hearing was scheduled for five P.M. on the first Monday following the weekend. His appearance was mandatory. The board had the power to try cases and render verdicts, which ranged from no action to disciplinary warnings to suspensions and expulsions. Failure to appear before the board, barring legitimate requests for a delay, was grounds for expulsion.

Tommy chose not to call either of his parents. They didn't have to know he was in trouble not entirely of his making. And they need never know. He logged on to the school's Web site, which listed results of hearings before the board. In the past year for first offenses on alcohol-related episodes a warning was the customary penalty without parental notification.

Tommy was seen with the beer in his hand, they had him on that and it would have been implausible for him to claim he was holding it, but not drinking it. The other possible accusation was that he brought the beer into the room, which was also against school regulations. If Kevin tried to raise that before the board there was no proof of it. As for the marijuana, they all seemed to be in the clear. Calley claimed she smelled it, she didn't see anyone smoking it, and Kevin's threat that it was Tommy's pot, too, was irrelevant—there was no evidence of pot. Whatever the result of the hearing, he was going to request that either he or Kevin be transferred out of the room. He couldn't imagine ever speaking to the guy again. He wondered what someone's background was for doing this. His parents were divorced and for a brief moment Tommy thought this might give them a connection. He was self-centered and selfish, merely a bad roommate until now, having moved to the nightmare level.

He called Brian in New York, whose advice was to take the hit on the single can of beer, a first offense, it wasn't a big deal. He should just say he drank a beer, that's all he did, there was no proof of anything else, and by all means he should get rid of the roommate.

"A can of beer. It's just a can of beer," Brian said.

A handbook was available for use of students called before the board and he studied it. Tommy was faintly ill all day Monday in anticipation of the hearing. He saw no trace of Kevin and the slow winding day finally reached the time for his hearing. These matters were in the province of the deans of the college and the hearing was to be held in a conference room in the administration building, where the deans' offices were located. He entered the area. A female secretary in her thirties asked him to sit on a chair outside the conference room until they were ready for him. After five minutes, Kevin emerged from the conference room and Tommy saw that he and Kevin had been dealt with in separate procedures.

"Got your turn first, did you?" Tommy said. "Try to sink me in there?"

"I've made a request of the dean for me to vacate the room, effective immediately. With exams coming up I don't want you as my roommate any longer. You're a bad influence."

"You scheming sonofabitch."

Kevin walked away. He went on record first to say Tommy was the bad guy. Tommy assumed he used the room request in the hearing as part of his act. He told the secretary he needed a few minutes and hurried to the men's room with the runs.

When he returned he was asked to enter the conference room. Windows overlooked the campus quadrangle and the walls were lined with books. At one side of a wide mahogany table sat the hearing committee, a bookish-looking young woman in glasses, a pretty face masked by the seriousness of her demeanor, which was the general attitude of the other students—a hulking young man, broad shoulders and a square head that ran by way of a wide neck to his torso, a football player for sure, Tommy guessed. He was going to be judged in this room by another athlete like Kevin. Completing the panel was a freckle-faced girl with auburn hair and blue eyes, the closest to looking pleasant, but she also adopted a serious judge's manner. Looking on in a chair near a side door was the faculty advisor, the freshman dean, Andrew Roberts, an African-American in his late twenties, the freshmen girls' heartthrob, and Tommy was encouraged to see him there. In his speeches to the freshmen he had been sensible and direct. He knew the advisor was present only in an administrative capacity, to see the rules were followed; still Tommy was encouraged, looking for something to encourage him.

"I'm Donna Wright," the bookish-looking girl said. "This is Bart Moss and Sandy Goodman. We're seniors. We're very familiar with the student guidebook on rules of the campus and we want to make sure you are."

"I've read it, yes."

"And the handbook for the hearing?"

"Yes."

"So you know this is not a court of law. It's a hearing. We hear the facts as we can determine them and we issue a verdict. This is not a place for lawyers or parents. This is not a police matter, although the minimum drinking age in Massachusetts is twenty-one, as you must know. Do you?"

"Yes."

"But you weren't arrested by the local police, you were found by campus security. This is about a college self-policing itself in matters private to the college."

"I understand."

"The reason we're here," Bart said, consulting notes, "is you were found by campus security with a beer. Another security guard discovered beer cans in your room. The university prohibits alcohol consumption by students on campus and inside the residences and campus buildings. Are you aware of those regulations?"

"Yes, but as to the beer in the room—"

"We'll deal with that accordingly," Donna said. She looked over at the advisor. "May we have the security officers, please."

Marijuana hadn't been mentioned, given the apparent absence of evidence. A can of beer, it's just a can of beer, Tommy said to himself.

The security guards entered the room and the one to find Tommy, Officer Claire, was asked for his account of Saturday night's activities.

"I entered the rear area of the campus bookstore and at seven twelve P.M. came upon Mr. Burrows with a beer in his hand."

"Did you see him drinking the beer?" Bart asked.

"Not bringing it to his lips, but he had it in his hand and there was the smell on his breath."

"Mr. Burrows, were you drinking the beer?" Bart said.

"I was. One beer. I didn't even finish it, just a beer with my pizza."

"So you admit to consumption of alcohol on campus?" Donna asked.

"Yes, to less than one can of beer."

"Officer Claire, what happened next?" Sandy asked.

"I called into the main security desk, learned that Mr. Burrows' and Mr. Wilkins' room was the subject of an inquiry by Officer Stark and asked Mr. Burrows to go there with me."

"And what did you find?" Sandy said.

"I found Officer Stark and—" he consulted his notes "—Kevin Wilkins, Robert Hardaway, Nikki Cole, and Samantha Biers in the room with the dorm advisor, Calley Shea."

"Officer Stark, why were you there?" Bart asked.

"Ms. Shea called in security."

"Why was that?" Sandy asked.

"She told us it was because she was unable to gain access to the room after suspicious activity."

"What kind of suspicious activity?" Sandy said.

"She said she smelled marijuana."

"Did you find any marijuana or see anyone smoking marijuana?" Bart said.

"No, we did not," Officer Stark said.

"So that's not an issue here and Mr. Burrows was not in the room at the time anyway," Bart said.

"That is true."

"What *did* you find in the room?" Bart said.

"While investigating I found beer cans scattered in a wide area outside the window, but nothing to specifically link that to the room other than circumstantially. I did find two opened beer cans in the room. We concluded our investigation and since no unlawful activity was taking place at that moment we left the premises."

"So the only time Mr. Burrows was seen with an alcoholic beverage was in back of the bookstore?" Sandy said.

"Yes, that would be the only time," Claire said.

"He was not seen by either of you officers bringing beer into the building?" Donna asked.

"Not by me," Claire said.

"Nor by me."

"There's nothing you observed that told you the beer cans in the room belonged to Mr. Burrows?" Bart said.

"Nothing. As you know, we're not into fingerprinting beer cans," Officer Stark said. "That's not the kind of campus anyone wants."

"Mr. Burrows, is there anything in this account you find fault with, anything you'd like to ask the officers about?"

"No."

"Officers—" Donna said, dismissing them, the advisor showing them out.

"So—" Donna continued, "what it comes down to is an offense of drinking an alcoholic beverage on campus, which you admit to, and a second possible offense, bringing the beer into the dorm."

"Did you bring it into the dorm?" Sandy asked.

"No. I came back to campus around five on Saturday. To do some work on a paper. When I got to my room it was trashed. My roommate, Kevin, his girlfriend, Nikki, Bob and his girlfriend, Samantha, were passed out, beer cans all over the place. Garbage on my bed. I tried to rouse them.

They weren't interested in moving. I had work to do and didn't want to be bothered dealing with them. I was feeling really intruded on and, maybe in anger, maybe for a payback, I just grabbed a beer from the fridge, their beer, went to the library, did my work, bought some pizza, sat down back of the bookstore for privacy, ate the pizza and sipped the beer, which is when Officer Claire found me. I never bought that beer. I didn't make a scene at the time when I found them all over my room. I figured I'd do my work and eventually they'd leave. I drank a beer. I shouldn't've. It's against the rules. I know that. Just a single beer. It was a mistake and I'm sorry."

"You should know your roommate appeared before us to answer to Officer Stark finding beer in the room. He said *you* bought the beer. That you have a serious drinking problem," Donna said. "And that he can't room with you anymore."

Tommy was working hard to contain himself.

"He's lying. He's on the baseball team and he wants to make sure he doesn't get in trouble, so he's dumping on me."

"One of you is lying," Donna said. "We're not into fingerprinting beer cans, as the officer said. It isn't the kind of school we want to have. We just want to police ourselves in a way that makes sense."

"Anything else you want to add to your story?" Sandy asked.

"If you can picture that scene in your minds when I walked into my room and they didn't think I'd be there, it was not the way you want to come back to school. The beer cans out the window. I think they tossed them out and just happened to miss a couple, but it wasn't beer I bought. I haven't been in trouble all semester. I can handle a beer, which is all I had. As I said, I shouldn't have, but I wasn't disruptive to anyone and it was just a beer."

"Thank you," Donna said. "We'll have a verdict for you in a timely manner."

He returned to the room and found Kevin had already cleared out his clothing and some of his books. He was probably going to come back for the rest when he knew Tommy was in class. The board couldn't connect Kevin to marijuana. And no one saw him drinking beer. The beer cans on the ground couldn't be tied to him. Tommy surmised his roommate was going to walk away clean, not even a disciplinary warning, while he was going to end up being the only guilty party in the episode. The board members seemed reasonable. Serious, but reasonable. He assumed his being a first-time offender on a minor offense would be taken into consideration. The next day he found a letter in his mailbox on the Student Judicial Board letterhead.

> Dear Mr. Burrows:
> Concerning the charge against you by campus security of drinking alcohol on campus in violation of the college's regulation #12 of the code of non-academic conduct, which prohibits alcohol consumption, the board finds you guilty. You are to report within 48 hours of receipt of this letter to Health Services for mandatory counseling and for an educational assignment. A notification has been sent to Dr. Mary Hughes, director of Health Services, and to the contact names on your school records, Karen Burrows and Rob Burrows, who will receive a copy of this letter by registered mail.

No one in a case like this gets any more than a disciplinary warning. It's insane. And telling my parents. They're going to think I'm a falling-down drunk.

ELEVEN

• • •

Karen rehearsed speeches in her mind. She loved him, he had to know that, but if he were a secret drinker they had best deal with it now. And what about drugs? They had to face it. The loose compact between parents and children in their culture was a form of "Don't ask, don't tell." The more realistic version of that compact was "Don't ask, don't tell, unless there's trouble." He was going to have to be absolutely honest with her.

She was unable to motivate herself to go into the store and busied herself with tasks around the apartment waiting for Tommy to return her call. The phone rang and she rushed for it. Rob was on the line, how serious was it? She couldn't assure him, she needed assurances herself. She would let him know when she spoke to Tommy and he should do the same.

She called Polly at work and read her the letter.

"He's not been in an accident, he's not in trouble with the police. He got caught drinking," Polly said. "Is he a drinker?"

"They all drink sometime, don't they?"

"If he's a boozer, obviously that's not good. If it's innocent and it's just that he got caught, then it's being dealt with. What's the drinking age there?"

"Twenty-one."

"So it's being handled internally by the college."

"It's got to be serious for them to contact you."

"He's a good citizen, Karen. My guess is, it's just an incident."

Tommy was occupied for much of the day with his circumstance, which accounted for Karen's difficulty in reaching him. After consulting with Brian and Jill the consensus was that he had no alternative. The student judicial board was a final arbiter in these matters. A student didn't even have a right to appeal. He could protest, organize a committee on campus to object to the nature of these proceedings. His friends agreed the energy expended would not be worth it—accept the verdict and move on. He should, though, for his own satisfaction, tell the dean of freshmen who sat in on the hearing exactly what he thought about this finding. At five in the afternoon, after waiting over an hour while other students with previous appointments filed in and out, he was allowed to see Andrew Roberts.

Tommy angrily made his case. He wasn't found drunk or destructive. He didn't have a record of previous offenses. He had one stinking beer off by himself, bothering no one. His roommate and friends made a goddamn mess of his room and he took a beer out of their stash. This was a mockery of a court. He had logged on to the college Web site. Nobody ever got a sentence like this for his offense. Just a beer and he had to go for counseling and what the hell was this educational assignment and why the hell did his parents have to be told? This was a second, a third offense type of punishment, or worse. Not a first offense. Roberts listened patiently, interjecting "I understand" several times. And what happened to the others, Tommy wanted to know, his roommate—did he have to go for counseling and an educational assignment and were his parents and the baseball coach told? Tommy knew what the answer would be.

"Kevin Wilkins was not seen drinking, nor were any of the other students. There was insufficient evidence to find them guilty of regulation twelve."

"He tells the board I bought the beer and I have a drinking problem and he gets off totally clean. The beer cans in the room and the beer cans out the window. They were mine, I suppose?"

"There was nothing to link them to the beer cans."

"And he makes me out to be the bad guy!"

"Mr. Burrows, if you logged on to the Web site you know alcoholic offenses are up. The administration wants to cut that off before it gets any worse. Basically, we're putting in a zero-tolerance policy. By the old standards this *is* a second or third offense sentence, but it's the way we're going now. You were caught in the first wave of a new policy."

"I hate this. I hate having to sit here. I hate the idea I'm going to have to go through this nonsense. What *am* I going to have to do?"

"There's some private counseling, a workshop, and you'll have to write a paper on something like the dangers of alcohol."

"Wonderful."

"You may not have a problem, but the people on the panel, they couldn't be sure. They had a good sense about what happened that night. But there was no evidence against the other people. There was against you. Faced with erring on the conservative side they decided to have you do the counseling. If you have a problem, it can help. If you don't, it can't hurt. And with that, unfortunately, goes the parental notification."

"And if I don't show up?"

"You'll be expelled right before finals. It doesn't pay, Tommy."

"This system sucks."

He returned to the dorm room, replayed Karen's message, and called her. He recounted the events of that night, the hearing, and the meeting with the dean. He was going to accept the counseling, but he was furious about it.

Tommy, what is happening? My sweet boy, accommodating everyone on Thanksgiving. How did we get here in just a few days?

A seemingly routine college incident was becoming larger than the details. For Karen, it went to the heart of whether her son was lying to her. The roommate had moved out. Was it, as Tommy said, a clever strategy for the roommate to make himself the injured party, or was Tommy the undesirable? Karen was not unlike the student board, she just didn't know. She asked him to go over the events again to make sure she understood and he did, unhappy about it; he had just told her. When he finished his account he asked, "Don't you believe me?"

"How much *do* you drink, Tommy?"

"I have a beer now and then. Never again here, that's for sure."

"And drugs?"

"I don't do drugs. If there's pot around sometimes I'll smoke it. Same as my friends. I'm not a pot head. I'm not a drunk. I'm the least likely person to have to do counseling and now I'm going to have to, goddamn it."

"Didn't you say the dean told you if you don't need it, it's not going to hurt you?"

"Depending how much time it takes. I have a lot of work coming up. I wanted to do better in college. Damn! What did Dad say?"

"He's waiting to hear more."

"It was an invasion of privacy, to tell you. I don't have a problem, Mom, believe me."

She delayed a moment and said, "I believe you."

He talked about his study plans for the last portion of the school year. The courses on short stories and on the Vietnam War required papers in lieu of exams for final grades and he had a substantial amount of reading in advance of his writing. He worried the mandated counseling would cut into the amount of time he had for his schoolwork. Karen sympathized. She didn't know what else she could do but sympathize and trust he was telling her the truth. They ended with Karen giving him assurances for his course work and good riddance to his roommate. Now he would have the room to himself for the end of the term and Tommy wanted to be free of him anyway.

She called Rob, who was in his hotel room in Detroit, and tried to accurately reconstruct Tommy's account. Rob didn't like hearing that Tommy's roommate requested a transfer.

"It's a weak link. The other boy asks for a transfer because it'll make his position in a hearing look better, according to Tommy. I'm really so-so on that."

"You have to buy it all to believe him. I don't think Tommy's lying in spots."

He checked an incoming call on his call-waiting. It was Tommy and he said he would be right back to him.

"He's on the other line. We'll talk. And we'll hope for the best."

"Of course, we will."

Tommy gave Rob the same version of the events he presented to Karen. With Tommy's first set of college grades at stake Rob made the decision to keep his doubts to himself. They could deal with the rest later. He advised Tommy to grit his way through the counseling and do as well as he possibly could in his schoolwork.

Rob returned to New York and when he told Vickie about the incident, he expressed his reservations about Tommy's account of the incident.

"Where there's smoke there's fire?" she said.

"Something like that."

"First of all, these college judicial boards, or whatever they want to call them, are hardly models of justice. When it's serious, say a rape charge or theft and the college wants to keep it in the family, they allow lawyers to defend their clients. In a case like this, somebody caught with a beer, it's a joke to give Tommy, who doesn't have benefit of counsel, any kind of sentence. Sounds like the college is protecting itself, building a case for their diligence if anything serious happens in some other instance."

"The smoking gun is the roommate moving out."

"It isn't a smoking gun. It doesn't prove anything. The roommate says Tommy—bad. Tommy says the roommate—bad. Now which of these people am I to believe, a boy I've never met who makes a love nest out of his dorm room and tells a student board they were drinking beer bought by Tommy, who wasn't even part of his soiree, or a boy I know and love whom I would trust with the welfare of my own children?"

"Thank you, counselor," he said somewhat placated.

Karen and Bill were at her apartment getting ready for bed after seeing a Broadway production of *La Boheme* at the Metropolitan Opera House. She started telling him about Tommy earlier in the evening and with the incident still troubling her she continued, describing her most trying moment, listening to her son and not knowing whether he was lying to her. Bill wanted to be thinking about Puccini. How did we get back to Tommy? This boy!

"What do you think?" she asked.

"Cindy was such a good student and never got into trouble, so I always seem to be a step behind on Tommy's problems. What I worried about when she went off to college was that she might get pregnant. That's funny because now I'm waiting for her to *get* pregnant. But it just must be different for girls and boys."

"That's very philosophic," she said ending the conversation for the night.

Tommy made an appointment by phone and reported to the offices of Health Services located in its own building on campus. The receptionist was a slightly built girl of five feet four, her brunette hair in bangs, a small nose, blue eyes, an angelic face, the prettiest girl he had seen on campus.

"I'm Tommy Burrows. Here to see Dr. Hughes."

"Would you have a seat?"

"I haven't seen you before."

"Have you been here before?"

"I mean, I haven't seen you around."

"I work part-time. I'm at Pittsfield High."

He hoped she was at least a senior. He didn't want to think he was attracted to a junior, or younger.

"What year?"

"Senior."

"I'm a freshman. I'm here because I'm in trouble with the law."

"Serious. What did you do?"

"Got caught with a beer on campus."

"That's pretty stupid."

"I'm not a computer wiz. I'm just an English major."

She smiled. "Still pretty stupid. So you're a mandatory."

"A mandatory."

"Some of the most interesting people around here are."

"I'd like to think I'm interesting, but I don't believe I'm guilty, so I don't know where that leaves me."

"Possibly interesting."

"This is not so bad, you know. I thought the therapy would be worse than this."

She laughed at the remark. A door to the inner office opened and the therapist, Dr. Helen Hughes, came out, an intimidating six feet two with broad shoulders in a shapeless suit and a blouse with a rounded lace collar, a severe-looking woman with wire-rimmed glasses, who looked to Tommy like a very tall nun. This wasn't going to be pleasant. He could already feel the wrath of God. "Mr. Burrows?" The therapist motioned for him and reentered her office and he turned to the girl.

"Will you be here when I come out?"

"No."

"What's your name, is this where I find you?"

"Elena Garrity and you'll find me in the cafeteria in an hour."

In the room with the therapist, Tommy had the sensation of being in a class being timed without clocks. He recalled a line of Brian's when they went to see a particularly witless comedy supposedly tailored for their age group and Brian said, "We have to leave. This movie has no end. They are prepared to show as much movie as we're prepared to sit for." In this session there was no leaving until excused. The therapist spent what Tommy regarded as an unconscionable amount of time on the details of his apprehension with the infamous beer can in his hand. She kept pressing him to admit his guilt, but his difficulty was the degree to which he was guilty.

"What you don't seem to recognize," she said, "is from the standpoint of campus regulations there is no distinction between your one beer and five beers." She asked about his drinking patterns and he insisted he didn't have a pattern he could call a pattern; he had a beer now and again.

"Do you have fake ID?"

"Yes."

"That's revealing."

"All my friends in New York had fake IDs. The minimum age is twenty-one. It was understood in the clubs that we had fake IDs. It was the deal."

"So you weren't guilty of any illegality. It was the deal. It's never you, is it?"

"I had the beer. I admit to that. That's all I did, drink a beer."

"Have you spoken to your parents since the hearing?"

"Yes."

"And how did that go?"

"Awkward."

"You're close to your parents?"

"They're divorced. I think we're pretty close, though."

"How did you feel about their being notified?"

"Not good."

"How did you feel about their getting divorced? When was that?"

"Five years ago."

"And how did you feel about it?"

"Also not good."

"And now?"

"You live with it."

"And to live with it, is drinking part of your coping mechanism?"

"No."

"You've had a fake ID. You've been drinking illegally in New York. Drinking illegally in Massachusetts."

"Not all of Massachusetts. Behind the bookstore."

"Why, Thomas?"

"To go with the pizza."

"I want to consider this, and what might be of value to you. I'll send a note to your box."

He didn't think much of the therapy. She might have been on to something, asking about his reaction to the divorce. If he were the therapist he would have spent the entire session on that.

• • •

Elena was reading a schoolbook in the cafeteria. In the larger setting she looked even younger than when he first saw her, and compared to the other women, even prettier.

"How did it go?" she asked.

"If you think you didn't do anything bad it's hard to feel you got something out of it."

She asked about the incident and he told her, including the fact that his parents were notified, which he found needless and embarrassing. He was trying to be honest. He hated everything about it. She didn't question his account; she believed him.

"You *were* stupid. But your roommate, he's the roommate from hell."

They decided to stay on and eat dinner there. She, too, was on a meal plan by virtue of her job at the college. She talked about herself. She lived near campus with her mother, who worked as a waitress in a restaurant in town. Her parents divorced seven years before. Her father was in Galveston, she thought. She planned on going to college. They could save money by her living at home so she applied to the local colleges, Marlowe and Berkshire Community College. She was also applying to Wesleyan, Connecticut College, Brown, and Boston University, with Brown her first choice. She hoped that being the features editor and writing for her school paper could help. Wherever she was accepted, apart from Berkshire Community, she wouldn't be able to attend unless she received substantial financial aid. Elena was direct, reportorial, this is the way it is, matching Tommy in his candor.

"These articles, could I see some of them?"

"You're really interested?"

"I am. Also I'd like to keep this going," he said lightly.

They strolled to her home, a fifteen-minute walk from the campus. Elena told him competition for college was intense at her school. As she described it, the competition didn't seem nearly as intense as Bantrey and the New York schools.

"I'm going to ask you something, completely inappropriate and I apologize, but I'd be curious to know."

"Am I seeing anyone?" she teased.

"Worse. What was your SAT score?"

"Now *that's* personal. 1510."

He feigned doubling up in reaction.

"And, of course, without expensive tutors," he said.

"I bought a book on it."

"1510 in your sleep!"

She lived in a two-story tract house. Her neighbors on either side were local service people, a carpenter and a landscaper, their vans in the driveways. In Elena's driveway an old Toyota was parked, the hood up, her mother crouched over the carburetor with a spray can.

"Mom, this is Tommy Burrows."

He saw Elena's features in her mother's, a hardened version with streaky brown-auburn hair, a cold, skeptical expression on her face, as though it were a skepticism that fit everything, anything said, anyone new. Surely this new boy standing there was worthy of it.

"And where are you from?"

"Marlowe."

"That's where you *go*. Not where you're *from*."

"Had a bad day, Mother?"

"New York," Tommy answered.

"A slicker."

"I'm sure you'll find people slicker-er," Tommy said.

"Yeah, well, I'm off to work." She closed the hood. "Not late," to Elena and then for Tommy's benefit, sardonically, "You, too, Slick."

The living room was decorated with low-budget matching pieces. He read several feature articles she wrote for her school paper and thought she was an excellent writer. Living in a modest house with a mother who fixed her own carburetor and who, if she ever caught them in bed, something he was already thinking about, would probably whack him with a baseball bat, this girl managed to flower.

They began to meet for dinners in the cafeteria. He had no other time to see her. The educational assignment was given him by Dr. Hughes, to write a twenty-five-hundred-word essay on the dangers of alcohol consumption, due by the end of the term. The assignment was punitive. He was required to write it during the same period he was preparing for finals and writing term papers. Elena told him she heard in the office the timing was intentional and that he was not the only one with a mandated essay. They wanted to make their point—in the future don't drink. On the next Saturday, the next to last Saturday before the term ended, when he needed the time for schoolwork, he was required to attend an all-day workshop on alcohol abuse.

Seething, he sat on a folding chair with six other Marlowe students, five men and a woman facing Dr. Hughes in a bare room in the Health Services building. They were required to tell about the offenses that brought them there. When it got to him he detected snickering, you call that drinking? He was the person with the least serious offense, caught in the college's newest policy on alcohol consumption.

A common denominator among young drinkers, according to Dr. Hughes, was denial. They explored how comfortable they were with denial in their everyday lives, then went on to the effects of alcohol on them, what it felt like to drink, what they thought they gained by drinking, what were the peer pressures. Tommy found himself increasingly alienated by the themes and by the people. Some seemed to him in love with their own stories about getting wasted. He had no argument with the point Dr. Hughes spent the day trying to develop in the room. He couldn't connect what any of this had to do with him. If he expressed that, he was in denial. He tried to use the time to formulate ideas for his term papers while he was sitting there. When it finally ended after six hours he thought he needed a beer.

His original plan was to use the night for work in the library. He was too drained to concentrate and called Elena hoping she would be free to meet him for dinner. She told him she stayed home in the hope he would call when he was through—and how did it go? The best thing he had to say for it was that it was over. They went to a pizzeria and then he took her back to the dorm. Kevin performed a service. Tommy had the room to himself. They made love and afterward she said it was just a week, she couldn't imagine she would ever do it with anyone after just a week.

"I must have fallen in love with you. In a week," she said.

"I could say the same."

"But are you? Saying the same?"

"I must have fallen in love with you. In a week," delivered with a smile to protect himself from looking overly committed.

Neither was willing to risk her sleeping over and answering to her mother. They walked back toward Elena's house and as they left campus they passed three female Marlowe students talking among themselves. Wistfully, Elena turned slightly to watch them. Tommy saw it as his opportunity.

"Something I've been thinking of. Not to offend you or anything. With your SAT score and the newspaper articles . . . and I bet your grades are high, too . . ."

"Yes."

"I bet you can get a good scholarship. I've got a couple of friends and we've all been through the college thing. I mean, it's crazy where we come from and I'm sure we can help, on your applications."

"Really?"

"We know how to do this."

Tommy called Jill and Brian the next day and told them about Elena. Jill was dealing with her own final exams period, which was the same as Tommy's, ending before Christmas. Brian's were scheduled after the Christmas–New Year's break. They were willing to help and would meet with Elena in Pittsfield the Saturday after Jill's and Tommy's semesters ended. They would only have two weeks before the application deadlines for the remaining colleges on her list. She already submitted applications to Berkshire Community, Marlowe, and Connecticut College, so they were down to Wesleyan, Boston University, and Brown. Brian thought it wasn't ideal, but it could be manageable with the time remaining.

The paper on alcohol consumption made a serious dent in his time. Elena came to his room to help drill him on vocabulary for his Italian final and they stole some time for sex. He worked hard, as college students do during these periods, and then he was done. On the last night of the term, when all the exams were completed and his papers handed in, he could hear the sounds of release, parties and hooting and hollering around campus. He would be by himself. Elena was obligated to attend a party for people on the school newspaper. Apart from the two sophmores he met through tutoring the elementary school children, and with whom he would chat when he saw them on campus, he developed no particular relationships in his first semester. His roommate had been a disaster. Elena was the most important person he had met at Marlowe and she had appeared at the end of the semester, and she wasn't even a student at Marlowe. As he looked out the window of his room he wondered if they were drinking at any of the celebrations, whether they had lookouts, whether they were smart enough to avoid his punishment.

He dressed in his gear and went jogging into the winter night, circling the campus, taking it in, the sounds, the lights. It all felt very distant.

• • •

Karen called him on Saturday morning to find out how he fared with the last of his tests. He was apologetic, he had to go, he had people coming, he thought he did okay. As to when he was coming home, he said he would let her know, and too quickly for her to question him, which was his intention, he said, "I met a girl I like and she's applying to colleges and Jill and Brian are coming here to help with her applications," and he was gone.

Rob called Karen to arrange for Tommy to spend time with him during Tommy's mid-semester break.

"Who knows who this girl is," she said to him. "It's like Enigma. You try to piece something together out of the code."

"If he got Jill and Brian to come from Boston to help, she must be important."

"Those kids would go to Timbuktu for each other. But she still might be important. Sounds like he'll show up when he shows up. We'll work it out."

"And he thought he did well?"

"I imagine. That was sort of coded, too."

Brian rented a car in Boston. Tommy and Elena were waiting in the dorm room when Brian and Jill arrived. They were interested in this new girl of Tommy's, but they spent little time on casual conversation. They sat on the floor and went over Elena's remaining applications. Tommy asked her to bring along a half dozen of the pieces she wrote for the newspaper. They came out of the aggressive, sell-anything-you've-got private school ideology. They chose two articles they liked best for Elena to submit. Brian was unhappy with the drafts of her personal essays. He thought the writing for the newspaper was loose and creative, but that she froze up in her essays. She was willing to talk about her background, that her mother was a single parent and they didn't have much money, but he felt she was being too formal in expressing those feelings.

"Write it as if you were doing a feature on yourself."

"I didn't think they were that good. I didn't know why."

"That's why," he said with certainty.

For the next three hours they worked on her essays, Elena at Tommy's computer, printing out pages that they group-edited. Then they examined the other aspects of her applications. She had recommendations from teachers. Jill wanted to know why, if she worked part-time in the Marlowe Health Services Department, she hadn't also asked her supervisor, Dr. Hughes, for a recommendation. She simply didn't think of it and she was going to ask for it now. The applications were taking shape. Elena would need to do the fine-tuning, but they all felt the improvement. Elena teased that she couldn't put a number on it, but it was 42 percent better.

They went to eat in a diner. Tommy was jumpy at the table, moving his water glass around, fiddling with silverware and his napkin.

"What's wrong with you?" Jill said. He didn't answer at first, gathering himself. "Tommy—"

"I'm not going back to school next semester." They were shocked. "I didn't like it very much and it probably isn't the school. The courses were sort of interesting. I'm just burned out."

"You worked so hard to get in," Brian said.

"Probably harder than you did to get into Harvard. I'm just tired of school. Also I hated what happened these last few weeks. Not a great thing to say about this place."

"If they're morons you can't let it affect you," Jill said. "You don't make a decision on that. If it's so terrible, you transfer."

"I'm not transferring. I'm done with college."

"What would you do?" Elena said, worried.

"Get a place here in Pittsfield. Get a job."

"What kind of job?" she asked.

"I don't know. Something. I have a little money. My grandfather left me a few thousand dollars when he died."

"What do you think the world is for college dropouts, Tommy?" Brian said.

"I just can't do school anymore."

"I feel awful," Elena said. "I feel if you never met me you wouldn't have this incentive. Like it's attractive for you to drop out and stay here."

"I'd do this even if we hadn't met. I might've gone back to New York, but I don't think so. I'm tired of the living arrangements there," he said with a weary tone. "I want to be on my own."

They marshaled their arguments, economic, social, the-stay-in-school arguments, as if they were guidance counselors. He rejected everything they had to say. Looking for something hopeful, Brian offered that some people don't go directly to college from high school, they take time out for a year or so, work, travel because they are burned out, and maybe Tommy would have been wiser to delay college.

"College still might not have been the thing for me. All I know is, I hit a wall."

His friends were moving slowly as they left the diner, still trying to deal with the news. He was being brisk, already on a schedule. Marlowe shut down between the fall and spring semesters and required students to vacate their dorm rooms. Since Tommy would not be a returning student he was obliged to clear everything out of the room. And since he was not going back to live in New York he needed to find a place immediately. Once he was situated in Pittsfield he intended to tell his parents about his decision.

Brian originally planned to drive back to Boston when they finished working with Elena. Jill assumed she would be going by bus to New York with Tommy. He asked if Brian would stay on a while and drive him around so he could look at places to live. Two fifty a month. That was his budget for rent, assuming he could get a job and supplement his expenses out of his savings.

Over the next several hours into the early part of the evening his friends became increasingly solemn as Tommy followed through on newspaper listings in the drabbest sections of Pittsfield, given the limited amount of rent he could afford to pay. They left an attic apartment on the third floor of a house, a noxious mildew smell permeating the interiors. Just before they returned to the car Elena squeezed her eyes in tension. Jill said softly to her, "This has nothing to do with you. It's about stuff long before he met you."

A gray two-story house with white trim and a small front porch was next, the house without peeling paint or missing shingles, an exception thus far. Across the street was a parking area containing upwards of thirty interchangeable yellow school buses. The lot was screened by a chain-link fence with barbed wire along the top and signs at intervals announcing a guard dog. Five other houses were on the street, which had trash littered along its length soaking in the Pittsfield winter snow. The owner introduced himself as Carl, a Swedish-accented white-haired man of six feet four in his sixties, wearing chinos and a work shirt. He told the group he was a retired carpenter and now did odd jobs and that was why his house looked so good. He was proud of it and the extension he built in the rear with its own entrance, a ten foot by twelve foot studio apartment with a tiny bathroom. The place was smaller than the dorm room Tommy shared with his roommate. Carl was offering clean space. Decor was not his strength. Wallpaper featured robins on tree branches, an excessive number of robins and tree branches for the space. The furniture looked as though it might have been discarded from jobs Carl worked on. A twin bed against a wall had a decent mattress. The main window in the room faced a stockade fence in the rear of the property, and yet it was a model apartment on a house tour compared with what they had seen on the day. No pets, no noise, no loud parties, three hundred dollars a month. He wouldn't rent it to a group and Tommy explained he was the sole renter, the others were his real estate experts, the humor not translating. They dickered for a while and Carl accepted the two fifty a month, Tommy's limit. Carl didn't bother with leases, they shook hands on the deal and for good measure he shook hands with the others for the additional legality.

The last bus from Pittsfield to New York had left. The dorm was open until Sunday afternoon and Tommy could put up Jill and Brian in the dorm. Brian offered to use the rental car to move Tommy into the new place. They made two trips from the dorm to the house alternating people staying in the dorm to allow more room in the car, stopping for sandwiches at a grocery store in the middle of the move. The time was after ten, Elena was falling asleep in the car, and they dropped her off at her house. Tommy told her he would figure out the transportation for getting around from his place to hers and he would have a phone installed. They would talk. She had started the day with a new boyfriend who went to Marlowe College and who recruited his friends to help her with college applications and ended with a new boyfriend who had dropped out of college and was jobless.

"You take a person's breath away," she said. "I don't know who you are."

"That's two of us. If you want to quit on me, that's okay, we haven't known each other that long."

"I don't, I don't think."

"Okay, then. We're solid."

Tommy, Jill, and Brian returned to the dorm. Tommy spotted a female student who lived down the hall whom he knew from his Italian class, which made her one of his closest relationships on campus. He asked if she had an extra mattress in her room. Her roommate had already vacated for the semester, so he was able to borrow the mattress and the trio crashed for the night in Tommy's room. He set the alarm so Jill could make the morning bus to New York. They went out for breakfast and took Jill to the bus terminal. She wanted to know about New Year's, if they could spend it together, was Tommy coming into the city? He didn't know what his plans were and she departed.

Tommy and Brian had one more trip to make and everything would be out of the dorm. Kevin had already removed his belongings. Except for the school-supplied furniture, the room was empty when Tommy closed the door on the room and this phase of his life.

Everything Tommy had taken to college was in the new place somewhere. Brian wanted to know if Tommy was really, really sure this was the right thing to do? Tommy said it was the only thing to do. After Brian left Tommy walked to a public phone two blocks away. He would have liked the package to be complete before presenting it to his parents, a place to live and a job. Little thought had gone into the job. He wanted to pay the rent and his bills and take a long breath after fourteen years of school and parental expectations.

His first call was not to Karen or Rob. Impulsively, he called Karen's mother in Florida.

"It's Tommy, Grandma."

"Tommy, how are you, dear?"

"Grandma, I dropped out of college. I finished the first semester, but I'm not going back."

"Oh? Why is that, Tommy?"

"It's hard to say. So much went into my getting in, the tutoring and the SAT and all, when I finally got there it was like I was worn out."

"What did your mom and dad say?"

"I haven't told them yet."

"Do you have a plan?"

"I just got a place in town. In Pittsfield. And I'm going to look for a job and stay here. You know, I have that money Grandpa left me."

"Wouldn't it be easier in New York? Live at home until you work things out?"

"I'm worn out from New York, too, Grandma."

"I see. Would you like to come here?"

"Thank you, but I'm going to do it this way."

"So what kind of job, Tommy? Do you have anything in mind?"

"Not yet. Something while I catch my breath."

"When you're worn out you *do* have to catch your breath. Tommy, whatever you do, the tutoring—I think you should keep that up. Have something that's grounded. It'll be good for the little children, of course, but it'll be good for you, make you feel good about yourself."

"All right, Grandma, I will."

"You're healthy, Tommy, no other problems?"

"Didn't even get the flu this winter. So far."

"Do you have a phone, an address?"

"I'll get it to you. Don't worry about me, Grandma."

"I've got to worry a little, Tommy."

"A little then."

"You'll work it out. I have faith in you."

It was the reason he called her.

He couldn't decide. Did he get on a bus and go to New York, tell them in person, or do it by phone? The spring semester payment was due on January 1st. He called the twenty-four-hour customer service number at the bank and learned a check could be stopped for up to several months, so he assumed that even if his father had sent in the tuition he wouldn't lose the money. He wanted a finality, to have his parents understand he was through with college and going out on his own. He presumed it would be better accomplished in a room with them and he also understood he owed them more than a phone call. He packed a small canvas bag with overnight items, returned to the grocery store, and asked about the bus service to the Pittsfield bus terminal.

He chatted with the local driver on the way to the terminal to get his bearings on the various bus routes. His new place was about twenty minutes by bus to Elena's house and a few minutes to the center of town. He thought he might get a bicycle when winter passed.

He called Karen from the terminal, trying the store first. She was not in and he asked John to tell his mother he would be home that evening. She was not in the apartment either and he left a more personal message on the answering machine asking if she could have Rob there at around nine P.M. when he arrived. He was unable to reach Rob directly and left a message on his cell phone service asking him to be at the apartment.

He had picked up the local papers and during the bus ride he read the want ads. The ads were sparse and he assumed it was a poor time around the holidays to be looking for work. But he knew that every day in Pittsfield people got up and went to work—in stores, in offices, in the malls, in the shopping centers. Jobs existed.

The simple messages he left for his parents were read as ominous when they reached each other by phone early that evening. What was going on? He never asked for both of them to be present. Did it have to do with the trouble he was in? Was he in trouble again?

The thought came from the anger Rob heard in Tommy's voice when he told him about the beer incident and the unusual request for both of them to be there when he came home.

"I think he's dropping out of school," Rob said.

"No."

"I think we should be prepared."

Rob arrived a few minutes before nine. With the tension they were experiencing they neglected even a polite kiss. He sat in the living room and she went into the kitchen to bring him a drink of scotch he asked for, pouring one for herself. He was extremely uncomfortable sitting there, the first time he had been in the apartment since the divorce. Many of the pieces in the place were bought when they were together, including one he always liked, a naive painting of a farm scene. He had gone with her to the Brimfield, Massachusetts, antiques–flea market show. The place was famously frantic as crowds of dealers and civilians hurried from booth to booth looking to buy before someone else did. He and Karen laughed as they rushed along. "Last chance to beat the other couples," she said. A dealer from New Hampshire was selling the painting. Karen was uncertain, but because Rob liked it so much she bought it. Karen never resold it in her store. She placed it on a wall in the entrance foyer, it stayed there and was still there. Rob never thought to ask for it when they separated, it was part of her world, her business. But I liked it. It wouldn't be here if I didn't like it. Those were good days. When everything was for the first time.

Tommy entered the apartment carrying a small overnight bag, which immediately indicated he didn't plan on staying long. He sat gravely before his parents in the living room. The four-hour bus ride from Pittsfield gave him time to frame his presentation and he had the benefit of the run-through with his friends.

There were worse things to hear from your eighteen-year-old son than his announcement that he was dropping out of college. Karen and Rob each came to that conclusion while listening to him. In a world of AIDS and sudden illness and accidents and terrorists killing people for incoherent political arguments, it was not a tragedy. But it was a numbing disappointment, greater than any they ever experienced with him. The school meetings over the years, the discussions between themselves, the watchfulness, the anxieties intensified by his mediocre school performance and then the apparent victory. Karen and Rob felt they had done their best to create an environment where he would not be damaged by the divorce. His getting into a front-line college confirmed for them that they had succeeded. He was launched. It was to be a shining passage, college and a sunny future. How could it possibly be that he was unable to handle more than one semester?

Karen wondered if he had become physically run-down. It happens to some freshmen. His physical state may have contributed to his sense of feeling burned out, as he claimed to be. She raised the possibility and he countered by saying he jogged about three times a week. He even came to his decision while jogging, so he must be in decent physical shape. She then echoed Brian's thought, perhaps it would have been better for him not to have gone directly from high school to college. He doubted a delay would have had any effect. Eventually, he would have arrived at the same place, tired of school. Marlowe itself may not have been the right fit for him, Karen suggested. The way the college dealt with the drinking incident also might have contributed to his sense of not belonging there. He knew the way they handled it was stupid, but he didn't think this college was the problem. And he didn't plan on transferring to a different one.

Rob was growing impatient. Did Tommy know the facts of life after high school for someone with only a high school diploma? The world was brutally competitive. People were laid off periodically in every possible job category. To move up from an entry-level job, and that's all he would get, major ambition and drive was needed. Tommy showed something working his way through the SAT and getting into Marlowe. He was going to have to show even more of that drive to overcompensate for his lack of education, which is how it would be regarded, a lack of education.

"Nearly anything you can think of that's worthwhile requires more than one semester of college," Rob said.

"I'm not looking to build a career, Dad, not right now anyway. I just want to get started paying my way."

"You need college today, Tommy. It's required. You have to be thinking of transferring, trying some other kind of place."

"Dad, I'm done with school."

"Did you flunk out?" Rob asked.

"I don't know what that has to do with anything. I don't even know what I got."

"This is how you feel tonight," Karen said. "You have to keep your options open."

"School is over. I'm prepared to have you be angry with me and disappointed in me and all that. I'm not prepared to change my mind."

"Why don't we just take it a semester at a time, so to speak? Why don't you reevaluate as you go along instead of this big pronouncement, 'I'm not prepared to change my mind'?" Karen said.

"Because unless I say it that way, you don't get how sure I am."

"Tommy, you went to private school and you got into a good college," Rob said. "It's an elitist system. Which isn't fair to people who aren't in it. But it's not all bad. The system produces people, some who do wonderful things in the world. You get the chance to be special if you stay in the system and get the college degree they want. You have so many more chances to be an important person than if you quit school now. Step outside the system, you'll be in the lowest level of the job market. You're more than that. The cartoons you did for the paper, the way you willed yourself for the SAT. That was someone special in the making. You can't stop now."

I can't say it better. Tommy, listen to me. Please, listen to me.

Tommy shook his head negatively. Karen was downcast.

"I have the store," she said, "and people think it's very creative and it is. But remember, I came to it from being an anthropology major. That came first and then I could branch out. You're absolutely limiting your choices if you limit your education."

"Maybe. Maybe not."

"There are so many schools," Karen added. "You weren't at the right school for you. It's still out there."

"You might want to go to school here. Could be you're just a New York kind of person and that's part of why it didn't work out. I'm not saying Columbia, but there are a bunch of other colleges here. Maybe after a while you could go to one of them."

"This isn't where I want to be. I spoke to Grandma Sally. She said I should keep up tutoring little kids, that it'd be good for the kids and good for me, but I think it'd also be good for you guys, so you don't think I'm like a vagrant. I'm going to get a job. I almost don't care what, as long as I don't have to think about school. And I'm going to be on my own. And that's what I need right now."

"You're only eighteen," Rob said. "You're too young to be on your own."

"Eighteen, you can go off to college, can't you, and that's not too young?"

"Because you're at college," Rob said.

"You can join the army and it's not too young. People get married at eighteen," using the argument he prepared on the way in on the bus. "They go off with bands and tour around at eighteen. They graduate from high school and move to cities to find jobs at eighteen, or from one coast to another at eighteen. What is it you think I don't know how to do at eighteen?"

"It's still too young," Rob responded. He was like a gambler at a blackjack table drawing cards against the dealer. "Suppose you came and worked for me. I could find interesting things for you to do. Better than what's out there."

"I appreciate it, but I don't want that, Dad, and I don't want to be in New York."

"It needn't be permanent if you don't want it to be," drawing another card. "After a while, well, I wouldn't discount the transferring thing. You could change your mind."

"No, Dad. I already have a place, and that's where I'm going."

"What kind of place?" Karen said. "What kind of neighborhood?"

"It's in a house. It's Pittsfield. It's not New York. Anyway, I'm getting a phone. We can call, we can e-mail."

"You should have a cell phone. For emergencies," Rob said.

"The service is too expensive, Dad. I'll do without it."

"I'll pay for it."

"I don't want you paying for my cell phone. The idea is for me to be on my own," he said, exasperated. "And that's what I'm going to do. End of discussion. Really."

"Tommy, it can't be the end of the discussion just because you say so. It's too important," Karen said.

"Mom is right."

"This is what I've decided."

"No matter what our best judgment is?" Karen said.

"College didn't work out. That's it. I'm hooking up with Jill now. I love you both, but tomorrow I'm taking the afternoon bus back to Pittsfield."

He picked up his jacket, kissed them, and walked out the door.

"He's going to compete with no skills and no plan and just a high school education? What does he expect?" Rob said.

"He expects to be done with college, obviously, and everything we wanted for him. It's not only college. He just announced he's leaving home."

She thought darkly about the guidance counselor, Jesse Parsons, and the educated pessimism of her observation, "One of them goes off the tracks, the likelihood is you'll never get them back on."

TWELVE

• • •

The leverage parents held over children his age was based on mutually agreed upon goals, college is good for you, these are the steps you have to take to get into college. Or it was based on trust, parents know best. Or it was economic, the parents paid the bills. If Tommy at eighteen announced he was through with college, that he knew what was best for him and he would pay his own bills, they had no recourse. He was a high school graduate, not even subject to truancy laws. If he said he wanted to be on his own and was prepared and capable of paying his way, he was on his own.

They decided to restate their case in a gathering of adults. Karen called Bill and gave him an outline of the developments and their intention to meet with Tommy at noon the next day at Karen's apartment. He could have lived without the call. This kid. He sucks the air out of a room.

"Fine, I'll be there," he managed to say. "Sorry you're having this trouble. Only there's something we don't like to think of, college may not be for everyone."

"I'd appreciate it if you don't make that point tomorrow," she said sharply.

"It's just a thought between us. I'll try to think of people who might be able to hire him."

"That's a little more like it," she said, annoyed with him.

Vickie was reading in bed when Rob returned home with an account of the evening. She was upset for him and for Tommy, too. Not wanting to trouble Rob any further when he was so distraught she didn't raise the question on her mind, whether Tommy dropped out of college because he was burned out, as he said, or because it was an unconscious act of rebellion against his parents and the life he was required to lead since the divorce.

Karen left a note on Tommy's pillow before she went to sleep asking him to be present at noon the next day, Rob, Vickie, and Bill were coming by to speak to him. He sighed audibly when he read it, but figured it was part of the deal, you decide to go home to tell your parents, you have to deal with this, too.

They were spaced around the living room and Karen began by reiterating her belief that even serendipitous journeys like becoming the owner of a store required a solid foundation and he would shortchange himself if he cut off his source of academic knowledge at eighteen. He repeated his lack of interest in going on with college.

Rob made another foray on the college front. Tommy resisted again. He then promoted the idea of an apartment for Tommy in New York, where he had far more employment opportunities, it wasn't even comparable—the jobs in New York against the jobs in Pittsfield. They would help out on an apartment. Tommy responded that if he wouldn't accept money for a cell phone, he wasn't going to accept being set up in an apartment. Rob moved to the next position, perhaps Tommy could handle the rent with a roommate, or in one of the other boroughs where young people congregate, and they could contribute part of the money. No sale.

Looking uneasy, Bill offered to arrange interviews for Tommy with people he knew in New York. Karen noted he didn't seem very persuasive. And Tommy was not persuaded. He wasn't interested in a job in New York.

As it rambled on Vickie was starting to think he should try a period of independence for a while, but in the city; she was allied with his parents on that point. He could still be independent in New York, she told him, the very act of working in his first job would buy him that. "I've always lived in New York," Tommy said firmly. "I need to be somewhere else."

After an awkward hour of Tommy declining their advice and offers the adults acknowledged they were out of advice and offers. At the time of the incident at school Rob didn't press the issue of his drinking; Tommy needed to get through his courses. Rob was not going to avoid it any longer. "I'm seriously concerned about your drinking," Rob said. "We would be negligent, criminally negligent, if we allowed you to go off with a drinking problem."

"You don't have to worry," Tommy said calmly. "I don't have one."

"How would I know that?"

"Because I'm telling you." Rob looked unconvinced. "You can ask. You want to talk to Jill, to Brian?" he said defiantly. "Ask them."

Tommy went to the phone in the kitchen and dialed a number.

"Hey, Jill, my dad wants to talk to you."

He handed the phone to his father.

"It's Mr. Burrows, Jill. I need to know something. It's terribly important you answer me honestly. We're worried about Tommy. This decision of his—"

"I wish he wouldn't do it, but we couldn't talk him out of it."

"I'm concerned about his drinking."

"His drinking?"

"That business at school—"

"It was ridiculous."

"Does Tommy have a drinking problem, Jill? You have to tell me the truth."

"No. I mean, he'll have a beer or two like we all do, but no, Mr. Burrows."

"That's the absolute truth? You know how important it is for me to know, if he's going off on his own."

"The absolute truth."

"What about drugs?"

"What about drugs? We're not druggies."

"You have nothing to tell me that I should know? Nothing you'd prefer not saying about a friend that at a later date we could come to regret your not saying?"

"That sounds like an essay question, Mr. Burrows, but I'm going to do it short answer. Nothing."

"You're sure."

"Yes, Mr. Burrows."

"All right. Thank you, Jill."

The call exonerating Tommy brought the family council to an uncomfortable conclusion. Tommy said he was taking the four fifteen bus to Pittsfield, he would get them his phone number as soon as he had one, and after embraces as awkward as the previous hour's discussion, Tommy withdrew to his room.

• • •

Rob and Vickie paused a moment on the street outside the building, Rob rattled. Bill followed them out. The uneasy expression on Bill's face vanished as soon as he reached the sidewalk. He hailed a cab and waved an inappropriately hearty good-bye to them.

"He was elsewhere," Rob said disparagingly about him. "What a waste. I messed that up."

"Tommy saw that you care."

"But we didn't convince him."

"He's an unusual boy and very self-composed—the way he handled that."

"Pittsfield! Doing *what*?"

"Rob, this is today. Nothing is permanent."

Vickie went to see a client. Rob headed for Seth's advertising agency and waited in the reception area until Seth came out of a meeting. In Seth's office Rob gave him the scenario from his viewpoint, his son skittering out of control and his inability to do anything about it.

"You think you were going to say the one right thing to save the day? Not possible. He's telling you—the hell with college, the hell with my life, I'm starting over."

"He's only eighteen."

"Remember how Jimmy the Greek used to handicap teams? Two points for the quarterback, two points for home field, one point for the offensive line . . . He's an eighteen-year-old who comes out of a divorce. That's got to be worth a year or two."

"Thank you so much."

"In terms of work he probably would be better off in New York."

"That's what we tried to tell him."

"I can understand why he might not want to work for his father, if what he wants is to be independent. Now my field, they're always hiring college graduates to be trainees because that's what they think they should be doing. But you learn on the job. Everybody knows it. Those cartoons he did, nothing in terms of artwork, but the gag lines were good. Maybe he could be a copywriter one day. Maybe he could do account work, production. Let's get him in here. Make him an all-around assistant. We just picked up a couple of accounts—I could use some help. I'll pay him twenty-five thousand dollars a year, which is standard for these kinds of jobs."

"It's a tremendous offer, Seth."

Seth thought a moment and said, "However—"

"However what?"

"He'll be okay as long as he works for *me*. In this business he won't be able to move too well without a college degree."

"Exactly what I've been saying."

"Look, let's get him working. Put some money in his pocket. Get him past this. Want me to talk to him? Might be better from me."

"Please."

Rob dialed Tommy's number and handed over the phone.

"It's Seth."

"Hi, Seth," apprehensively.

"Tommy, I don't know how much you know about our agency. We do different kinds of accounts, Topps running shoes, Aunt Mary's Barbecue Sauce, Vexon Tires, MayPole. Anyway, your dad told me you weren't going back to school and the thing is, he showed me some of the cartoons you did when you were at Bantrey . . ."

"He did?"

"A proud father. And they were pretty impressive. So here's what I'd like to propose. Come work here. You can be a general assistant. Help with all the departments. We'll both find out what you like and what you're good at. 'Advertising Trainee,' if you need a job title. Pay you twenty-five thousand a year to start. You can start right away."

"That's very . . . generous." He was touched by the gesture.

"It's not generous if you turn out to be good, Tommy. I think you will be."

"But to be here, working for my dad's friend, in a job that came through my dad . . . it's not what I need to do."

"This is usually a college-grad type of job."

"It really is amazingly generous, but I've got to get out of New York," he said with an element of desperation in his voice. "I don't want to be here anymore."

"That's pretty strong."

"It's the way I feel."

"Tommy—"

"—I just can't, Seth. I'm sorry," definitively, his tone a door closing.

"If you change your mind—but don't wait until you're forty."

"Thank you very, very much."

"Good luck, Tommy."

He clicked off and turned to Rob.

"Says he's got to get out of New York. Doesn't want to be here anymore."

Rob placed his hands over his face and lowered his head.

Karen stayed in the apartment waiting for Tommy to leave, fussing over him when he emerged from his room. When would she hear from him, when could she come up?

"Mom, let me get settled. It's not the end of the world. I'm not even going to the end of the world. It's Massachusetts."

He was carrying the bag he brought with him and a trash bag with other items he wanted that he hadn't taken to college. She put her arms around him, kissed him, and touched the sleeve of his jacket as he left the apartment.

The phone rang and she let the machine record a message from Bill. He wanted to know if they could get together that night to talk. She was not interested in talking to him. She felt he had mailed in his part. He told Tommy he would make calls in his behalf with so little enthusiasm it was as if he were saying—I'll do this because your mother wants me to, but you don't really measure up. Not a time for seeing Bill. She called Polly and asked to come by for dinner, that it was a day beyond dreadful.

Polly favored the deferred acceptance premise. He was undoubtedly one of those students who benefit from taking a break from the grind before starting up again.

Joe said, "My father, he had a ninth-grade education. My mother was a salesgirl in a lingerie store in Brooklyn. That's what I had to work against. Polly's parents were small-town business people. That's what she had to work against. Your mother was a teacher. Your father was a dentist. Professionals, but not high profile. That's what you had to work against. Tommy has to work against you and Rob. The very definition of high achievers, short of being in show biz. It's a generation of kids trying to make their way against achieving parents. And this dopey ride they're on, the grades and the SAT and the whole college thing, it's no wonder more of them don't just say, 'I'm mad as hell and I can't take it anymore.' My daughter, too. You think Becky, when she gets out of Princeton—nuts that I've got a daughter in Princeton—you think when she gets out she's not going to be looking over her shoulder at us? So Tommy jumped off. He's going to land on his feet and you know why?"

"Yes, I'd like to know why," Karen said.

"Because he's white. America the Beautiful is set up for a kid who's white. In the open market a white male with a high school education trumps a black male with a high school education, maybe even a black male with college and it stinks because he also trumps other minorities with the same education and that stinks, too, for all the Republicans claiming they'll leave no child behind—"

"Joe, you're rambling," Polly said.

"He can do menial jobs for a while, no real future, but they're out there. He can go into retailing or restaurants or sales or health or clerical. He can become a manager of something one day. He can think up his own business, who knows what? He can work for himself or work himself up. He can do things on the job or outside the job to make himself a person of value. He can function without a college degree. He'll have to deal with his parents' expectations. Or maybe he won't. He already took a stand against your expectations. That's what this is, you know? If Becky did something like this I'd be disappointed, but I'd hope she'd become a person of value. I'm not going to deny the odds for him would be better if he finished college because that's America, too. And it is possible he might never find himself—"

"Joe!" Polly said.

"—but that's true of any kid today," brushing her off.

"So you're willing to concede I shouldn't be floating in a sea of calm," Karen said.

"But it's not like there are zero odds in his favor. He'll survive, Karen, because he's white and good-looking and with you and Rob in his bullpen, he's also got money as a backup."

"He's not taking money from us. He has five thousand dollars from his grandfather. That's not going to last."

"He'll do fine."

"Why should I believe that when he does something so hostile to his parents, so unbelievably irresponsible?" Karen said.

"Not irresponsible. Responsible. To say to you, I'm marching to my own drummer and I'll pay my own way. I love him. He's fucking audacious."

"You give a curious kind of pep talk, Joe," Karen said.

• • •

Karen tried to find comfort in work, but the Christmas sales season for Karen was disappointing, as it was for most retailers downtown. Tourism in New York was off dramatically after the disaster. Street traffic had not returned to pre–September 11 levels for SoHo and certainly not for the area adjacent to SoHo where Karen was located. When Karen spoke to other retailers along her street she found the mood was—a write-off of Christmas. Karen felt, as did most other local merchants, that they were spared and still there, and others weren't.

Tommy spent a grim month looking for a job. At the end of the holiday season most employers had already hired their people and in the first weeks of the new year they were paring their post-holiday payrolls. He followed the want ads and went door-to-door to businesses, discovering he had little chance of getting a full-time job with his lack of work experience. Companies knew the rules and kept their entry level employees part-time, under twenty hours a week, to avoid paying employee benefits. As a consequence many people in the Pittsfield area at Tommy's age and experience level tried to hold two part-time jobs. He was competing with students from town willing to work for spending money at or near minimum wage and a pool of unskilled workers.

After a New Year's Eve party with Elena and her high school friends they saw each other a few times, movies, pizza, teenage dates with the advantage of his having a place of his own. She was uncomfortable with whatever it was she found herself in—taking up with someone who was suddenly without direction. The responsibility for his dropping out of Marlowe and staying in Pittsfield concerned her, even if he claimed she was not a factor in his decision. She was trying to find a level of integrity for herself. She didn't want him to become dependent on the relationship at the expense of more important matters, such as getting himself established. So she limited them to no more than a couple of dates a week on weekend nights.

Elena's mother seemed even cooler to Tommy when he showed up at the house now that he was a college dropout and now that they seemed to be going with each other. She did, however, in deference to Elena make a few calls to local people toward getting him work, but without success.

He landed a job on his own, hired as a general assistant at Sport, a clothing store in competition with Old Navy and the Gap, located in the

Berkshire Mall. The assistant store manager, a perky young woman in her twenties who hired him, said his lack of retail experience was not necessarily a drawback. "You make a nice appearance, which we like." The job paid $7.25 an hour, fifty cents an hour above minimum wage.

"I figured something out about you," Elena said when they were together at his place. "Makes it easier for me to understand you."

"Go on."

She smiled in anticipation of her own observation.

"Would you like to share it?"

"You're going through your ski-instructor phase, only you don't ski."

He smiled in reaction. "That's good. I may use it. A girl from the Berkshires, that would be your reference."

"Would you like to ski? We all do around here."

"No, thank you. But I admire that you do. Everyone is very physical around here. The cold, the snow. Even when the weather calls for sunny, it snows. Even when the sun is out, it snows."

"Something I have going for me? I can handle cold weather?"

"Something you have going for you is you're smart."

"I think you are, too."

"Ah, you're just saying it," he teased.

"No. I just don't know how smart you are, how much is hidden," she said with seriousness.

"I don't know either," he said quietly.

Karen drove north along the New York State Thruway. On leaving the city she realized it was a trip without a radio. Something was apparently wrong with the electrical connection and she was making the approximately three-hour journey unprotected, alone with her thoughts. In the four weeks that passed since Tommy came into New York to make his announcement, he found the part-time job and settled in sufficiently to invite his parents to visit. Rob admitted to Karen he wasn't up to seeing Tommy yet, feeling his best efforts in behalf of his son had been rebuffed. He spoke to him several times, as she did. He would go there soon. Karen was welcome to be first.

Without a radio and unable to escape anxieties, the trip felt longer than the last time she went to Pittsfield. She was convinced he had placed himself in a double bind, functioning without a college degree and in a geographic area of limited options. As she passed the highway signs, Sloatsburg, Harriman, Kingston, Hudson, she sensed a falling away of economic opportunity the farther north she traveled. Several inches of snow had fallen recently and the areas surrounding the highway, the fields, the trees, and occasional house were covered with snow. The landscape seemed anything but picturesque to her, it was desolate, no population, no respite, hour after hour of trees and fields in unremitting whiteness. She pulled off the main highway onto the country roads along the New York–Massachusetts border, passing homes in snowy fields, possibly beautiful to others. Each mile she traveled became more painful. He had to go all this way, another mile and another and another to place this cold distance between himself and his parents.

Two weeks earlier an envelope had arrived from the college and he asked her to send it to him unopened. She presumed it contained his grades and she asked about it the next time they spoke. He received two Bs and two B pluses. He thought he could have done a little better if not for the school-mandated assignment at the end of the term. The result was startling to her. He actually fulfilled the promise of his application essays and improved on his high school performance. Wasn't it important for him to know he was capable of doing the work? He answered that his decision was never based on his ability to do the work.

She headed toward the center of Pittsfield. Although snow had been cleared on the main streets, the side streets were unplowed. Having arrived in Pittsfield a few minutes early she parked the car at a parking space in the middle of town facing a ridge of plowed snow. Tommy advised her to bring boots and she was glad she did, snow banks were everywhere along the streets. She made her way toward a drugstore to pick up a local newspaper. The sidewalk was barely shoveled with a thin strip for pedestrians largely created by previous footsteps. It seemed to her so much snow accumulated in Pittsfield they gave up or simply ignored it. This, too, did not build her confidence in the commercial viability of the area. Here was the hub, the main street of the town, and the banks created by the snow plows were nearly impenetrable and the sidewalks virtually uncleared. On crucial streets in Manhattan snow blowers and trucks would come and get the stuff the hell out.

She bought the *Berkshire Eagle* and sat in the car, browsing through it, local news sharing the front page with international stories. This was his paper now. She would be surprised if he still read *The New York Times* and even if she offered him a subscription he would probably decline.

He asked her to pick him up after his shift at the mall so he wouldn't have to take a bus back to his new place and his directions required her to continue on through the middle of town. Apart from a high-rise hotel a block from the main street and a few small modern office buildings along the way, the architecture had the look of time, of many towns in New England, low-lying buildings containing storefronts along the main street with an old movie theater in the center. The main street was also the principal artery, Route 7, which ran right through the center of several Massachusetts towns, a holdover from the period before highways, the connecting artery becomes Main Street.

She hadn't seen it as clearly as this moment, the snow ignored, the old architecture, the movie house on the main street, the road running through. It wasn't that he conveniently remained in the place he went to college, or that he stayed there because of the girl—another factor was influencing his decision. He had chosen to reject New York City and live in small-town America.

With this awareness, when she walked into the mall food court and saw him sitting in his winter jacket, his jeans, and boots, amidst other local people of various ages with their outerwear and boots, Tommy blending in, sipping a soda in the mall where he worked, in the town where he lived, she burst into tears.

"Mom! What is it?"

"I'll be okay," she said. "It's just I miss you and seeing you in this setting, on your own, all these hours away. It's an awful trip without a radio." Trying to settle herself, "So this is the mall."

The Berkshire Mall consisted of food stalls, small shops, chain stores, a movie complex, everything indoors as an answer to the weather. "When you said mall—it's nicer than I expected."

"I'll show you where I work."

The store was a large space with several people Tommy's age manning a row of cash registers and placing merchandise in bags. He waved to a young woman in her early twenties, a brunette of five feet three, blue eyes, with a friendly smile.

"This is my mother. Karen Burrows, Joni Clarkson, my supervisor. Joni's the one who hired me."

"Nice to meet you, Mrs. Burrows. Tommy hasn't been with us long, but we already know he's a good worker."

"A good worker" added to her distress. A few months after dropping him off at college with such hopes for his future she stood with her son who had a part-time job in a mall and was being told by a supervisor who looked not much older than Tommy that he was a good worker.

"Nice meeting you," Karen said and she turned to leave. "Looks like a very well-run operation," she said to Tommy.

"There's a lot to learn. But I think I'll get the hang of it."

Do I hope you will? Or do I hope you won't and move on? I guess I have to hope you will.

At $250 a month she presumed he would not be in a better section of Pittsfield. As she drove, he directed her away from the Berkshire Mall past a shopping center and along a row of auto agencies, gas stations, and retail stores. They made a turn. Two blocks from this strip in an area of small one-story houses was the street where Tommy lived, unpassable for the snow. They parked at the foot of the street and walked in. The parking area for the school buses confirmed what she expected about the neighborhood, and to add a flourish, a snarling Rottweiler behind the fence suggested that Karen should not entertain any notions of stealing a bus.

His landlord's house seemed presentable, the exterior in better shape than the other houses on the block. Tommy opened the door to his place and she found herself immediately inside, the space offered no true entrance foyer, merely a three-foot width allowing for a clothes closet. The robins on the trees were virtually leaping out at her to command attention.

"It's small, but it's clean. I have what I need and my landlord, he's good about heat."

She had no incentive for disapproval. The larger thought, his need to be in Pittsfield rather than New York, dominated anything at stake for her in the decor or the size of his apartment. He could be in a fine home in a good section of town with excellent furnishings and it wouldn't matter against the essential element, that he needed to be there at all. The curious, random furnishings, the odd wallpaper didn't go with an eighteen-year-old boy. She would have found a decent store, given him a modern look, and that wouldn't have mattered either.

"It's fine. Small, but you seem to have, as you say, what you need."

"And if I get a second job, I'll be able to handle it all right."

"You don't want to run yourself down with too many jobs."

"That's what people do around here, juggle their hours. I'm looking, just haven't gotten lucky yet."

"The place is fine," she said again.

"What I was thinking is, you could meet my friend, Elena. She works at Marlowe after school, but she'll meet us for something before she goes to work."

He wanted to show her everything he had, his place of work, his apartment, his girlfriend, I'm okay, Mom.

"I'd love to."

Then she noticed the bulletin board, a corkboard near the small stove. With pushpins he had affixed a bus schedule for Berkshire Regional Transit, a laundromat ticket, a small calendar, and a photograph of Karen, Rob, and Tommy. He was twelve and they were on the last vacation they would ever take as a family. They went to a motel on the ocean in Montauk. Another guest snapped the picture of them in their bathing suits, Rob and Karen on either side of him, their arms around him, everyone smiling. The spirit was draining from the marriage by then, but it wasn't quite over and for that instant they were happy to be at the beach with their son, hoping to hang on, and it was there in the snapshot, a last, captured happiness. Somehow he got hold of the picture. She didn't even remember it existed. It wasn't in his room. Had he kept it in a drawer? She remembered the moment, seeing the photograph again. He took it with him as one of his possessions in his unsentimental relocation, a picture of himself with his parents when his world was different. She excused herself to go into the bathroom, ran the water so he couldn't hear, and wept.

Elena was waiting outside Pittsfield High School when they drove up. She was wearing a ski jacket and carrying a backpack. It wasn't the girl who caused his decision, Karen knew that now. But she must have possessed some non-big-city virtues that were part of the appeal of this place for Tommy. He came out of the car, kissed her, and brought her over to Karen's side.

"This is Elena Garrity. My mom, Karen Burrows."

"A pleasure," Elena said.

"My pleasure."

They went to a coffee shop and Tommy directed the conversation to Elena's college applications, unconcerned with any reflection on his own standing. Karen went to the traditional adult portion in dealing with high school students, where would you like to go, what would you major in, Tommy proudly inserting Elena's SAT score, "without tutoring," causing Elena some embarrassment. Karen could see the physical attraction for Tommy and, incrementally, Elena's other virtues began to reveal themselves.

"Did you tell your mom about the library?" she asked brightly.

"I tried to keep up the tutoring like Grandma suggested, but they have a specific program with Marlowe and not being a student I couldn't do it anymore. So I went over to the library. I do a few hours a week in the children's room, reading to the kids and helping with some crafts projects."

"That's wonderful."

"And the Italian," Elena said prodding him.

"I liked Italian. '*Belleza.*' '*Doloroso.*' Beautiful sounding language. So I'm keeping it up. I have some CDs and some books."

Do you get it, Mom? College isn't everything. I'm not a bum.

"You're keeping busy. Terrific."

"And looking for another job. Tell my mom what you said about me, about my phase."

"Tommy—"

"Elena said I was going through my ski-instructor phase. Only I don't ski."

"That's very good."

"Helpful, right, Mrs. Burrows?"

"Yes, Elena, helpful."

Elena was due to be at work and they dropped her off at the entrance to Marlowe, Tommy without a reaction to being at the campus again. He wanted Karen to see the Pittsfield Library where he volunteered. The librarian at the front desk greeted him warmly and Tommy showed Karen around the two-story Pittsfield library, an attractive, open space, Tommy proprietary about it.

They went to a Radio Shack, where Karen bought an inexpensive tape recorder and batteries so on the way back to New York she could play some of the cassette tapes she brought. She planned to stay at the nearby hotel and leave in the morning. Tommy was scheduled to be at work at eight A.M. the next day for a shift unpacking merchandise and they set out for an early dinner at Arturo's, an Italian restaurant on Route 7.

At dinner Tommy was straining to get the focus off himself and he steered Karen to discuss her work. Business was off, as everyone's was—people hoping life would get back to normal. She discovered from a listing in the paper that one of her customers, a young woman who worked for the Port Authority, had died at the World Trade Center.

"A picture book came out about it and the librarian read it to the little kids. And then they did drawings I helped with. They don't even know what tall buildings are, some of these kids, but it was good for them."

"Nice you could do that, Tommy."

They gravitated to the movies each had seen lately and the dinner approximated the time when he lived at home and they spent a meal together catching up. She drove him back to his street and kissed him on the forehead.

"I love you."

"Love you, Mom, thanks so much for coming."

"She's a lovely girl."

"Thanks. Mom, tell Dad I'm going to make it."

He walked through the snow back to his place. She watched him enter the house then drove to the hotel. She called Rob from the room and described the visit in detail.

"You really think this is his statement, to be small-town?"

"Looks that way. Nothing I saw led me to believe he thinks this move is temporary."

"Bottom line is what we said. He's working practically minimum wage in a low-level job, which incidentally he could get anywhere. What's so unique that he needs to be in Pittsfield?"

"He doesn't want to be in New York. That's *his* bottom line. He's very optimistic. Proud of the volunteering and the Italian and the girlfriend. He wanted me to tell you he's going to make it."

"A little early for that conclusion."

"He thinks it's a start."

"Going to college is a start. Ironic. You worry about your child being learning disabled and he turns out not to be. And then he chooses to live exactly the life he'd have to live if he were."

"That's pretty harsh."

"It's what it is. One of us has to face it."

"We'll talk."

• • •

She woke at four thirty A.M. and decided not to fight her wakefulness and checked out of the hotel by five. The trip back was longer by an hour than the trip north as she picked up commuter traffic heading into the city, grateful for the tape recorder and music, which did not entirely ease her mind. She thought Rob was being rough on Tommy, yet she couldn't be sure if he would make it. They didn't have more to go on than his first initial steps, as if he were like a toddler again, holding his hands out for balance.

Rob's mother called him in the office, irate.

"What in the world is going on? Tommy called to wish me a happy birthday. Thank you for the flowers by the way. And thank your wife."

"She has a name. It's Vickie."

"I asked how school was and he said he's not in school. He decided not to go back. He's working in a store in Pittsfield. Why?"

"What did he tell you?"

"He didn't want to go to college and he didn't want to live in New York and he wanted to live there."

"That seems to be it."

"I never heard anything like it. He's college-age. He should be in college."

"We tried to tell him that, Mother. Believe me we did."

"So did I. He said he made up his mind. How does a father with two degrees allow his son to quit school? And this wife of yours. She's a lawyer. And Karen. She has a college education. What are you people doing?"

"It's not completely within our control, Mother."

"He's a bright boy. He should be in school getting brighter. You have a lot to answer for."

"I can't tell you how reassuring this is."

"You're an intelligent man. Fix it."

"If it can be fixed."

Karen and Bill went out for a light dinner in a bar near her apartment. At one point she stopped eating, holding a hamburger in her hand, suspended by the image of Tommy walking back to his place on the dark street in the snow.

"Karen?"

"Sorry. My mind is elsewhere."

"Anywhere but here."

"I do have a lot on my mind. And you can have more on yours."

"What does that mean?"

"Obviously I'm worried about Tommy. And where are you in this? Would it ever occur to you, if I tell you I'm going up there, to say I'd like to go with you so you don't have to sit in a car for six or seven hours by yourself and so I can see how he's doing? Maybe give him a little encouragement, like I was a teenage boy myself once."

"He has a father, Karen. He was also a teenage boy once."

"Would it ever occur to you to pick up the phone and call him and say, 'Hey, Tommy, it's Bill, how are you?' "

"We didn't have the closest relationship."

"And whose fault was that?"

"He's a little remote, or haven't you noticed?"

"He doesn't have the personality of a cheerleader, but you make an effort."

"I've been impeccable with the boy. I didn't invade his privacy. I didn't patronize him. I have nothing to reproach myself for."

"You are the man in my life. He is my son. You could do more."

"All right, next time you go up I'd like to go with you. You think he'd like that?"

"I don't think he'd mind."

"But he wouldn't be thrilled by my being there. No more than he was thrilled by my offer to help. He was completely into himself."

"You couldn't wait for him to say no. Come on, Bill. Did you really want him to work at some place where they know you?"

"Stop it, Karen."

"Did you think he'd reflect badly on you?"

"I don't know how good he'd be, if you must know."

"Because?"

"Because I don't know how motivated he is. What he seems to be best at is calling attention to himself."

"Oh?"

"He's got everybody jumping through hoops. This is so dramatic, dropping out of college after a semester. He's got a bit of the drama queen in him, your son."

She reacted as though she were slapped.

"Now I know. It's not that he's remote—you simply don't like him."

"Not true. I went too far. I apologize. We're both a little overwrought from his adventures."

"Adventures?"

"He does have a propensity to struggle and enlist people in the struggle."

"He hasn't enlisted us. He didn't ask for that meeting we had. He's gone off and doesn't want a penny. He's totally on his own. How is that enlisting us?"

"Emotionally then."

"I'm his mother. I can't be as cut off from him as you. But it seems to me the whole idea for him is to *not* enlist us. At eighteen. Good-bye. You've got it upside down if you think this is some kind of ploy for attention. He doesn't want our attention. 'Drama queen.' What a loathsome thing to say."

"Karen, it's an emotional subject. It brings out emotions."

"Dinner's on me. I'm going home. Don't see me out." She dropped money on the table.

"Karen!"

"*We're* not jumping through hoops. Don't you see that? *He* is."

Vickie arranged for Tim to take the children on a February Saturday so she could go with Rob on his first visit to Tommy in Pittsfield. He was in New York to do the voice-over for a television commercial, walking around money, by way of explanation. She asked the teenage sitter who had slept over in the past to be on call pending any last-minute Tim behavior and to take over from Tim in the evening. Rob went to get the car and was spared the sight of the boys greeting their father, whom they had not seen in two months. They tackled him in the living room, pulled him to the floor, and piled on, giggling as he tickled his way out from under them. Vickie smiled slightly. The scene was unfathomable to her in terms of Rob and the boys. He was back to traveling after the holiday season, a day or two here, a day or two there, a trip to the foundry, visits with the contractors, calls on clients—and sullen when he was home, preoccupied with Tommy, never short with the boys, polite, not much more than polite, a stepfather who was barely present.

Rob chose a jazz collection of Rodgers and Hart to counter the drive north. The day was rainy, the snow on the sides of the road soggy and pockmarked.

"If our moods are affected by light I'm going to arrive there totally depressed," Rob said, "even with this music."

"Don't you think you're due to take the boys to something?" she said without a transition, expressing exactly what she was thinking. "Like a movie some time."

"What do you mean, due? Is that judgmental?"

"You haven't done much with them lately."

"I've been busy, Vickie."

A line he carried along through two marriages.

"I understand. But you were doing things with them and you stopped."

"When I can. In two Saturdays."

"Good. We're a family, Rob. Not the original family, but the family that's evolved. They're going to spend more of their lives with you around than with Tim, so it would be good if you *were* around."

"You're right. I'll try."

"Okay."

They stopped for coffee at a rest stop and Rob's cell phone rang.

"Dad, it's me."

"What's up, Tommy?"

"It's not such a good idea for you to come today."

"We're three quarters of the way there. What's wrong?"

"I had sort of a problem."

"What kind of a problem? You okay?"

"I am. Turns out it's not the greatest day for a visit."

"It's not. It's the dreariest, worst day, but we're less than an hour away and I'm not turning around. What is it, Tommy?"

"I'll explain when you get here. You have the map?"

"I do."

"I'll see you at my place. Appreciate it, Dad, to come out on a day like this. See you when I see you."

After he clicked off Rob looked grimly at Vickie.

"Some kind of problem. He'll explain."

On Tommy's street the layer of snow in the gutter was brownish-black from traffic and on the sidewalks the snow had turned to slush. The rain continued to fall and Rob shielded Vickie with an umbrella as they hurried to the door. He rang the bell and paused to take in the immediate area, the rows of buses parked with agricultural uniformity, the slushy parking lot, a location that was not about to be featured by the Pittsfield Tourist Board. Tommy opened the door, Rob embracing him, Vickie kissing him. Rob barely glanced at the room, having been prepared by Karen to expect a small, functional place. And he had a pressing concern, Tommy's last-minute reluctance to see them.

"What's the problem?" Rob asked as Tommy took their coats and tossed them over the top of the shower rod.

"It's cozy," Vickie said to Tommy with a reproachful look at Rob, there are amenities to be honored here.

"Thanks. It works for me."

"So, what's happening?"

"I got fired this morning," he said heavily. "Got a call from my supervisor. The main office, which is in Denver, ordered a cutback. Me and two other people like me got fired."

Telling them was an effort, his face tense.

"What are your plans?" Rob said.

"Find another job. Or two. I really need two part-time or one full-time."

"It took you how long to get this one?"

"Four weeks."

"It's not your fault, obviously," Vickie said. "Seems to have very little to do with you."

"Except this is the kind of job he's chosen to work at," Rob said. "I know this sounds like 'I told you so,' but you're on a very difficult side of the street. The turnover in these kinds of jobs is enormous."

"I'll have to find something else, which is why I thought you shouldn't come. It's an important day to look, on a Saturday, and I'm going to make rounds."

"We should have lunch, Tommy," Vickie said.

"Oh, sure. I meant later."

"What's the best place for lunch?" she asked.

"There are a couple of nice places."

Tommy went back to get their coats and his. Rob scanned the room and noticed the picture on the bulletin board of the family on the beach at Montauk.

"Oh," he said, a soft sound that was close to a moan and he held his hand to his chest. He tried to recover as Tommy returned with the coats.

Tommy chose the Italian restaurant where Tommy went to dinner with Karen. He pointed out places along the way, stores where he shopped, and the library. Vickie asked a few questions. Rob was withdrawn, still affected by seeing that image.

Over lunch Rob allowed Vickie to take the lead as Tommy talked about his possibilities. He was on the waiting list for a telemarketing job for ski resorts. He left a résumé with the *Berkshire Eagle* indicating he worked for his high school newspaper and was told they sometimes had openings for part-time clerical workers. He planned to go back to the mall. He heard that retail was an area where jobs came up. He was prepared to try again even though it hadn't worked out in the first place.

"With Seth you could have earned real money and you would have learned something, too. I don't know how you turned it down."

"I would have had to be there. I'm here."

"It was a fantastic opportunity."

"Not if I didn't want to be there. In some patronage job. *That's* not being on my own."

"Tell me about the girl you're seeing," Vickie said.

"I like her a lot. She's a terrific writer for her school paper. She's pretty. Smart. We helped with her college applications, Jill and Brian and me. Brian thinks she's a lock to get a scholarship somewhere. I wanted you to meet her, but she had to go to a birthday party."

"Tommy, if she's one of the reasons you're here, then what does it tell you about the choices you're making if she's going to college and you're not? Staying in Pittsfield you're limiting yourself in really profound ways."

"You're trying to connect dots, Dad, that don't connect. Even if I didn't know her, I'd be here. And I didn't leave college because of her."

As he did with Karen, Tommy directed the conversation away from himself and shifted it to them, what was new with Rob in the office, what projects was Vickie working on, how were the boys, what movies did Rob and Vickie see lately? They finished lunch and Tommy wanted to get on with making the rounds at the Berkshire Mall. He asked Rob to take him over there after he went back to the apartment to change into better clothing for job-seeking. En route to Tommy's place Rob parked near the traffic circle at the center of Pittsfield.

"Tommy, could you get out for a moment, please?"

"Why?"

"Please."

Tommy stepped outside and Rob put his arm around him.

"Look. It's the middle of the day. It finally stopped raining and there's barely a handful of people on the street. I know these towns very well. Not many people on the street because they operate at a small-town frequency. That's the strength, small-town values, good, decent people with good, decent values, but it's also the weakness, because you don't have the same opportunities in a place like this."

"It's not a small town, Dad, they call it the City of Pittsfield."

"A small city then, but it's like a small town when you compare it to a place like New York or Chicago or any major American city."

"You're leaving out how much cheaper it is to live here. I can get by on so much less."

"I never dreamed for you that what you'd want someday is 'to get by.' Tommy, to be in a place like this without a college degree, any place, really, it's going to be incredibly more difficult to find something that can make you special, which you are at eighteen. But that's off of what you've done so far. How long will it last? How special will you be at thirty?"

"I'm sorry if you can't accept it. This is where I am."

Rob and Vickie remained in the car while Tommy changed his clothes.

"I'm a broken record. Can you say that anymore? A broken CD."

"He's not lying in bed with the shades drawn." She said it to encourage Rob, but when Tommy emerged from the house walking slowly, starting over again to look for a job, she thought he looked like someone seriously overburdened.

At the mall Rob and Vickie came out of the car to say good-bye and Tommy manufactured a cheerfulness that was transparent. As he went into the building, Rob said quietly, "He's a lost boy."

Vickie and Rob were both restless that night and she arose shortly after four and looked in on her children sleeping. How are you going to turn out, guys? Are these the coming attractions? Will you get tired of performing just so your parents can say to themselves the divorce was benign? She adjusted the blankets for each child. We kid ourselves with these divorces, don't we? The bill always comes due.

THIRTEEN

• • •

This was their ritual now, meeting in public places, divorced people consoling each other, the bond between them deeper than anything that existed in the last years of the marriage, connected by their son, talking it out, looking for magic. They were in an espresso shop in Greenwich Village assessing the latest news. After three weeks Tommy managed to find a new part-time position. He admitted the job market was tight and it was the best he could manage. He was a security guard in the mall. Minimum wage. He wore a uniform.

His orders were not to physically intervene in any altercations—so they shouldn't worry. He was to answer questions, give directions, watch for trouble, and call in to the main office or the police if there were disturbances or emergencies. The hours were five days a week, Wednesdays through Sundays from two to six P.M. for Secure-Com, the company that provided the security service for the mall. He could still volunteer at the library and he was still studying Italian, he assured them.

Rob couldn't believe the rapidity of the descent. In less than a year he went from someone wearing a cap and gown graduating from one of the best private schools in New York, headed for an excellent college, to someone wearing a security guard's uniform. Karen and Rob were worried despite his assurance. He was in a public place, dangerous things could happen. And what would this do to his mind, sitting for long stretches doing nothing? Karen thought it was like accepting a prison sentence for his independence. And what if he did well, they wondered, watched well, would that mean he would be offered a full-time job as a security guard? Rob passed Vickie's opinion along, that he needed something quickly for his morale and took this particular job out of expedience. Reaching, Karen suggested his situation might be similar to the students who worked in jobs like this so they could be with working people and understand the world of work before moving on. Rob thought her analogy only made sense if he did move on. And what could he move on to with one semester of college, Rob's main theme. He believed Tommy did have the capacity for being special. He feared by doing this kind of work, inevitably, Tommy would lose the possibility for specialness.

Rob took Karen's hands in his and kissed them and she leaned forward and kissed his. In this moment of intimacy born of their troubled hearts they couldn't bear going over it any longer and took leave of each other.

Attaching himself to Valentine's Day, Bill tried to use it to coax himself back into Karen's good graces. He sent a dozen roses to the store with a note asking if they could celebrate Valentine's Day with dinner at a bistro Karen liked, Cafe Luxembourg. Two weeks had passed since she bolted from the table and he called twice, but she hadn't returned the calls. She softened, reaching him in his office, and told him she would celebrate Valentine's Day with him. She bought Bill a scarf from Bloomingdale's as a present, he bought her cultured pearl earrings from Saks. At dinner she told him about the security guard job and waited expectantly for his reaction. He suggested people change jobs and careers far more than in years past and this job sounded as temporary as anything could be. She felt the response was rather dry and would have preferred him to be closer to her feelings—it's absurd, what can we do to keep ourselves from screaming? Yet it was a sympathetic response and she thanked him for the thought.

At her apartment afterward, the first time they made love in three weeks, he was ardent, as if promoting his relevance and viability. She didn't know what it meant and didn't want to dwell on the implications; she hadn't missed the sex with him and was not overwhelmed to be in bed with him again.

Bill went to dinner at the apartment of his friends, Mack and Beth, and confided in them about the difficulties he was experiencing with Karen.

"Maybe she wants to get married and it's not moving toward it," Beth suggested.

"Marriage never comes up. I doubt she'd want it. I certainly don't. It was fine the way it was."

"If you're going along, uncommitted, anything can throw it off," Mack said. "And this boy, he doesn't sound like he's just anything."

"She wants me more involved with him. But he's a great pain in the ass. Dropped out of college after one semester and he's working as a security guard in a mall in the Berkshires."

"I've heard worse. Why does that make him a pain in the ass?" Mack said.

"It's a pretty obvious attention-getter, wouldn't you say?"

"I don't know his psychology."

"There's nothing like it in my experience."

"He's not your daughter?" Mack said with a touch of sarcasm.

"Right. I was spoiled. Cindy did so well," he replied, not reading the sarcasm.

"You know why she did so well?" Beth said. "Jane, the woman, was watching out for her. You were off at work."

"So was she."

"Bill, I would never characterize you as having your consciousness raised. I'm not saying you weren't a responsible father. But Jane was the one who stayed home if Cindy was sick. Jane was the one who made the major decisions. Jane was the psychological parent. So I don't see where you can compare Cindy with this boy. Your experience with Cindy was filtered through Jane."

"I miss her so much," he said.

"She's irreplaceable," Mack said. "You do your best. You were doing pretty well with this lady."

"If you're more open about the son, things might go smoother with the mother," Beth said.

"I'm sure you're right. Only as far as I can see, he'll never amount to much. Frankly, he's completely unexceptional."

Karen invited Polly and Joe for dinner ostensibly to say the words, to get them out there, "Tommy has a job in the Berkshire Mall as a security guard."

Joe smiled. Polly was not smiling. After a beat Polly said, "There's a context, this mission of his, to break away. You have to look at it in that context."

"I'm trying to. And hoping this, too, will pass."

"He's growing larger in stature for me," Joe said.

"Oh, please, Joe," Polly said.

"He's taken himself out of the private school–private college category and he's in with the common man. It can develop. He could end up being any number of things, a grass-roots politician, a labor organizer."

"Right now he's wearing a uniform, which you can imagine doesn't thrill his parents," Karen said.

"A uniform! You know how determined he must be? I am definitely in love with this boy."

Embellishing his point, Joe began to sing "This Land Is Your Land" in a twangy Woody Guthrie voice. To stop him Polly grabbed his mouth.

"I'm so happy this amuses you," Karen said to Joe.

"I think he's great. Whatever it took for him to put on a uniform and work as a guard to pay his bills so he can make his statement is going to stand him in good stead. Be proud of him, Karen. You raised a young culture hero. An anti-hero maybe, but a hero."

"I'm not there yet," Karen said.

"Then I'll be there for you," he said with sincerity.

Working in the mall gave Tommy a passing acquaintance with the other regulars, the employees, the managers of the stores, and he learned a cashier slot was open. He was hired by Assortments, a newsstand-sundries shop, to work at minimum wage five mornings a week. He now worked Wednesdays through Sundays, ten A.M. to one P.M. as a cashier and two P.M. to six P.M. as a guard. He was off two consecutive weekdays, which meant he could still volunteer at the library. He tried to jog a minimum of two mornings a week, weather and snow permitting. He also continued to maintain a social life on weekend evenings with Elena.

Tommy became assimilated into the dating routine of Elena and her friends, going to a few of their parties, not calling attention to himself, never mentioning his New York City private school background. One of Elena's classmates worked after school at Old Navy in the mall as a part-time stock clerk. Kit MacDougald was on the high school football team, a wide-bodied five feet six, with a stone-chiseled face, and surprisingly soft-spoken. Tommy chatted with him in a corner at some of the parties, usually about their jobs and people who worked in the mall. He learned from Kit that Elena had had a boyfriend at Yale, but they stopped seeing each other a few months earlier. The guy was from Lenox, Massachusetts. Kit only met him a couple of times and didn't like him. Kit said he was full of himself and that he liked Tommy much better, which Tommy appreciated.

Elena's best friend was the editor-in-chief of the school paper, Jocelyn

Brandt, a bouncy girl of five feet two, always ready to do the next thing, the party after the movies, the bowling after the party, the ice-skating after the bowling. Her boyfriend was a skinny boy with glasses, Teddy Briggs, the editor of the yearbook and passive with Jocelyn; his life being managed by his girlfriend and Teddy too passive to notice. Jocelyn was going to Connecticut College on an early admission, Teddy was accepted at Middlebury College also on early admission and Elena was expected to get in somewhere. They reminded Tommy of his own trio, although he missed Brian's humor and Jill's sophistication.

Jill and Brian were in classes on his days off. Tommy worked on the weekends and they couldn't get together. He maintained an e-mail correspondence with them and they spoke intermittently. Tommy's friends, troubled by his situation, tried to focus on the selling points he offered, his continuing study of Italian, volunteering with children at the library, which meant something to them, the part of Tommy that was recognizable.

With the second of the two jobs he was making a living at his modest level. He did not have to become a hermit in order to live on his own. He had small-talk relationships with people who worked in the mall, he had a girlfriend for as long as she would be around, his girlfriend had friends, they went to the party after the movies, and the bowling after the party. He began with a stumbling start, but he was satisfied now. He said, "Enough," and changed direction.

On a Sunday afternoon he was sitting in his chair behind a desk at an end of the mall wearing his uniform, black shoes, black socks, black pants, a black knit tie with a two-toned white and black shirt, a nameplate over his left pocket, and patches on both sleeves that said "Security." Walking through, carrying shopping bags, was Elena's mother. She noticed him and stopped.

"So, Mr. T. Burrows," referring to his nameplate.

"Hello, Mrs. Garrity."

"How is it going in the security business?"

"Fine. Everything's secure."

" 'Everything's secure.' A little New York humor there?"

"No offense intended."

"Elena tells me you're a cashier, too. Quite the resourceful fellow."

"Just working."

"And it gets you your own place." The remark was unmistakable, a sexual reference regarding her daughter.

"Yes."

"Something you should know, Mr. T. Burrows. Elena is going to college. The best college I can afford. I don't want anybody stopping that from happening. She's not going to be a teenage mother who loses out, if you understand me."

"I understand you."

"I asked her if you flunked out. She said you passed all your courses."

"I did."

"So what *is* this?"

"I needed to do something different."

"This'll do it. Listen, young man, Elena is going to have a good life. It starts with college."

"I'm with you on that. We worked on her applications, my friends and I."

"I know. That was nice of you. But she could be accepted in Boston, it could be in Providence, wherever, and I don't want her making a decision because of you, because you're here."

"That wasn't the idea. It was to get the best package from the best school."

"And if she gets into, say, Brown, does that mean you trail after her to Providence and work there as a guard or a cashier to be around her? College girls have boyfriends, I can live with that, but they're usually other students. Not some town guy."

"Hadn't thought of it quite that way, but if we were still together, it's what I'd be, a town guy. I'm not going to trail after her, Mrs. Garrity. I'm not going to be a distraction for her. I'm staying in Pittsfield and I'll see her when I can see her, if I can see her."

"Good. I'm glad that's understood. I don't want you holding Elena back while you're figuring yourself out."

She walked away and he watched her go. All these adults running a scoreboard on me.

Karen conceived a new policy in the store to feature a different artisan every month with the same kind of attention an art gallery would bestow on a one-artist show. The entire store would not be given over to the featured artist, she needed to maintain her sales from the rest of her merchandise, but she would use the window space and a large portion of the selling area. Working with her manager, John, she started to make the selections from her painters, sculptors, weavers, basketmakers, quiltmakers, carvers, from the serious and from the whimsical. The new approach was also going to require the creation of mailing pieces, follow-ups to the media, parties for openings. She went through the planning stages while keeping up with the usual activities for the store. She was working intensely and Bill was less and less a factor in her week. She went a few weekends without seeing him. She was still waiting for that moment when he would ask to accompany her the next time she drove up to Pittsfield to see Tommy. A test, she realized, and yet he continually failed. She was hoping to visit Tommy again. She and Tommy returned to the pattern of his first semester in college, she would call, he would usually recapture the call from his answering machine and they would eventually speak, Tommy generally uninformative. The second job he took was a disappointment to her. What was he going to build on by being a cashier in a sundries store, being a cashier in a larger store?

She spoke to Rob, who had been traveling, locating him in Sumter, South Carolina, a familiar location to her, Rob there for Atkins Welding, echoes of past friction between them—You were just there last month, Rob, why do you have to go again? Because I do, because it's my work and that's the way it is . . .

"I was wondering if you've got plans to visit Tommy any time soon," Karen said. "I'm not so free these days."

"I'd like to. I've been on the road so much. I was kind of hoping you'd get there."

"I can't right now. You know, I want to see him, but there's a part of me that doesn't. He's so *in* his world there."

"I know what you mean."

"I was walking along Broadway," Karen said, "and I saw a woman with a little Yorkie under her arm, another one on a leash, and a third one peeking out from her pocket, and I thought, that's cute. Then I looked closer and she had a fourth Yorkie in her handbag, and what started out cute, looked like she was just a crazy lady. It was the fourth Yorkie that tipped it. I feel like that about Tommy. It was the second job that tipped it. He's now officially entrenched in Pittsfield."

"I was hoping he wouldn't find anything and he'd have to come home. He's there, that's the reality, there's nothing else. Like the old comics used to say, 'These are the jokes.' "

"You're a regular laugh machine."

"You, too."

"Let me know if you go up."

"You do the same."

Atkins Welding had been doing business with MayPole, first through Rob's predecessor and then through Rob, for thirty years. Sam Atkins, seventy-four, who owned the company, was a burly, weathered six feet two, an L.L. Bean guy. He was hinting about something he wanted to discuss the next time Rob was in Sumter. They talked in his office for an hour about the various MayPole playground pieces in the works. Then Sam walked Rob toward a metal shed on the grounds.

"We captured some aliens," Atkins said, "and we've got them with their space ship. But don't let it get out. Just wanted you to see it."

"Appreciate the courtesy."

"You're looking grim, Rob. Been noticing since you're here."

"My kid's on my mind a lot. Quit college and he's working up in Massachusetts."

"Doing what?"

"Nothing much."

"You don't know how your kid is going to turn out until he's not a kid anymore and then it doesn't matter what kind of kid he was."

"There's some sage advice buried in there, Sam. Deep in there."

Atkins opened the door to the shed, revealing a variety of wrought iron garden furniture, benches, chairs, patio table sets, exquisite pieces elegantly designed with floral embellishments.

"They're mine. I designed them."

"Beautiful work, Sam."

"Been thinking about it for years. A side activity for my old age."

Rob looked more closely at the pieces.

"Really beautiful."

"I'm going into business with them. Atkins Wrought Iron Furniture. But I don't want to get stuck in the business end. I just want to cook the ribs, let someone else do the rest."

"Okay."

"I want you to be my guy. I'll design them, I'll make them, you be my distributor. You know how to move merchandise. Wouldn't be much for you to take on a consumer business."

"It's a question of time. I'm overbooked as it is."

"You hire people."

"That takes time, too, and overseeing them takes time. By the way, it's a terrible name, Atkins Wrought Iron Furniture. You want something that sounds like it's a real line, maybe a little English. Something-shire. Gardenshire."

"I like it. See? I'm telling you, this'll be a piece of cake for you."

"Sam, what do you know about the field?"

"Nothing. I just know what I like and what it'll cost me to make the pieces."

"Let me do some research, come up with a business plan. I'll show it to you. You can try to run it yourself if it looks feasible. Or give it to someone else. Or possibly I'll do it, if it can work out."

"Here's to Gardenshire," Sam said.

Rob's plane arrived in New York shortly after four P.M. Normally he would have gone directly to the office. The boys would be home and he had spent so little time in their company of late this was an opportunity. They gave him a casual "Hi, Rob" greeting when he came in. They seemed disappointed Rob would be relieving the teenage girl from the building; they were in the middle of a New York City Monopoly game on the floor of their room. Rob took over and he was on the floor with them when Vickie came in close to six. She was surprised to see him playing with the children and she remained in a good mood until the time after the boys went to sleep, when he told her Sam Atkins offered him the distributorship.

"I didn't say yes. All I'm going to do for now is develop a business plan for him. Then I'll see."

"When I came home and you were playing with the boys I had a strange reaction. It wasn't 'how nice.' It was 'how unusual.' You have such a narrow life with these children. And with me, too. We find our moments. But if you walked out the door I don't know if they'd even miss you."

"That's pretty sad."

"You always say you'll do better, then you slide. This business with Tommy—"

"What about it?"

"It's eating you up. You're filling yourself up with work to will it away. I ache for you. I ache for him. It can't be easy for him, scrambling around, living the life of an adult when he isn't. But it's like you've got nothing left for these little boys when your own boy is in trouble. You're used up, Rob."

"I must be aware of it or I wouldn't have done this today."

"Yes, that was good. You're a good and valuable man. You do good. It must be terrible for you to see your son like this. But *we're* here. You have a wife. You have, what shall we call them, alternate sons, substitute sons, stepsons? You can get something out of them and they can, too."

"You're right, of course."

"This Atkins thing. If after the toll Tommy is taking on you, and after the way you travel in the normal course of business, you take on another business, with all that's going to come with it, well, I'll make it easy for you. If you go into business with Atkins, I'm going to leave you."

They spoke little for the rest of the evening and he left before she did in the morning. He called Seth and asked if they could have breakfast. Seth's office was on Fifth Avenue and 26th Street and Rob was early so he sat on a bench on the street side of Madison Square Park to pass a few minutes. Short of sleep, he had the physical symptoms of a hangover when he hadn't taken a drink. He thought the winter air might help. He watched people hurrying to work on this February morning, people in good overcoats and in ski jackets and some underdressed in windbreakers, the coats defining income on a cold day, Rob in a decent coat, a British warmer from Brooks Brothers in its sixth year, not looking shabby yet. A Hispanic couple in their twenties in matching ski jackets, arm in arm, hurried past. Were they married, would they get divorced? How many of you are divorced? The divorce rate is so goddamn high, has to be some of you. He had no idea he was that close to the edge with Vickie. He thought he must be completely unconscious. He started to get chilled and put the collar up on his coat. He was wearing a scarf and no hat. Are you cold up there, Tommy? You had to go and be in such a cold place? Tommy. Tommy! He started to cry. The tears were stinging his cheeks and he brushed them away with his sleeve. A woman of about thirty in a dufflecoat carrying a briefcase passed by and looked at him, a well-dressed man sitting on a park bench at eight thirty in the morning crying. She slowed her stride for a moment as if considering assistance, but chose not to stop and continued along. He noticed her and appreciated her moment's hesitation and also her decision to let him be.

He walked to the coffee shop where he was meeting Seth. He was still early and sat with *The New York Times* in front of him, unable to concentrate on it. His mind drifted to Tommy trudging into the mall trying to find work.

Seth slipped into the booth opposite him.

"You look like shit."

"This is what falling apart looks like."

"What's up?"

"Sam Atkins offered me the chance to distribute a line of garden furniture he's going to make and when I told Vickie she said if I took it on she'd leave me."

"And what do you want to do?"

"I want to stay married. I want my son to be all right. When I came back on the plane I was thinking a new business might not be such a bad idea. Could be something Tommy might like to get into, or something I could turn over to him when he's ready. Working at MayPole with me might be too much for him, but this would be a different business."

"Assuming Tommy wants to sell garden furniture," he said. "Rob, you having a nervous breakdown?"

"No, but I bet I have some of the symptoms."

The waitress came and took their order, two former college runners in vanity watching their waistlines ordering orange juice, and dry cereal with skim milk.

"This was the day to order ham and eggs and home fries," Rob said. "What is eating healthy going to do for me?"

"On Tommy, I don't know what you can do. On Vickie, at least you have a choice."

He looked out the window absentmindedly and turned back to Seth. "I never thought I was a candidate to be divorced twice."

Karen cleared the second Tuesday in March for a visit to Tommy. She gave Bill ten days' notice to arrange the time so they could go together. He apologized, he couldn't possibly, he was scheduled for lunch with someone at the Soros Foundation and he was courting them for funds to contribute to his foundation. She didn't understand why, out of the possible breakfast meetings and lunch meetings and drink meetings and dinner meetings and five days a week and four weeks a month, he couldn't reschedule a lunch. She let it pass with "That's too bad, maybe another time." She mentioned to Polly on the phone she was going up without Bill, who found an excuse not to go. Polly said she was obliged to be in Washington that day or she would have gone with Karen. Joe overheard the conversation from Polly's end. He offered to accompany Karen.

Traveling in a car with Joe was like having a radio that picked up the audio portion of the Sunday morning television talk shows. He went on about the cynicism of the political parties, not even sparing his beloved Democrats. As they passed the Catskills region he switched gears to the social and economic evils of casino gambling and it was better for the Catskills not to be another Atlantic City, gambling was like sports stadiums, it never brings the money into an area the advocates promise and worse, it steals from the poor. She thought about what it might be like to be in a relationship with a man like Joe, high-energy, opinionated, rather than someone like Bill, correct and deliberate.

"Bill didn't score too many points by not coming today," she said.

"If I had someone for you, I'd fix you up in a New York minute."

"That's subversive."

"I should care about this Bill's feelings?"

They were approaching Albany and she said jokingly, "Talk to me about the state legislature. It gets me excited when you talk that way."

He laughed and proceeded to go right ahead and talk about the state legislature and the disproportionate allocation of funds by the state to New York City.

Tommy's street was passable this time and Karen parked next to the house. Their arrival signaled the Rottweiller in charge across the street to report for duty and he took a run at the fence, barking and snarling.

"Scenic," she said.

Karen rang the bell.

"Hi, folks," Tommy said, Karen kissing him, Joe giving him a hearty handshake.

"Compact. Nice," Joe said, looking over the room, and Karen smiled at his effort to be complimentary.

"Get you anything, use the facility?"

Karen went into the bathroom and noticed the aroma of Ajax. He cleaned up the place for their arrival. When she emerged, Tommy said, "I thought we could do some things. There's a Norman Rockwell museum in Stockbridge I hear is good and I've got a couple of restaurant recommendations around there."

"Sounds great," Karen said.

"We can be off then." He went for his coat and Joe spotted the photograph on the bulletin board. He glanced at Karen and she nodded, frowning.

The museum displayed Norman Rockwell originals and printed versions of the *Saturday Evening Post* covers, along with a commentary on Rockwell's life. Tommy was eager for them to like it as though it reflected on his being there. He was pleased when they did enjoy the exhibit. The temperature was in the fifties and they walked around Stockbridge. Karen mainly wanted to buy Tommy clothing, a shirt, a sweater, socks, anything. He insisted he had everything he needed. They went for an early dinner at the Red Lion Inn, a Berkshires landmark. Tommy revealed he didn't consider himself locked into these two particular jobs.

"Tommy, you were a camp counselor. You volunteered in the rec center. You're volunteering with children in the library. You must like children. Why don't you consider being a teacher?" Karen started in an even tone. By the time she reached the end it was closer to a plea.

He reacted to the emotion in her voice.

"I appreciate that, Mom, very much, that you're not tied into my being something that's only about money."

"Teachers should be better paid," Joe said firmly, the conversation landing in his sweet spot.

"But to be a teacher you need a college degree and I'm not going to college. So it isn't possible."

"It's something to think about as time goes on. I know the children in the camp loved you. Dad said you're good with the little boys. I know you'd be a wonderful teacher. Meantime you might get a job in a day care center with your experience," she said.

"I tried. Weren't any openings."

"But I wouldn't exclude teaching as an idea."

She excused herself to go to the ladies room, unsettled by how rigid he was, leaving Joe and Tommy at the table.

"How is it here, Tommy?" Joe asked directly in the manner of—it's just us guys, we can talk.

"Good. The weather's a little on the cool side," he added wryly.

"It has to get warmer. It always gets warmer. Stick it out, Tommy. I want you to know I think this was a gutsy move. Now you won't accept anything from your parents and that's fine, it's what you have to do. But if a job comes up and it's a better opportunity, except it's hard to get to, you can get yourself a car—off me. You should be able to get something that passes inspection for under a thousand around here. I'll buy it for you. Get you wheels to open up your options. If you want, you can think of it as a long-term loan against your future. I'm with you, Tommy. I think you're great."

Tommy was silent, looking down, afraid to make eye contact or his eyes might water up and you didn't do that among guys.

"That's really terrific of you, Joe."

"Your parents don't have to know. It's between us."

With a three-hour trip in the dark ahead of them, Joe offered to drive home. He wasn't going to tell Karen about his offer to Tommy, nor was he going to tell his wife and burden her with keeping a secret from her friend. He merely felt Tommy's parents were so disappointed and anxious they were in a state of shock and the boy needed to know someone was willing to give him support.

Karen was disturbed by how swiftly Tommy brushed aside the notion of becoming a teacher. Joe thought teaching might be a good idea, but Tommy was saying over and over that college wasn't anything he was currently interested in. Joe was convinced Tommy would find something worthwhile eventually. Worn down by the strain of seeing him in the place he had chosen to live and being confronted directly by his unwillingness to accept anything from her, advice, clothing, no thank you, she slept most of the way home.

The following week when Tommy arrived at Assortments to begin work, the gate was down. Usually the manager for the store opened in the morning and went on to the next location when Tommy took over at the cash register. He dialed an emergency number from a pay phone. No one answered, not even a recorded message. He spoke to the manager of a fast food stall nearby who told him the store hadn't opened for the last couple of days, Tommy's days off. He heard they went out of business. Tommy went to the next Assortments location in a shopping center, a twenty-minute walk, and found it was also shuttered. He appeared to have lost another job. He was paid through his last work day on Sunday and presumed the unceremonious end to Assortments meant he would not receive severance pay. His father was coming up to see him again in four days and he didn't want to be in this situation when he arrived. He made the rounds in the mall. An assistant manager at a drug store told him a cashier's slot might open in a few weeks. Tommy found nothing immediately available, not even jobs at the food stalls.

"I might try to reverse it," he said to Elena. She met him at a coffee shop in town after he finished his guard shift. "See if I can switch to mornings and get something else afternoons."

"One good full-time job would get you out of this."

"Can't seem to get one. What do I do about my dad?"

"Tell him the truth. It's not your fault they went out of business."

He sighed, unguarded with her.

"All I wanted was to be on my own."

Rob was coming from Boston and drove to the mall on the succeeding Friday night at six to meet Tommy when he finished work. They were then going to dinner and Rob would make a late drive back to the city. Tommy waited inside the doors in his winter jacket, jeans, and boots. Rob caught sight of him before Tommy saw his father. A man and a woman in their thirties wearing maintenance worker's jumpsuits were leaving the building and cordially greeted Tommy as they passed, and he responded with a smile. To his father he was so radiant, Rob squinted as though he were looking into the sun.

Tommy suggested they go to Arturo's, the Italian restaurant where they had been before. Rob asked how Tommy was living, what did he eat, where did he eat, was his place warm enough, did he need clothing, did he have enough for spending money on dates with his girlfriend, how was that going? Tommy handled those questions without difficulty.

"Tell me where you think these jobs of yours are leading?" Rob was attempting to position himself on the subject of the distributorship. "A guard, a cashier, that's not altogether consistent, you've got to admit."

"Actually, I'm not doing the cashier thing anymore. They went out of business."

"What's that?"

"They folded. I'm looking for something else. I hoped I could find something before you came up," he said dryly.

"To put a good face on it?"

"Yes. But jobs turn up."

"Tommy, I'm thinking of a new business, distributing garden furniture for Sam Atkins."

"He does garden furniture?"

"It's going to be a side business and he wants me to be his distributor. I'm not going to do it instead of MayPole. It would be a different company and you could be a part of it, in on the beginning. We can figure out what kind of job."

"Dad—"

"I know you're not interested in working for me, but you'd only be in a bookkeeping sense. It wouldn't physically be in my office. I'm going to hire people and it'd be separate in a separate location, if I go ahead with it."

"I don't want to be in New York, Dad. Why doesn't anybody listen to what I'm saying?"

"I'm listening, Tommy. I just don't want to hear you."

"I'm sorry. Please don't keep asking things where I have to say no."

"All right. I haven't even decided about it. Might've been an incentive if you were interested. So—I see there's a minor league baseball team up here. Maybe some time when I come up we can go."

"Sure."

"You used to be a good Mets fan."

"I lost interest. But I'll go to a game, Dad. It'll be nice."

They descended into small talk, both of them seeking refuge.

Driving home along the northern reaches of the Thruway, Rob called Karen and told her about his visit, and Tommy losing another job.

"Selfish of me. It's a 'why should I bear this alone' kind of thing."

"I don't blame you. I'd tell *you*. An interesting job offer you made."

"So was Seth's."

"He'll find something else."

"I suppose. He's become like a migrant worker."

Rob told Vickie when he returned home that Tommy was going to careen from job to job like a ball in a pinball machine. She thought Tommy would find another part-time job and then eventually a full-time job and, when he developed skills, he could arrive at a degree of job stability. The person she saw in a major crisis was Rob.

"When are you going to decide about Atkins?"

"I have to get an appraisal of the market, the competition, figure out costs of distribution, expenses for a distributorship. It'll take a little more time."

"What's the goal, to ship three pieces a month or three thousand?"

"I'd say on the lower end. Or maybe not if it builds."

"You've got decisions to make."

"I'm well aware of your ultimatum, darling."

"I'm glad you are, darling."

Bill was on a tour of programs his foundation funded, which included a sweep through New England. If he couldn't arrange his calendar to accompany Karen on her recent trip she doubted he was going to visit Tommy by himself. He never brought up the possibility and she didn't promote it. She was tired of administering little tests about Tommy that Bill failed, annoyed with herself for testing him and disappointed in him for failing. After another two-week lull of not seeing each other, they met on a Friday night after she finished work. He planned the type of evening he regarded as the essence of their relationship. They went to a performance of the musical *Cabaret*, then on to supper at Trattoria Dell'Arte, cold antipasto with white wine, a tasteful, sophisticated evening. Wanting to be at his best, Bill was wearing new clothing, a pinstriped gray suit and mauve shirt from Barney's, a gray silk Armani tie, light brown shoes from Paul Stuart. She wore a black suit and white blouse from Che, a SoHo boutique, Karen marking their first night out in a while by upgrading from the strictly comfortable clothing she usually wore to the store. For Bill, this was who they were, stylish New Yorkers. In the restaurant she listened to his opinions of the differences between stage musicals and the movie versions. *Oklahoma!* surprisingly good, *Cabaret*, very good, *A Chorus Line*, disappointingly bad. She thought of Noel Coward's lines from *Private Lives*—"Very big, China." "Very small, Japan,"—but kept it to herself. Bill seemed to be on top of his game, a handsome, verbal man, and they could go on like this forever, talking forever, in a relationship forever, so long as the plays and the references to the plays lasted.

The waiter cleared their dishes and they ordered coffee, Bill smoothly shifting the conversation to the store, performing his role of the well-rounded man with business intelligence.

"What seems to be at a stalemate is Tommy," she said and with the mention of the name Bill became tense. Was she going to do the boy now? Were "The Further Adventures of Tommy Burrows" going to ruin the evening?

"He wasn't willing to take anything from me when I went up to see him. Seems overindependent to me. By the way, Joe went to keep me company."

"I would've gone, hon, but I told you, I couldn't clear my calendar."

"Any particular reason you didn't ask about the trip?"

"I assumed we would have gotten to it."

"I made a suggestion to Tommy, that he think about being a teacher. He brushed it aside. Said he's not interested in college."

"There are other things he can do for children without a degree."

"He said he looked. Nothing was available."

Bill was extremely unhappy with the turn the conversation had taken. They were descending from New York sophistication into what he considered the banal travails of an unexceptional teenager.

"He's still a guard, but he lost his other part-time job. This newsstand, or whatever it was, went out of business."

"Does he have money?"

"Some. Who knows how long he'll last up there on one part-time job."

"You don't want him to last up there."

"No, but I want him to be as comfortable as he can while he's there."

He didn't sign on for this. The beautiful woman on his arm as they glided into rooms, a woman who was creative, prestigious, evenings at the theater, concerts, dining in good restaurants, being well-dressed, engaging in intelligent conversation, that's what he signed on for. She wasn't his wife, nobody could be his wife for him. She was as elegant a substitute as he had been able to find. But Bill had enough of hearing about this boy. These labored discussions of his problems weren't leading anywhere. And they would go on interminably because her son was strictly mediocre by his standards and he had enough.

"Karen, I think you should prepare yourself for the possibility this is going to be his life, in and out of routine jobs, you worrying about him and his disappointing you."

"How's that?"

"You have to get on top of it, make peace with it. This is who he is. The only solution for your own well-being is to modify your expectations."

"Is that so?"

"He's a guard in a mall. All right. He does honest work. He also volunteers. He's obviously a fine person. You can't keep beating yourself up over who he's not. He's average, no more than that. I would imagine it's difficult for a parent to accept. But not accepting it causes pain. And you obsess."

"Obsess?"

"Looking for more out of him. It's not going to happen."

"I didn't realize adolescent psychology was your specialty. He got into several colleges. He passed all his courses his first semester."

"I've seen what he is and what he's not. He is not a particularly unusual person, as much as you'd like to think so. A fine person, not unusual. Let it go at that. Because it's beginning to affect our relationship."

"Oh."

"He's like a weight. Let go. Let him be. He's finding his place and it's not going to be what you hoped for. So let's all live with it."

"For his high school paper he wrote a cartoon line, 'You think I can list my SAT tutoring as community service? My tutor is, like, poor.' "

"And?"

"It's witty. It's self-aware."

"You're his mother. You see something there. It goes to my argument. It's just a joke line."

"But he made it up. He observed the world he was in and he thought of it."

"Karen, you're grasping at straws."

"You really have very little affection for him."

"I always respected him. But I don't see an exceptional boy there, I have to say. And the expectation that he's out of the ordinary has serious implications for us, how we spend our time together, what we talk about."

"I'd rather believe he's special and hasn't found himself, than accept he's not."

"A loving sentiment. It's unrealistic, which is my point."

"I hear your point. Too bad you feel he's a weight on our relationship. Too bad my expectations have serious implications for how we spend our time together and what we talk about. Wouldn't want anything unpleasant to interfere with your social life."

"Karen, you take a risk when you're honest. I assumed I could do that with you."

"You can. You did. Now I'll be honest with you. I don't want to see you anymore. I'll put it in the simplest terms. Love me, love my son. Even love me, like my son. But it can't be love me, dismiss my son. Good-bye, Bill. Thank you for everything. Truly."

He didn't come up with a last, saving remark. He went too far on the boy, he knew that, still it was how he felt. She could deceive herself, he didn't have to sit still for it anymore. Her son was second-rate.

Karen soaked in a bubble bath. She thought Bill was a decent man, often helpful, good, literate company until he was not—and wrong about Tommy. She wondered how Rob managed to get married and stay married, unaware of the trouble there. The shock waves of Tommy's decision to be on his own had affected both his parents' relationships. Karen and Rob attempted to rewrite a failed marriage with a successful divorce so their son could move gracefully and unharmed into his future. Neither of them were prepared to accept that his difficulties might have begun the day they told him, "We can't stay married. We tried."

FOURTEEN

• • •

The circular, accusatory quality of deteriorating marriages—people believing *I'm* the injured party, no, *I'm* the injured party for you thinking *you're* the injured party—dominated the household even while ordinary transactions occurred, children going to school, put to bed, adults going to work, returning from work, seemingly normal routines except for the absence of sex and the brooding silences in the time before and after sleep.

Rob worked on the business plan for Atkins while conducting his normal work activities, not coming home until close to eleven each night and going into the office on weekends. He was angry with Vickie's ultimatum, angry that she would say it, angry that she didn't understand Atkins was crucial to his business, that he was obligated to help him even if it didn't lead to an eventual business arrangement. She was angry at his unwillingness to value his marriage and his home life, or what could be his home life, for allowing it to be at risk because of his business life. She didn't suspect he was with another woman, the one good thing about his work hours. She believed he was a man who wouldn't have the time or the attentiveness.

In a mingling of nostalgia and sexual fantasy Rob found himself remembering Claudia Wright, with whom he had a relationship for four months, the last serious girlfriend before Karen. Petite with long black hair and dark eyes, she worked as an art director for Columbia Records. Claudia spoke rapidly, moved rapidly, always on the verge of frantic. She was said to have had an affair with Miles Davis and for a time whenever Rob heard one of his plaintive solos he wondered if Miles had been able to get her to come to a rest. Rob had not. She disappeared from New York without a word in the midst of the relationship. He was told by someone in her office that she had gone to the west coast. He tried calling; her number was unlisted. After he was married to Karen for a year he received a note from her, "Belatedly, sorry I had to split. I liked you. Am working in an ad agency here in San Fran, living with a guy, a photographer. Am pretty happy—for me. Love." What came back to him most vividly about Claudia was something she once told him. She asked if he ever considered suicide and he said no. Claudia said she had and the interesting thing about it was how everything took on equal weight, that you were in such disarray you didn't know whether to buy the container of milk you needed, or stick your head in the oven. In her case, she bought the milk. But it could have gone the other way.

He worked in the office on a Saturday dealing with the Atkins proposal and came home a few minutes before the boys went to bed. He said good night to them and went into the living room to continue working on his laptop in the living room. By the time he went into the bedroom it was eleven fifteen. Vickie, with whom he had not spoken more than a few words since he came home, was asleep. He slipped into bed. He wondered, even if he passed on Gardenshire, whether they could recover. It was then he thought of Claudia. Not only with the contemplation of suicide did everything take on equal weight. He was balanced squarely in the middle of letting the marriage end and going on.

Karen wanted a formal recognition for herself that the Bill period was over and spoke to Polly with Joe on an extension to say she wanted to go on a "date." "God help me for using the word, but I'm ready to sit opposite a man and he'll be thinking how long it'll take to make me and if I'm lucky I'll be thinking the same thing about him and I'll be back in the whole awful game again. Meaning, in my head it will be completely and officially done with Bill."

"I've got the guy," Joe said. "Just met him. Democratic fundraiser from Stamford. Comes into the city. About fifty. Divorced. Not the greatest-looking guy, but really bright."

She was at the bar of the Mercer Hotel with Joe's discovery, Ted Coleman. He had an extremely narrow face and nose and as he droned on about Democratic Party politics she thought he was a person built for physically burrowing into things. She imagined him going under fences or digging in backyards for bones. Not good images for a first date. As Joe said, he was bright. Joe happened to leave out that he was excruciatingly boring. I bet people donate money for the Democrats just to get him to stop speaking. I'm prepared to donate money myself. They each had a glass of wine, he pushed the idea of continuing with dinner, but she felt it was done. I'm back in circulation—with a faint heartbeat.

She walked several blocks and wandered toward Chinatown, slipping into a small six-table restaurant. She ordered a fish soup, which she thought was delicious. With Bill gone she could count on dining alone for most meals unless and until someone else appeared. She was certain being alone was a better state than being with the Ted Colemans out there. She amused herself to think this could become her place. She was the only Caucasian of five customers. She could come in once or twice a week and they would get to know her. She would begin to order off the menu. They would make special dishes for her the Caucasians never get to eat. No one would bother her. She would have a zone of privacy after the tension of being in the store, her place where she could sit anonymously. The windows were steamy and covered with menus so she couldn't be seen from the street. She needn't feel awkward about eating alone and reading a book or a newspaper over dinner, but no eels, she wasn't going to eat anything with eels.

Polly told Karen to come by for dinner any time or they would go out any night, weekday or weekend. She and Joe would also do a search, see who was available, have a dinner party or parties, the population didn't end with Ted Coleman or with Bill. She went to dinner at their apartment for Polly's reliable meat loaf and a good bottle of red wine Joe received as a gift, too good for the cuisine, but he didn't care, it was his celebration of no more Bill. Polly suggested this could be an interesting period for Karen. She had been unavailable for a couple of years. Here was a chance for her to act on any fantasies she may have had. Karen told them Moses Clark was the most interesting man she knew, an African-American from Greensboro, North Carolina, who was seventy-two years old, a carver of duck decoys, as well as a stride piano player, who sent her a CD he recorded for an off-brand label.

There was another possibility. She began to think of Peter Briggins on and off over the next few days, imagining the contours of a possible relationship. If he happened to have lived in New York she would give them about ten weeks, an affair with a slightly different cultural tone than with Bill, a couple of book parties, possibly a reading or two of authors at the 92nd Street Y, theater tipped more to off-Broadway than Broadway, the possibility of what *Cosmopolitan* magazine used to refer to in their advertising as "cliffhanging sex," whatever that was, and then he would break it off for a former student from Lafayette whom he would not see when she was there because of the ethics involved, but since she had transferred to NYU it was only the ethics of sleeping with *a* student as opposed to *his* student. That was if he lived in New York, but if he were still at Lafayette she would give them a bonus of six or seven weeks more for the infrequence of their contacts and then he would break it off for a former student who transferred to NYU.

She called Peter Briggins at Lafayette on the premise it surely was doomed, but it wouldn't be dull, unless he turned out to be more self-involved than he seemed to be. On the other hand, if being self-involved was a disqualification, Karen presumed she would have difficulty ever again making a social engagement with a male. The operator said Peter Briggins was no longer connected with the college and transferred her to a woman who told Karen he was at Vassar. He was even closer to New York at Vassar. She left a message on a machine with her cell phone number. She was in her office the next day when he returned the call.

"Nice of you to call back."

"How are you, Karen?"

"I'm well."

"And the store?"

"The store is good. So you're at Vassar now?"

"Teaching a course. I obviously enjoy teaching. And I'm living here. Working on a book."

"What is it?"

"A collection of short fiction, pieces that have some relationship to each other."

"And the relationship is?"

"Sounds pretentious, but it's survival."

"Sounds excellent."

"Let's hope. How is your son doing?"

"Thanks for asking. He left Marlowe after a semester. He's working in Pittsfield now. Odd jobs. I don't know what his plans are."

"Odd jobs—that's okay. I like odd jobs. Learn the value of work. More of these kids should do it after high school."

"He's testing your premise."

"Working isn't going to hurt him. He was clever, as I recall. I wouldn't worry about him."

She barely knew this man and she felt in one minute he was more encouraging about Tommy than Bill had ever been.

"Why I called, Peter—when we first met I was in a relationship and at the risk of sounding like something out of a magazine article, what the modern woman should do, I wanted to let you know I'm not in that relationship any longer, so if you ever get down to New York maybe we could have a drink or lunch."

"You're fabulous, that business of yours, and not meaning to sound crude, all that and to *look* like you. But I'm remarried."

"Oh." Her voice dropped slightly. She recovered. "Congratulations."

"Really remarried. I remarried my ex-wife."

"Did you?"

"After five years we both realized we made a mistake."

"And you can do that?" she said lightly.

"Attempting to. She teaches here. A Shakespeare scholar. Reflected glory. She makes me seem deeper than I am."

"I don't think I knew, do you have children?"

"No. We're talking about it, though."

"Good for you. Peter, I wish you the very best. I'll be looking for the book."

"I'll send one to you. Good luck, Karen."

She remained at her desk absorbed with the phone call. How can you admit a mistake of such proportion and act on it, say you were wrong, set aside your pride, ignore the blame and the acrimony? Surely that must be the bond, if you can do that, say you were wrong together, if you can be that courageous together, then it binds you and you can be together again. The marriage to Rob was untenable. They both knew it at the time. They came to the decision to end it nearly simultaneously, it seemed. Six years later she couldn't see the jagged edges of the marriage as clearly. She wondered if they, too, made a mistake, if their life without each other was so demonstrably better than their life had been together, if the upset for Tommy was necessary, if he would have dropped out of college had they stayed together. Was this the magic? They remarry and Tommy is transformed into a young man with a glowing future. But Rob was married. And Karen, unable to deal with the possibility that the difficulties of these past years was the result of a mistake, settled back into accepting that the true mistake would have been to continue with the marriage.

Vickie's problems with Rob exposed her isolation. She was the classic working mother arranging her work hours to be with her children as often as possible and gave up income, sheer billable hours, so she could be home for their dinners and bedtimes. The rotating teenage sitters who filled in for her were just that, teenage sitters. The two lawyers who were partners in the real estate law office where she rented office space were married men in their fifties who lived in Westchester and played golf and sometimes wore ties with golf symbols on them. She didn't view them as confidants. The three secretaries in the office were single girls in their twenties with active social lives and Vickie chatted with them casually about movies and dating. She talked briefly to her parents in Cleveland a couple of times a week. They mainly wanted to hear about the latest triumphs of the children and also liked to discuss Tim when an item about him appeared in print or on one of the television entertainment shows. Her friend Dori and her husband, Jim, moved to the west coast, where he took a job with the *Los Angeles Times*. A woman lawyer who was also a mother worked in another office on her floor. In the ladies room or waiting for an elevator they sometimes compared notes about managing their schedules and occasionally they had lunch together. The woman moved to Houston. Vickie and Rob saw Seth and Carlotta. Vickie considered them Rob's people. She had gone to college and law school in Evanston, Illinois. None of the people she knew at school came to New York, except for Tim. She was essentially without close friends.

Vickie went to see a therapist whose name was mentioned favorably in an article in the *New Yorker* magazine. Helena Matthews was a distinguished-looking woman in her fifties who advised Vickie that she didn't have to draw a line in the sand with Rob. She was a lawyer, she could negotiate. After two sessions at $175 per session, Vickie already disliked the sound of her own voice in the room and thought the process was going to be long and expensive. And she didn't agree with the therapist. If she didn't challenge Rob about taking on a new business they would go on for years with Rob, disengaged, making limited appearances at home, and she would be in therapy the entire time.

She confided in Tim. He was in New York briefly on a press junket. He came to the apartment with a set of racing cars that rode on tracks. The boys were happy to have him for whatever amount of time he was there and he took them out for hamburgers. When they returned, Vickie asked if he could have a drink with her. She called one of the sitters and she and Tim went to a nearby bar.

"Tim, my marriage is not in good shape."

"I thought you guys were okay. He's a regular guy. Wasn't that the idea?"

"He works long hours, travels, and now he's thinking of taking on another business. Some of it is so obvious psychologically. His son is having a hard time getting himself centered and Rob is looking to lose himself in work."

"Vickie, men work. It's what we're supposed to do."

"Except he doesn't leave much over. And he doesn't relate that well to the boys. I told all this to a shrink. Basically, she said I should wait it out and I suppose if I wait long enough he'll retire and the boys will be in their thirties and it won't be a problem anymore."

"Is he mean to them?"

"No, no, no, nothing like that. More like a car radio that loses its signal."

"Sounds like me."

"They love you."

"I should see them more."

"That would be good. That would be *really* good if my marriage breaks up. It shouldn't just be their mother and sitters."

"I'm going to Toronto on a movie. In three months I'll be done. Instead of going right back to L.A. I can hang out here for a few weeks, spend some more time with them."

"And in general, Tim. Having Santa Claus as a daddy is great—"

"I know."

"Divorce is not nothing for children."

"Are you picking up something?"

"I don't see anything so far. But kids react in different ways. Rob's son, it was like a time bomb ticking."

"Drugs?"

"Not as far as we know. Might be he just got worn down from the divorce."

"I'm going to do this. I'm going to stay in New York a while. But calmer. The Santa Claus thing. Every time doesn't have to be Christmas, right?"

"Calmer would be nice."

"With your husband, how bad is it?"

"I did something, Tim. I said if he goes into the new business I'd leave him. I thought it was the only thing to do. Now I'm not so sure. I saw a shrink. She said I could withdraw the ultimatum."

"You could."

"It wouldn't eliminate the problem. If he goes into this business it'd be terrible."

A round-faced woman in her forties materialized next to them.

"Mr. Grove, I'm a great admirer. Could I have an autograph please?" She produced a paper napkin and a pen. "It's for my daughter. Could you make it out to Megan?"

He signed the autograph and with a nod handed the napkin and pen back to her. As the woman walked away she said, "Thank you very much. I've seen all your movies."

"So have I," Vickie said.

"I'll give you my autograph. I'll give you a blank check."

"Just show up, pal."

Rob came home after eleven and it promised to be another cold interlude between two people who were barely speaking and who were keeping out of each other's way until they got to sleep. Rob was at his laptop again in the living room. Vickie waited in the bedroom for him to enter.

"How is it going?" she asked when he entered the bedroom.

"Taking a little longer than I planned. Another week or so."

"Rob, make whatever decision you have to about this business. Make a business decision. That's what it should be."

"I've said that all along."

"Maybe you won't take it on, and if you don't, you're still going to have to pay attention to your family, and if do, you're still going to have to pay attention to your family. But an ultimatum, you shouldn't have to deal with that."

"I'm glad to hear it. I didn't see any 'linkage,' as they say in foreign policy. Okay. I suppose it wouldn't do any good if I told you I know if I took it on there'd be ramifications and I'd have to be really conscious of how it affects us."

"Just decide what you have to. I'm not part of it."

"A little while longer."

The conversation didn't get them to a reconciliation. They didn't make love. By the time he was ready for bed she was already sleeping and he allowed her to sleep.

Once a week Vickie called Tommy at home. She didn't tell Rob, no reports back, merely a chat with Tommy so he could know she cared about him outside parental judgment. Intentionally, she veered away from the questions his parents were likely to ask about his job prospects and his plans. She staked out nonthreatening areas—where he had been recently with Elena, movies they had seen, general conversation. Tommy always stayed in the designated safe zone with her. This time it was he who brought up the subject of work, obviously uneasy about it. He found the second job he needed for his expenses and worked for a couple of weeks as a cashier in a drug store, but was let go. Evidently, they needed to fill a slot temporarily while someone was out sick and led him to believe the job was to be more permanent.

"I'm not even going to tell my parents. It'll confirm all my father's worst prejudices."

"It's a process. You'll find something else and then a full-time job you like. I'm betting on you."

"Thanks, Vickie. My dad, is he betting on me?"

"I want to tell you something and you have to know it's true. Your dad loves you *so* much."

"I must be a major disappointment to him."

"It's too early for you to be a disappointment to anyone, Tommy. It's a process."

She could feel how he was struggling in his quest to live on his own terms. If the marriage ended would she become his *ex*-stepmother? What would she be to this boy she considered so admirable?

"I appreciate the call. Keep calling, okay, Vickie?"

"I always will."

One of the guards who worked Mondays asked Tommy to swap days with him so he could go to his daughter's birthday party, and as a result Tommy had a Sunday free. He sent e-mails to Jill and Brian. They were going to meet at Brian's dorm and walk over to the Charles River and eat lunch along the river. He took a morning bus from Pittsfield and the MTA to Harvard Square. Jill was sitting on the steps of the dorm when Tommy arrived. She was waiting for Brian to come down. They hugged each other and she stepped back in a mock appraisal.

"You look great," she said.

"Doing some jogging. Trying to eat all right. *You* look good."

"I gained six and a half pounds. I'm like a cliché freshman."

"Six and *a half* pounds? Did you just weigh yourself?"

"This was almost the debut of the very Debby Simmons, Brian's girlfriend. Got to say that again to hear how it sounds, Brian's girlfriend."

"He never said anything to me."

"Sort of just became official."

"What's she like?"

"I only met her once. Seems funny. Bright. A photographer on the paper. A total roly-poly. Roly-poly face, roly-poly body, roly-poly hair. But I think she's one of the most beautiful girls in the world because she likes Brian."

Brian appeared in his dumpy splendor, a knit cap askew, his shirttail sticking out of his windbreaker, a perfectly acceptable look on a campus, but for it being one shirttail in and one shirttail out in a Brian touch. He gave Tommy a bear hug.

"Hey, man."

"Brian. A girlfriend?"

"Wanted you to meet her, but she had to cover something. You're here! How great is this?"

They bought sandwiches, strolled along the river, and found a spot. Brian was having a typical time with his mother and stepfather, his mother sometimes taking several days to return his phone calls, which he thought might be worthy of the Guinness Book of Parental Records. He invited his father in Chicago to visit just so he could see Brian at college. He was figuring on giving him lead time and if his father was ever in Boston and if he ever had an hour to spare Brian thought perhaps by his senior year his father might make it there. Debby was going to dominate the highlight film of his freshman year. Jill thought the classes were good, she didn't give very good grades to herself. She had run through two guys already and was feeling she was getting fat and easy. Her father was talking to her about working in his office for the summer and beginning to learn the business so she could go into it when she was finished with college. This led them into a discussion of the upcoming summer. Jill wanted to stay in Boston and work in the Tufts admissions office. She didn't want to be programmed by her father into her future so soon and didn't want to be in New York and deal with her mother's increasing complaints about her own love life. Jill wanted to lose the six and a half pounds, not be easy with any more guys, be productive, in that order, and not be mediocre. It was her greatest fear, that she was on track to being mediocre. Tommy jumped all over that. "If you're worried about being mediocre," he said, "worrying about mediocre isn't mediocre and you can't be mediocre."

They had come to Tommy. His summer was going to be spent in Pittsfield, hopefully with two viable part-time jobs or one good full-time job. Brian came prepared for Tommy with an index card he took out of his pocket.

"I get your wanting to be free of that whole living-with-divorce thing. But here's what you should think about. You can still go your own way and still finish college. If you establish residential status in Massachusetts for one year," and he referred to the index card, "twelve consecutive months, which means you have an address, pay bills, get mail, vote, etcetera, you qualify for in-state admission into the UMass system. That's UMass Amherst, UMass Lowell, UMass Dartmouth, UMass Boston, or UMass Worcester—"

"Brian—"

"This is my speech. I planned it out. Tuition is about five thousand a year. Room and board is another five thousand. You'll get in for sure and they'll take your credits from Marlowe so you've only got another three and a half years."

"You're like my parents. I'm done with college."

"You can be done with college after college. Then you can be a guard. Maybe they'll make you captain of the guards. By doing it this way, you're still making it on your own terms without your parents. You would've earned your status legitimately. Working and paying taxes in the Commonwealth of Massachusetts. And with a college degree you're reducing the chances of banging around. Ten thousand a year. You can get a student loan. And this is important. You ready for this?"

"No, but go on."

"I'm a fucking rich kid. That's what I am. If you need money to do it, I'll give you the money. You can pay me back someday or not. Who cares?"

"I can't take money from you, Brian."

"Sure you can."

"No. I can't. And it defeats the purpose."

"Get a different purpose."

"A friend of my mother offered me a car. But this is unbelievable. Why?"

"You, me, Jill, we've all been through our parents' 'marital arrangements.' Why the hell should *you* cripple yourself to get free of all that? Why, he asks me? Because you're my golden boy," he said, his voice breaking.

They were sitting on the grass and Tommy leaned forward and pressed his forehead against Brian's, Tommy's arms around Brian's shoulders.

"I can't take your money."

Jill slid over and put her head next to theirs and they huddled together, Tommy holding Brian, Jill holding both of them.

For her first one-artist show Karen chose Moses Clark and his elegantly carved waterfowl decoys. She also liked the idea of his stride piano CD playing in the store and she ordered a quantity for sale. The windows were decorated with a selection of his pieces and others were placed in the store on mounts to give them importance. An Avedon-like blowup of the artist, taken by his son, a photographer, dominated one wall—Moses Clark's noble, wrinkled face. Karen wrote an accompanying wall text that she mounted near the blowup. The compelling image of Moses Clark became the focus for publicity and it appeared in *The New York Times* along with a photograph of one of his pieces. At the opening on a Friday night the store was crowded with people. Fred, her accountant, came, as did Polly and Joe, who made purchases over her protests that they didn't have to support her that way. Karen noticed a man handling a decoy of a pintail drake, examining it closely. He talked to John, who shook hands with him looking pleased, an apparent sale. She made her way toward the man. He was in his mid fifties, five feet seven, stocky with a prominent Adam's apple and long brown hair with a cowlick, a man in serious need of a haircut, but the way he was looking at the decoy, obviously someone with other preoccupations.

"Like the piece?" she said.

"He just bought it," John said, taking the man's credit card to the cash register.

"It's lovely. They're all lovely. Reminds me of the work of Elmer Crowell."

"I'm Karen Burrows. This is my place. You're a collector?"

"A dealer. Jeff Wells. I have American Pleasures. I do shows."

"So you're going to resell it and I underpriced it?" she said lightly.

His expression was very serious.

"It's for me. It's very good. How did you find him?"

"On a sweep through the South some years ago."

"It's a wonderful presentation. The store, it's a gallery really. Wonderful. You know, a Crowell went for eight hundred thousand dollars at Christie's recently?"

"Then if Moses reminds you of Crowell you got a real buy."

"Uh—I'm not too good at this, but with what I'm saving on my purchase . . . you think I might take you to dinner?"

A man with taste who knew the price of a decoy at a recent Christie's auction—he definitely seemed an improvement over Ted Coleman.

"And when did you have in mind?"

"See, I'm *not* too good at it. Tonight. After you close. Tomorrow. Whenever."

"Why don't you meet me here in an hour and a half."

"My lucky night."

He suggested they go to Il Cortile in Little Italy. Karen nearly sold out the show in these first few hours and she was in a mood to take her customer out for dinner, but he declined when she offered. She inquired about his background in the field. He had an art history degree from Pratt, worked at Sotheby's and then for the American Folk Art Museum before going over to the retail side ten years earlier. He said he was a widower, skipping rapidly past it. He lived on Riverside Drive and 116th Street with two teenage children, a girl of fifteen and a boy of sixteen, both at Hunter College High School. She told him about her journey from anthropology to retail with a mention in passing about Rob. She described Tommy as living independently. They exchanged shop talk. Gradually he became animated, engaged, as the conversation went from the business of the business to the aesthetics. Because of his sensibility, this average-looking man was beginning to seem better looking to her as time went on and she repressed a smile over this. His Chevrolet station wagon was parked near the store and he offered to drive her uptown.

He double-parked outside Karen's building on Lexington Avenue and turned to her with a look of sadness.

"I shouldn't have done this."

"I beg your pardon."

"When I saw you, you were so pretty and the store is so beautiful and your taste . . ."

"What is it?"

"Five months ago my wife stepped off a curb on Park Avenue and was killed by a drunk driver running a light."

"I'm so sorry."

"It's too soon. I tried tonight. You're so—"

"Shhh."

She put her hands over his lips.

"It's too soon," he said, his shoulders slumped as if he had become exhausted.

"Thank you for dinner. Enjoy Moses' piece. You're a lovely man."

She retrieved a message from Polly who wanted to know how the opening went. Karen told her about its success and the aftermath.

"The poor guy. He was battling it. I figured the evening went great. How stupid am I?"

"If that's how he is in grief, he must be pretty nice. Karen, I do not envy you. This is hard."

"I'd settle for hard. It's impossible."

At four in the afternoon Tommy was in the middle of a typical uneventful shift at the mall. He saw Elena and her mother coming toward him. Elena was running, her mother trailing behind. Elena leaped onto Tommy and he grabbed her legs to hold her and she smothered him with kisses.

"Tommy, I got into Brown! They gave me everything! A full scholarship! Full tuition. Room and board! Everything!"

He kissed her lips and let her slide down.

"I am so happy for you."

"You did it! You and Brian and Jill. You did it!"

"Don't you think you had something to do with it?"

"I'll have to work in one of the offices, but they said it shouldn't be a problem to handle it. You did it, Tommy. Tommy!"

By now, her mother reached them. She was carrying a gift box.

"I don't know how to thank you enough," she said.

"Congratulations, Mrs. Garrity."

"If you didn't help her—"

"It's debatable how much we helped."

"I know what you did, you and your friends."

"I don't think we did any harm. It's what we know."

"We wanted to tell you in person. And my mom wanted you to have this."

"Please, Mrs. Garrity."

"I want you to take it. And I want to get something for your friends."

"They don't need anything."

"Open it, Tommy," Elena said.

He opened the box and it was a white Ralph Lauren cotton cable knit sweater.

"I can't accept this."

"I want you to have it."

"Mrs. Garrity!"

"Don't insult me. You think your friends would like something similar?"

"Don't spend any more money. My friends don't need anything. They'll be happy just to know, believe me." He turned to Elena. "Brian predicted it. Where else did you get in?"

"Everywhere. But I'm going to Brown, Tommy." And she said it again as if to make it real for herself. "Brown!"

The reversal in their status, that he was now somebody from town and she would be going to an Ivy League school, did not concern him. His girlfriend had what she wanted and he was happy for her.

"If you come to the restaurant tonight after work," Mrs. Garrity said, "like at seven, we're having a celebration dinner. It's on my boss."

"I'd be happy to. The sweater, really—"

"You'll look nice in it," Mrs. Garrity said. She straightened his tie with affection. "Not many security guards in Pittsfield who can help someone get a scholarship to Brown, Mr. T. Burrows."

In William Steig's children's picture book, *Amos & Boris*, Amos, the mouse, saves the life of his old friend, Boris, the whale. In Vickie and Rob Burrows's marriage, Amos and Boris collaborated on saving it from possibly coming to an end.

Rob was still not finished with the report for Atkins. On this particular night he was home first. Vickie was working late at a meeting with a client.

The boys were at the dining room table with one of the teenage sitters Vickie engaged, Jody, an ebullient girl of fifteen. They were playing with the racing track and cars given them by Tim. Rob said hello and the boys said their hellos, barely looking up, watching the cars. The girl, whom he had seen before, gave him a broad smile and he was aware of how completely insulated he was from these children. Vickie covered the bases, a cheerful sitter, the boys taken care of, he could or could not show up, early or late, and it wouldn't have mattered to anyone. As Rob observed, the younger boy, Tod, the eight-year-old, appeared to have a vacant look on his face.

"Something wrong?" Rob said to him.

"I'm sad."

"Why?"

"My daddy is away for three months."

A child unhappy because his father was away, a scene playing out in front of him in his apartment where he was not a participant and not even expected to be—it was never more apparent to him how he was barely a presence here. Rob went into their room and checked through their books. He didn't find what he was looking for and announced he would be back in a while. He went to a bookstore and found a paperback edition of *Amos & Boris* and bought it. They were done with the racing track and cars and were in their room watching a cartoon on television. He stood in the doorway watching with them and when it was over he said, "I have a book I'd like to read to you. It was a favorite of Tommy's."

Tommy was a key word. They became alert at the mention of his name.

"When will we see Tommy?" Tod asked.

"He's not in New York now, but I'm sure when he comes in."

"He's in Pittsfield, Massachusetts," Keith said. "Mommy told us. He lives there."

"Yes, that's where he lives. Well, this was a book he liked."

"Shall I read it to them, Mr. Burrows?" Jody asked.

I'm not expected to do *anything*, am I?

"No, I will. You can go, actually, Jody. We'll be fine here."

"Their baths?"

"I'll take care of it."

She said good night to the boys and left. Rob suggested they take their baths first and then he would read to them. They had their order established, Tod, then Keith. They came into the living room in their pajamas and sat on either side of Rob on the sofa. It didn't matter to them if they were getting too old for picture books. They were intrigued, he had a book Tommy liked. From the opening lines and the distinctive rhythms of the language Rob was transported back to the times when Tommy in his pajamas curled close and Rob read this book to him. Tod and Keith were captivated by the story and the pictures. When Boris, the whale, lies dying, washed up on a beach, and Amos, the mouse, who was once saved at sea by Boris, rushes off to find help, an impossible task, and then in one of the great page-turns in all of children's picture books, returns with "two of the biggest elephants he could find" and they roll Boris back into the ocean, the boys' eyes widened with a joy Rob recognized.

After reading the book to them he went into the bedroom and tapped his head softly against the wall in self-reprimand. These children were an opportunity he was squandering. He couldn't deny his travel and his work hours, they were constant when Tommy was little, but he believed he was there when he was there. He thought he was a good father. He had to have been, there were too many memories of times spent with Tommy, sledding, snowmen, children's plays, movies, swimming, balls tossed, kites flown, books read, *Amos & Boris*.

He tucked the boys into their beds, leaned down and kissed each of them on the top of their heads.

Rob was in the living room, not working, thoughtful, when Vickie came home.

"Hi. The sitter still here?"

"I sent her home. I put the boys to bed."

"You did?"

"Vickie, I made my decision. I'm not doing the thing with Atkins. I'll give him the plan to work with, but I'm not taking it on."

"The numbers didn't add up?"

"Has nothing to do with the numbers. What cute boys you have," and he came toward her with contrition and held her in his arms.

FIFTEEN

• • •

By June, with spring finally driving out the New England winter, signs of renewal in nature failed to translate into a discernible change in Tommy's work life. He was still in search of the full-time job or the second part-time job to give him a measure of financial stability. While working afternoons in the mall he held various temporary morning jobs, distributing flyers for Radio Shack, conducting market research surveys in shopping centers, handing out free pens for a bank, all at hourly rates, as far down the economic scale as delivering newspapers, which he also tried, finding it insufficiently remunerative to continue. The guard position was the anchor to his work week. If he were to be promoted to a full-time slot he would be, by definition, a full-time guard. He heard nothing in the guards' locker room to suggest a change in status was in his near future, but he considered the consequence of accepting such a job if offered. He would have to do this work for a forty-hour week. Some guard's positions in other venues allowed for reading books while on duty, listening to a Walkman, watching a small television set. The nature of his job was to be alert to the area in his field of vision and he was not permitted personal electronic devices. Tommy was undeterred in his desire to stake out an independent path for himself. Six months into the attempt he was no longer confident that the little incentives he built into his schedule, the Italian lessons, the volunteer work at the library, the jogging, were sufficient to sustain him. He was increasingly worried about the sameness of his hours, the yawning quality of sitting and watching while in the service of people shopping and eating. He had little hope of being able to continue the relationship with Elena once she went to college. He was convinced the dullest guy at Brown or any college would be more interesting than he was now.

• • •

He and Elena went to see Françis Truffaut's *The 400 Blows* at a film series at Pittsfield Community College. Tommy was shattered by the ending of the movie. The stark, haunting image, the boy played by the young Jean-Pierre Lèaud, stopping at the sea with nowhere to turn, nowhere to run, was still powerful for the audience and perhaps no more so for anyone than it was for Tommy. He was so affected by it he couldn't speak when they left the auditorium.

"It's supposed to be one of the great movies," Elena said at the bus stop. "I can see why," trying to get a conversation going.

The bus that ran near her house approached.

"You go home. I'll talk to you," he said.

"I'm not going to leave you in this mood."

"I'm no good in this mood." He gently nudged her toward the bus.

"Tommy?"

"I have to be by myself. Please!" As she boarded the bus, he said, "That was me up on the screen."

Rob hired a salesman to relieve him with his work hours, Cal Meadows, who was his colleague when Rob first came to MayPole. Cal was forty-nine and had been working for a playground manufacturer in Houston where he moved with his partner, a NASA engineer. They were back north and Cal contacted Rob. He was prepared to take on some of Rob's travel responsibilities and Rob knew he would be a major asset to the company. It would mean a substantial personnel expense, but one that might pay for itself in terms of Rob's home life. He didn't indulge in self-recrimination as to why he never made a personnel move of this kind during his first marriage. He always believed it was a budget expense he couldn't afford in those years and that his personal involvement was critical on the road. He still believed it about his involvement. He was going to continue to call on Atkins and maintain his relationships with the local contractors. But he was now open to allowing Cal and Marty to assume more of the new business development.

He donated playground equipment for a refurbished playground on 114th Street near First Avenue in Manhattan. The refurbished stepfather brought his stepsons to the dedication ceremony, held on a Saturday morning. The donation, a large tree house with climbing equipment and slides, was made through the City Parks Foundation, which supplemented resources for the

New York City Department of Parks & Recreation. During the week he received two calls from someone at the foundation confirming his attendance at the ceremony. Parked outside the center were two television news vans and when they entered the area several photographers and television news people were standing around. A young woman with the foundation ushered Rob and the boys to a section where chairs were set up and others were already seated, including several Parks Department officials he recognized. He presumed this was going to be a dedication similar to many he had attended in the past. Approximately sixty children in the custody of adults squatted on the ground in the play area. The mayor of New York, Michael R. Bloomberg, suddenly arrived and Rob understood why the press people were present. The children recited "Trees" for the mayor. The commissioner of parks, Adrian Benepe, spoke about the public-private partnership for parks and playgrounds and surprised Rob by citing MayPole Manufacturing of Long Island City. He asked Rob to come forward and Rob took the boys with him. The commissioner introduced the mayor, who read from a plaque thanking MayPole Manufacturing and its president, Rob Burrows, for years of generous gifts of play to thousands of children of the city of New York. The boys were in awe. They knew who Mayor Bloomberg was, they had seen him on television, and here was the mayor talking about Rob, who was married to their mommy, whom they lived with in their apartment. Rob accepted the plaque and posed for the cameras with the mayor and the parks commissioner, the boys standing nearby. Asked to speak, he said it was his company who should be thanking the city for the opportunity to be of service. He turned to the children assembled and told them they were citizens of the city. As citizens, one day they would have the right to vote. As citizen-children they still had rights and one of those was the fundamental right to play and have fun, which appealed to them.

Rob, Vickie, and the boys watched the television coverage of the event that evening on New York One, the local cable news station. Vickie was proud of Rob and jubilant that he took the boys. He delayed going to sleep and sat in the living room sipping cognac, thinking about the irony, he had been acknowledged for contributing to the well-being of thousands of children of the city of New York and he couldn't do a damn thing about the well-being of his own son.

Karen rented a car at the airport and drove to Moses Clark's garden apartment in Greensboro, North Carolina. When she first met him twenty years earlier he lived in a shingled house with his wife, Nelle, and their teenage children, a boy and girl. The boy was Sam, the photographer who took the portrait of his father and who now worked for Duke University. Their daughter, Celia, an elementary school teacher, was married and living in Charleston. Moses, a former school custodian, and Nelle, a former post office worker, lived in a one-bedroom place on their retirement funds and the added income from his wood carving and his weekly appearance at a roadside restaurant where he played stride piano. They expected Karen for lunch and Sam was taking time off from work to be there. Moses in person was Moses in portrait, a man as elegant as his wood carving. Nelle was a woman in her seventies with a welcoming face, her hair speckled with gray, who kissed Karen on greeting her as if she were family. Sam, in his mid thirties, was a lanky, younger version of his father.

"You did your dad proud, Sam," Karen said and she showed them the press coverage featuring the photograph of his father.

Every piece was sold and a publisher expressed serious interest in a monograph on Moses. She planned to assemble the decoys to be photographed from a list of owners of previous pieces sold. She would write the text and wanted Sam to do the photography. Her question to Sam was whether he had an interest in doing the work and the resources available for studio photography. He was eager and suggested taking photographs of his father in the physical settings that inspired him and then Sam would come to New York and rent studio space to photograph the decoys, rather than ship the pieces South and back North again.

The lunch was celebratory. She gave Moses a check for five thousand dollars for a new group of carvings. As a matter of policy and principle Karen never took items from the artisans on consignment, they were always outright purchases. They followed Karen out to the car and she could see them in the rearview mirror still waving as she drove off.

Karen made a North Carolina loop which she had not traveled in several years, to a quiltmaking group in Winston-Salem, a pottery cooperative in Charlotte, and a whirligig maker in Asheboro, buying the crafts, arranging for shipment, and returning to New York from Greensboro. On the last stretch she stopped for lemonade at a produce stand north of Asheboro and looked out on an expanse of farmland. The morning was hot and she recalled other trips and other mornings when her clothes did not come from SoHo boutiques, but were simple cotton outfits, the time when she was a young girl who made a turn in the road. Leaning on a fence outside Asheboro, North Carolina, she was in touch with her original impulses. Crafts people like the ones she had seen on this trip were her motivation. She had fallen in love with them and with their work. If you couldn't find someone who understood the feeling, understood it inside you, it was all right to be alone. Part of her was comfortable with the concerts and the theaters and the talk about the arts Bill enjoyed so much and he was always excellent on the business side of her business. As to the uniqueness and the excellence of these people and their workmanship, he never really felt it. A person like Jeff Wells did. If only he weren't so wounded. She never could have married Bill if they ever got to considering marriage. He couldn't have made a trip like this and taken the pleasure from it that she did. Years ago, when she was first married, before Tommy was born, she stopped on this particular road with Rob. He had been to see Sam Atkins in Sumter, South Carolina, and Rob met her in Greensboro and made the loop with her. He loved the idea of their being on the road together and said it was too bad they couldn't do the same thing, work together, travel together. She was thrilled about finding the potters and he understood, he always had a feeling for the aesthetics and for the people who did the work. He always wanted to see which new things she found, which new people she discovered. She wondered if it were possible for a marriage to end in divorce and still for you to have married the right person. She answered it for herself. He was the right person at the time. Which meant he was the right person.

Tommy was developing a nervous tic out of boredom, tapping on the guard's desk with his right hand, and he became conscious of it. He knew he had to get out of the job. Brian was in a summer internship at the *Boston Globe*. Jill was working in admissions at Tufts. Elena was working at the Pittsfield High summer school before leaving for college. He was a part-time guard. The most exciting thing to happen on the job for days was his aiding an elderly woman wandering around the mall disoriented. He called in to the office and an announcement went over the mall public address system. To calm the woman he let her sit in his chair. Her daughter, a middle-aged woman, ran up and started shouting at the mother for getting lost and took her by the arm and led her away without acknowledging Tommy. He noted there was little to distinguish him from the elderly woman. They both occupied the chair, disoriented.

• • •

He conducted a session at the library for fourteen five- and six-year-olds, reading Maurice Sendak's *In the Night Kitchen* to them and then guiding them to do drawings of what they imagined their night kitchens might be. He was walking home from the library. In the window of a photocopy store in the middle of town was a HELP WANTED sign he had not seen before and he entered the store. The place was twelve feet in width and three times that in length. Behind the front counter the work area contained two Xerox photocopy machines, a color copier, a fax machine, and a computer and printer. A woman in her early thirties with sandy-blonde hair falling into her eyes, five feet four with a strong outdoors physique, which made her look like a skier or a swimmer in the wrong environment, was bedeviled by a stack of papers she was trying to collate. He asked about the job and was told she needed someone afternoons five days a week, did Tommy have a résumé? He said he would return with one, rushed home and rewrote his résumé on the computer. Under "Business Experience" he placed the cashier job at Assortments in the number one position, followed by the library volunteer work. For "Education Background" he included his computer course at Marlowe. He was going to delete the guard position entirely, thinking it would be irrelevant for a photocopy store and possibly even a negative. Here was his economic mainstay for the past few months and it wasn't usable. He needed to account for the time, though. He wasn't unemployed, so he listed it below the library work. He hurried back with the résumé. The woman read it carefully.

" 'Cashier' tells me you're honest, but it doesn't tell me if you can learn the machines and do the work. The computer course tells me you should be able to. 'Security guard,' I don't know what that tells me. Thomas, is that what people call you?"

"Tommy."

"Tommy, your résumé is a mess. What are you set up to do?"

"I'm sure I can learn anything."

"It's making copies and doing some desktop printing. Can you use the computer?"

"Sure. I designed Web sites at school."

"Why aren't you there?"

"I had enough school and I liked it here, so I stayed."

"Here's the deal. I'm in the store most of the time these months of the year. I work in the family business, food service at the ski resorts. This is what I do off-season. Ski season comes and you work out, you could be full-time. I pay eight dollars an hour to start. Monday to Friday, one thirty to five thirty. Are you interested?"

"Absolutely."

"Who should I call for references? This Assortments place?"

"They went out of business. I would call the library. I just came from there."

She dialed while he was standing in front of her and requested information about Tommy. She was connected to the director's assistant. Yes, they knew Tommy and would vouch unhesitatingly for his integrity and reliability.

"When can you start?" she said, a person in serious need of help.

"I have to give notice at the mall. Two weeks, I guess, unless they'll accept a week."

"Meantime, could you start mornings? That way I can break you in and you could move over to afternoons when you're done there."

"Sure."

"I'm Cathy Collins, by the way. Call me Cathy. Work rules— I don't have any. Just do the work. If it's slow, it's okay to read, but do it in the back. Same as with eating. I don't want anybody coming in and seeing someone out front eating or reading."

"Fine."

"Tomorrow at ten?"

"Ten it is."

He was retiring his uniform. He called Elena that evening and she was glad to hear he was leaving the job. The next day in the locker room he spoke to his immediate supervisor and was told they had a few applications on hand for jobs and he could finish on Sunday, the last day of his weekly shift. He didn't have to come in the following week. This worked out perfectly for the new job, but it was disturbing how easily he was replaced and how insignificant was his function, just another guard in a mall.

Within a day he learned the basics of the copying machines, the desktop printing program on the computer, and his general duties. His co-worker in the mornings was Cathy's cousin, Bonnie Collins, in her early twenties, another sturdy, physically fit blonde who was off the slopes for a few months.

• • •

He saw Elena on Saturday night. They went to a bluegrass concert in the basement of a church and then back to his place. In bed with him she pressed her fingers across his brow.

"Not so many frowns now. Some. Not so many."

"I'm potentially happy."

"I'm potentially happy for you. Think you're going to like it?"

"I do. There's more going on. And it could be full-time. Not bad if that happens."

"Tommy—"

"What?"

"It's so much simpler for me. I never see my dad, this is our life, my mom and I. For her, anything I do is like a miracle. Getting into an Ivy League school, it's a miracle."

"Would've been a miracle for me, too," he said.

"I can't begin to fathom the complications of your life."

After a week at Quick Quopy Tommy considered the change secure enough to inform the family and he made a round of phone calls loading up the announcement, how it was more interesting work than sitting in the mall, and you made creative judgments in the work orders, and it could lead to a full-time job since it was clear his boss didn't want to be there and she gave him responsibility, trusting him with the cash register and important orders, and he could walk to work or ride a bike; he bought a secondhand bike in a garage sale. Rob and Karen spoke to each other after Tommy called them, agreeing that whether or not this job was temporary or permanent was less important to them than the fact that he was out of the job in the mall.

Karen's mother asked Tommy detailed questions about his duties. She hoped he would be able to make a trip to Florida to see her and if she got to New York—he finished the thought, he would come to the city to see her. His grandparents in Kingston, Frank and Anne, lived a few hours away by bus and he had not seen them lately either. He took advantage of his Saturday off to go there. They were set up at a flea market and he slipped in the announcement of his new job while they were between customers. His grandmother was interested in SUNY Albany—why didn't he go there or transfer to somewhere else? He had anticipated this line of questioning and was prepared. He wasn't interested in college "at this point in time," hoping she would accept it, even though he couldn't foresee at what point in time he *would* be interested in college. After more questions, Anne said she was going to let it pass "at this point in time." His grandfather didn't remember at first where Tommy had even gone to college and by the time they finished eating dinner at a diner, he offered to take Tommy into the flea market business. His grandmother was furious. Tommy wasn't going into the flea market business. Was the man demented? Caught in the middle, Tommy said it was probably a fascinating business, but it wasn't for him.

They dropped him off for the bus in the morning. Anne thanked Tommy for visiting and tried to give him five hundred-dollar bills. Tommy declined the money, promising to take it at a later date if he needed it. Frank insisted he accept a present and he slipped into Tommy's pocket a Tom Seaver Mets baseball card, a gesture Tommy recognized as dotty, but sweet.

Karen went to Florida to visit her mother. She needed arthroscopic surgery on her right knee, an outpatient procedure, and assured Karen she didn't require assistance. Karen insisted on coming down. Karen drove the rental car from the airport to Delray, where Sally lived. She made an exit off the main highway past several gated communities. Sally's older sister, May, lived in one of these places, and on visiting her, Sally observed it was a culture where women outnumbered men by the simple fact of outliving them. Sally presumed a woman alone in her declining years would not feel like an outsider there. And she was weary of the northern winters. She had chosen this particular development, Palm Lakes, for its clubhouse facilities and because it was the place where May was a resident. The architecture was functional, stucco sand-colored two-story buildings, row after row like a semitropical Glasgow.

Sally's apartment was adjacent to a small outdoor pool. A dozen people were reading, talking, bobbing in the water. Here, too, the women outnumbered the men. Karen parked the car and as she walked to her mother's apartment she could overhear one of the poolside conversations. Three women were discussing their dinners the previous night. This was not how her mother spent her time. Sally kept active as a volunteer at Palm Lakes Cares, a service area in the clubhouse for administering to the eldest and neediest within the complex. Listening to the conversation and seeing these people passing time poolside in the middle of the day, Karen decided never to retire. When she no longer owned the store, even if economics required her to leave New York, she would continue to sell crafts and set up booths at shows similar to the activity of Rob's parents. She would stay busy. They'll have to cart me off with a decoy under my arm.

She took Sally to the doctor's office and waited a couple of hours for her, the procedure pronounced successful. Karen settled her mother in a recliner in the bedroom and went to do some shopping for her. She returned and her aunt May was there, a pixielike woman of eighty-one, gray-haired like Sally, neither woman opting for bleaching their hair. May was a widow with a daughter in Minneapolis who had two children. Before retiring she had worked in New York as a buyer of children's clothing. She heard about the breakup with Bill from Sally and wanted to know how Karen was faring. Karen recounted her experience in North Carolina, the realization on the trip that someone like Bill was not the man for her.

"It's a curse. The women in this family are too sensitive for these drips," May said.

Karen laughed out loud.

"I can't remember the last time anyone used the word 'drip.' I wouldn't call him that."

"I would. He let you get away."

"Then I guess Rob was a 'drip,' too," Karen said.

"No, he wasn't," May responded seriously. "He was a fool."

"Then so was I," she said reflectively.

"You were. I love you anyway."

"And how is *your* love life, Aunt May?"

"I'm waiting for Mr. Right," she said in a perfect deadpan delivery.

After May went off to a book group at the clubhouse, Sally said to Karen, "We have to talk about Tommy. He called about this photocopying job."

"My feeling is, he's out of the guard thing so it's a step up."

"Could be more than that. People do that kind of work for a living, Karen. They work in photocopy stores. And that's what he could end up doing."

"I wouldn't rush to make any assumptions about this job."

"I keep hearing that in your voice. This is temporary. This doesn't count. What if it does count? He could learn the business. He could even open his own store one day."

"He's been in the job two weeks and you've got him going into the business?"

"I don't. But it could happen. He's been struggling. We know it and I think he knows it. But this could be a turning point. Are you ready for the possibility he'll never go back to college and he could be some kind of clerk or a small business owner, like a photocopy store?"

"No."

"I didn't think so. It's why I'm telling you this. I don't think you're ready for what could happen. I doubt Rob is."

"This has been the question, do you root for him to succeed, or fail in these jobs and move on to something better?"

"Except here's something he could move on to—from working to owning. I doubt he'd ask you for money to go into business. Seems unlikely with this independence idea of his. He might ask me, though."

"Has he?"

"No. If he did, if he asked me for the money, or to co-sign a loan, if he said, 'Grandma, I want to open my own . . .' well, let's just say, photocopy store, you have to know this is my grandson. Who had that stuffed alligator he used to take everywhere he called 'Allie.' Who was one of the most beautiful little boys I ever saw in my life. Who, when you got divorced, looked like an injured child."

"That's not fair."

"And if he comes to me and asks me for money, I'm going to give it to him, Karen. I'm his grandmother and I won't be here forever and if that's what he needs from me . . ."

"This is an extremely baroque scenario."

"It is not. It is eminently possible. If you think it's a bad idea for him to start a business like that, I don't want you thinking I'm disloyal to you, or I'd be going behind your back. I'll make all the right speeches about college, and is he sure, and he should be very careful about committing himself, and when I'm done, if he still needs money from me to go into something or other, I'll give it to him."

"That's telling me."

"My opinion—you and Rob are holding on to the fantasy he's only going through a phase and it will all work out in the end. It may, but this may be the way it works out."

"He didn't even fail anything, Mother," she said plaintively, the entire college situation tumbling in on her. "He passed all his courses."

"This is apparently what he needed." She reached out and stroked her daughter's hair to console her. "I only hope I'm still around to see him succeed in whatever it is. Can you say that, my darling? '*Whatever* it is.' "

"Not yet."

Rob, Vickie, Tod, and Keith came to Pittsfield to visit Tommy and go to a home game of the Berkshire Black Bears. The Bears were the Pittsfield entry in the Northern League, the equivalent of Double-A baseball. The game against the Allentown Ambassadors was a Sunday 2 P.M. start. They were going to lunch, then to the ball game and then Rob, Vickie, and the boys were returning to the city. The boys were keyed up about seeing Tommy again and he was bringing Elena, a special feature for the adults. They met outside the pub in town and the boys rushed up and Tommy swung each of them around off the ground. He introduced Elena, who was wearing a Brown sweatshirt, jeans, and a Boston Red Sox hat. As they entered the restaurant Vickie gave Rob a nod of approval. With the boys electric about being with Tommy, he wanted to know everything they were doing and they interrupted each other telling the dramas of their lives. Tommy answered Rob's inquiry about the new job with a favorable report, he liked the work, a certain amount of creativity went into the printing decisions, and his boss allowed reading on the job as long as it wasn't busy, so it had a far different intellectual component from the job as a guard. Vickie asked Elena if the Brown sweatshirt had any significance and she told them of the Tommy-Brian-Jill intervention. She said it holding Tommy's hand, this fantastic thing that was done for her. Tommy went to his original response in modesty, Elena had far more to do with it than they did. Rob was focused on the fact that this girl was going to Brown on a scholarship and Tommy, who helped her, had dropped out of college.

The ballpark was the embodiment of minor league baseball, fewer than five thousand seats, mostly in a shed behind home plate with no outfield seating. Tommy placed the boys on either side of him and kept up a running commentary about the Berkshire Bears players from notes he printed out from his computer. He had known nothing about the Berkshire Bears players until the previous day when he researched the ball club on the team Web site in preparation for the boys' arrival.

As the game was played Rob measured the passing of time and the changes in their lives by ballparks. Once he sat with Tommy in Shea Stadium, immense compared to this place. No divorce occurred yet. No race to a college finish line. No dropping out of college at the end of a semester.

The possibilities he imagined for his son were as expansive as the Shea Stadium outfield. And here they were in a ballpark again, only it was a minor league ballpark in his son's hometown where he was working in a store.

The Berkshire Black Bears won 8–6. The boys said they were Berkshire Bears fans now and Rob bought them Bears baseball hats. After the game Rob made the offer Tommy always rejected—could they go shopping, did he need anything in the way of clothing or anything else, and Tommy declined. Tommy guided Rob to the photocopy store and Rob parked the car so they could look inside. Rob said it seemed like a good operation. He restrained himself from expressing that even this business symbolized the limited options of Pittsfield, a photocopy store and it was closed on Saturdays.

They drove to the Berkshire Mall, where Tommy and Elena were going to meet her friends and see a movie. Last offer before the highway from Rob with the spread of clothing stores in the mall available to them. Tommy declined again and they said their good-byes.

As they left the parking area, Vickie commented, "Better, wouldn't you say? And he's out of that job."

"He's lucky to have any jobs the way the jobless rate is for people in his category," Rob said.

"I'm not talking economic indicators here. He seems better than the last time I saw him, is what I mean."

"I would agree."

"This girl, she must be very bright. And she likes him a lot. You can tell."

"A nice girl. Ivy League. She'll have nothing to worry about."

He turned on a National Public Radio station and the programming carried them along for a while. Tod and Keith fell asleep on the drive home, their baseball hats pulled over their eyes. Suddenly, Rob said, "You can fit every person in Pittsfield, Massachusetts, into Shea Stadium."

"It was fascinating. The size of that ballpark. Like it's the scale of how he wants to live now."

"Small."

"He seems to be saying—this is where I am and there's something to it. And there *was* something to it in the greenness of everything, and the scale of that field. Being there must feel manageable to him."

"I wish I saw all that. All I saw was a bunch of ballplayers in a minor league baseball game and I thought about how few of them are ever going to make it."

Rob promised Karen a report on the visit and suggested they meet at the store so he could see the Moses Clark show he read about. He came the next day after he finished work. The Moses Clark pieces would be on display for a few more days and then she was featuring a quiltmaker. Karen discovered her at a crafts show in Newark. Tammy Ashford was a relatively young artist for the work, in her late twenties, a maker of austere, near-abstract quilts. Karen relished the idea of going from Moses in his eighties to Tammy in her twenties.

Rob entered, greeted John, then directed his attention to the decoys on display.

"Moses—a great man."

"He's aging gracefully," Karen said. "His son, Sam, took the photo."

"Lovely shot. Sam's a photographer?"

"Works at Duke. In the public information office."

"He went to Duke?"

"He did."

"Good for him. And the girl?"

"Celia. She's a teacher. I was there recently to visit. I made the loop."

"The loop," he said. He made no further comment. Each of them knew the other remembered their trip together.

In her office he described the day in Pittsfield with Tommy.

"He's out of that guard thing, which was always unthinkable," Karen said. "Joe made it out to be wonderful, but that's Joe. I adore him, but he has a vision of the world as a Diego Rivera mural."

"How are they?"

"Good. Polly's working hard and he's always at his verbal best as the party out of power."

"Their daughter?"

"She's at Princeton."

"Princeton. And Sam Clark went to Duke. I'm impossible. *My* vision of the world is where other people's children went to college."

"I know. Rob, I saw my mother. She had a procedure on her knee."

"Is she all right?"

"She's fine. The knee was not the headline of the visit. She thinks this job could be a turning point for Tommy. Says it's a business he could conceivably work in for a living, or possibly own a store like that. And she doesn't think we're being realistic. Thinks our fantasy is, he'll go on from here, and we don't realize this is how he may end up."

"End up? It's a little soon. What is she thinking?"

"Basically, she wonders if we're ready to accept what might happen—'whatever it is.' That's how she put it. I told her I'm not ready, not yet."

"Exactly."

"Here's a tough question. How much of what's turned us upside down is about status?"

"Status, as in what will people think?"

"Yes."

"From my end, it's in there, I have to admit. But I also know he's put himself in a terrible bracket. I worry more about that, about what he's doing to his future, than what it looks like to other people. Unless I'm kidding myself."

"I'd also like to think I'm worried more about *him*. But my mother may be right. This could be a turning point."

"Vickie thinks something positive is going to evolve, but that's from someone who went to Northwestern *and* Northwestern Law. Where is Bill in all this?"

"We're not together anymore."

"I didn't know. I'm sorry. He seemed like a classy guy."

"That's what he was, and that's what he was."

"Are you all right?"

"I am, actually. Making that trip was clarifying."

"That's good. So—what are we supposed to do about Tommy?"

"Love him, my mother is saying. But if it does come to something . . . ordinary, can we give him our hearts?"

"Thing is, when you hold your little boy in your lap in front of you, and you look into his eyes, you're thinking the moon."

"Or whatever it is."

"Or whatever it is."

They sat for a while without speaking. He rose, touched her cheek, and left. She tried to do a little paperwork, couldn't concentrate, and went home for the night.

SIXTEEN

• • •

The spring of renewal and rebirth arrived a few weeks before Labor Day for Tommy. The job was turning out to be an excellent work situation for him. Five mornings a week he also worked as a temp answering phones for a ski condo broker during the office staff's summer vacation period. The second job came through the store; the owner of the business was a customer. He moved his volunteer time at the library to a Saturday morning and everything at Quick Quopy was pointing to his becoming a full-time employee when his boss went back to the slopes.

He celebrated his nineteenth birthday with dinner at Elena's home. He was still technically a boy from town, not the college student boyfriend Mrs. Garrity had in mind for her daughter, but she knew objecting too strongly would only create a rigidity in Elena. Mrs. Garrity took the position of modified acceptance of Tommy, not embracing him, not rejecting him. He had in his favor a major asset for which Mrs. Garrity would always be grateful: He helped Elena with her scholarship. So she asked if he would like to invite his friends—and Jill and Brian came over from Boston to celebrate. Mrs. Garrity prepared a steak dinner and baked a birthday cake for Tommy. As a present Jill and Brian bought him nineteen scratch lottery tickets that paid back eleven dollars. Over his objections Elena and Mrs. Garrity gave him a more serious gift, a new sports Walkman for jogging. He raised his glass to toast them, and with particular emphasis for Elena, declared himself no longer potentially happy—he was happy, and spring finally arrived.

Along with congratulatory phone calls and birthday cards from parents and grandparents, a little family conspiracy resulted in his receiving gift certificates for J.Crew and Old Navy. Later in the week he set out to go jog ging in the morning with the new Walkman and a T-shirt and shorts purchased with one of the gift certificates. The Rottweiller ran toward the fence. Through familiarity the dog no longer snarled and barked on seeing Tommy, the dog's nasty behavior a common occurrence when he first moved in. One of the workers in the yard told Tommy the dog's name. Guard-dog humor was surely an oxymoron and in a clear example of the genre the dog was named "Killer." "Hey, Killer," Tommy called as he jogged by. Tommy came to a stop, amused, knowing he had definitely turned a corner in his life in Pittsfield. The dog wagged its tail.

Rob was being consistent, home earlier from work, and with his new salesman in place, conservative about travel plans. Stringing days on either side of the Labor Day weekend, they were going on a family vacation, taking Tod and Keith to Disney World. He asked if they could make a stop in Atlanta for a few hours en route to Orlando. He received photographs from Ronnie Blakemore on the progress of the playground and Lars in his office had been to the sites recently. Rob was overdue for a visit. He didn't want Vickie to think this was going to be a business trip with Disney World merely tagged on. He needed to check on what was happening and he wanted Vickie to see it, he was proud of the project. She imagined him getting stranded with work in Atlanta and saying they should go on without him, he would catch up. He insisted he had nothing like it in mind. He would be on the plane with them to Orlando.

They made the detour, took a cab from the airport, and met Ronnie Blakemore at the first site. The main castle was in, a sprawling, elaborate structure, the largest piece MayPole had ever constructed. Ronnie was excited, it was exactly what she hoped for, and the children of the area were so keyed up they were ready to burst through the fence protecting the site. Tod and Keith wanted to climb on it themselves, but Ronnie explained it would cause a commotion if anyone saw them, everyone would want to come in. When Ronnie learned Vickie was a real estate lawyer she was eager to tell her about the politics, the fundraising, and the obstacles to the clearing of the sites. After they traveled in Ronnie's car to the next locations, Vickie told Rob she understood why he wanted her to come. The project was extraordinary.

At Disney World Mickey Mouse shook hands with Tod and Keith and the boys got the giggles. Vickie knew he had been in this place before with Tommy and noticed his tension.

"You don't want to get too nostalgic," she said. "It'll spoil the fun."

"I'm in the moment. Mainly."

"There's a big argument for us to stay together forever. If you get married a third time you might have to do this again."

"*We* can do it again."

"You're getting to be the perfect man. Mainly."

They made love that night at a high level of performance.

"Great sex in Disney World," Vickie said afterward. "It's like a sin. Did Mickey and Minnie ever have sex?"

"They had Huey, Dewey, and Louie."

"Those are ducks. We should stop speaking. We're ruining a good thing," she said.

"It is a good thing. Right?"

"Don't ask. Like you said, be in the moment."

On the night before Elena left for college Tommy came over to say goodbye. Mrs. Garrity opened the door with an acknowledging nod, down the middle, neutral. The living room was occupied with Elena's college-bound belongings.

"She's in her room on the phone. Have a seat." He pushed a carton to the side and sat on the sofa. "So, Tommy, what are your plans?"

"What do you mean, Mrs. Garrity?"

"Are you going to move to Providence, get a job there?"

"I live in Pittsfield. I work in Pittsfield."

"You're staying here?"

"Of course."

"Makes me feel better. I didn't like the idea of you being an Elena-groupie."

"I never intended to. That's something you made up, Mrs. Garrity."

"The job's working out?"

"Full-time would be better. I'm hoping it happens."

"And that other thing, mornings, Elena told me."

"It was temporary. It ended."

"I can't say you're lazy. You've worked. From what I can tell . . . frankly, I can't tell anything. You're a mystery to me. Anyway, I'm going to miss her like crazy. I guess you will, too."

"I will."

"You've got nobody here now, like if you got sick or anything—"

"I've got parents in New York. My friends in Boston. And I work with people."

"But nobody here. What I'm getting at is, I can be an emergency number, Tommy."

"I appreciate it, Mrs. Garrity."

"I'll get her for you."

She went inside for Elena and he looked around the room. The familiar sight of transferring things to school had no effect on him. Elena came in and led him from the house. They walked along the street, holding hands.

"Your mom just said something really nice. Said I could call her in an emergency."

"Momentous. See, get a girl into college and you can call her mother in an emergency."

"Elena, if we never met, you'd still be going to Brown."

"I don't know that. What do you say we go back to your place, spend the night, wake up in the morning together, which we've never done—"

"—and your mother will come in and beat me up with a baseball bat, but that's all right because I'll have *her* number to call in an emergency."

"So what's going to happen, Tommy?"

"You're going off to college and I'm working."

"I mean, are you going to see other people?"

"Which of us is going to be in a place with two thousand guys, both sexes in the dorms, and which of us is going to be living alone? I would say you're a lot more likely to see other people than I am."

"You're my boyfriend. I have a boyfriend at home, is what I'm going to say. I love you."

"I love you."

"*Will* you see other people?"

"No. Not unless you do first."

"Good. We got something settled. You can visit me, you know."

"We'll get together when you come home. I don't want to distract you."

"Who says you will?"

They circled back toward her house and she leaned against a car and touched his face, tracing the outlines with her fingers.

"Something. Something in you. I know you're going to turn out to be somebody excellent. I know it."

"Well, you just said you loved me so that kind of clouds your judgment."

"Maybe you're dumber than I think. It's *why* I love you."

He kissed her, a good-bye kiss.

"Good luck, Elena."

"What you may not know about me is, I'm very competitive. In school ever since I was a little girl I never liked it when I got the wrong answer. I'm not going to be wrong about you."

Karen and John regarded Tammy Ashford to be a gifted quiltmaker, but Karen was obliged to accept the reality that she was not going to get media coverage for every artist featured in the store, not with so many competing galleries, retail stores, and museums. Nothing appeared in the media on the Tammy Ashford show. She sent mailers to her regular customers and the opening night party was fairly well attended, not like the turnout for Moses Clark. She found herself checking to see if the intriguing but woebegone Jeff Wells, who was now on her mailing list, would appear. He did not. The first night she sold two quilts of the twelve on hand and another the first week. Karen was out of the store when John sold the fourth quilt. He threw his arms around her when she came in and said, "We sold a Tammy to the American Folk Art Museum."

"Oh, John."

"A couple of people came in. They took it off the wall. That was all right, wasn't it?"

"Yes!"

She called Tammy immediately and gave her the news. She screamed on the other end of the phone. They printed out a sign and put it in the window, THE WORK OF TAMMY ASHFORD IS INCLUDED IN THE COLLECTION OF THE AMERICAN FOLK ART MUSEUM and went out at closing time to celebrate at a nearby bar with champagne.

"I learned a lesson here," John said. "It isn't all about sales. Sometimes you want to be vindicated."

"True. But in retail, sales are not bad."

She wasn't able to stay for dinner with John. Polly set it up for Karen to see someone she recommended, Garth Keaton, a public relations man Polly met recently at a luncheon. She described a man about Bill's age, well known in the field, who just came on the market with a divorce. Karen was skeptical about someone divorced that late in life, which sounded like an aberration. Polly urged her to meet him and they were having dinner at Frankie & Johnnie's Steakhouse. Karen thought it a peculiar choice in this day and age. He was eager for them to go there and she surmised he wanted to show he was a real guy, as in real guys eat steak.

She called Polly when she arrived home after the dinner.

"So?"

"A fabulous day. We sold one of Tammy Ashford's quilts to the American Folk Art Museum."

"Good for you."

"Then I went out with John to toast the sale with champagne. And then I met your friend. We went to Frankie & Johnnie's."

"And wasn't he impressive?"

"He was. And impressed with himself."

"Oh."

"It's all right. Most successful men are. Only thing is, and don't get alarmed, he's fine, but he choked on his steak."

"What?"

"The waiters are great in a place like that. They must be trained. Like lifeguards. One of them immediately applied the Heimlich maneuver and the food came up, all over the table. And he truly was fine, kind of. Polly, if I'm going to do this, you really have to find people for me who know how to eat."

"How awful."

"He talked so much about himself that when he was choking, I swear, his life flashed before *my* eyes."

Arturo Colletti was the proprietor of Arturo's, the Italian restaurant on Route 7 where Tommy went with each of his parents. Four times a week he came into the store for photocopies of the menu. His wife wrote it in longhand and two dozen copies were run off on cream-colored paper which Arturo placed in leather binders in the restaurant.

He was a fastidious man in his sixties, six feet tall, slim, with a thin, European-style mustache, who favored suits with vests even in summer, someone who could have been a boulevardier in the Italy of the 1920s. He entered the store on a Friday afternoon while Cathy was dealing with a rush job for a sales meeting at the Crowne Plaza Hotel. Tommy was running off the copies while Cathy was placing the material in folders. She took over for Tommy so he could work on Arturo's menus with the second copier.

After the job was run off he asked if it might be possible for a handbill to be made for him. His cousin, a chef in Florence, was coming to visit and they were cooking together for a weekend. Arturo wanted to call it an "Italian Festival," create a special menu, and promote it with ads in the newspapers and with handbills that would be placed in the restaurant and at locations around Pittsfield. He had a piece of paper with the information. Harried by the rush job, Cathy, who ran the business as if she had never spent more than a day indoors in her life, gestured toward Tommy; perhaps he could help. Tommy looked at the paper. After overseeing so many children's crafts projects Tommy presumed he could figure out some kind of collage that would work for a handbill. He told Arturo he thought he could do something for him. On their equipment they were able to print copies up to eleven by fourteen inches on cardstock, which was fine with Arturo. Tommy was going to work on a design over the weekend and show it to him on Monday. Arturo wanted to know how much it would cost for designing it. Tommy deferred to Cathy, who said she would pay Tommy for his time and since Arturo was a good customer, if he liked it, he should give her a hundred dollars and allow her to put a credit line for the store on the bottom. He left with his menus and they went back to the rush job.

The next day at the library after his session with the children Tommy went through travel books, art books, encyclopedias, film histories, wine digests looking for images of Italy. He was able to take reference books as well as circulating volumes out of the building on the promise he would return them in a few minutes. He had a key from Cathy to open the store and preferred to use the store's copiers rather than the library's, since he could make more adjustments on those machines. He made photocopies of two dozen images then returned the books to the library. At a table in the rear of the store he looked at the images, not making any judgments yet. He began to move them around, bringing a half dozen to the forefront. Not knowing why, it merely felt interesting to him, he formed off-center patterns with the images, turning them at angles, taking a head shot and placing the bottom where the top should be and then tilting it, working against symmetry, creating a pattern out of an aerial view of Florence, a box of pasta, Sophia Loren, the Colosseum, the Sistine Chapel, a bottle of Chianti, a map of Italy, the interior of La Scala. With a pair of scissors he cut away extraneous backgrounds, rearranged the images, adding Luciano Pavarotti and the Piazza San Marco. He pasted them on a sheet of paper and ran off a copy. He saw a major adjustment that would have to be made. The images were of different tones and he worked with the individual pieces to get a relatively uniform master copy for each and repasted them. He ran it off again, made a few adjustments on the original, repositioning images, and printed another copy. He printed it darker, printed it lighter, going up and down the scale. He thought the lighter it went, the more visually interesting it was, a suggestion of images rather than a heavily detailed pattern. At the computer he typed in the copy Arturo had given him, playing with different type faces. Considering the artwork he didn't feel the copy would look good with heavy type. He chose a simple Courier font, a typewriter face, that seemed clean and appropriate to him. His intention was for the handbill to reflect the elegant Arturo Colletti. He set the copy in different sizes and ran off a sheet on the printer. After a few tries, adjusting for the point size, he settled on the type and pasted it to the center of the art background. Then he made a copy of the entire piece on cardstock. He gathered all his work in a pile, stood the handbill against the wall, and thought it looked pretty good to him.

On Monday when Tommy arrived in the store the first thing Cathy wanted to talk about was how hard she had to work that morning because her cousin, Bonnie, called in sick.

"What do you think of the restaurant thing?"

"I like it, sort of."

"Sort of?"

"It's not very poster-y. More like a big greeting card."

"It was supposed to be elegant. Like Mr. Colletti."

"Maybe he'll like it. I like it. Just doesn't knock me out. What the hell. What can he expect for a hundred bucks?"

She handed him a job order and he was into the day's routine. Several people came in for photocopies. An hour later Arturo entered the store and by then Tommy was in the flow and after Cathy's reaction he wasn't expecting very much. Perhaps he would ask him to try something else or would just tell him to forget it. He showed him the handbill. Arturo looked at it for a full minute.

"It's beautiful. Better than I expected."

"Really?"

"Beautiful."

Cathy wandered over, looking to be entrepreneurial.

"Unusual, isn't it?" she said. "It has the elegance you have, Mr. Colletti."

"I'll take thirty. If I need more—"

"We have the master copy," Cathy said. "We'll just run some more off."

"What is your name?"

"Tommy."

"Tommy, you come to the restaurant when my cousin is here. You have a meal on the house. You, too, Cathy."

After Arturo left, Cathy asked how many hours Tommy worked on it and he said about five. She took forty dollars out of a cash box and handed it to him. He figured it was a neat deal all the way around, some extra cash and a free meal in a good restaurant. Cathy hoped the credit line might lead other people to ask for handbills to be made and Tommy could do those, too. They had little time to deal in Quick Quopy futures. A lawyer rushed in, upset. His copying machine had broken down and he needed several copies of a long contract for a meeting. Cathy went to talk to the phone company about a loss of service on the fax machine line and Tommy, back to work, ran off the copies for the lawyer.

The handbill went up in store windows where Arturo had friends and customers. He used it as artwork for ads in the local newspapers and Tommy didn't think it looked good in that form, the background images were barely visible in the transfer to newspaper reproduction, and the Courier type came through as too light against competing ads. Nonetheless, when Tommy went to the restaurant on the Friday night of Arturo's festival he was informed by the maitre d' the restaurant was at capacity and they were fully booked for the entire weekend. The maitre d' said Mr. Colletti had been talking about the event with his regular customers. Tommy didn't assume it was his work alone that brought out the people.

The dinner was the highlight of the experience, the best meal Tommy had ever eaten. He was at a table with Cathy and her boyfriend, a rangy ski instructor in his thirties from Vermont named Stefan, who found a theme for the dinner, trying to convince Tommy to get out on the slopes when the ski season began. Tommy's lack of interest in skiing didn't discourage Stefan, who seemed to have little other than skiing to discuss. Arturo and his cousin, a cherubic, heavy-set man in his forties, came out of the kitchen in their white chef's aprons and walked through the dining area greeting customers and receiving compliments. They reached Tommy's table as dessert was served and Tommy tried out his Italian in thanking them for the meal, which went over well with the two men.

He and Elena had spoken a few times since she started school. Largely they communicated with chatty e-mails. She called this time and he told her about the handbill, the forty dollars, and the dinner, one course more delicious than the next and the conversation in Italian at the end. Alert to any possibilities for Tommy, Elena focused on the handbill and asked if he ever considered studying graphic design. His response was that it never occurred to him. Possibly he might think about it if he had more work like that to do.

With his parents he was more descriptive about the dinner than the collage, saying he gathered a few pictures and put them together like projects he had done with children. Karen and Rob knew he was doing letterheads and small printing jobs with the desktop software and assumed this was another example of his duties in the store.

After two weeks of the handbills displayed in town prior to the restaurant event and lingering in a few locales afterward, no one made note of the credit line and came looking for anything else to be created. Tommy concluded that the design, chosen specifically for Arturo, was not in keeping with the bold style of most handbills for flea markets, concerts, and fairs, and his work was not going to encourage people to seek out Quick Quopy for their handbills. Other than Arturo's response he didn't have a sense it was noteworthy.

Rob and Vickie celebrated their third anniversary with dinner at the Union Square Cafe. As they clicked champagne glasses, he started to smile.

"Yes?"

"For a while there I didn't think we'd get to three."

"There are probably some statistics on this. If you can get to three, you can get to six."

"If I took on the business for Atkins, you wouldn't have left me, right?"

"When I first said it, I meant it. But I felt foolish about it after a while. Here's the thing, though. If you did it, I wouldn't have bet on six. Now it's easy sailing," she said playfully.

Tommy was in the store by himself reading in the rear when an elderly couple entered. They didn't look like the usual customers for photocopies or like any Pittsfield couple he had ever seen. They were in their seventies, the woman was stately looking, slender at five feet seven, wearing a severe outfit in black, a black sweater, black skirt, with black sandals, and wore a silver pendant of a lightning bolt around her neck. Her gray hair was pulled back tightly away from her face, a luminous face with light brown eyes. The man was pugnacious looking, his head was shaved, he had a close-cropped white beard and his nose was flat and full, a boxer's nose. Five feet five, he wore overalls with shoulder straps, work boots and a blue T-shirt that revealed his physical fitness. Everything about him suggested compact strength. He had thin, piercing brown eyes he directed at Tommy.

"We saw the announcement for the restaurant," he said, his voice deep and resonant in contrast to his bantam appearance. "Was that done here?"

"It was. Interested in our doing something for you?"

"We were just curious who designed it," the woman said.

"I did."

"Your name is?" the man said.

"Tommy Burrows."

"Tommy, what's your background? Have you studied design?" she asked.

"Why are you asking, ma'am?"

"This is rude, you're right, to walk in and start interrogating you. My name is Portia Jackson. And this is Philip Jackson. Do you happen to know his name? He's an artist."

The name was vaguely familiar to Tommy.

"I think I've heard—"

"I'm a very well-known artist," he said in a dry tone. "I suppose I could be a little better known and then you'd know who I am. This piece you did, my wife and I were impressed."

"It jumped out at us. You don't see anything like it around here and we wanted to find out who did it," she said.

"Are you a design student, did you take courses?" Philip asked.

"No. I mean, I've supervised collages—with children."

"You have no training?" she said.

"We put the credit line on so people would come in and ask for work to be done. I don't think I'm supposed to be saying I never did it before."

"We're not potential customers," she said. "We're admirers. It's very good, Tommy."

"I'm glad to know that."

"You don't know that? Well, it is. And I'd like to think we can tell."

The lawyer whose copier was not functioning, a man in a rumpled suit in his forties, nearly staggered into the store, opened his briefcase, and spilled contract pages on the front counter.

"We'll leave you to your work," Portia said. She wrote a number on a piece of paper on the counter. "We'd very much like to have you to dinner at our home. To talk."

They left the store and the lawyer said to Tommy, "What do they want to talk to you about?"

"I don't know. How many copies?" Tommy asked.

"Three. That's Philip Jackson. He's famous."

At home Tommy did an Internet search on Philip Jackson and found pages of listings. He was seventy-six, born in Pittsfield, an abstract expressionist whose paintings were in the collections of museums and collectors throughout the world. Tommy was embarrassed. He was somebody in a photocopy shop who vaguely knew Jackson's name. A biographical note stated Jackson's wife was an art historian who had taught at Wesleyan and a published author of a book on her husband. The idea that these people admired his handbill and invited him to dinner was astonishing to him.

He made a call and accepted an invitation from Portia Jackson for dinner on Saturday night. He figured it would offset a Saturday night alone. He couldn't imagine why they wanted to see him, it couldn't be anything weird, they were too famous. Perhaps it was one of those pick-the-brains-of-the-younger-generation deals, and what do you think of the administration's policies, young man?

They lived a two-minute walk from a bus stop on a street of large homes in a three-story Victorian shingled house with a front porch. Behind the house stood a barnlike structure a third of the size of the main house with a skylight along one side of the roof.

Tommy wore a new windbreaker from J.Crew and his best shirt, sweater, and slacks. These were important people and he wanted to be crisp for the occasion. Portia Jackson opened the door wearing another dark outfit, all navy blue highlighted by a Native-American silver necklace.

"Welcome, Tommy. Mr. Jackson is finishing up in the studio. He'll be with us in a few minutes."

She led him inside to a house completely renovated with new walls, modern oak floors, and track lighting. She guided him to a library of dark leather furniture and floor-to-ceiling bookcases containing, by his estimation, as many art books as the Pittsfield Library. Portia went to bring him the soda he asked for and he looked at the framed pieces on the walls—art gallery posters, corporate brochures, and book jackets.

"Those are our daughter's. She's a graphic designer in Chicago. So we really do know something about graphic design around here."

Philip entered in what appeared to be his signature outfit: overalls, boots, and a T-shirt. He extended his hand cordially.

"Ah, we're all here."

"All" gave Tommy a start. Was he going to be able to handle it, just the three of them, and hold up his end? Philip took over, taking them through the overdevelopment of the Berkshires, which carried them past drinks to dinner. The dining room contained a long country pine table. Portia served a salmon and wild rice dinner, which Tommy found pretty good for fish. The art changed in this room, an Edward Hopper watercolor, a Picasso lithograph, a Dubuffet sculpture and, as if in keeping with the shift in the art, Philip tilted the conversation toward art critics, primarily a dialogue between Portia and Philip.

Portia led them into the living room for dessert and the art changed again, a Willem de Kooning, an Arshile Gorky, a Mark Rothko, a Franz Kline. Tommy knew enough to realize the gravitas of the art in this home. The man is sitting there in overalls and he's the richest man I've ever met. Portia asked Tommy about the poster for Arturo's, what did he have in mind, and he told them he was thinking of Mr. Colletti himself and his elegance. Philip wanted to know how long it took him to do the work and when Tommy replied several hours to get the images and find the right darkness or lightness as it developed, Philip appeared to be pleased with the answer.

He invited Tommy to take a look at his studio. He threw a switch and flood lights filled the space, a large room with exposed beams and walls finished with Sheetrock. A long work table with paints and supplies stood in the middle like a floating kitchen and along the sides of the studio were rolled canvases and works in progress in various stages of completion. On the extreme wall as they entered was a large, commanding painting nine feet tall and six feet wide held by a wood framing apparatus. Tommy was drawn to the painting, which seemed to be completed, a dripping, menacing shape beginning at the top in dark blue, becoming darker, bleeding into black, pressing down on an uneven white area at the bottom of the canvas, the white appearing to be decreasing, savaged by the weight of the black, the painting seemingly fluid, in motion, as if one were witnessing the extinction of the white. Tommy walked up to it and had the feeling of standing in it, part of it. He was overwhelmed. He stood in front of the painting for a while and then turned back to them. They were observing him. Tommy was now looking at the artist after looking at the artist's work, fascinated that this little man created this overwhelming painting.

"Awesome," Tommy said. "I mean, sometimes kids use awesome for everything, but it's really awesome."

"Your first review on it," Portia said.

"I'll take it," Philip replied.

They returned to the living room and Portia said if it wouldn't be too intrusive to ask, she was interested in Tommy's background. How did he come to be in the job? Tommy gave the minute-waltz version of his life, Bantrey in New York then burned out on academics at Marlowe, deciding to stay in the area, wanting to be independent of his parents, who were divorced, waiting for the first snow when he would probably be full-time in the store.

"And your parents, what do they do?" Portia asked.

"My dad is a playground equipment manufacturer. He's remarried to a lawyer. My mom has a store, more of a gallery really, with American crafts in New York."

"Young people are under a lot of pressure today," Portia said. "You can get fed up with it. But you've taken another kind of pressure on yourself, to be on your own like this."

"Except it's *my* pressure."

Philip nodded in response to Tommy's remark and stood and crossed over and patted his hand.

"Exactly right. It's *your* pressure. Would you excuse us a minute?"

He gestured to his wife and they went out of the room. Tommy examined the paintings and then they returned and sat next to one another on the sofa.

"We called a cab for you. We have an account," Portia said.

"It's all right. I can get a bus."

"Please," Philip said.

"Tommy, what we have to say you don't have to give us an answer on right now. Think about it, talk to your parents if you need to, but I suppose you've been making most of your decisions by yourself. Mr. Jackson had an assistant who's left and he needs a replacement. It's a full-time job to assist in the studio, preparing canvases, working with paint, but it also has an office component, and that's to do the clerical work involved with our foundation, mailing applications, answering inquiries, and some work for us. It's a combination job, in the studio and in the office. We have a housekeeper so you wouldn't have those kinds of duties, but you might have to run errands for supplies and such. You'd be paid by Philip Jackson, Inc." At this point, Tommy's mouth was literally open. "Loosely it's a five-day week, but you'd be paid overtime at fifteen dollars an hour for everything over forty hours. We're very organized here. You'd be on a payroll, workman's compensation, taxes. The base pay is four hundred dollars a week to start. You'd have withholding out of that, but that would be true of any real job."

"I'd just like to say I think you're a young man of character and I'd be very happy to have you working here," Philip said rather formally. Then he added, "And you liked my latest piece so you have very good taste."

"I'm . . . I'm . . ."

"Yes?" Portia said.

"I'll take it. Definitely."

"Wouldn't you like to sleep on it?" she asked.

"No. I'll take it."

The taxi arrived. He could have run home. The time was not yet eleven P.M. when he was back in his apartment, still early enough, and he called Rob, who was awake, and told him to conference Karen, he had some interesting news and they got on the line, Rob, Vickie on an extension, and Karen. He announced he had a job at four hundred dollars a week as an assistant to Philip Jackson, the artist. He would be working in the studio and in the office for his foundation and was starting as soon as he was out of the store. They all paused to absorb the information. Karen spoke first.

"Philip Jackson. *The* Philip Jackson?"

"Yes!"

"How did this happen?"

"They saw the handbill I did for the restaurant and they came into the store and had me over for dinner and I liked his painting and they liked me." He held the phone away and shouted, "Yahoo!"

They congratulated Tommy and peppered him with questions about what he thought his duties would be and where the place was located and how much of the time would be in the studio and how much in the office. He tried to answer, and finally he said, "Enough. It's fantastic!"

After the call from Tommy the adults consulted, still trying to process this turn of events. They speculated about whether a job working for an artist was transferrable experience or limited to this one artist. The office aspect of the job was promising to them as a new entry on a résumé.

"I wonder if this is the 'whatever it is' my mother referred to," Karen said.

"Whatever it is," Rob said, "it's better than what he was doing."

Vickie cut off these speculations by saying, "Folks, we should leave it alone. This is what he's doing now. It's the very meaning of a gift horse."

Tommy called Elena next. She knew the Jacksons. For years they had been coming into the restaurant where her mother worked and she first met them there. She loved Mrs. Jackson and admitted when she was a little girl Mr. Jackson frightened her. She thought he was a mad elf.

"Tommy, it's so terrific! I wish I were there with you. I miss you so much right now."

"Full-time, Elena, finally."

"And what a great job! I'm going to tell whoever asks, I have a boyfriend at home. He's an assistant to Philip Jackson, the artist. My boyfriend, he's *very* interesting."

Jill was in her room with a date when Tommy reached her. The guy had passed out in her bed. "I'm so happy for you. If I'd known this was going to be such a good night, I wouldn't have hooked up with this bozo."

On hearing about it Brian said, "It's super, Tommy. And if he ever gives you an insider price on something, take it."

"What do his things go for?"

"I don't know. Hundreds of thousands."

"This is very helpful advice, Brian."

The next day he called his grandparents. Karen's mother said Tommy must have done something special with the poster to attract Philip Jackson's attention and could Tommy send her one? Rob's father advised Tommy to put any extra money into government treasuries. Rob's mother cautioned him not to fall off a ladder.

Tommy came to the store a few minutes after Cathy opened on Monday morning. They sat at the table in the rear and she listened with a dour expression as he told her of the offer from the Jacksons. She admitted that she hated the store. Her father thought it would be a good diversification for her so she took it on. With Tommy leaving she might as well turn the entire operation over to her cousin, Bonnie, who had been lobbying in the family to take on the business with her younger brother. If Tommy stayed and worked full-time in the winter Cathy would have ignored the place knowing he was there and it only would have delayed the inevitable. She gave him her blessings and asked him to finish out the week until Bonnie and her brother could rearrange their work schedules. Tommy wanted her to know he was grateful to her, he never would have been hired by the Jacksons if she hadn't allowed him to do the restaurant piece. She didn't even think it was so good, she joked, which only proved she shouldn't be in the business.

Tommy read everything he could about Philip Jackson before starting the job. The art section of the library contained the published companion volumes to his one-man shows at the Whitney Museum of American Art and the Museum of Modern Art, the biography by Portia Jackson, and four books on abstract expressionism that made reference to Philip Jackson and contained illustrations of his work. Using the library's Internet resources he was also able to read some of the articles about him in art magazines. Tommy made notes on the characteristics of Philip Jackson's work, as observed by writers on the subject, in the event he might have to demonstrate some knowledge about his employer. He learned Philip Jackson lived in New York from 1950 to 1952 after his graduation from the Rhode Island School of Design, then returned to Pittsfield where he was born. Known for his large, drenched color field abstractions, he was considered something of a nature artist in abstract expressionism. Fifty years after his first paintings he was still working when the other artists were gone.

Tommy sent his parents and grandparents copies of the handbill. Karen and Rob thought it showed surprising ability.

"We should be encouraging him to study graphic design," Rob said to Karen on the phone.

"It's an entire course of study. You think he'd be up for it?"

"Maybe not right now. Maybe after working in the job for a while."

"I'd wait a little to suggest it. Otherwise we're undermining him. He just got the job and we're already pushing him in a different direction."

• • •

Rob brought the handbill to Seth's office, and Carlotta, an art director, came in to see it. In her opinion, given that he had no background, it was a very promising piece. She agreed with Karen—becoming a graphic designer was a path unto itself. Considering the roller coaster ride he had been on, she thought they would be better advised to allow him to focus on the new job for the time being before pressing him to study graphic design. Tommy was nowhere near these adult speculations. He wasn't thinking about alternatives or his future. After meeting Philip Jackson and reading about the man, he was only concerned with the present and whether or not he could measure up to the task of doing the work.

Rob and Lars were on a plane to Atlanta for the opening of Ronnie Blakemore's first playground. Away from the office with a few hours to spend together encouraged Lars to breach the careful social distance Rob maintained between them. From a remark Rob made a few months earlier, Lars knew Tommy dropped out of college. With his daughter, Toby, beginning to talk about going to Yale and his boss's son obviously troubled, Lars avoided discussing their children. He was concerned about Tommy, though, and he used this opportunity to inquire.

"Tommy has a new job. Assistant to the painter Philip Jackson."

"Really? That's terrific, Rob."

"Jackson lives in Pittsfield and Tommy's going to be helping him in the studio. Doing some administrative work, too."

"Good for him. Very unusual."

"It is unusual. Something you don't need college for," Rob said for his own reaffirmation.

Ronnie Blakemore's playground dedication ceremony surpassed any event of its kind Rob ever attended. He was aware that when Robert Moses ran the parks system of New York City he was famous for turning dedication ceremonies into community events. In the 1930s he would open a new facility like a neighborhood swimming pool with parades, bands, bunting, entertainment, and Mayor Fiorello H. La Guardia to charm the crowds. Ronnie Blakemore ran a Robert Moses–style opening in Atlanta. She brought in a local high school band, break dancers who called themselves "The Atlanta Breaks," a disc jockey playing rap music over a sound system, a rapper, 2Morrow, performing live, and a church choral group completing the entertainment in a revival-meeting atmosphere of high spirits and hand clapping. A temporary grandstand was filled with politicians, business people, and funders who made the project possible, with the spectators consisting of more than five hundred predominantly African-American children from the area and as many adult spectators. The principal of the local elementary school cut the tape. Shouting with excitement, the children spilled over the MayPole equipment.

As Rob looked out at the scene, a jewel of a playground in an inner city neighborhood, he was reminded of his favorite Robert Moses project, the Hamilton Fish swimming pool on the Lower East Side of Manhattan. It was a generous and surprising facility carved right out of tenement life. Along with his well-documented drive for power, Robert Moses possessed a visionary civic nature. With this playground in Atlanta Rob thought he approached the highest of Robert Moses's standards. He was glad Vickie had a chance to see it under construction; he would bring her down again now that it was completed.

With the sound of the children playing, the jubilation in this open, inviting space, he thought—this is what I'm about. It's as good as I can be. He found himself recalling the arguments with Karen over his business life and his work schedule and his travel. If she could ever have seen this she might have understood. Something like this doesn't just happen. It takes years of commitment and work.

He closed his eyes in recognition of what he was doing. At a time like this he was thinking of Karen.

SEVENTEEN

• • •

The playground was featured in a front-page story in the *Atlanta Journal-Constitution* and led to articles in the three major news magazines with images in color showing the vista, a modern playground against the backdrop of an inner-city neighborhood. It was one of the largest pieces of playground equipment ever constructed in the United States, sixty yards long and thirty yards wide. Contained within the structure were sliding and climbing units, monkey bars, walkways, and sitting areas. The highest platforms were six feet above the cushioned ground. The illusion of height was created by steelwork in a castle design rising above the platforms. In other parts of the playground were swings, seesaws, and slides also in a castle motif. "The Castle in Atlanta," as Seth named it, became the centerpiece of a new MayPole advertising and promotion campaign he created.

Rob, Vickie, Seth, and Carlotta went to Atlanta on a Saturday so they could see the site when children were out in force. More than two hundred children were there with accompanying parents, none of it arranged by Ronnie Blakemore, the public simply turned out. She provided a box lunch for her guests and they ate on benches facing the castle. Rob took Seth by the arm and they entered the structure and climbed on to one of the platforms, giving them a good view of the playground with the sound and sight of the children beneath.

"Best project of my life," Rob said.

"Gorgeous."

Seth looked over at the three women together.

"Vickie looks happy."

"We're doing much better. But you want to hear something wild? At the opening ceremony I found myself thinking about Karen. I was thinking—if she could've seen this, she would've understood something. Strange, isn't it, at a time like that for my mind to go to her?"

"No. This is the ultimate of what you do. And she was there for you in the beginning."

"Until she wasn't."

"Can say the same about you. The two of you, you killed each other on careers, but you might not have had them if you weren't there for each other."

"She's doing well in the new place. Had a beautiful show of Moses Clark decoys."

"It's Karen. What do you expect?"

"All those arguments we had, this would've been a great visual aid."

"Timing. This is coming in a little late."

Karen was experiencing another success on the next of her one-artist shows with Gail Sinclair, a potter from Rutland, Vermont, seventy-five years of age, one of the veterans of her craft. For the show Gail created a series of bowls, plates, vases, and serving trays in swirling blue against soft cream backgrounds. The *Daily News* writer who featured the show in a weekend guide referred to the work as "dreamlike." They were sold out in a few days. Karen had to ask purchasers to allow the work to remain on display or there would be no exhibit for people to see.

She was in the store on a late Saturday afternoon when Bill entered, surprising her. He was wearing a suede overshirt, a brown cashmere sweater, twill slacks with a perfect military crease, and suede shoes.

"Hello, Karen."

"Bill—looking splendid."

"As are you."

She was wearing a brown turtleneck sweater and simple beige skirt. She rushed out of the apartment that morning with no time to blow out her hair and took the compliment as hyperbole.

"Do you mind my coming?"

"Not at all. It's good to see you." John was at the cash register with a customer. "John, you remember Bill Withers, don't you?"

"Nice to see you again," John said.

"You're a mainstay here." It seemed to Karen he was trying to remind her of his influence in hiring John.

He looked at each piece and read the wall text on the artist.

"Lovely. I saw something about it somewhere."

"The *News*. We've learned you can't get into print on every one of these shows, but the *News* was a bonus."

"How are you?" he asked.

"I'm well. And you?"

"Holding on."

"Holding on" was the giveaway. The man was not on a ceramics buying mission. As if he suddenly remembered the old complaints about his disinterest he rushed to say, "And Tommy, how is Tommy doing?"

"Tommy is working as an assistant to the painter Philip Jackson."

"Really?"

"Guess he's not 'completely unexceptional.' "

"I was trying to be candid about the boy and I made a mistake there."

"In being candid or in judging him?"

"Both. I'm sorry, Karen."

"It's not important anymore. How's work going?"

"Busy. There's so much interest in reading programs, we're in the middle of it. Karen, I'd like to buy something of hers. Doesn't look like anything's still available."

"You don't have to buy anything to say hello."

"I'd like to."

"Then we'll take your name. And when merchandise comes in we'll give you a call."

He filled out a sheet and nodded, aware that the visit had run its course. She gave him a light kiss on the cheek.

"Appreciate your stopping by," she said. She did not want to resume the relationship. As she watched him leave she thought he did look splendid. He always did.

Richard Cryer, a restaurant owner, recently divorced, whom she first met at a downtown merchants association meeting, invited her to dinner at Options, his Tribeca restaurant, a man with an inexhaustible capacity to discuss his business deals. Doug Valens, long divorced, a men's clothing designer, who came to her by way of her dental hygienist—you've got to meet this guy—invited her to lunch, a man with an inexhaustible capacity to discuss his clothing design deals. Neil Marshall, divorced two times, a retired mergers and acquisitions expert, another Polly entry, invited Karen for a drink, a man with an inexhaustible capacity to discuss his shares in thoroughbred race horses. Of the three, Marshall seemed the most promising; she didn't know a thing about race horses, so there was a possible educational advantage to seeing him and she consented to a follow-up dinner at Orso. She was interested in the beginning, but he couldn't get off the track and buried her with information, a dinner companion version of the *Daily Racing Form*. Plus, the nose was troublesome, a broad, pink nose glowing reddish after his second martini and third glass of wine. I'm just not somebody who can be with a man with a W. C. Fields nose.

After three weeks of working for the Jacksons Tommy told Elena, "It's the best job ever." He arrived for work each day around nine. Philip was already in the studio. Tommy's first duties were clerical and he worked at a computer in a small bedroom converted into an office, answering inquiries for foundation grants, addressing applications, and typing letters for Philip and Portia from dictation they left on a cassette tape. Portia was intrigued by Tommy's knowledge of Web site design. She wanted an official Web site for Philip so that when people searched for his name on the Internet they would get accurate information. Portia kept a photographic record on slides of Philip's paintings. Tommy began working on the Web site, converting her slides for inclusion on the site. He showed her how a digital camera could accelerate the process and she was going to use it for Philip's future pieces.

A housekeeper, Mrs. Feeney, an efficient woman in her fifties, sturdy-looking, vigorous with a lilting brogue, came in every weekday to shop, clean, and cook for the Jacksons. According to Portia's instructions she included Tommy in the lunch distribution. Portia was working on a new book on abstract expressionism. Mrs. Feeney stopped at her office, at Philip's studio, and at Tommy's office, the same lunch every day for Tommy, a tuna salad sandwich, potato chips, and a Coca-Cola. He estimated the Jacksons were saving him twenty-five dollars a week on lunches. He sat in a dining alcove in the kitchen and ate his lunches undisturbed while reading *The New York Times*, which was delivered to the house. After lunch he went to the studio and remained there for the rest of the work day unless Philip needed him to pick up paint or supplies and he would drive the Jacksons' Buick station wagon.

Philip had a long-standing relationship with a carpenter, Dave Walden, who lived nearby, and who supplied him with prestretched linen canvases on wood frames, according to the sizes Philip specified. Philip told Tommy that when he was a younger artist he constructed his own, preferring now to save the time and effort and he trusted this carpenter to meet his specifications. With Philip taking him through the procedures Tommy began mixing paints and preparing canvases for future use, applying a base of rabbitskin glue for sizing and then gesso, a soupy acrylic, to create the foundation for the application of the oil paint Philip used. He also showed Tommy how to paint an initial field of lead white on some of the canvases to give them a brilliant brightness.

Philip worked silently, methodically, never speaking except occasionally to ask Tommy for materials. Tommy presumed, given how talkative Philip was when he came to dinner the first night, he would have to deal with an old guy rattling on. As Philip's social needs dictated, he sometimes made comments when he took a break or stopped for a drink of water, talking usually about art and artists. Otherwise he never spoke. Tommy learned quiet was part of Philip's work environment and it was not appropriate for Tommy to initiate a conversation.

Philip would first make a study on a canvas of no more than three feet by five feet size, creating dense fields of color working with house painters' brushes. If satisfied, he moved to a larger canvas.

"If I don't like it, even full-size, I paint a white X across the surface and I throw it out."

"After all that work?"

"It's the process. If I'm happy with ten percent of what I start out to do, it's a good percentage. When I was younger the percentage was higher. Either I'm getting pickier, or I'm not as good. Let's say I'm getting pickier."

Once he was satisfied with the finished work he destroyed the study so as not to have "lesser versions hanging around," he said. As a result of this deliberate method his output was limited. In the library Tommy read an article in a back issue of *Art in America* that said the small number of paintings he produced each year had the effect of maintaining demand for his work. The article contained a quote from a curator: "Jackson continues at a high level and there's an unquestionable integrity to him, he doesn't flood the market. It's as though he's saying, 'I'm one of the last of the old boys standing and I'm going to make it count.' "

• • •

After a few touch-ups, Philip determined the large piece, which Tommy first encountered in the studio, was completed. The work was earmarked for the Philadelphia Museum of Art. He used wood vises top and bottom to support his large canvases and he released the painting from its mooring with Tommy's assistance. The art moving company was on its way to place it in a wooden crate. Philip appraised the piece which was leaning against the wall and nodded his own approval. He turned to Tommy. "One of the great things ever said about painting was said by Franz Kline. He said, 'If you meant it that much when you did it, it will mean that much.' "

Home for Thanksgiving, Elena borrowed her mother's car to pick up Tommy at work, looking for the opportunity also to say hello to the Jacksons. Philip and Portia came out when she arrived—how was college, her mother was so proud of her and they were, too, and what a nice coincidence that Tommy was her boyfriend. As Tommy left arm in arm with Elena the Jacksons were beaming from the porch over the appropriateness of these two young people being together. Tommy and Elena went back to his place, teenagers in heat for each other, and then they separated, Elena off to a family gathering for the holiday in Bennington, Vermont. Tommy was headed for New York to visit with Karen. He didn't have to go through convolutions on this trip—Rob and Vickie were taking the boys to visit her parents in Cleveland.

Polly and Joe were the home team for Karen and Tommy's Thanksgiving. The others present were their daughter, Becky, Joe's father and mother, and Polly's mother, a frail woman in her late seventies. Brian's parents were in Europe and he was having dinner in a restaurant with Jill and her mother. The friends were going to meet later in the evening.

Becky was a twenty-year-old brunette, thin-boned, nearly six feet tall, with her parents' intensity and their kindness. She took Tommy into her room to learn how he was doing and he told her how excited he was with the job, which she was pleased to hear.

"It's been a bumpy few years for you, hasn't it? I still remember when my parents found out your parents were getting a divorce. It was such a sad night for them."

"Your parents are so good to my mom. And your dad—he's the greatest, Becky."

"I know. So I hear you've got a girlfriend."

"I do."

"I was sort of going with somebody. It's on-again, off-again. I just want to get done, then I'm going to do 'Teach for America.' So all in all, you're okay, Tommy?" she asked with sincerity.

"I am. Becky, you're such good people. A terrific family."

With both Joe and his father at the table political matters dominated the meal. As it was nearing an end Joe shifted the attention to Tommy.

"Tell us what it's like to work for Philip Jackson."

"Good. I'm working for his wife, too, office work."

"Does he tell wonderful stories? Wasn't he in with Pollock and all those guys?"

"He talks a little when he feels like it. It doesn't sound like he was really in with those people. He was in New York a while, but then he went back home."

"So what's the most interesting thing about him?" Joe asked.

Tommy thought a moment, picturing the bantam champion of abstract expressionists.

"How serious he is when he's working. And how quiet. That's interesting to me. He's so—still."

Tommy went to Brian's apartment. Jill came by and they filled each other in on their activities. They would not be spending the upcoming Christmas–New Year's holiday together. Brian was still seeing "the highly regarded Debby Simmons," as he referred to her, and over the holidays he was going with Debby to her home in Bangor, Maine. Tommy suspected he needed to remain in Pittsfield to work and would just go to a party on New Year's Eve with Elena and her friends. Without the fellows around Jill thought she would do some things in the city with her mother. Tommy, Jill, and Brian arranged to go to Long Island City the next day where the Museum of Modern Art was temporarily located so they could see a Philip Jackson in the permanent collection. None of Philip's paintings were on display in his home and one day in the studio Philip explained the reason to Tommy. He didn't want any old images in his day-to-day life because it might inhibit his current work. He also told him nearly everything he ever painted was in the hands of collectors and museums, with a number of paintings warehoused by his dealer, Arnold Glimcher in New York, "for financial security in our old age," he said, amusing himself.

Tommy was involved in what was, essentially, a home-study course on modern art. Portia encouraged him to borrow books from the Jacksons' collection and gave him a copy of lecture notes from the course she had taught at Wesleyan. He was very interested in looking at art now with his new eyes. They entered the area where several abstract expressionists were displayed, including a nine foot by seven foot Philip Jackson. The painting was a color field with gradations of pink and intermittent royal blue ripples, an insistently brash, sunny work, a contrast to some of the brooding canvases nearby. It was playfully titled "Miami Beach."

"Very bright," Brian commented.

"And big," Jill added.

"He's in here, with all these artists I read about."

"What do you think?" Jill asked.

"Fantastic. And he did it in 1952. And he's still going. Unbelievable I work for this man."

Tim Grove was back in the city after his last film and planned on staying for a month to spend time with the boys. In a sea change Rob was even feeling a little jealous. With Tim in New York, Rob and Vickie were able to schedule a trip over the Christmas–New Year's week and decided on London. Vickie was maintaining her phone call relationship with Tommy, but missed seeing him and suggested she and Rob rent a car, get together with Tommy on Christmas Eve in Pittsfield, and fly to London from Boston. As Tommy had anticipated, he was not going anywhere for the week. Philip paid no attention to the holidays and started a new canvas and Tommy was fascinated to be in on the gestation of a new piece.

Rob and Vickie drove into town late afternoon of Christmas Eve. Pittsfield looked to Rob exactly as the last time he stopped at the traffic circle with Tommy, hardly anyone on the street, snow everywhere. His observations about the limited opportunities in a place like this had proven to be irrelevant. Tommy found the one job where he specifically needed to be there in order to get it. Philip Jackson was from Pittsfield.

They went to Arturo's. The handbill was framed and placed in a prominent place in the entranceway to the restaurant and Arturo treated Tommy as if he were one of his most important people, fussing over them, giving them a complimentary bottle of wine. Vickie reached for Rob's hand under the table and squeezed it in response to Tommy as he described Philip Jackson's process and the intensity of the man.

"I've never heard you so excited about anything," she said.

"It's exciting."

Tommy liked to stop by the workshop of Dave Walden on Saturdays after his session at the library to watch him stretch and reinforce Philip's canvases. Walden worked on home construction during the week and this was the time he allotted to Philip. Sixty-five years old, six feet four and three hundred pounds, Tommy envisioned him being able to snap the pieces of lumber in his bare hands. Walden had been working with Philip for over thirty years and was in the same category for Tommy as Morris Blenheim of Pittsfield Art Supplies, Philip's vendor for materials. In his early seventies, a trim five feet seven, Blenheim wore warmup suits and sneakers to work and fast-walked two miles to the store and back in clement weather. He was a landscape painter and won several juried competitions, the ribbons hanging in his store. He had been supplying Philip for forty years. Tommy admired these people; he thought they were substantial. And he had come to love their materials, the lumber, the canvas, the paints—the pigments, the viscosity.

Karen was selecting merchandise for the next show, by Bramden Sellers, the whirligig manufacturer from Asheboro, North Carolina, a maker of brightly colored spinning toys. He was a discovery of Karen's from her first trip through the South.

John answered the phone.

"Homecraft."

"Is Karen Burrows there?"

"Who's calling?"

"Tell her Jeff Wells. I bought a Moses Clark decoy—"

"Jeff Wells?" John said, and she raised her eyebrows and went into her office to take the call.

"Hello, Jeff."

"Do you remember me?"

"Of course."

"What a performance. I was horrible. Before I called I was trying to think what it must have been like for you. Like that date Woody Allen and

Dianne Wiest have in *Hannah and Her Sisters* where he says he had a lovely time, like watching the Nuremberg Trials."

"No, I understood."

"What did you say to people? Did you tell anybody? About this guy who kind of collapsed mid-sentence?"

"I really understood."

"Remember in that movie they run into each other again? And it works out. So maybe there's hope. Of course, it's just a movie. What I'm trying to say is, it's over a year since my wife died and even my daughter, who's sixteen now, says—well, she doesn't say 'Dad, you should go out *more*,' she says, 'Dad you should go *out*' and I don't believe you ever get over it, but you do get to go on and, frankly, I had a really good time with you until I fell apart. That's not the greatest line in the world."

" 'I had a really good time with you until I fell apart'? There's room for improvement."

"Well—I thought of you. You have a place as the woman I most wanted to see again if I hadn't messed up."

"That I like very much, the woman you most wanted to see again if you hadn't messed up. Were there women you *sort of* wanted to see again if you hadn't messed up? Or women you *didn't* want to see again and *didn't* mess up?"

"Honestly, this is my first call," he said with sincerity.

"Sorry, I was just teasing."

"I've got a booth at the Pier Show and I was hoping you could come by Saturday around five thirty, it closes at six and that way you could see what I sell, the kind of things I like, and then we could go for dinner if it's not too early and . . . we could do all that."

"Yes. Let's do all that."

The booth for American Pleasures was spare, only a few pieces on display suggesting to the public they were premium, museum-quality items, a weathervane, an Amish quilt from the 1920s, an oak bench, a naive rendering of a farm scene, a portrait of a woman in the flattened perspective of the unschooled early American portraitists, a weathered wood sign for "fresh fish" in the shape of a fish, and, in a glass case, a collection of antique dolls. Jeff was with a customer, a beefy man in his forties wearing sunglasses and an expensive suit. Retailer's decorum—she made eye contact with Jeff and stayed in the background. When the customer left she went over to him.

"This is a beautiful display."

"I'm so happy you came."

"Who was that?"

"Monsieur Deep Pockets. A collector from France. I do some business overseas."

"I'm very impressed. We're consonant, but not. I sell crafts. You sell folk art."

"It's found art, certified as art. Years to come a lot of what you sell will be in a booth like mine."

"Wonderful pieces. But if it's all right with you I'm not going to return the compliment by buying something of yours, not at these prices."

"You came. I thank you and my daughter thanks you."

They went to Pastis, a restaurant downtown, and talked about the ways their businesses were alike and the ways they were different. In Karen's operation she was able to cultivate artisans. The creators of the pieces Jeff sold were no longer living so he worked with other dealers and collectors. Wandering into a country flea market or an antiques store and finding a resaleable item was such a rare occurrence for him he had given up traveling to do so. Especially now that he was a single parent.

"What did your wife do?"

"She was a pediatrician. Somebody who helped people, as opposed to the bastard who killed her," he said, his rage and hurt so close to the surface he couldn't restrain himself. "Maybe he helped people. He's a Brazilian banker. There's going to be a substantial settlement. If someone is going to run down your wife, might as well be a banker." He was reflective for a moment—too long, he realized. "It's a conversation-stopper. I apologize."

"I asked. Has to be said for us to move on."

"We're dealing with it. My children are heroic. Tell me about your boy. He was somewhere on his own."

"He's an assistant to the painter Philip Jackson, in Pittsfield."

"Philip Jackson? I want to *be* him. When I'm older I want to still be at it. And your boy works for him? Spectacular."

"It's nice of you to say."

"Karen, are you—at large? Did I really completely mess up with you and am I getting another chance?"

"Looks that way."

"You know what I'd love to do? It's a few months off so we've got to figure out a way to get a relationship going and get that far. But I would love to go with you to Brimfield and slog through all that insanity and just have the greatest time. To be with someone like you—"

"Isn't it a little too flea-market for you?"

"I love all that flotsam and jetsam. Stuff that doesn't make the cut for the business, I've got it all around the apartment. You're not into it?"

"I used to be."

"We'd have so much fun. And we could go to the Shelburne Museum. We could go to folk museums the way baseball buffs go to different ball parks." He caught himself. "I'm getting too far ahead."

"I haven't heard a bad idea yet."

He drove uptown and they stopped outside her apartment building, where he had had his previous collapse. She was not quite at the point of inviting him in, nor was she about to let this person get away. She leaned toward him, kissed him, a serious kiss, and said, "Tell your daughter you did very well," and let herself out of the car.

In the kitchen sipping tea she thought about this man with his grief and his two children, somebody battling to be part of life again and she saw it was possible not only to be happy in his company, but to be his way back in.

The Chelsea Piers sports complex was a project Vickie worked on for the developers during their negotiations with the State of New York. One of the Chelsea Piers partners, Roland Betts, was now with the Lower Manhattan Development Corporation overseeing the rebuilding of the World Trade Center site. He asked Vickie to meet him there. Betts, a strapping man of six feet one, walked her along the base of the cleared area. From this vantage point Vickie was moved by the enormity of the space, the madness of the act and loss of life, and the potential for transformation. Betts offered Vickie the opportunity to work for the Development Corporation as plans went forward for the rehabilitation of the site. The need was for someone to deal with the various constituencies, private and public, a real estate lawyer who would be less concerned with contract language than with being a liaison between the various entities and the Development Corporation. Given the ebbs and flows on a long-range project, the offer was for Vickie to be on retainer at her hourly rate. She could maintain her law practice, although it was logical to assume this work eventually would dominate her time. Betts asked her to consider it and give him an answer as soon as she could.

The opportunity went to the essence of her marriage. She knew Tim would continue to be a dramatic but inconsistent figure in her sons' lives. She could hire a full-time housekeeper, or continue to alternate sitters. Still, a parent was sometimes needed at home and if she were tied up with work, could she count on Rob, only recently dependable?

After the boys went to sleep she described the meeting with Betts. Rob understood the issue without her articulating it—if need be could she count on him to be there for the boys? From nothing, from the previous day when the engine on the marriage was running comparatively smoothly, they were in a major test of Rob's commitment.

"The World Trade Center," he said. "It's enormous. About America, really."

"And New York."

"So if you were a man and you had children you'd make the decision solely on the merits."

"But I'm not."

"How many times does anyone get to work on something like this?"

"Not often."

He considered before responding then he said, "I'm there. Say yes."

Philip took his brush and marked a bold X in white paint across a large canvas he spent weeks refining through several smaller studies. Philip noticed a perplexed look on Tommy's face.

"What is it, Tommy? You liked it more than I did?"

"I did, Mr. Jackson."

Without harshness, lightly, he said, "That's why I'm the artist and you're the assistant. But you can be the artist. Have you made anything since that poster?"

"No."

"Mrs. Jackson tells me she sends you home with books. Books are important. Doing is also important. Would you like to do something? Use the material here. Work when you're done for the day. Weekends, whenever. Feel free."

"I appreciate it very much, Mr. Jackson, but I'm not sure what I would do."

"You're not sure. Years ago, Mrs. Jackson and I were in New York and we were taken out by a wealthy collector from Milan. This man only wanted to go to the Plaza Hotel, where Sergio Franchi was performing. So Sergio Franchi comes out and before he can sing a note, a woman in the audience yells, 'Sing Sorrento!' Sergio Franchi looks at her and says, 'Please, madame, it's called—the act.' It's called—the art, Tommy. Not—the science. If you were sure, what would be the point? Explore. Create something."

In a corner of the studio was a piece of plywood Dave Walden had used temporarily to cover a window while he ordered replacement glass. The piece was three and a half feet by five feet and Walden neglected to take it away when he fixed the window. Tommy stood the plywood vertically against the wall and then horizontally, studying it as he had seen Philip do with a blank canvas. He thought it was good material for the backing of a collage, a form he felt most comfortable working within. An autobiographical motif appealed to him. He would use elements that expressed his time in Pittsfield. He asked Portia if he could borrow the digital camera and he took a photograph of Portia and Philip, surely important to his Pittsfield life, a view of his room, and he wanted to get one of Killer in his killer mode. This was impossible with Killer now his buddy so he settled for, in effect, a smiling Killer, which he accepted as part of his Pittsfield story.

He worked at night as Philip suggested and on the weekends, using a table at the side of the studio, embarrassed for his unfinished collage to be seen so he covered it with a drop cloth whenever he stopped. He accumulated items he was considering and tacked them to the plywood with pushpins, rearranging them, discarding some, adding others, working deliberately, emulating Philip's careful style. When he created the collage for Arturo's he was working with paper. The solidity of the plywood encouraged him to use other materials. He spread out facing pages of the classified advertising section of the *Berkshire Eagle*, part of the Arturo's handbill, an old pair of running shoes, the photographs of the Jacksons, another of his room, one of Killer, and of Elena—a photograph she gave him—a flyer from the mall, and arranged the elements in an off-center, off-balance pattern in which everything drifted without foundation, which he hoped expressed his experience. Finally, the pattern, as with his life in Pittsfield, settled into a solid base at the lower right hand corner, where he placed the photograph of the Jacksons and a paint can with brushes. In one of Portia's books he had seen color plates of Jasper Johns's "Savarin" series of a rendered paint can with brushes. He used it for reference here, but with an actual paint can containing actual brushes. He glued the paint can directly to the plywood, as he did with the *Berkshire Eagle* pages, his sneakers, and the other elements. Then he applied a coat of varnish for sheen and permanence. Using the materials, organizing them, physically gluing them to the surface so they had dimension, doing the work and seeing it evolve was exhilarating to him. He came back to it the next night when the surface was dry. He picked up a painter's brush and made sweeping movements with his hand, practicing to get a fluidity of motion. When Philip used his brush Tommy thought his movements were like liquid. And in the Hans Namuth video of Jackson Pollock at work that he borrowed from the library he was impressed with the artist's freedom of movement. So he made his moves as if he were a baseball player taking practice swings. Then he dipped the brush into a tray of acrylic white paint and swept it across the surface of the piece, his representation of the cold weather months of Pittsfield. He took a tray of forest-green paint and with his brush swept the paint up and through the white representing the warm weather months.

It was done. He created something. Whether it was good or bad, he had no idea.

He left the piece standing in the corner of the studio uncovered. The next morning he entered the office and found a note on his desk, "Please see me in the studio." Nervously, he walked into the studio, where Philip was making pencil sketches on a study-size canvas.

"Ah, here he is. I wanted to talk to you about your piece. You're telling a story here?"

"It's my life in Pittsfield. So far."

Philip stood over the collage.

"The elements, for the most part they're disorderly."

"And then at the end it comes together with you and Mrs. Jackson and the paint can."

"I saw that. What I wondered is how much *you* saw that. It was intentional?"

"Yes, Mr. Jackson."

"I brought Mrs. Jackson in a while ago. We were curious, whether the disorderliness was accidental, or your intention. We assumed it was intentional. We hoped it was. And the green and the white?"

"Winter and summer."

"It's good."

"It is?"

"For someone completely untrained, definitely. My only criticism is—perhaps it's too literal. On second thought, I take that back, it's supposed to be about you. I would encourage you to do more, Tommy. Can we keep this here for a while?"

"Absolutely."

"That'll be your side of the studio. Fill it up with some pieces. Any materials you want, use what we have, order them."

"Really, Mr. Jackson?"

"Out of curiosity, how are your drawing skills?"

"Bad. When I was in high school I drew cartoons but they were stick figures."

"So you'll naturally gravitate to found elements. That's fine. But think of this, just for the experimentation of it. Think of the surface as color and light. And as you do more work, imagine how you might render some of the elements you want to portray not with found objects, but as color and light representing those objects. You follow?"

"Abstraction."

"Yes, Tommy. As an experiment."

"I will, Mr. Jackson."

Philip took the collage leaning against the wall and ceremoniously placed it on a long shelf in the area he was defining as Tommy's side of the studio.

Simple moves. From one side of 53rd Street to the other, first to the folk art museum, then to the crafts museum, both getting a chance to be verbal about their expertise.

They stopped for an early dinner at Isola, an informal Italian restaurant. Karen allowed herself a Sunday away from the store to be with him, an indulgence. He wasn't exhibiting in a show for the weekend and yet, in the couple of hours they were together, he received three calls on his cell phone from other dealers.

"Seems rarefied, folk art," he said, after excusing himself for a few minutes to return the calls. "But it's a business. You're always checking, trading. I spend the week on the phone or on the Internet."

"Is that a complaint?"

"No. Someone who works as hard as you do—I just don't want you to think you're with a playboy, but without the money."

"I wouldn't take you for a playboy."

"The clothes give me away."

He was wearing a tan corduroy suit with a blue dress shirt open at the neck, something Bill might have worn when he was twelve years old.

"Even with a few calls to bother you, to get weekends off—" she said wistfully.

"Work saved me. And knowing I had to be strong for the children." However social he was trying to be, his loss was a reference point impossible for him to avoid. "But the thing about work—and I have to keep reminding myself—is you have to find a balance."

She didn't respond, knowing she and Rob never did find that balance.

She invited him back to the apartment and he looked carefully at the crafts pieces in the foyer and living room.

"Beautiful. Just what I expected." He took a closer look at the naive painting Rob encouraged Karen to buy. "This is pretty nice. Where's it from?"

"Found it at Brimfield."

"We're going to get there. I hope."

Suddenly he kissed her and it was so sudden and adolescent she sensed the struggle even here—if I don't do this now I'll never do it, and I have to do it, I have to start. She said, "I don't know about Brimfield, but we can go inside."

He was eager in bed, passionate, but it seemed to her this was the first time he had been with a woman since his wife died. She looked at him as they lay in repose and she couldn't tell if he wanted to smile or cry. Possibly both.

"Thank you," he said.

Thank you! It was either one of the most awkward things he could have said, or one of the sweetest. Again, possibly both.

Just as Rob found himself thinking about Karen at an untimely moment—in bed with Jeff Wells for the first time she found herself thinking about Rob and Brimfield as they rushed between the booths, laughing, happy. "Last chance to beat the other couples."

EIGHTEEN

• • •

The war in Iraq played on television all day in the Jackson home, Mrs. Feeney leaving the set in the kitchen playing as she moved within the rooms of the house. Tommy came out at the top of each hour for the latest news bulletins. His brief conversations with Kit MacDougald, Elena's classmate in high school, had the appearance of two local guys with something in common, chatting in social situations. But because of their different backgrounds Tommy never considered the military, while Kit was with the Third Infantry Division in Iraq. Kit was always pleasant to Tommy and said he favored him over Elena's previous boyfriend, amounting to local support. Tommy recognized here was where the war came home. The Kit MacDougalds were, in a sense, serving for the privileged. Because these young people from small towns joined the volunteer military neither Tommy nor his high school classmates would ever have to fight in this war. He followed the news reports closely, the war personalized, a local boy his age who had been kind to him, was there and he was not, and he rooted for Kit to come home safely.

Philip Jackson's newest canvas, at nine feet by seven feet, was a large deepening field of green, the merest suggestion of green at the uppermost portion gradually growing deeper to its dense, verdant culmination at the lower portion. Tommy read in it the emergence of spring and thought it especially beautiful and optimistic, spring comes and it is rich and full, and the war would end and a true spring would reemerge.

His own pieces occupied the side of the studio Philip designated for him. His initial feelings for the very smell and viscosity of the paint were magnified when he started to actually apply paint to canvas. In his intensity he could have been any of the children he supervised in art projects, nothing existing but this moment, this material, this surface. For his first painting he started making sketches in a pad, continually revising, eventually transferring the pencil lines to a canvas. He hadn't gone near paint and it was four hours after he began. Only when he drove home in the station wagon, which he had permission to use, did he realize he was hungry and stopped at a McDonald's and would have gone back to work on the piece if it weren't so late.

The subject of the work was Jill and Brian; he found it helpful to be dealing in narrative. Philip took back his criticism that the Pittsfield collage may have been too literal—Tommy kept it in mind. He preferred working in a mixed media format with printed pictures to give himself a starting place and to anchor the narrative. So as not to be too literal he went for a loose method of portraying his friends, in a visual code, a picture of François Truffaut signifying Brian, the teenage film critic, a computer for his intelligence, sunrise over the Grand Canyon for Jill's sunniness, and a bottle of beer from an advertisement for her partying. He glued the pictures to the canvas and applied a coat of varnish to them, leaving the rest of the canvas free for the oils he was going to apply. He gave over more of the surface to abstract renderings than in the collage on plywood, creating drifting strokes in a variety of pigments as he imagined his friends in color and light, applying a dark underscoring to some of the brush strokes with gray and black. The darker pigments were intended to represent the darkness he was aware of in their lives, which they attempted to conceal, but which he allowed to show through. He found that confronting his feelings about his friends, trying to represent them on canvas, these other children of divorce, was more emotionally demanding than he ever would have thought. He understood being affected by the process of writing something. He never imagined you could be affected by something you painted.

For his next piece he borrowed Elena's graduating class yearbook from her mother and made a photocopy of Kit MacDougald's graduation picture. He used it actual size and glued it to the center of the canvas. The piece he created around it was a rendering of colors from the television war coverage, green for the night images, black for smoke, yellow for the explosions, a blatant red for blood, the pigments applied in a chaotic tangle of brushstrokes, Kit's face looking small and overwhelmed by the pattern. The shorthand he was adopting—this is how I feel about my friends, this is how I feel about the war—was working for him as a starting point.

Philip encouraged Tommy after each of the canvases was completed while not inhibiting him with specific critiques.

"Excellent," he said after the first.

"Thank you, Mr. Jackson."

"Why don't you try another?"

After Tommy completed the second, Philip asked, "Who is the boy?"

"Someone I knew from around here who's in Iraq."

"And that's the war?"

"Yes."

"Good. Keep it up, Tommy."

Portia also gave him encouraging, but muted, reactions. She said, "I like what you're doing in the studio," after he finished the first painting, and told him, "Stay with it, Tommy," after the second.

He next attempted to express how he felt about his parents' divorce. He began with a picture he looked for in a medical book in the library, a color plate of the human body. He went to Quick Quopy and the new owner, Bonnie, his former colleague, allowed him to run off his own photocopy. He was working with a four-foot by five-foot canvas with a bright white lead paint undercoating and he placed the canvas horizontally on an easel and glued the seven-inch by ten-inch picture to the center of the surface. He took a permanent marker and drew arrows pointing to the head and to the heart. Working from pencil sketches in a pad, Tommy painted a pattern resembling a latticework in shades of blue, the lines breaking, which he intended as a representation of his parents' marriage. The picture of the human body with the pointing arrows was chosen to show where he felt the pain. He was forcing himself to confront that pain and it was exceedingly difficult for him to deal with these feelings. He tried to transfer his emotions into his application of the paint itself and he used a narrow painting knife to drive the paint into the canvas with hard, slashing motions. When he was done it looked sloppy to him. He took white paint and X-ed out the canvas. He began again with another canvas, narrowing the lines of the latticework, this time using a narrower knife so the pattern of lines was clearer, and the discontinuation of each line more pronounced, digging the paint into the canvas. He was surprised to find no lessening of emotion. He was as racked by the process as the first time. When he considered it complete and was satisfied with the result he sat in a chair looking at it without any sense of catharsis. He couldn't even look at it very long. He felt as if he were looking directly into his own pain.

He left the painting on the easel without a drop cloth so Philip could see it the next morning when he came into the studio. The collage and the two succeeding canvases were now in a line on the shelf with the newest piece on the easel in front of the shelf. Philip entered with a cup of coffee, looked at the piece, and went into the house to ask Portia to come in and see it. She appraised it and said, "Undeniable." Philip looked at each of Tommy's pieces and remarked, "Simplistic, and you're right, undeniable."

Tommy was in the office at the computer when Portia came by.

"I saw your new work, Tommy. Very strong."

"Thank you, Mrs. Jackson."

"What launched you into it?"

"Frankly, my parents' divorce."

"And the human body and the arrows?" He was reluctant to answer. "It's all right. I don't need to know if it's personal."

He chose to tell her.

"Mr. Jackson would probably say it's too literal and it probably is. I was trying to show where it hurt."

"Not too literal for my taste. Strong things can come out of directness. Good work, Tommy."

He answered inquiries for the foundation, took his lunch break and read the newspaper. Philip never came out, nor did he ask to see him, and Tommy assumed this latest piece didn't warrant particular attention. He entered the studio and saw that Philip was working intently on repainting the lower portion of the green canvas and he knew his own effort was of little importance in this studio. Philip acknowledged him with a slight wave and Tommy busied himself preparing canvases. After nearly an hour Philip stepped away from the painting.

"Now let's talk about *your* piece, young man. I spoke to Mrs. Jackson a while ago. She said you used your parents' divorce as inspiration."

"Yes."

They walked over to the painting.

"And the broken lines, the discontinuity, what are you trying to express, the discontinuity of their relationship?"

"And our family."

"Of course, your family. Broken connections. Mrs. Jackson told you it's strong and I agree. Well done, Tommy. I hope I'll see more."

• • •

Tommy went home without staying on in the studio to start another piece. He didn't have a good thought about what he might like to create next. With rain predicted through Sunday night he was going to spend the weekend watching television and reading. Now that he had four pieces occupying part of the studio he wondered whether the Jacksons would object. They hadn't said anything. He didn't want to remove the pieces. He had little space in his apartment and he wasn't going to give them to his parents or anyone else. They didn't know he was doing the work. The only person he told was Elena and he only mentioned he was experimenting with material in the studio. She was eager for information, but he wasn't comfortable in elaborating, just as he didn't want to discuss it with the adults. The experience was too raw and new. And he wasn't sure of the quality of the pieces and whether these nice people were just being nice in encouraging him, as though he were an art mascot.

At Jeff's urging, he and Karen took a flight to Burlington, Vermont, rented a car and drove to the Shelburne Museum, a vast collection of objects from tobacco tins to Grandma Moses paintings. He was so enthusiastic about being there with her, and animated, he reminded her of the best of Joe when he was on his subject. When they left the grounds, she tousled his hair, something she never would have done with correct Bill, and said, "This was perfect."

With Vickie at a Saturday meeting for the World Trade Center site, Rob brought the boys to see the musical *Frog and Toad*, and went to a sports restaurant for dinner with the emerging sports fans. A few days later, Tod came home with a watercolor he made in school. Vickie showed it to Rob, a rendering of a family holding hands. At one end, a blond man taller than the rest, and in succession, a red-haired woman, two red-haired boys, and at the other end, a brown-haired man.

"Better than getting to order your own pizza," Rob said to her.

A week after Tommy completed the divorce canvas he was at his desk in the office. Philip and Portia entered the room. This was so unusual in the normal pattern of everyone's day his first reaction was that they came in to tell him there had been a change in their needs and he was going to be let go.

"Morning, Tommy," Portia said.

Apprehensive, he stood.

"Morning, Mrs. Jackson, Mr. Jackson."

"Sit, please," she said. He settled back down, warily.

"Tommy, Mr. Jackson and I have been talking about the art you've been creating. We think you have undeniable talent. You lack technique and that's understandable. You don't have any training. And I understand you don't have skills as a draftsman. What you do have is passion and a feel for color and material, which we think explodes off the canvas."

"Or the plywood, as it were," Philip added.

"Granted, it's a youthful explosion and unrefined, but it's real. It's especially clear in that last painting where you're dealing with a very difficult part of your life. You seem to be able to take your emotions and express them through art, and that's the definition of an artist. Given your potential, it would be wrong for us to hold you in this job."

He knew it. Nice people finding a nice way of firing him.

"We think you should go to art school," Philip said. "You'll probably have trouble with illustration and there's probably a way around that."

"If you were a photography major you wouldn't have to draw," Portia said. "You can make it up in other ways. Now as far as art schools go, we like the Rhode Island School of Design very much. Mr. Jackson went there a long time ago. And our daughter went there. They do an excellent job and it's well rounded. You take academic courses, too, and that will be good for you."

"We took the liberty of sending them photographs of your work. And naturally I gave them a very high recommendation, which I must say counts for something."

"I FedExed it over and they liked what they saw and why not?" Portia said. "They're going to give you a scholarship, Tommy. Acceptances go out in a few weeks for the fall semester so they want to meet you. You have an appointment tomorrow at noon. Take the day. Drive the wagon."

"A scholarship?"

"I explained to them you're living on your own and that's what we expected them to do," she said. "They do it for some people. Who better?"

"This can't be."

"You were tired of school, I understand," she said. "But this is a completely different kind of education. We definitely urge you to do it."

"You can work until you start there. My old assistant left to have babies and now they're older and she'd like to come back. And we thought you could work here summers when she'd like to be off anyway."

"Please, Mr. Jackson, Mrs. Jackson, this is going too fast. You recommended me and they looked at my work and they gave me a scholarship? I already *have* it?"

"With room and board," she said. "They expect you to hold down a job at the school to contribute toward expenses, but that's apparently standard."

"And I'm supposed to go there tomorrow?"

"They want to meet you and formalize it. You have an appointment with Ellen Dawson in Admissions at noon."

He couldn't absorb it and sat speechless, shaking his head.

"Mrs. Jackson, Mr. Jackson . . ."

"Isn't it wonderful? You don't have to *say* anything. From now on, you can put it on a canvas."

On the drive to Providence he had to pull the car off the road a couple of times to try collecting himself. Is it truly happening? Do I really have any talent? He knew what it felt like to express himself with these works and with these materials. He never experienced anything like it before—to tell something about yourself and your feelings and sweep it across the surface or dig it into the canvas. He had no sense of how he measured up creatively. The previous night after he left work he researched the Rhode Island School of Design in the college guides in the mall bookstore and when he went home he logged on to the school's Web site. It was known to be a major art school. I'll flunk out. They're only taking me as a favor to Mr. Jackson. I have a scholarship to RISD?

He entered the admissions office, his palms sweating, and he wiped them against his chinos. He wore a jacket, shirt, and tie out of respect for the person he was going to see, but now thought it was a mistake; the students he passed were dressed like college students, art students, not fake art students. A woman in her thirties with blondish hair in a ponytail, five feet five, in a white blouse and navy skirt, who looked like a student herself, was leaning over the front desk of the outer office making a notation in a pad.

"Yes?"

"I'm Tommy Burrows. Here to see Ellen Dawson."

"That's me. Come in, Tommy."

She extended her hand and he knew she was feeling his wet palm.

In her office several art posters were displayed for exhibits at the RISD

Museum of Art. She sat behind her desk and motioned for him to sit opposite.

"This must come as a surprise to you, Tommy. Mrs. Jackson told me they did this without your knowing. They didn't want to say anything if it didn't happen."

"I had no idea."

"How much do you know about RISD?"

"By reputation."

"I'll give you a tour."

She walked him through the facilities. Along the way he saw classes in session and students at work in the studios, drawing, painting, and he thought—there is no way I can go to this place, I'll never make it. Followed by—I want to go here more than anything in my life. He was asked about his likes and dislikes in art and he worried any wrong remark would be fatal and expose him, but it was as if Portia had been prescient in offering her quasi-course, as if she were planning—one day you'll be walking through the Rhode Island School of Design with a scholarship in hand and you'll be asked about art and you'll be able to hold your own, more than hold your own, you not only read books, you were in a studio when Philip Jackson was creating paintings.

They went back to her office and she had some questions for him. She understood he had been living on his own for over a year and was this so, and he said it was true. She was curious about his skills for job placement and he offered that he was reasonably computer-literate and he also volunteered in the local library. She thought they would be able to find a suitable job to fulfill their work requirement. Portia told them he was a graduate of Bantrey in New York and completed a semester at Marlowe. They were in possession of his transcripts and wanted to slot him as a first-year student and not a transfer student so he could begin to fulfill their courses of study as an incoming freshman. They could assess at a later date whether any of his Marlowe credits would be accepted. Was that all right with him?

"Fine."

She handed him a packet of materials.

"You'll fill out the forms and get them right to us?"

"I will."

"Everything you need to know is in here, but if you have anything you're not sure about, please call me. Anything you'd like to know right now?"

"I think you've pretty well covered it."

"My last question's the most important. This was initiated by the Jacksons. But do *you* want to go to RISD?"

"It would be the greatest thing that ever happened to me."

"Then congratulations." She stood and shook his hand, which was still wet with nervousness, but he assumed it didn't matter anymore. "Philip Jackson was so complimentary I was curious to see what you'd done. I'm very impressed with your work."

"You *are*? Thank you."

He started to leave, then stopped.

"I have a question. Does Mr. Jackson do this often?"

She looked at him as if she didn't understand what he was asking.

"He's never done it."

Tommy tried calling Elena and could only reach her answering machine. He left a message saying he was in Providence and would wait for her at the dormitory. He walked over to the Brown campus, which was a short walk from RISD, hard for him to believe in itself. He located her residence. She was still not in and he sat on the ground with his back against a tree, reading the material. A half hour later Elena came toward the building. Tommy saw her and called out and she ran over to him.

"What are you doing here? Is something wrong?"

"Remember I told you I was working on things in Mr. Jackson's studio? Well, I did some art pieces and it seems people think they're pretty good. And the Jacksons recommended me and they just gave me a full scholarship to RISD."

He held out the material he had been reading as though to submit documentation. She looked at him and at the material and her eyes became watery. She pressed her face to his chest. "Tommy—I knew I was right."

Portia opened the door for him expectantly.

"Looks like I'm going," he said. "The admissions person said congratulations."

"Congratulations."

He entered the foyer and Philip emerged from the den.

"So?"

"At one point she asked me who was my favorite abstract expressionist."

"I hope you said Arshile Gorky," Philip told him.

"I'm afraid I said you, but they're giving me the scholarship anyway."

"Imagine that."

"Mr. Jackson, Mrs. Jackson, in the history of the world . . ."

"It's not so big a deal, Tommy," she said. "It's merely appropriate."

He delayed calling his parents until he received the official notification on a Rhode Island School of Design letterhead. The letter arrived four days after he submitted the requested forms.

Rob was in his office and Tommy asked him to conference Karen in the store, that he had exciting news. When they were both on the line, he said, "I just got a full scholarship to the Rhode Island School of Design. I accepted and I start in the fall."

"What?" Karen said and she struggled for breath.

"Hard for me to believe, too, but yes, Mom. Mr. Jackson recommended me and Mrs. Jackson, who's respected, she helped it along. I'll have a campus job as part of the package. I've got the letter and I bought a T-shirt in the bookstore, so it's officially official."

"Tommy, it's like a dream."

"I know, Dad. The Jacksons, they've been amazing. They asked me to work in Pittsfield until I go to school, then after that they're taking back their old assistant and I'll work for them summers. When I start school I'd like to give up the place in Pittsfield. I won't be off much if I'm working there summers—but I'd like to come home."

"I'd say it's all right," Karen responded.

"The Jacksons invited you up Saturday for a celebration lunch if you can make it. One o'clock. I'll send directions."

"Of course," Rob said.

"Absolutely."

"Vickie will come too, right?"

"I'm sure she will."

"I'll call her and I'm calling my grandparents. This is huge."

"What did it, Tommy?" Rob asked. "Working for Philip Jackson?"

Out of self-protection he hadn't told them about his art so they didn't have an accurate view of his candidacy, as the colleges use the expression. He wouldn't be able to properly explain his work on the phone. He chose to wait and allow them to see the pieces in the studio.

"Something like that."

When Tommy was off the line, Rob spoke to Karen, the news leaving them ecstatic. They made arrangements to meet at the Jacksons' home driving their own cars; Karen was going to a crafts show in Hartford on her way back.

"Unbelievable," Rob said.

"It's a great school."

Tommy made his other calls. Vickie congratulated him on being true to his independence, which she believed had a direct influence. Rob's mother focused more on Tommy, a college-age boy, back in college where he belonged, rather than the art school part of it, and Rob's father agreed. Karen's mother told him she suspected he had something unique when he sent her the poster and he should continue his volunteer work to keep himself centered. He promised he would, that for all he knew, working with children in the crafts projects helped him reach this point. He called Jill and Brian on their own conference call. Jill said, "I'm so proud of you I can barely speak." Brian told him, "I'm going to start collecting you. It's wide open." Lastly, he spoke to Elena's mother. Elena already informed her.

"The school just happens to be there. I don't want you to think I'm trailing after Elena, Mrs. Garrity, your worst fears," he said lightly.

"You looked very handsome in your security guard's uniform, Tommy, but this is better." She added whimsically, "You're a credit to Pittsfield."

Rob arrived at the Jacksons' home first, Portia greeting him at the door. Vickie couldn't make the trip, the boys were ill with chicken pox. Tommy was already there wearing his RISD T-shirt in celebration. Portia introduced Rob to Philip and they went into the den, where the graphic designs by the Jacksons' daughter were on display. From his years of dealing with graphics in business he was able to recognize it as superior work and passed that opinion on. Karen arrived and she was gathered into the discussion of graphics and Tommy's first public work. Philip opened a bottle of champagne and they drank a toast to the scholarship boy.

"May we show my parents the studio?" Tommy asked. Portia didn't know Tommy had yet to tell them about his work. She knew, though, this would be their first opportunity to see his pieces.

"I'm sure they'd be interested," she said.

They walked into the studio and there was the large, verdant canvas Philip created.

"Magnificent," Karen said.

"Really," Rob added. "Wonderful."

"Much obliged."

"What happens to it?" Karen asked.

"I'm contributing it to Berkshire Community College here in Pittsfield."

Rob noticed the pieces along the side, the plywood collage and the three paintings.

"These are very interesting, too," Rob said.

"Don't tell me. Tell the artist," and he indicated Tommy.

"You did these?" Karen said.

"I didn't want to explain over the phone. I got a lot of encouragement from Mr. Jackson and Mrs. Jackson."

"We're very pleased with Tommy's work," Portia said.

"I'd like to say it was Tommy's art that got him the scholarship. Closed the deal," Philip said.

They looked more carefully now and reached the last piece, Tommy's visualization of his feelings about the divorce. Philip was curious to see the subjects of the piece observing the piece. They couldn't know from its abstraction the literal inspiration, but they appeared to feel its emotion.

"Great, Tommy," Rob said.

"I'm absolutely in awe," Karen said.

She looked at Rob, both bewildered. How could they miss this in their son?

Portia prepared a lobster salad and with Karen's knowledge of naive art available to him Philip found a meandering topic for the lunch, the relationship between untrained, naive artists and the work of artists like Rousseau and Gauguin. Karen and Rob were in the conversation to a degree, still affected by the experience of seeing Tommy's first art, intense and complicated.

They left after lunch to further congratulations from the Jacksons, and fervent thanks on their part, and went with Tommy to his place. Sitting on the sofa between Karen and Rob he excitedly showed them the material from the college.

He went to the refrigerator to get them water and on returning to them, seeing his parents on the sofa as they read the material, the two of them together as when he was younger, but not together, his brow creased momentarily with a sadness that could never completely disappear.

Finally, it was time for them to say good-bye. Rob was on his way to New York, Karen to Hartford. His parents kissed him and looked at him with pride and wonder, their son headed in a direction they never would have imagined.

They drove their cars around the corner and when they were out of view of the house Rob pulled over to the side and Karen did the same. They emerged from the cars and embraced, joyful, relieved, and reluctant to let go. Then they drew back. Karen was involved with Jeff Wells, her work in progress. Rob was settling into his second marriage. They both had moved on, away from each other.

"We got lucky here," Rob said.

"He's the best of us."

She extended her hand and they held hands a moment. Then they returned to the cars, found their way to the center of town, and drove off in their separate directions.

Reading Group Guide

1. In the author's previous book, *Kramer vs. Kramer*, the ex-spouses end up in a court custody battle. Would Karen and Rob have been better off with clearer lines of responsibility for Tommy's upbringing, or was theirs the best possible arrangement?

2. Tommy and his peers are under considerable pressure to perform well on their SATs and to have stellar resumes for their college applications. Do we put too much pressure on young people in our culture today to perform well in school?

3. Tommy's parents can afford to hire SAT tutors. Do you think this poses an unfair advantage over other, less fortunate students? Should his parents have declined tutors for ethical reasons? Or do you think since students are all in a fierce competition, extra help is fair game?

4. Is Tommy's behavior, his diffident school performance, and subsequently, his decision about college, a direct result of his parents' divorce or should it be blamed on his academic limitations? Or is his behavior the result of a combination of factors?

5. When Tommy makes his crucial decision about his college career, do his parents behave responsibly? Should they be even more active in attempting to get him back on track and have they left too much to chance? Or is allowing him to find his own way responsible parenting?

6. Bill doesn't have much patience for Tommy, whom he regards as a high-maintenance teenager. Is his attitude appropriate, or is he being selfish and interested in his own social agenda? Is Karen overly sensitive about Tommy, or on-target in her assessment of her relationship with Bill?

7. Tommy's difficulties resemble the effect of throwing a rock in a pond, the ripples reverberating on all sides. Do the adults invest too much in the boy's success or lack thereof? Do they blur the lines between where their lives end and his begins? Can you relate to their position?

8. What would you consider a desirable balance between work and home life, since Karen and Rob never seem to find the time that allows them to have both a successful marriage and career? Is it possible for men and women to "have it all," or is that an impossible idea that jeopardizes our marriages?

9. Could Rob and Karen's marriage have been saved? Should they have found a way to work even harder on the marriage, or was it doomed by their personalities and by the nature of their individual professional needs?

10. Tommy and his friends Brian and Jill are all affected by their parents' divorces. Is divorce inevitably detrimental to young people? Or has divorce been successfully integrated into our lives and are the young people in the novel more sensitive to their parents' divorces than the norm?

For more reading group suggestions visit
www.stmartins.com/smp/rgg.html